WHAT the Heart WANTS

TEIRAN SMITH

WHAT THE HEART WANTS

ISBN-13: 978-0-578-78625-4

DEDICATION

To everyone who believed in and supported me (I know who you are and hopefully so do you), thank you.

To my fans... Thank you for your patience. This release has been a long time coming. I hope you enjoy this story as much as the last one!

Chapter 1

"YOU'RE CHEATING ON ME?" Everett bellows.

"I couldn't help myself," Dex, my soon to be brother-in-law, laughs. "She's so beautiful."

Everett points at the framed photo on the living room wall. "You put this print up in place of mine. How could you?"

Standing off to the side at the far end of the room, I stare at Everett. I swear the guy is more gorgeous every time I set my eyes on him. He's in his regular attire, a formfitting black shirt with the sleeves pushed up to his elbows, and jeans that hug his delicious ass just the right way. His salt and pepper dark blonde hair is perfectly coifed. And the beard… Very debonair. Closely trimmed and blonde like his hair, but with a tad more salt than pepper. No man has looked sexier with facial hair.

He causes me to salivate.

Too bad he can't stand me.

If Everett never saw me again, he wouldn't miss me. He wouldn't even remember me.

To him, I'm just his best friend's fiancé's annoying little sister.

A tongue-tying, sad label I have rightfully earned.

"Sorry, man," Dex says. "But you have to admit, it's a great piece."

"It is nice work." Everett admits and studies it with appreciation before turning back to Dex. "Who is the photog?"

With a devilish grin, Dex points at me.

My heart takes off into a full-blown sprint and I can't breathe.

Everett spins around to face me. His eyes widen and mouths falls open. "*You* took this?"

He does nothing to hide his shock. That he doesn't like me surely enhances his surprise.

I met Everett a month ago, in this very spot. I had been looking forward to the introduction for months. When I found out that Dex was best friends with a world-renowned landscape photographer, I went crazy. I'd heard Dex refer to his buddy "Everett" from time to time in conversation, but I didn't know he was talking about *Everett Shaw*.

I have been studying the man's portfolio for years. He is one of my favorite photog's. One of whom I've strived to emulate. And low and behold, he's Dex's closest friend. What are the odds? For me, that information was better than winning the lottery. It beat any Christmas morning as a child. It was more exciting than a trip to Disney land for a kid. This was my ultimate jackpot.

But when I met him, I made a complete and utter fool of myself.

I hounded the guy for two hours about his work and gushed about how big of a fan I am. I jabbered nonstop until he finally said—not verbatim, but in a nutshell—he was here to catch up with his best friend, not go over his resume.

In Everett's defense, he had every right to snap at me. My exuberance over meeting him was excessive, to say the least. Add to that his being the most handsome man I've ever laid eyes on and I was completely googly over the guy. I acted like a thirteen-year-old teeny bopper girl meeting my most beloved boy band member.

Yeah… I was *that* level of ridiculous.

I was and still am mortified. Since that unfortunate day, I've barely been able to make eye contact with him.

I nod in response to his question.

"You have a good eye." He spins back to the print. "You captured the light beautifully. The composition is perfect."

Did he really say that?

Trying to seem unaffected and cool, I shrug. But my chest is tight and I can't stop my face from flushing. *Everett Shaw* is praising my amateur work!

But that's just it. It's amateur work. He most likely sees flaws in it I can't comprehend. He's probably being polite by not pointing them out.

I move closer to where he and Dex stand. "It didn't turn out exactly as I'd hoped."

"Don't be demure," Everett chides, his electric blue eyes now on mine. Lord have mercy, those eyes… "This is genuine talent. You need to own it and take credit when it's due. This is something to be proud of."

Hope springs within me. Perhaps he's not just being nice. "You really think so?"

"I do," he declares. "And I'll tell you another thing, it wouldn't be hanging in Dex's house if it was anything less than stellar. It took years to get him to display my stuff."

I want to jump up and down, screaming and squealing with glee. And later, I will. But for now, I do my best to remain calm and collected. "Thank you, Everett." I smile. "That means a lot coming from you."

The instant Everett leaves, I run to the kitchen where my sister Maren is baking. It's all she does lately. It's her default whenever she's stressed out or upset.

"Oh, my god!" I squeal too loud and Mare covers her ears.

"What?"

"Everett saw my print in the living room. He says it's really good!" I bounce. "He wants to see more of my work."

"That's great, Liv."

"I know, right? He asked me to email some stuff to him tonight. I'm so nervous I could puke."

To look at Maren and I, one would never suspect that we are sisters. She has wavy blonde hair and blue eyes. I have straight, dismal brown hair and hazel eyes. She stands five feet nine inches tall, I'm only five-three. She's lanky with long slender legs and an ample bosom. While I have always been athletic, I've never been able to trim these curves. When I leave a room, my ass lags. That's just the beginning of our differences.

She's twelve years older than me, and we were born to different women who raised us in separate cities. Because of tensions between her mother and our father, my sister only visited one weekend a month. Growing up, Maren wasn't sure who or what to believe. Our dad left her mom when she was only four years old. The story Maren's mother spun was that he abandoned them. While he has admitted to some guilt, he left because Maren's mom was having an affair. It had been a long-standing liaison with a colleague, and it wasn't just sex. It was a full-blown relationship with feelings.

My dad and Maren's mom were high school sweethearts. It crushed my father when he learned his first love was cheating. When he took a job in Colorado Springs, he fought hard for joint custody but ended up with weekend visitation. As Maren got older, she lost interest in visiting. Her heart was in Denver with her mother and friends. When she started college and her adult life began, I hardly saw her.

Because of our age difference, we never had much in common. Maren was always good to me, but we didn't have a solid sisterly bond. I wanted it but didn't know how to ask for it or how to initiate it. When I turned sixteen and Maren was twenty-eight, she took more of an interest in me. She helped me prepare for dances and dates. She was the only person not afraid to be in the car with me as I learned to drive. When I had questions about boys, she was my go-to.

At sixteen, when my mom got sick and later died, Maren stepped up big time. She became a regular fixture in my life. She called each day, and every other weekend she either came to visit or took me to Denver to stay with her. Hers was the shoulder I cried on and it was her strength I relied to on survive my loss.

While we still have little in common, our bond is solid and unbreakable. Our love for one another is unconditional.

"Don't be nervous," she says as she vigorously stirs an enormous bowl of chocolate batter. "It's just Everett, and your pictures are beautiful."

She doesn't get it.

"Mare, Everett is an award-winning famous photographer. Having him look at my work is like having Martha Stewart taste test your pastries."

She scrunches her face as though I've offended her. "Martha is a hack. Pierre Herme, on the other hand…"

I roll my eyes. "Whatever. You get my point."

"Yeah, yeah. But even so, you have nothing to worry about."

I lean onto the island with my chin resting in my hands. "Do you think he will be honest? If he hates what I send him, will he say that?"

"He won't hate them."

I groan. "Don't placate me, Mare."

She stops working and faces me straight on. "I honestly don't think he'll hate them. But I expect he will offer you his professional and honest opinion."

I blow out a breath, but I'm no more relaxed than when I came in into the kitchen to talk to her.

"Why does he want to see them?" she asks and goes back to her task.

Her question comes off odd, as does her tone, but before I can respond, Dex enters the kitchen.

Dex is quite a catch with his sophisticated manner and dashing good looks. At five feet eleven inches, he's not remarkably tall, but has an athletic physique. He has dark hair with not a single gray and insists he doesn't dye it. Yes, I asked. He has broad shoulders and a killer smile. My sister is a lucky woman. They are bound to make gorgeous babies.

He goes to Maren and peeks into the bowl of batter. "We haven't gotten through the batch of brownies you baked two days ago. We gave away half of the muffins you made five days ago."

"This is for Mrs. Jones," she explains. "Her birthday is tomorrow."

Dex leans against the counter. "Oh, I didn't realize."

"Of course, you didn't," she scolds him. "You don't make a point to get to know our neighbors."

He presses a palm to his chest, feigning offense. "I talk to them all the time."

She stops stirring and stands with her hands on her hips. "Okay, how many children do the Albertson's have?"

"Three."

She holds up four fingers. "And another on the way."

He just shrugs. "So, I don't count people's kids. That doesn't make me a lousy neighbor. Besides, I bet none of them know much about me."

Maren rolls her eyes, but she's not annoyed. She's just pretending.

"They probably know more about you than you know about them."

"How could they know anything about me if I don't speak to them?"

"Because I talk to them."

"Perfect," he smirks, "that means I'm off the hook."

I snicker. These two are perfect for each other. "You two are so cute."

"Just wait until you get one of these," Maren nods toward Dex.

"I hope we're as adorable as you two," I reply.

After pouring her batter into separate baking trays, she turns to her fiancé. Once again, there's a weird tone to her voice, "Liv says Everett wants to look over her work."

"Yeah." Dex shifts to me. "He's quite impressed. He says if it's half as good as the print in the living room, you have a legitimate chance at a career in photography."

"Seriously?" I shriek loudly and they both make faces.

Dex nods with his palms over his ears. "Yep."

But my excitement withers fast. If Everett doesn't like what I send him, it will mean I have little to no chance at a photography career.

Three agonizing days later, Everett calls and invites me to his gallery to go over my work. He mentions nothing of the photos I sent or his thoughts on them. Perhaps he's unimpressed.

As I approach the gallery entrance, my heart palpitates and I feel faint. To try to calm my nerves, I inhale a deep breath as I pull the door open. When I step inside, I catch Everett's voice and find him sitting behind the counter talking on the phone. He holds up a finger and mouths, "Just a minute."

Just like that, my nerves disappear.

Well, not entirely.

But I've forgotten about them for the moment.

I'm hypnotized.

Everett could mouth the word cheeseburger, and it'd probably be the sexiest thing I've ever seen. Those lips are the definition of sexy. Everything about him is sexy. I bet his toes are sexy and I am not the least bit attracted to feet. I'll never understand foot fetishes. And yet...

I'm staring.

Though I hear his voice, I haven't a clue what he's saying. I'm just watching his mouth move.

A laugh follows his smile. What I wouldn't give to be the person making him laugh.

Stop staring, Liv!

Now.

Turning away, I walk into the gallery show room, studying the prints on display. Several of the pieces I recognize, while others are new to me. All are stunning, but when my gaze lands upon one called Enchanted Street, I fall in love. The colors are so vibrant, the image is so crisp it's as though I'm standing on that brick road. I can almost feel the concrete wall of the café. This… This photo is what I want to one day produce.

"You like it?" Everett asks and I jump. I hadn't realized he was standing beside me.

"It's incredible."

"It's one of my favorites." He beams with pride. His biceps bulge as he crosses them over his chest. "Oddly, it's not a fan favorite."

"They must be blind."

He shrugs. "Art is subjective."

I step closer to the print. "It's my dream to travel and capture places like this."

"I took this in Prague. A truly incredible place."

"I can only imagine."

A moment passes, my eyes lingering on the picture. Everett stands to my right, watching me as I all but drool over his work.

He places his hand on my elbow, bringing me back to reality. "Follow me. I have something to show you."

Following Everett to the back of the gallery to a narrow corridor, we enter an office on the right. He flips on the light and asks me to have a seat and close my eyes. Once I'm sitting and he's sure I'm not looking I hear rustling. A moment later he tells me to open my eyes.

When I do, I come face to face with a huge canvas print of a photo I took of the City Hall subway in New York City.

Last year, my best friend Grayson and I went to New York on a crazy whim and stayed for a week. Because it was all we could afford, we stayed in a crap motel and ate fast food every day. It was one of the greatest experiences of my life.

The memory of the day I snapped this picture is as clear as though it just happened yesterday. It was our second day in New York and I wanted to spend a day sightseeing and taking photos. As always, Grayson happily obliged. It was a long day. We walked and walked until our feet hurt. It was hot with one hundred percent humidity. We were both miserable. Grayson was ready to call it a day, but I needed to see one last place. The City Hall subway. He groaned and said, "Okay, but this is the absolute last stop. I'm sweaty, I stink, and I'm hangry." I almost laugh out loud.

"This is fantastic work, Olivia," Everett praises. "It belongs in galleries and magazines."

Upon examining the capture up close in print form, it's much more dynamic than on a screen. Still, my insecurities creep in. "I almost didn't send you this one. I wasn't sure the composition was quite right."

"Are you kidding? Everything about it is perfect. This picture is by far the best out of the collection you sent."

Everett's words take me by surprise. I wouldn't have considered it the best. I sent him ten images and almost sent another in place of this one. "You think so?"

"I do. In fact, I'd like to display it here."

I snap my head back in astonishment. "In your gallery?"

Everett nods with a grin. "I assume you don't mind."

"No. No, I don't mind. I just can't believe it." I haven't inspected every picture here, but I don't think he has any other photographer's work on display. His offer is a true honor.

"You have real talent, Olivia." After leaning the print against the wall, Everett steps closer to me. "Some of the photographs you sent me are better than I've seen from photographers with twenty years of experience."

Unable to believe my ears, I stand, mouth agape. "I don't know what to say."

"I'm going out shooting next Saturday and I'd like you to join me. I want to watch you in your element and observe your technique."

Somehow, I manage to not squeal. "Seriously?"

He chuckles. "Seriously."

"Yes, Yes! Absolutely." And then I remember…

Chapter 2

GRAYSON HAS REQUESTED THAT I be his plus one at his friend's wedding. My stomach falls. "Actually, I can't Saturday, but I'm free Sunday."

Crossing his arms, Everett casts his gaze to the floor. "Saturday is the only day I'm shooting."

"Perhaps another day?" I ask, my tone contrite yet hopeful.

Everett cocks his head to the side and shakes it. "You shouldn't look a gift horse in the mouth, Olivia."

"I'm not." This is a chance of a lifetime. My stomach is in knots that I might lose it. Grayson begged me to join him at a friend's wedding. His ex-girlfriend is in the wedding party as is the guy she left him for. It's only been a few months since their split, and he's still a little raw over it. He claims he needs me there for reinforcement. I won't let my friend down. When I make promises, I keep them. "I really want to go, I just can't on Saturday."

"We can't choose when opportunity knocks, so when it does, you should answer the door. It's the only way to make it in this business."

"The door is open."

He arches a brow. "But on your terms, right?"

"No." My voice is meek because my answer is a lie. It is on my terms. He's given me an extraordinary opportunity and I'm refusing it because it isn't on my timing.

"Why can't you shoot Saturday?" Everett asks and folds his arms across his chest. "Give me one good reason that is more important than your career and I'll consider taking you another day."

I shift feet and fidget with my fingers. "I promised my friend I'd go to a wedding with him."

"Let me get this straight," Everett rubs at his eyebrow, "you're declining an incredible opportunity to be someone's date at a wedding?"

My initial response is to correct him about Grayson not being my date, but that would probably just annoy him further. Instead, I swallow and nod. "We made the plans months ago."

"He can't take anyone else?" He throws a hand up. "You know what, never mind. Call me when you're serious about building a career."

"I can't believe you turned him down," Grayson says as he drives us to the wedding.

"You begged me to come today."

"Are you serious?" He sighs and stares at me with disapproving gray eyes. "I could've come alone. I'm a big boy. I'd survive."

"Grayson," I huff, "you and I both know that you being in the same room as Jenna and Alex is a bad idea. You need me there."

This will be his first time seeing Jenna since their breakup and seeing her with the guy she cheated on him with is going to be miserable. I can't let him go through that alone. If the shoe was on the other foot, I would need him with me. And knowing Gray, he'd stand by my side even if he was deathly ill. I can't do any less for him. That's what best friends are for.

Grayson closes his eyes and sweeps his fingers through his shaggy brown hair. "But you've lost an unbelievable opportunity. I feel so bad."

"*You* have nothing to feel bad about." Feeling high and mighty, I jut out my chin. "Mr. I'm-too-cool-Shaw completely overreacted. Who is he to tell me how to live my life or what's right or wrong for me?"

"He's a world famous, rich photographer who could literally make your career, that's who he is." Grayson narrows his eyes at me. "He may have been a dick, but I agree with what he said. You have to take those opportunities."

"I don't abandon my friends in their time of need." I use my most self-righteous tone. "I think that says a lot about my character and I happen to like who I am."

"I like who you are too, Liv." He lays a hand on my shoulder. "But this isn't a life-threatening situation I'm in. I would've been okay."

"Nevertheless, I believe I made the right choice."

"No. You don't."

I gasp and turn to him, ready to argue, but he continues.

"Don't lie to me," he snipes, "but most of all, don't lie to yourself. You totally want to kick your own ass right now."

This is why I love Grayson. He calls me out on my crap. And ninety-nine percent of the time, this time included, he's right on target.

"Yeah, I kinda do."

"You should call him, admit your error and apologize."

"I'm not sure it would do any good."

"You never know unless you try."

Grayson's last words stay on repeat in my mind. Every day I tell myself I will get in touch with Everett. And every day, I make excuses for why I can't. Or I convince myself it would be a futile attempt. It's just nerves. I'm too big of a chicken to make the call.

When I turned down Everett's offer, I wasn't completely honest with him. I wasn't even honest with myself. Yes, I offered to help Grayson. And yes, my word means something to me. When I tell someone I'll do something, I do it. But there's a bigger reason I declined Everett's offer.

His offer took me by surprise. It threw me off kilter. It was the last thing I expected, and I wasn't prepared. My insecurity got the best of me. To go on a photo shoot with Everett would be overwhelming and unnerving. I couldn't handle the pressure of him evaluating me.

It's now Thursday. On Thursday's, Dex and Maren hold "family dinner" at their house. For the past couple years, it's only comprised of me, Maren, and Dex. Since his return to the States, they now include Everett as Dex considers him family.

I'm a freaking nervous wreck. I should have called him. Calling would have been infinitely easier than facing him in person.

When I pull into the driveway and see his Jeep, my stomach drops. I knew this would happen. That at some point, sooner rather than later, I'd come face to face with him. Avoiding the inevitable is unlike me.

To make matters worse, I'm running late. Maren loathes tardiness. I wasn't able to call until the last possible minute to let her know work had delayed me. I imagine the scene now… the three of them at the table, waiting as the food gets cold.

"Look who finally made it," Mare says as I enter the dining room.

I do my best to appear normal instead of the nervous mess I really am. All eyes are on me, including Everett's. If I knew him better I would say there's a hint of regret in his. And he's smiling at me!

"Sorry, all," I say, "my boss kept me late. You didn't have to wait."

"Nonsense," Dex says. "Of course, we waited."

I take my usual seat across from Everett and glance to the covered dishes on the table. "It smells fantastic."

"It's a new recipe," Mare states, wearing a proud expression. "Pork chops romano in lemon-butter sauce with green beans and salad on the side."

Maren stands and unveils the food. The spread looks as excellent as it smells.

"I've been looking forward to this meal all week," I say. "I'm so tired of eating takeout and chicken salad."

"You have a kitchen," my sister points out, as she often does. "It's cheaper to eat at home than eat out."

"So you say," I argue. "You don't have two roommates who eat all your food."

Maren and I have had this conversation before. If she had roommates, they wouldn't be eating her food because she'd "nip that crap in the bud promptly." And she would. But Maren is stronger than me. She has a commanding presence. When she speaks, people listen and take her seriously.

"So, how has everyone's week been?" Everett asks as we each fill our plates.

Dex starts, "Mine has been a week from hell. My new chief of surgery is a pompous asshole."

"I thought you were up for that role?" I ask, my head tilted to the side.

Mare shakes her head, her brilliant blue eyes drilling into mine. Evidently, this is not a preferred topic of discussion.

"So did I," Dex answers matter-of-factly and leaves it at that as he takes a bite of pork chop.

"How about you, Maren? How has your week been?" Everett asks.

The dynamic between my sister and Everett is complex. Everett is Dex's lifelong best friend. They've known each other since they were young kids. They are more like brothers than friends. But Maren doesn't like Everett because of his well-earned, scandalous reputation as a lady's man. That wouldn't bother her so much if he hadn't slept with one of her close friends after she expressly asked him to exclude her cohorts from his extracurricular activities.

Nonetheless, they both make nice for Dex's benefit. I have noticed, however, that it's usually Everett making the effort. He always includes her in conversations and goes out of his way to be pleasant. She just accepts that he's here without being a bitch.

"Overwhelming," she replies. "Between work and wedding planning, I've scarcely had time to breathe."

"Why haven't you said anything before now?" I ask. "I'm happy to help any time."

I have told her this several times. I've sensed her stress for weeks. She works long hours at her bakery café. Most weeks she only takes one full day off from work unless Dex demands they both take an entire weekend off. He helps where he can, but admits he doesn't have the first clue how to plan a wedding and worries he'd make matters worse by trying. Maren is an "I can do it all on my own" type who never asks for help until it's practically too late.

"I know, I know. I should've said something, but you know me…" Yes, I most certainly do. "But I need you this weekend. I'm looking at wedding gowns *again*." The word "again" comes out as an extended groan. She looks no more enthusiastic than she sounds.

Choosing the gown is usually the part brides are the most excited about. It's the fun part of the wedding planning. Most girls grow up envisioning the gown they will wear when they marry their Prince Charming. Going out in search of said dress is thrilling for them. But Maren isn't a typical bride.

Luckily, I am excited enough for the both of us. "Ooh yay!" I clap. "I'm in!"

Maren smiles, but it's halfhearted.

My heart goes out to Dex. He's thrilled about the wedding. Maren, on the other hand… just… isn't. Mare has a serious marriage phobia.

She loves Dex deeply and wants to be with him for life, but she doesn't believe in happily ever after. Not after our dad and her mom's contentious marriage and combative divorce. If it was up to Mare, she and Dex would live happily *un*married for the rest of their lives. Dex wants a legal and binding marriage complete with kids and a white picket fence. His Christian values expect that two people raising a family together be married. His parents remain married even though his father has lived in a skilled nursing facility for the past six years following a stroke. Dex believes in the institution of marriage because he's seen the good side of it. Nevertheless, he understands Maren's feelings, and he respects them, which is why they've taken their time getting to the alter. His patience is remarkable as is his ability to accept her flippant attitude toward the wedding.

"I'm also stuck on the bouquet," she adds. "I can't figure out what I like."

"You should wait until you have your dress picked out," I suggest. "The flowers need to coordinate. You don't want a gigantic bouquet with a simple gown, and you don't want a dinky bouquet with a princess gown. They should be proportionate."

"You seem to know your stuff," Dex says.

I nod. "I have been in so many weddings that I've learned all the things to do and not to do."

It's only April and I've already been in seven weddings. One of which I was the Maid of Honor. Last year, I was in nine weddings. I am a perpetual bridesmaid. As such, I have picked up a lot.

"Such as?" he inquires.

Counting on my fingers, I run down the list. "Don't set predictable tables, but don't over decorate. Do your floral research. Stick with classics, never go trendy. Don't get DIY happy. Never invite non-wedding guests to pre-wedding parties. Don't get a spray tan and don't ignore your eyebrows… I could go on all night."

All three adults stare at me with open mouths.

"Since you have it down to a science," Maren starts, "why don't you plan the whole thing for me?"

"Ha, ha. You're funny."

The four of us spend the next thirty minutes making small talk. While Everett and I aren't ignoring one another, we don't address each other directly. I wonder if he's still annoyed with me. Despite his capacity for being a major dick, he remains the most gorgeous man on earth. I can't stop sneaking peeks at him. His smile drives me wild and when he laughs… my heart can't take it. His voice is deep and husky. I could listen to him talk endlessly and never tire of it.

Once we've finished dinner and everything is cleaned up, I say my goodbye's. I hug Dex and my sister before bidding a quick goodnight to Everett. The only words I've spoken directly to him all evening.

"I'll walk out with you," he says, and gestures to Mare and Dex. "Thank you both for a fantastic meal. Keep that recipe in the rotation."

Maren and Dex close the door behind us. As I approach my car, Everett calls my name. Stunned, I come to an immediate halt. I spin to face him and am surprised to find him standing directly behind me.

"I want to apologize for snapping at you the other day." His head is bent slightly down, but his eyes are on mine. "I was in a shitty mood. Truthfully, I've been in a bad mood for about three years. I shouldn't have taken it out on you. Please forgive me."

With marked contrition, his apology seems as sincere as it is unexpected. Now it's my turn.

"Only if you accept my apology." I glance down to my hands. "When I told my friend what I did, he called me an idiot for declining your offer."

"You were," Everett jests with a crooked smirk that is just too cute. "On a serious note, you have genuine talent, Olivia. I want to help you foster it."

Never did I imagine that Dex hanging my photo on his living room wall would lead to a famous photographer taking notice and offering to nurture my talent. I should say something, anything. But the only words that come to mind are thank you, and that's lame. I refuse to be lame.

Casual and relaxed, Everett leans against my car door. "Did you know eighty-five percent of photographers fail?"

"I didn't know the exact statistic, but I knew most don't make it."

"What's worse is, most who've made it don't have *half* of your natural ability. They only made it because they knew the right people or had a stroke of luck. Those who didn't make it failed simply because they couldn't get the right doors to open. They couldn't get exposure. It's really all about opportunities."

With embarrassment and shame, I cast my eyes to the pavement. I squandered a huge possibly career making opportunity because I was scared and insecure. *I'm such a moron.*

"Being a mentor has always been a goal of mine," he says and turns to me. "I'm finally at a stage in my career that it makes sense and you're the perfect student worthy of my training."

I am a "perfect student" with "genuine talent." My face flushes and butterflies take flight in my belly.

"Join me on a shoot," he urges. "We can check our schedules and pick a day that works for both of us. What do you say?"

I smile much too wide. "I say absolutely."

"Great." He flashes his megawatt smile and rests a hand on my shoulder. "I'll call you tomorrow when I have my calendar in front of me and we can figure it out."

My heart drums in my chest. I feel like I need to say something, but I'm at a loss for words. Again. "This is amazing, Everett. Thank you."

"*Thank you* for allowing me to put things right between us. I felt like such an ass."

"Me too. I wanted to call all week to apologize for being an idiot. I picked up the phone so many times, but I chickened out. And I figured you probably wouldn't want to talk to me anyway, so…" *Why did I say all that?*

He grins, thoroughly entertained by my rambling. "I'm glad we got this worked out. I'll talk to you tomorrow." He pushes off my car and walks toward his. "Have a good night."

The instant I'm in my car, I dial Grayson. Panting, he answers on the fourth ring. It's not like him to be on the treadmill this time of evening.

"Gray!" I yell.

"Damn Liv, either take it down a notch or move the phone away from your mouth."

"Sorry," I lower my voice to a somewhat reasonable decibel. "I didn't mean to scream in your ear, but you're never going to believe what just happened."

He whispers to someone telling them to wait a second. "What just happened?"

"You remember how I told you I was dreading seeing Everett at dinner?"

"Yeah." He breathes hard, there's a rustling in the background.

"Well I'm so glad I did. He offered to be my mentor! Can you freaking believe it? *The* Everett Shaw as my mentor!" I move the phone from my mouth and squeal.

"That's awesome, Liv. Really," he says, followed by a quiet moan. "Can I call you tomorrow?"

"Yeah." And it finally dawns on me. "Wait… are you having sex right now?"

"Kind of." He moans again.

"Yuck! Why did you answer?"

"It was an accident." He laughs as though he's being tickled. "I was trying to reject the call."

"Goodbye Grayson." Hanging up, I try to erase putrid images of Grayson getting it on from my mind.

I've barely slept. I'm too excited about going shooting with Everett. It's all I can think of since talking with him. As eager as I am, I'm also extremely anxious. He's going to be critiquing my technique and my skill along with my weak points.

What if he realizes I am a hack with far more weaknesses than talent and ability? I'm such a bundle of nerves that I'll probably screw everything up.

My stomach rolls. I can't breathe.

We agreed to meet on a Saturday since I work Monday through Friday. My boss is never amenable when I ask for days off. I've only had the job for six months. I haven't acquired any paid time off. Even if she granted me a day off, I can't afford to take it. I can scarcely buy food as it stands.

There's a knock at my door and my stomach flips. Everett has arrived to pick me up.

Here goes nothing.

Or everything.

Soon, I shall find out which.

Chapter 3

PRETENDING TO BE DISINTERESTED, MY roommates, Hannah and Jess, sit to the side. They are desperate to meet the "hot photographer God" that I've been gushing about for the past several weeks.

When I open the door, Everett stands before me with an enthusiastic smile. "You ready?"

"As I'll ever be." I reach for my gear that sits by the door, but Everett holds out his hand to stop me.

"Allow me," he says.

Ooh… Chivalrous.

As he picks up my things, I glimpse my friends who are making googly eyes and mouthing how hot he is. Somehow, I manage to keep from laughing.

It's not until we're on the road that Everett tells me where we're headed.

"I thought we'd hit Red Rocks. I assume you're acquainted with it?"

I nod. "I've been there a few times."

"Have you done any shooting there?"

"A couple times for fun."

"That's what I was counting on. Today I want you to try to see it with a fresh perspective, as though seeing it for the first time." He looks to me for a moment before turning his attention back to the road. "Look at every minute detail. Observe the way the light hits the rocks, the contrast of the blue sky and the redness of the rock. Don't just shoot something because it's pretty. Wait until you see something that *really* catches your eye."

I listen intently, hanging on his every word, all the while picking furiously at my cuticles.

"You seem nervous," he says.

I stop picking. "That's because I am."

His smile is soft and understanding. "Try to forget I'm there. Have fun with it."

I chuckle. Is he kidding? "That's not likely."

"The fun part or forgetting I'm there?" His tone is facetious. He's trying to loosen me up.

"It would probably be fun if I can forget you're there."

"Just pretend I'm one of your friends tagging along for something to do."

Let me put this into perspective for him. "Who is your favorite photographer of all time?"

He answers without hesitation, "Brett Weston."

"If Brett Weston was taking you out on a photo shoot when you were just starting out, would you be able to," I make air quotes, "forget he was there?"

His neck snaps in my direction. "Are you saying I'm your favorite photographer of all time?"

My face heats up. "You're in the top ten. Answer the question."

"No, I wouldn't be able to forget. You make a fair point. But Liv?"

"Yeah?"

"I may be a successful photographer, but I'm really just an ordinary guy who enjoys taking pictures."

We get to the park and start along the trail. Everett also brought his gear, which is distracting. I find myself watching him take pictures rather than observing the scenery for what I want to shoot.

We speak infrequently, but the silence isn't awkward. I can tell he's purposely being quiet so as not to distract me from the task at hand. Little does he know that just his proximity is befuddling. In the twenty minutes we've been walking, he's taken a few shots and I've taken none. This may be a fruitless trip.

Then I see it.

The sunlight hits the rocks to my left in precisely the right way to enhance the colors. Deep reds, light and medium oranges, and the sky is a bright blue with a few high clouds. Perfect contrast. I stop, set the aperture on my camera, and begin snapping. I must take three hundred shots as I try to encapsulate the entirety of the scene. Everett stands idly by observing, but I'm no longer distracted by him or intimidated that he's watching. I'm too caught up in the moment and the beautiful scenery to care.

For the next two hours, it's much of the same. We walk quietly until I spot the perfect scene. We stop. I take a bunch of pictures while Everett watches. We walk more. Everett snaps a couple pictures here and there. He even joins me in snapping a couple of my chosen scenes. Being much more methodical, he probably takes ten shots for every hundred of mine. That must come with experience. He knows how to get the shot he wants with ease.

Once we've finished for the day, he mentions a trendy café on the way home and suggests we stop for a coffee to discuss our day.

At the café, Everett pays for both of us and we take a seat at a corner table, tucked away from the hustle and bustle. Here comes the part where he tells me what he thinks. I'm more nervous now than I was when he picked me up. I recall a trick my mom taught me when

I was young. Whenever I was anxious or upset, she told me to focus on the sights, sounds and smells around me as a means of taking me out of myself.

I start with noises. The patrons are talking, a cellphone rings, someone drops their keys on the floor. Next, I move to scent. The room smells of toasted bread and cinnamon. I love the smell of cinnamon. I breathe in long and slow, and a sense of calm slowly wraps around me. Before I can move on to sights, Everett begins.

"I enjoyed today," he says. "Would I be mistaken if I said you did, too?"

I shake my head with a smile. "You wouldn't be."

Once I got used to him being there, it was a lot of fun.

Everett leans forward, hands clasped together on the table, and sets his eyes on mine. "I feel like the mission was a success. You showed me the one thing I needed to see... a passion for photography. Watching you shoot, it's plain to see. You go totally into the zone, fully fixated on the scene. You're intense, but completely in your bliss. It reminds me of a time long ago when I still got excited over taking pictures."

Blinking, I stare. Did I hear that right? One of the world's top photographers doesn't enjoy his work? Say it isn't so... "You're not passionate about it anymore?"

"Not so much." He shrugs and sits back into his seat. "Photography has become old hat for me. Just more of the same old same old."

"I can't imagine ever feeling that way." Mindlessly, I spin my glass of iced tea. "Every time I hold a camera in my hands, I get a rush of adrenaline. As though the world is a canvas and it's up to me to capture it just right. For me, taking pictures is like smoking. It's my vice. If I don't take at least one picture a day, even if it's just of a flower, I get twitchy."

Everett closes his eyes as if he's remembering something.

"I haven't had that feeling in so long. Seeing the passion and excitement in your eyes when you were shooting was inspiring." He swallows as he pauses. "I had more fun taking pictures today than I've had in a long time."

Based on his depth of tone, this is a big deal for him.

"Hopefully I'll continue to inspire you with my excitement and love of the craft."

"Hopefully." He clears his throat. "Now, on to the technical stuff."

My stomach tightens and I screw my eyes shut. *Here we go.* "Be gentle."

I jump at the sensation of his hand on mine. He chuckles. "Don't worry, Liv. Today wasn't a test where you pass or fail."

His warm hand is big and strong looking, much like the rest of him, and the contact is reassuring. But it's gone all too soon as he pulls his hand away.

"The second thing I noticed is, you're what we in the business call a sprayer and prayer."

"A what?" I ask, nose wrinkled. Whatever it is doesn't sound good.

He chuckles again. "A sprayer and prayer. It's when a photographer takes hundreds of pics of the same scene in rapid succession. It's called spray and pray. Taking a bunch of pics hoping to get the perfect one."

I nod. "I've always done that. Is it wrong?"

Everett shakes his head. "It's not wrong, but extremely time consuming in the long run. I'm guessing you took five-hundred pictures today, maybe more. Now you have to comb through them, which will take considerable time."

I nod again. He's right. I put in more time combing through my photos than taking them. It's my least favorite part of the process.

"Then," he continues, "once you've examined all of them, there's the process of elimination which takes even more time, am I right?"

"Yes," I sigh. The task seems never-ending, but I assumed all photog's go through the same.

"And then," he continues further, "you get them narrowed down to a few or even a dozen, but you're torn on which you like best."

He's reading my mind. "Right again."

"It's fine, and works for many photographers," Everett says, probably to make me feel better, "but unnecessary. Focus more on the setup. Imagine what you are trying to capture. What do you envision? Personally, I visit a location several times before taking a single shot. I'll spend days there deciding what I want to capture. The sunrise? A foggy morning? The low light of the evening? Once I figure that out, I watch the forecast, pick the date and time that matches my vision and I go out."

The man a genius. I have been going about things the wrong way! I slap the table. "That makes so much sense. I never thought to do that."

"What we did today, I rarely ever do," he confesses. "I do my due diligence. I plan out the photo shoot, set it up, and then and only then will I do any shooting. It takes time, but it's infinitely more enjoyable to spend a day out on foot than sitting behind a computer screen scouring through images."

"I agree. I'm going to try it that way."

"Over time, it'll eliminate your need to spray and pray. When I go out, I take several shots, but I usually end up with more than one winner and I always get at least one that is exactly what I was hoping for. How often does that happen for you?"

"Rarely," I admit and slink back into my seat. "I get good pictures, but seldom what I was wishing for."

"That'll be your first assignment. Choose a place and we'll go out and study it in all different weather. You'll decide what you want to capture and when the weather is right, we will set up the shoot."

I don't need time to consider where I want to go. "Is Bear Lake too far away?"

It's a good two-hour drive from Denver. Maren and Dex took me once. It's a stunning place, and I was so excited to take pictures. I was beyond disappointed to discover the battery in my camera was dead. All I had was my phone. I got some okay photos, but nothing like I could have taken with my Nikon. Unfortunately, I haven't been back.

"Of course not. Bear Lake it is," he says easily, and rubs his hands together with an eager smile. "Now enough with the business talk. Let's dig into these pastries. They are the best in Colorado."

"Don't let Mare hear you say that."

"I won't tell if you don't." He winks and just like that, I'm at ease and once again under his spell.

I don't know why, but Grayson and I spend most of our time together running. Well, it's more of a speed walk mixed with jogging than a run, but calling it running makes us feel better about ourselves.

"Inquiring minds want to know who you were boinking when I called the other night," I say.

"Boinking?" He screws up his sweet, baby face. "No one says *boinking* anymore, Liv."

"Mare does. In fact, it's her preferred term for doing the nasty."

"The nasty? There's another expression I've never understood. There is nothing nasty about sex."

I shoot him a look. "Alabama hot pocket."

Grayson chokes on his laughter. "Okay, point taken."

"So?" I bump him with my shoulder. "Who is she?"

He hangs his head with mock shame. "My boss's personal assistant."

My head whips in his direction. "The hot blonde with the giant stick stuck up her ass?"

He laughs again. I'm on a roll. "The one and only."

"I thought you hated her?"

"I did. I think I still do. But she said she wanted to deep throat my meat, so I let her."

It's my turn to choke. "She didn't say that."

"Literally, those were her exact words. It may have been the booze speaking, but she followed through so…"

My favorite thing about Grayson is his blunt honesty. I love the guy, honestly and truly. Like a brother. But whenever he says things like that, I end up envisioning him in the act and it makes me acutely nauseas. I push the repugnant vision out of my mind with memories of Everett's sexy smile and velvety voice. I haven't been able to stop thinking of him since he dropped me off yesterday.

We ended up spending an hour and a half at the café talking about this and that. We talked about his travels, Dex and Maren and what a perfect, if unlikely pair they are. Oddly, we didn't talk much about photography. It kind of felt like a date, even though it obviously wasn't. But when we said goodbye, his gaze lingered on my lips. I'm sure it was all in my head. I'm fantastic at seeing things I want to see when they aren't there.

To my dismay, Grayson continues. "She called me already and asked for round two. Guess she got a taste of something she likes. Pun intended."

I gag. He says crap like that on purpose just to gross me out. "Next subject."

"How was your photo shoot with Hottie McHotness?"

I throw my head back in laughter. "Hottie *McHotness*?"

"Yeah. All you've talked about for weeks on end is how brilliant and good looking the guy is."

"McHotness is a catchy nickname. I like it." All this talking while jogging has me out of breath and I slow down. "The shoot was great. He observed my technique and gave me good advice."

"It wasn't as nerve-racking as you expected it to be?"

"At first it was, but I got over it for the most part. Now I have to go through all the shots I took and send him my two best to critique. *That* will be seriously nerve-racking."

"He's seen your work before."

"Yeah, but what if they're shit? I don't want to give him shit to critique."

"You're being self-conscious, Liv. Your pictures are awesome."

"To the untrained eye, but Everett will notice every flaw."

"That's a good thing," my friend encourages. "When he points them out, you'll learn what mistakes not to make."

"True, but still…"

Grayson slows almost to a stop. "Can I make a suggestion without you biting off my head?"

"Of course."

"Spend your time with him honing your craft rather than trying to impress him."

I open my mouth to argue that I'm not trying to impress Everett. But that's not entirely true. Sure, I want to learn and perfect my craft, but I also want Everett to be impressed with me. "You know me too well Grayson Masters."

Before beginning my Bear Lake assignment, Everett is taking me to shadow him on a shoot at Mount Falcon Park. We arrive at his chosen location two hours before sunset. The sun is already low in the sky, casting a golden hue on the landscape. The calming scent of pine needles and earth hangs in the cool Spring air. Everett sets up his equipment and gets ready. We each have a chair placed on either side of his tripod.

"How are you coming with the Red Rock photos?" He glances my way.

It's been two weeks since we were at Red Rocks. I'm still sifting through all the photos I took. It's been a grueling process. "I've narrowed it down to seven. I'll process them this week and decide which are my top two. But I'll warn you, they aren't my best."

Unimpressed with the photos, I need him to know up front that I'm aware it isn't stellar work.

Everett shrugs. "I'm not seeking perfection, Liv. I just want to get a sense for how you work. What's your style? Your signature, so to speak. Then I can help you refine it."

I take a chance and ask the question that's been burning in my mind since the day I met him. The question I would have asked that day had I not been such a complete spaz. In all the interviews I read, I've not found his answer to it. "You probably get asked this a lot, but how did you become a photographer?"

His expression turns thoughtful, and a moment passes before he answers. "I never set out to be a photographer. If you were to ask me twenty years ago if I envisioned this as my profession, I would've laughed."

His response doesn't answer my question, but I assume there's a reason he doesn't want to discuss it. Probably the same reason I never found the answer in all his interviews. If I had to guess, I bet it has something to do with his father and the Shaw family legacy that Everett was expected to continue. His dad owns a conglomerate. A multinational business Everett's grandfather built from the ground up. According to Dex, Everett's father was none too pleased when his only son didn't follow in his footsteps. He cut Everett off financially and their relationship remains nonexistent.

His choice to walk away and venture out on his own astounds me. The man was born into incredible wealth and privilege. He would never worry about anything for the rest of his life. He gave up everything to follow his dream, even if the decision meant being broke and scraping to get by. I have immense respect for him for making that choice. Few people would, or could, do what he did.

Reaching into the cooler between us, Everett retrieves a bottle of sweet tea. After taking a long swig, he answers my question.

"Photography found me when I was struggling to figure out who I was. It was therapy for me, in a way. I carried my camera everywhere I went. I'd sit in places for hours snapping one picture after another, fooling around and tweaking the settings. It became a love of mine. I started hanging my work at home and people took notice. I actually sold my first print at a garage sale."

"No way!" *The* Everett Shaw sold his photography in a garage sale?

"Yep. It was complete happenstance. It wasn't for sale. I had intended to put it up in my living room. The photo was leaning on the wall of my garage and a guy asked how much I'd sell it for. I sold it to him for double what I paid to have it printed. That's when I decided to go into business."

"I can't imagine what it would feel like to sell a print."

"The first sale is exhilarating." As though recalling the day, he has a faraway look. It isn't long before he returns to the present. "I've had a lot of interest in your City Hall print. That's what I named it. I hope you don't mind."

I couldn't care less about him naming my picture. I just can't believe he went ahead and displayed it. After our disagreement, I assumed he changed his mind. "You put it up?"

He nods. "I told you I was going to. It's also featured on my website. I've been meaning to ask you to come in and sign it. Makes the piece more valuable that way."

Valuable? My amateur photo has value? I try my hardest not to seem too excited and fail fantastically. "Of course! I'll come sign it whenever you want."

Everett chuckles at my over the top enthusiasm. He laughs often, which I adore. I also like the way the corners of his eyes wrinkle when he smiles.

But even his gorgeous smile isn't enough to keep my insecurity at bay. "Do you think it'll sell?"

"I know it will." Full of confidence, he gives an easy nod. "In addition to the print I have hanging, I'm offering prints in a variety of sizes. I expect a couple people to place orders in the next week or two."

Oh. My. God. If it sells, I will be a bona fide photographer! "You have to call me the instant you sell one!"

"It won't be me making the sale," he says. "It'll be you. But yes, I promise to call."

With that, Everett stands and snaps a series of photos. Soaking everything in, I watch his every move. At first I'm studying his technique and how he works. But I'm swiftly distracted. I find my eyes wandering to his angular jawline and broad shoulders. Even his nose is attractive.

After spending a little time with Everett, I'm starting to really like him. And it's not about his good looks or the fact that I am a fan of his work. With his laid-back vibe, he's pleasant company and he's easy to make conversation with. Given his extensive travel, he has a plethora of stories to tell. Everett is an incredibly interesting person with an abundance of life experience. The more I learn about him, the more I want to know. The more time I spend with him, the more time I want.

Chapter 4

AFTER OUR PHOTO SHOOT, I stop by Mare and Dex's to pick up some hot plates. Maren takes pity on me and sends me home with food a few nights a week which is more than fine with me. Nothing beats a home cooked meal that I didn't prepare.

Since I'm arriving later than usual, I get to hang out in the den with Dex while I wait for Maren to get out of the shower.

"How's it going with Everett?" he asks, and motions for me to take a seat in a chair across from him.

"It's great. We've only gone out a couple times so far, but he has given many great pointers already."

"He's good at what he does. You can benefit a lot from his experience."

I nod. "I agree on both counts."

Leaning forward in his chair, Dex clasps his hands. "Can I be straight with you, Liv?"

I shrug. "Sure."

"Ev is my best friend," he starts, and I instantly see where this is heading. "I love him like a brother, but I know him. Better than he knows himself, I think. And you are my sister now that I'm with Maren."

Holding my hand up, I stop him from going further. "Please don't worry, Dex. He has been a perfect gentleman."

"I'm glad to hear that." He casts his gaze to the floor and shifts in his seat. "But that's not all I am worried about."

What is he getting at? I arch an eyebrow, waiting on him to continue.

"Your sister and I are aware of your infatuation with Ev and frankly, we're concerned."

My body freezes and tingling sweeps up the back of my neck to my face. Am I that transparent? "You really have no reason to worry, Dex. Any time Everett and I spend together is strictly professional. And honestly," the words I am getting ready to spill are an utter lie and I hate myself for it, but oh well, "the little crush I had on him is *long* gone. It was more about being inspired by his work."

Not buying a word I've said, Dex crosses his arms and draws his eyebrows together. "Getting involved with Everett would be a bad idea, Livvy. He isn't an evil guy, and he never does anything with ill intentions, but—"

"May I stop you there?" I interrupt and he nods. "I can tell you unequivocally that nothing has or ever will happen between me and him."

With his eyes trained on mine, Dex sits back into his chair, arms still crossed as he ponders my words. Based on his expression, the jury is out. "Liv, you understand I am just trying to protect you?"

Although I lied on the subject of my crush on Everett—I'm crushing harder now than I was before I knew him. Odds are, by this time next week, my infatuation will be even stronger—the feeling clearly isn't mutual. Not once has Everett indicated that he's the least bit interested in me. He has never looked at me in *that* way. He treats me like a student. Looks at me like I'm Maren's little sister. Nothing will ever come of it, no matter how attracted I am to him.

"I do understand that, and I appreciate your concern, but it isn't necessary. There's nothing to protect me from where Everett is concerned."

He blows out a breath. "You're a beautiful young woman, Liv. And while you may think Everett doesn't see that, I guarantee you he does. If he hasn't acted on it, it's only because you're Maren's sister."

Wait. Does Dex know something I don't? Has Everett said something? Is that what this is all about? If I ask, I will show my cards and reveal my lie.

"Exactly. I'm Maren's little sister, and for that reason alone, you have nothing to worry about."

For that reason alone, even if Everett is attracted to me, which I seriously doubt, he'll never come near me. He learned his lesson when he crossed Maren the first time. He won't do it again, especially not with her sister.

I wasn't planning on coming out to Bear Lake today. Originally, I was supposed to spend the day at Hannah's boyfriend's pool party. But they got into a fight and he uninvited Hannah and her friends. Call me crazy, but that is just fine with me. I'd much prefer spending my time at Bear Lake than at a party getting hit on by sloppy drunk guys that I have less than zero interest in.

Since this was a spur of the moment trip, I didn't tell Everett. I figured he had plans and didn't expect him to drop everything at the last minute and make the journey with me. Besides, he and I are coming out next Saturday. But Maren and Dex let it slip that I was driving out here today, and Everett called and offered to tag along.

After forty minutes of walking, I find the perfect site for my photo shoot. Off the beaten path is a breathtaking view of the lake, with evergreen trees and mountains in the background.

I remember this spot from my previous outing here. I was able to get a couple pictures with my phone, but couldn't spend a lot of time because I was hiking with Maren and Dex. When Everett told me to pick a location for a shoot, I chose Bear Lake for this specific view.

"This is it."

Standing to my right, Everett takes in the scene before us. "Are you sure? We haven't done much walking."

"I'm positive." I remove the cover from the lens, select my settings, and start snapping away.

The words "spray and pray" slide into my mind and I stop. I step back and thoroughly examine the landscape, taking my time to deliberate the image I want to capture.

Although the assignment was to choose my setting, not to do any actual shooting, I still brought my camera. I couldn't help myself. Thankfully, I'm not the only one. With his own camera in hand, Everett joins me in getting a few shots.

Once we've both taken a good number of pictures and our cameras are put aside, I stand staring in awe of the gorgeous landscape.

"Have you ever seen a place this beautiful?"

"I've seen places that blow this away."

I should've considered the person I'm talking to when I asked the question. Everett has traveled the world over. Still…

"You don't think this view is incredible?" I motion toward the scenery before us.

"Sure, I do. But there are thousands of views far more incredible. Hopefully, one day, you'll get to see them."

Tearing my eyes away from the beauty before me, I look at Everett. It's a fair trade. "What would you say is the most beautiful place you've traveled to?"

He answers without hesitation, "Angel Falls, Venezuela."

Angel Falls… I have studied his work extensively. It doesn't ring a bell. Surely if it's so grand he would have shot there. "How come there aren't any photos of Angel Falls in your portfolio?"

His eyes widen and he smiles. Is he really surprised by my familiarity with his portfolio? "You're right. I haven't released any."

"Why not? If it's so beautiful?"

"That's why. It's too magnificent." He gets a far-off look and sighs. "No photo can do Angel Falls justice. Not even I could capture its beauty."

"But you took pictures?"

"Of course. I have one up in my condo." He sits on the trunk of a dead tree. "That was the best trip I've ever taken."

Again with the distant gaze. He must be remembering. After a moment, he scoots to the side and offers me a seat beside him.

"I'd like to see the pictures… if that's okay."

He glances my way with soft eyes. "I'd be happy to show them to you."

Having already chosen my site, we settle in for the next two hours watching the sun lower in the sky and making small talk about photography, his travels, and Dex and Maren.

The sun is almost set, and we will have to leave soon. I snap a final picture and realize this is *it*. *This* is what I wish to capture. The colors are so vivid. The sky is a deep blue, the sunlight casts a yellow and orange glow on the clouds and the mountain. It's pure perfection.

I hear a series of clicks coming from Everett's camera and assume he's capturing the scene. But when I glance to my right, I am stunned to find him shooting me. I throw a hand up to cover my face.

"No," he waves my hand away. "Keep sitting there."

"I can't now."

"Please do this for me," he implores. "Look out at the sunset."

I do as told, but I'm not nearly as relaxed and awe-inspired as I was three minutes ago. I figure it'll only last a couple more minutes, but time continues to pass as Everett snaps one picture after another, walking all around me. He takes shots from the front, both sides and even my back. At least ten minutes pass before he finally stops. He thanks me and puts away his camera.

"I don't need to come back," I say as we pull out of the parking lot and onto the main road. "That sunset is exactly what I want to capture."

He shakes his head. "Nope. That's not the assignment. The assignment is to come out in all different weather and times of day."

"But—"

He cuts me off. "Imagine that view on a foggy morning, or right after a rain shower when the clouds start to break up and the sun comes streaming through. You have to see it all."

"Okay. But I still want to shoot that."

"Then you can. But I bet that's what the majority of photog's would do." He shifts sideways in his seat to look directly into my eyes. "Liv, if you want to make a name for yourself in this business, you need to be different and stand out from the crowd. To do that, you must think outside the box. Don't always go for the obvious shot."

Think outside the box. Don't go for the obvious shot. Good advice. "I'll keep that in mind."

"May I turn on the radio?" he asks, and I nod. "What music do you prefer?"

"I'm not picky."

"Do you like stuff from the nineties?"

I shrug. "Sure."

"You're not being very helpful," he chuckles.

There's a reason for that. I don't enjoy telling people what music I like. When someone puts down a song or musician I enjoy, it feels like a jab. I realize that is absurd, but it's how I feel. For me, musical preference is extremely personal. It reveals so much about a person. As such, I must be comfortable with a person before sharing my taste in music with them.

"Whatever you put on is fine."

"Nineties it is."

What he doesn't know and what I won't say, however silly it may be, is I love nineties music. I was born in the nineties and grew up listening to this music. Maren playing it on blast was also a major influence. To this day, whenever we are in the car together, Oasis and No Doubt are our go to's.

"I hope you didn't mind me taking your picture earlier," Everett says and continues before I can respond. "I should've asked first. It's just that there are times when you get a certain look on your face. An expression so serious that it's as though you are pondering the meaning of life and might have stumbled on an answer."

This isn't the first time I've been told I wear a severe expression. My closest friends often tell me I'm too serious. That I should lighten up and live in the moment. I think I live in the moment, I'm just a serious person most of the time. I do a lot of thinking and analyzing. And yes, I have pondered the meaning of living. I do it often.

"You aren't far off," I confess.

He twists to face me. "So have you figured it out? The meaning of life?"

Few people I know want to delve into deep conversation. Grayson comes the closest, but even he prefers to keep things light and fun. Though I don't know Everett well, I relish the opportunity to hold a thoughtful discussion.

"Actually, I believe I have a pretty good idea."

"Care to share your divine knowledge?"

"Simply put, I believe life is a gift that we are meant to make the most of. But most people squander it. They let time go by, doing nothing worthwhile." When I glance his way, he appears truly engrossed in what I'm saying, so I continue. "People live for work and to accumulate things, but they hate their jobs. They spend so much time working their hated jobs that they can't enjoy the things they've achieved. Making matters worse, they spend more time with co-workers—some of which they loathe—than with their loved ones.

That's not living. *I* choose to *live*. I love photography. I love capturing moments and making them immortal."

Seemingly impressed, Everett watches me with a thoughtful expression. But he doesn't have a chance to chime in because I'm speed talking.

"Even the sad moments are beautiful and worth capturing," I say. "*Everything* about life is beautiful and meant to be cherished. So even though the odds say I'll fail, I will follow my dream, even if it means living in a dumpy studio apartment and eating ramen for the rest of my life. Because I realize living isn't about making money and acquiring things. It's about *moments* and enjoying them to the fullest. And *that* is what I intend to do. If everyone lived that way, the world would be a much happier place."

I suck in a much-needed breath.

Staring at me, mouth agape, Everett places a palm on my shoulder. "You're wise beyond your years, Olivia Bell."

As always, my skin tingles from his touch. My pulse accelerates and butterflies take flight in my belly. I could probably count on one hand the number of times he's touched me, and my physical reaction is invariably the same.

"I wish I had half your optimism," he says. "But I agree with everything you said. I've always lived in the moment, enjoying life to the fullest, but I'm sorry I didn't spend more time considering the bigger picture and the future."

"It seems to me you've done pretty well for yourself."

He nods, but his lips turn down into a frown. "Looks can be deceiving. I'm forty years old and stuck in a rut with no idea where I am going."

Based on what I've gleaned from the limited time I've spent with him, and what Dex has shared, Everett doesn't open up to just anyone. That he's speaking so openly after knowing me for such a short while is unexpected.

"I've felt that way before, unsure where I'm headed or what I want." Whenever it happens, I do what my dad taught me to do and it always helps. "Try imagining your life five years from now and be *very specific*. What exactly do you see?"

Doubtful, he looks to me and scratches his beard.

"Try it," I encourage. "Take your time."

Everett sweeps a hand through his hair and sighs. Silence lingers as a few minutes pass. He closes his eyes and leans his head on the headrest.

"I'm ready to slow down." He pauses, ducks his chin to his chest and speaks in a quiet voice. "In five years, I see myself traveling less and putting out less work. Perhaps being semi-retired. I'd like to spend more time with friends and loved ones. Honestly, I just hope that within five years I've found peace."

He releases a long breath, as though he's relieved to have spoken the words.

His last sentence makes me want to dig deeper. What does he mean? Why isn't he at peace? Is he not happy with his life? Has something happened? Perhaps there's something lacking in his life?

But I don't know him well enough to ask those deep questions. Perhaps one day… when we know each other better.

Also, it's not lost on me that he didn't say he'd like to spend more time with *family* and friends. In the short while I've known him, he's never mentioned any family. Not even during our weekly dinners with Dex and Maren.

From what Dex told me, Everett's mom is dead, something we have in common, and he isn't close with his dad. He was an only child. His parents, or rather his father, viewed him as an accident and made sure not to make the same mistake twice. I know nothing of his extended family or if he has any. My heart goes out to him. While my life hasn't been perfect, it overflows with love.

Wanting to offer him some form of comfort, I reach my hand out and place it on his, giving it a slight squeeze. "You'll find your peace."

"I can't believe this!" I say, while examining the vintage Leica M3 camera Grayson's grandmother has gifted me. It's in excellent condition and looks as though it's never been used, even though it's almost seventy years old. "Why would she give this to me?"

Grayson shrugs. "When I found it in her den, I commented that you would love it and she said to take it."

"No way!" Awestruck, I stare at the camera. When Grayson called last night and said he had a surprise for me, I never guessed this. "This is a highly sought-after vintage camera, Gray. It's worth a lot of money."

He shrugs. I may as well be speaking mandarin. He knows zero about cameras and photography. "It's yours now."

"I feel like I should pay her something for it."

He waves off my idea. "Drop her a thank you note. You know how old people are about their thank you notes."

Boy, do I ever… My dad's sister, Evelyn sent me a gift card for my birthday last year. I called her to thank her, but I didn't send a thank you card. Still, to this day, she won't talk to me over it. It's not like I didn't thank her. I'll never understand why a phone call isn't acknowledgment enough. When I give gifts, I do it with zero expectation. I do it because I choose to. No thanks required. But that's just me.

Gazing at the camera, I almost say out loud that I can't wait to show it to Everett.

I've thought about him constantly since our trip to Bear Lake. Thoughts of the man consume me. It's getting out of hand. Our time together and the conversations we've had play on a continual loop in my mind. I'm like a giddy teenage girl whenever I think about seeing him again. I've never been one of those girls who puts much thought into what I wear or my makeup. But when I know I will see him, I spend hours in my closet and in front of the mirror.

"I'm in trouble, Gray," I say and flop onto his couch.

"What kind of trouble?" He joins me on the sofa with a look of concern. Grayson is always ready to swoop in and save the day.

"Everett Shaw trouble," I sigh.

Grayson blows out a breath and drags a hand through his dark hair. His stare is accusatory. "You hooked up, didn't you?"

"No, but God I want to." I sit up and grab a handful of Hershey's Kisses from the bag on his coffee table. "The more time I spend with him, the more I like him. I really, *really* like him, Gray."

"Despite the fact that he's a manwhore who has bedded women on every continent?"

"That's just it… He doesn't come off as an egocentric manwhore at all."

"His past tells a bit of a different story." He steals a kiss from my hand and pops it into his mouth.

"Have *we* never made mistakes?" I counter. "Are we the same people we were in high school? Would we make the same decisions today that we made back then?"

Grayson sits upright and angles his body to face me directly. "What are you getting at, Liv?"

"People change. We learn and we grow." I stand and pace the living room. "We shouldn't be judged by our past but rather by who we are *today*."

He arches a brow. "Do you *know* who he is today?"

I stop pacing and face him head on. "I'm starting to and Grayson, he's a really nice guy."

"Maybe that's because you aren't sleeping together."

My gaze flicks upward as I cross my arms and tap my foot. "Or perhaps it's because he *is* a nice guy."

Grayson listens intently as I recount my conversation with Everett on the way home from Bear Lake. I explain that there's so much more to Everett than what others say about him. He isn't just a horny guy looking for his next piece. He's thoughtful and introspective.

"Liv," Grayson starts with a careful tone, "did you miss the part where he didn't say he sees himself with a wife and kids? Unless you left something out, he said nothing of a relationship or family. All he said was he wants to retire and spend more time with his friends. That's a warning sign."

"It is not," I protest.

"The dude is forty years old. In five years, he'll be forty-five. His life will be halfway over or more. If he doesn't see himself with those things by then, he doesn't want them."

"You don't know that." Or does he?

"Yes, I do," he insists. "I'm twenty-five and while I may not be ready for marriage and kids yet, I know I want them one day. I see myself married with kids by the time I'm Everett's age. If you asked me what I see myself doing in five years, I'd say, I hope I'm married or at least engaged to the love of my life and that we are planning our family together."

"That's you, Grayson," I sigh, exasperated. "Everett doesn't have to be the same as you to be a good person."

"You're right," he allows with a nod, "but if he doesn't want marriage and a family, how is that good for *you*?"

"You're getting way ahead of yourself here. I'm not saying I want to marry the guy for shit's sake."

"Maybe not, but you want to get married one day." Grayson stands to face me, eye to eye. "I know how important it is for you to be a mom. Why bother getting involved with someone who doesn't want the same things you want? It's counterintuitive."

"Not every relationship has to end in the fairytale."

"No, but if you're with Mr. Right Now, you could miss out on Mr. Right."

It's annoying when he's right, and really ticks me off. Realizing Everett probably isn't the man I'm meant to be with doesn't change what I feel for him.

"It doesn't even matter because he'd never look at me that way." My stomach tightens.

"Don't be mad at me, Liv." Grayson clutches my hand. "I'm trying to put things into perspective for you. We always promised we'd be honest with one another."

"Yeah, but sometimes the truth sucks Grayson."

"I know." His voice is low, his smile is tentative. "Please tell me you aren't angry with me."

"I'm not mad at you," I say, but it's only half true. I may not be mad, mad but I am irritated. Why is he always so levelheaded? I just want to enjoy my infatuation with Everett without having reality thrown in my face by the one person whose opinion I can't ignore.

Chapter 5

"THIS IS REMARKABLE," EVERETT SAYS and picks up the Leica gingerly, as though it's the most precious thing he's ever seen. "I've always wanted to shoot with one of these."

"I know, right?"

He turns to me with raised brows. "The woman just *gave* this to you?"

"Yep." With a nod, I step closer to him. Like a magnet, I'm drawn to him. "I can't believe it either."

"She must have no idea what she had, or she wouldn't have given it away." He examines the Leica from every angle. "It's in pristine condition. Did she ever even use the thing?"

I shrug. "Dunno. Grayson says it belonged to his grandfather, and he hadn't used it in years."

Something about having this man in my bedroom has my senses on overdrive. He smells so good my mouth waters. I lean forward to be closer.

Everett grins wide and there's a sparkle in his blue eyes. "I'll pick up some film and we can try this baby out this weekend."

Equally excited to hang out with him as I am to try out the Leica, I clap. "Yes!"

"I won't be offended if you say no, but do you mind if I take this with me and play around a bit?" I start to answer but he cuts me off by whispering, "Please, please, please?"

Not that I would tell him no, but if I was going to, I can't now. He's just too cute. "Of course you can take it."

"Really?" he asks, clutching the camera to his chest like a little kid holding his most cherished toy.

"Sure, I trust you. You know a heck of a lot more about using it than I do. I've never used a film camera."

Maren marches into my room unexpectedly.

What is she doing here?

Her gaze flits back and forth between me and Everett, her surprise clear as day.

"Everett," she says, "fancy meeting you here."

"Yeah," Everett starts with a slight stutter. "Olivia asked me over to look at this camera her friend gave her. It's vintage and highly coveted."

Maren crosses her arms and juts out a hip. Her phony smile doesn't conceal her displeasure or skepticism. "Is that right?"

"Yep," Everett answers. "I'm here for the camera." He holds it out for her to see.

"Looks like you found it… in my little sister's bedroom," Maren says, her fake smile still intact. "If you don't need anything else, I'm here to take said sister out for dinner."

"You're being rude, Maren," I grumble.

Her only response is the roll of her eyes. She would never tolerate me being unpleasant to a guest in her home.

Everett turns to me. "I promise to take excellent care of this."

"I'm not the least bit worried."

He flashes his sexy as ever smirk. "Send me a text to let me know when you want to go out this weekend."

With her eyeballs bulging out of their sockets, Maren looks like she's ready strangle Everett. Has she forgotten he is mentoring me?

"I will," I say. "Thanks for stopping by, Everett."

"Thank you," he says with a giddy smile. Ignoring Maren's blatant rudeness, he voices a kind goodbye to her as he departs.

My sister stares daggers at me. "What did he mean when he said, 'go out this weekend?'"

"We're going shooting like we usually do on weekends."

"Oh."

As soon as I hear Everett exit through the front door, I holler, "I don't appreciate you being rude to him."

She raises her voice, "Well excuse me for being surprised to find Everett the womanizer your bedroom. Couldn't you have handled your business in the living room?"

The gall of her!

With hands on my hips, I return her fierce stare. "The camera was in here and I'll handle my business where I want. I am a grown woman! Besides, *he* was invited. *You* are the one who showed up unannounced."

She flinches. "Are you saying I'm unwelcome?"

I hate arguing with Maren, and the last thing I want to do is hurt her feelings. As annoyed as I am with her, the words I spoke were uncalled for.

I take a deep breath to calm myself. "I don't want to fight with you, Mare. Of course, you're welcome. I just don't appreciate being treated like a child."

"I'm only looking out for your best interest. If you were aware of the things I know about that man…"

"I know enough," I insist. "And I already told Dex, but I will tell you again, there's nothing to worry about between me and Everett. *Nothing at all.*"

Her ice blue eyes are teeming with skepticism. "Do you promise?"

I roll my eyes. "Enough with this, Mare. I've told you nothing is going on. Please let it go."

Maren purses her lips in thought. After a few seconds she nods, but her pinched expression conveys her doubt. "Okay, I'll drop it. Do you want to grab some sushi? My treat."

Only Maren would show up at one's house, get into an argument, and then ask the person to dinner. She's lucky she's my sister and I love her.

"One condition… no more talk of Everett."

"Deal."

"Hey there," Everett greets me with familiar grin as I enter the gallery Wednesday evening.

He texted me earlier and asked me to pop by on my way home from work. Without going into detail, he said he has a couple things he wants to discuss. I assume it's regarding the images I sent him from our Red Rocks shoot.

"Hey back," I say.

"Come sit," he motions to a pair of barstools behind the counter, "I'll lock up."

I set my coffee and handbag down on the counter and glance about the area. He's changed his displays since the last time I was here.

"Thanks for coming by," Everett says on his way back from locking the doors and turning off some lights. He takes a seat on the stool beside me. "First, the images you sent over were good, but like you said, they aren't great. We'll go over the details when we have more time, if that's okay?"

So that's not why he called me here… "That's fine."

"Tonight, I want to discuss a couple other things with you. I'll start with the good news. Your City Hall print sold."

My jaw drops. Even though he said he expected a sale, I hadn't allowed myself to believe it would happen. "No way!"

"Yep. The buyer picked it up today." He hands me an envelope. "It sold for eight hundred bucks."

I almost choke. He can't be for real. "You're joking."

"Nope." Shaking his head, he presents the receipt. "That's a pretty good ticket for a first sale."

"Oh. My. God. I can't believe this." Happy tears pool in my eyes and I shake my head in disbelief. "My first sale."

"Before you get too excited," he warns, "you don't get the whole eight hundred. I deducted my printing cost and a thirty percent consignment fee. Your take is just shy of five hundred."

I stare in awe at the envelop in my hand. "That's more than I make in a week at my job."

"Congratulations, Liv," he says, looking every bit as thrilled as I feel.

"Thank you, Everett. This is all because of you."

"This has very little to do with me. You took the picture. All I did was hang it where people can see it."

I stand and wrap my arms around his shoulders. "You did so much more, and you know it."

After a moment, but he returns my gesture, draping his strong, warm arms around my waist. His beard isn't nearly as rough and scratchy against my face as I'd imagined it would be. I like how it feels. I don't want to let go, but if I hold on any longer, this will get awkward. Dropping my hands, I step away from his warmth.

"I can't tell you how much this means to me," I say.

"I think I know," his voice is low.

Am I imaging his burning gaze?

He clears his throat. "And now for the second item I asked you here to discuss. I want to hire you as my assistant."

"W—What?" I stutter.

"It would be easier for me to mentor you if you worked with me full time, and truth be told, I could use the help here at the gallery."

This can't be real. "You want me to work here... for you?"

He chuckles. "That's what I said."

I throw my arms around him again. "Yes! Yes, yes, yes, yes!"

He hugs me back, again. "We should probably go over the details before you agree."

To hell with the details. No way will I pass up a job at *Everett Shaw's* gallery. This is a dream come true.

"I'm listening," I say, and pull away.

"The hours will be nine to six, possibly a couple later nights but not too many. I prefer to keep my evenings free. As for the weekends, we'll still go on shoots like we have been, but that won't be paid time as that's time I'm spending teaching you."

"Sounds good." It sounds freaking fantastic!

"The salary is forty thousand a year, but I can't provide insurance right now."

"I already have insurance." When I fell off my dad's insurance plan, he insisted on getting another for me. Knowing I can't afford it, he pays the premium. "Forty thousand is more than I earn now and honestly, working here would be a dream. My answer is yes."

"Fantastic," he claps his hands together. "When can you start?"

I would start tomorrow but... "I should give my boss the customary two-week notice."

"That works." He extends his hand for a shake. "Welcome to Everett Shaw Photography."

Maren has called me over to pick up a few days worth of dinners she prepared specially for me. While here I intend to tell her about my new job. I'm not exactly champing at the bit to share my exciting news. She won't be happy. In fact, I wager she'll tell me what a horrendous idea it is and try to talk me out of it. Just thinking of the conversation about to ensue is exhausting.

Maren opens the door and greets me with a smile and a quick hug.

"I made your favorite," she says as I follow her into the kitchen, "baked ziti."

"You're spoiling me with these home cooked meals." Hopefully a little sucking up will soften her up before I tell her my news.

"I hope your roommates aren't eating them." She retrieves a large baking dish full of ziti and two additional containers of what I don't know out of the fridge.

Hannah ate my last serving of chili. Her excuse was she thought I didn't like it. Having scarfed down a bowl right in front of her the evening before, I'm not sure where she got that idea. But mostly, she and Jess don't touch the food Maren sends me home with. Probably because they are afraid of her. Maren can be quite intimidating. The last time she was at my place, the night she was rude to Everett, she told both girls in a roundabout, yet clear manner that the food she gives me is not for their consumption.

Without giving me a chance to respond to her previous statement, she says, "I made this one for you. Just bring the dish back when you're finished with it."

"Thank you, Mare. I really appreciate it. But I feel bad about you spending all this time and money feeding me."

She shrugs. "It's what family does, Liv. I'm happy to do it."

As soon as I open my mouth to inform her of my new job, she interrupts me with a pointed tone.

"Dex told me you're going to be working for Everett full time."

My stomach falls. I wanted to be the one to tell her. "Yeah, I was just about to tell you. He hired me as his assistant."

"Are you not happy where you are?"

"Not really." She already knows this. "I have no interest in portrait or studio photography. I can learn a lot more from Everett."

"But you'll be working in his gallery, right?" She rubs her chin. "Isn't that more retail?"

"That's not all I'll be doing. I'll have the same responsibilities I have now with the addition of helping with the gallery which will be beneficial for me."

She tips her head to the side. "How so?"

"There's a chance I'll open a studio of my own one day and this way, I'll learn how to run it."

She chews on her cheek as she mulls over my answer. "I guess that makes sense."

"It makes perfect sense."

Her pursed lips and lifted chin tell me she's about to try to change my mind.

"I'm going to be straight with you, Liv. I don't like the idea of you being around Everett every day."

Groaning, I lay my head on the cold marble countertop of the island. "You have to stop with this. I already told you, nothing is going on."

"Are you sure?"

I lift my head to see her cross her arms and jut out a hip. Her blue eyes narrow in on mine.

"Why would I lie to you?" I ask, exasperated.

"Because you know I'd be pissed if you were involved with him."

I throw my hands in the air. "For the millionth time, *nothing is going on*. But even if there was, that's none of your business. I love you, Mare, but you get zero say in my personal life."

"That's not very comforting."

"It's not meant to be." Frustrated, I tug on my hair. "I'm tired of having this conversation. I am sorry your friend fell for the guy and expected a relationship from a one-night stand, but that's on her. And if I'm being honest, I don't blame him at all for what went down between them."

Maren's face reddens. I've pressed a button. *Good.* "What a shitty thing to say. I bet you'd feel differently had it been you, which is what I'm trying to avoid."

My body tenses and heat flushes through my system. "That's my point! It would never be me! Not only can I can differentiate between a relationship and a hook-up, I don't do one-night stands. I never have."

"Do you have any idea the number of women who've fallen victim to Everett's charm? It's astounding! That man has lured more females out of their panties than Casanova himself!"

I laugh at her absurdity. "I highly doubt that."

"It's true!"

"Mare, I've spent quite a bit of time with him lately and I can assure you, he hasn't tried to charm me once. It's strictly business."

"Yeah, for now. But *I assure you*, as soon as he catches on to your infatuation with him, that'll change. The man is in heat twenty-four-seven. He can't help himself."

"You know what astounds me?" I ask, but don't allow her time to answer. "You treat Everett like a friend whenever he's here, but you talk about him like shit behind his back."

"He's Dex's best friend, and while I don't care for his womanizing, I admit, he's a loyal friend to my fiancé. As such, yes, I'm cordial to him."

"Maybe, just maybe, he'll be a good friend to me, too."

She closes her eyes and shakes her head. "Not even remotely possible."

"How can you say that?"

"Because you have boobs and a vagina."

I gasp. "I don't even know how to respond to that."

"Do yourself a favor and turn down his offer. Trust me, if you go to work for him, it will end in disaster."

I stand to leave. While I hate to depart on a sour note, I am done with this argument. Nothing she could say will change my mind. "I appreciate your concern, Mare, but I'm taking the job. It's a once in a lifetime opportunity for me to learn from the best. I can't turn it down."

She blows out a breath. "Mark my words, Liv, you will rue the day you took this job."

Two weeks into my role at Everett's gallery, it's going even better than I expected. Helping him run the gallery is a dream, and I've learned so much already. The icing on the cake is I've sold a couple more of my City Hall prints. They were smaller than the last print, but I made a few hundred bucks. If this keeps up, I'll be able to afford a place of my own. But I'm not getting ahead of myself just yet. I'll give it a few months to make sure it works out before I make a move.

Everett spends a few hours each day going over technique with me, as well as what he looks for in his shots, and how he processes his images. He is a wealth of knowledge for which I am eternally grateful. He answers every question patiently, no matter how stupid and is an excellent instructor.

The best part is, we've developed a remarkable rapport. He talks a lot, except for when he's processing. He's super serious when he processes. But the rest of the time we joke and laugh and have a great time. Truth be told, my time in the gallery isn't like a job at all.

It's Saturday, and he made the early morning trek with me to Bear Lake to check it out on a foggy morning. He even provided a thermos of coffee and some bagels for the trip.

We've been shooting for an hour. Everett has chosen to shoot with the Leica. He's been using it a lot lately.

"You were right about coming out in all different weather," I admit. It never would have occurred to me to come out on a foggy morning. "The shots I'm getting are phenomenal. So much better than our first trip out here."

To curb my habit of spray and pray, I'm taking a more methodical approach with my shots. With that thought in mind, I stop shooting and take a step back to observe the landscape. Everett joins me in taking a break.

"I love shooting in the fog," he says, staring at the Leica with adoration. "I also love this camera. I may never go back to my DSLR."

"I was beginning to wonder. I haven't seen it in your hand in weeks."

He gazes with reverence at the Leica. "Shooting with this and then processing the film, I feel like a little kid opening a birthday present. I don't know exactly what I'll get, but I can't want to see it."

"I can tell," I chuckle. "You're like a giddy little boy every time you go into the dark room."

He wrinkles his nose. "Is it that bad?"

"It's cute." Like his wrinkled nose.

Embarrassed, he tucks his chin. "I haven't been described that way in a long time."

I bet not.

I grab a tea from the cooler and sit in my chair. When his camera clicks, I look up to find him taking a picture of me. I hold up my hand to block my face. Laughing, he snaps another picture before sitting in his chair next to me. Returning the favor, I pick up my camera and snap a bunch of pictures of him. Not a bit camera shy, he makes an array of funny faces. Not that he has any reason to be bashful. He's the perfect subject.

"I belong behind the camera," I affirm, "not in front of it."

"Nonsense," he argues. "You're very photogenic."

I recall the day he took the series of photos of me. I'd forgotten until now. He never showed me the pictures. But he speaks before I can mention it.

"You once asked me how I became a photographer. It's my turn," Everett says, and I put my camera away. "How did you know you wanted to be a photographer?"

"I've been obsessed with taking pictures since I was a little girl. My poor parents burned through so many cameras because of me." I smile at the memory. "Whenever I saw a picture I'd taken, it was like… magic. With that snapshot, I could transport myself back to that moment and remember exactly how I felt. I still feel that way when I see pictures I took."

"Yeah, I agree. It can be magical."

This is usually where I stop. The rest isn't a story I share with many people. It's not a tale I enjoy telling. I've only told it to Grayson, Maren, and Dex.

"As for knowing I wanted to be a photographer, I was around seventeen." Glancing out at the lake, I try to tamp down my emotions. Otherwise, I'll never get through the story. "My mom became sick when I was sixteen. They diagnosed her with breast cancer. As soon as I got the news, I started photographing her constantly. I had this feeling in the pit of my stomach that my time with her was nearing the end. My parents never said as much, they kept my life as normal as possible. She had surgery and went through chemo. She fought so hard and was so positive and optimistic. But I knew. I just *knew*." Choked up, I pause. Everett watches me intently, engrossed in my story so I push to finish it. "I wanted to immortalize her and the only way I knew to do that was through pictures. I keep those photos in albums beneath my bed. They are my most prized possession. She passed away when I was eighteen. It wasn't until last year that I could look at them again."

"Dex told me about your mom. I understand the loss. I'm sorry."

"Not a day goes by that I don't think of her or relive a memory of her. I'll always miss her, but the acute sadness I used to carry is gone. I'm thankful that I made the most of the time I had with her in those last two years."

"I was younger than you when I lost my mother. I remember being sad, but the pain wasn't acute. We weren't much of a family and I never spent a lot of time with her. Still, losing a parent has a profound effect, especially on a young person. The best way I can describe it is, it's like losing a piece of yourself."

Everett gets it. Only someone who's been through it understands. As incredible of a friend as Gray is, and as sympathetic as he is, he doesn't get it. It's so nice to discuss this with someone who genuinely understands.

"Yes." I swallow. "And it's a piece you never get back. When my mom died, all I could think about was the things she won't be here for. My college graduation, my wedding, the birth of my children… My kids will never know my mom. That really sucks because she was an exceptional woman."

Placing a hand on mine, Everett's gaze is soft and understanding. "She will be here, Liv. Not in the way you want, but she's here. She'll see it all and she'll be proud."

"I hope so." With the back of my free hand, I wipe away a solitary tear. "Sorry, I didn't mean to depress you. I didn't intend to get that deep into it."

"You didn't depress me. It's nice talking with someone with a similar experience. I don't know anyone else who lost a parent as a kid."

"Me either. It is nice." I smile. "Thank you for listening."

"Anytime."

Staring into one another's eyes, a silent understanding passes between us. Our shared experience has bonded us.

Chapter 6

I'M MEETING GRAYSON AT HIS place for an after-work jog. When I told him I had taken the job with Everett, he congratulated me, but his concern was clear. He never voiced it, but it was there. Now, whenever we talk, the first thing Grayson asks is whether Everett's made a move on me yet.

"How is work going?" he asks the second our feet hit the pavement. "Is it still everything you had hoped for and more?"

Here we go… I nod. "Yep. It's great. I'm learning a lot."

"Your boss is still being professional and keeping his hands to himself?"

I roll my eyes. "Why is it that the first words to come out of yours or Mare's mouth is whether he's come on to me?"

"Because we care about you, and because we know the instant he makes his move, you'll reciprocate."

I love how they assume it's only a matter of time before Everett "makes a move."

"Yes, I would reciprocate. I've never lied to you about that. But… it won't happen. The man doesn't see me that way."

"Sure he does," Grayson insists, "he just does it discreetly."

I suppress a groan. "You realize you're basing your opinion of Everett off things my sister has said. You don't even know him. And you've never seen the way he looks at me or how he treats me. So why don't you try taking my word over Maren's for once?"

"I'm not only basing my opinion off what Maren told me. I've met the guy."

"Once, for five seconds."

"It was an entire evening," he corrects me with a fair argument. They met at a cookout held by my sister and Dex. While the two only spoke for a moment, they were in the same space for hours. "You know I'm an excellent judge of character. I read him, Liv. He's a lady's man through and through."

"I am well aware of his reputation. Neither you nor Maren let me forget. But I keep telling you both that nothing is going on. That he has been completely professional with me. And yet, that's not enough for either of you to let it go! I am so sick and tired of having this conversation I could puke nails!" I quit jogging. "Never mind Grayson, I'm going home."

He takes me by the arm to stop me. "Please stay. I'm sorry. I won't bring it up again."

Aggravated, I stand hands on hips, hesitant to believe him. Grayson is my best friend and only says what he does out of concern for me, and he has a valid reason to worry.

If Everett showed me the slightest bit of attention or interest, I would jump on it. However irrational it is, his past doesn't bother me. I don't care that I'd end up like all the other women he's bedded and fall for him, while it'd be nothing more than a casual hookup for him. I'd still dive in headfirst. And odds are I would get hurt.

Grayson is just trying to shield me from disappointment. I can't be mad at him for that. Or at least I shouldn't be.

"I love you, Grayson. I realize you're trying to protect me, and I appreciate it. But we've talked about this ad nauseam. Nothing has happened, and I doubt it will. But even if it does, that's my business. It's my choice. No amount of harping at me will change that."

"I know. I'll stop."

Skeptical, I give him the eye. I know him as well as he knows me.

He chuckles. "I'll *try* to stop."

"Try very hard," I plead. "Because as much as I care for you, these conversations make me not want to be around you. Imagine if every time I saw you, I told you what an idiot you are for sleeping with your boss's assistant. It's sure to backfire, which you know, but you continue to do it."

"True."

"Do you hear me nagging you?"

"Rarely."

"Then please do me the same kindness."

"Done."

"Thank you."

We start walking and he asks, "Can I just say one more thing?"

Growing super impatient, I shoot him a glare.

He holds his palms in the air. "One more point and I promise to drop it."

"Go ahead." I close my eyes and ready myself for whatever he is preparing to say.

"Look at me," he says, and I comply. "When it happens, and you get hurt, I *will* tell you I told you so. *But* I'll be here with a shoulder to cry on. I am always here for you."

I can't be angry with Gray. He's too sweet and caring. He always has my best interests at heart.

When I arrive to work Everett has a bunch of sold prints ready to ship to their buyers. I never imagined how much thought and precision goes into the job of packaging them. It's a time-consuming chore that takes up a quarter of my working hours. Today the task is even more tedious thanks to my pounding headache. The Tylenol I took upon waking didn't touch it.

Thankfully, Everett is assisting, which will turn a two-hour job into one hour.

"Is everything okay?" he asks. "You're not your usually cheerful self this morning."

I shake my head. "Last night was lady's night at The Thirsty Stone. My roommates forced me to go out with them." The outing was fun, but I drank too much and stayed too late. A choice I'm paying dearly for today.

"Ouch, the dreaded hangover."

Rubbing my temples, I groan. "I am never drinking tequila slammers again."

He chuckles. "The good ole days. Enjoy them while you can. They'll be over before you know it."

Everett resumes taping a box closed while I stand pondering the question that came to me in the middle of the night in my drunken haze.

I haven't known Everett very long, but out of everyone, he is the best person to discuss my dilemma with, taking into consideration his *experience* in the department.

"I realize you are my boss," I start, "but I consider us friends. Do you agree?"

He nods. "Sure."

"Given the time we've spent together these past few weeks, you've had the chance to get to know me pretty well. Do you think I take life too seriously?"

Everett sets his tape down and gives me his full attention. "No. I think you're the just right amount of serious. Why do you ask?"

"My friends insist that I'm too serious about life and my career. That I don't act like a normal twenty-four-year-old." And the rest spills out as super speed word vomit. "They say I need to party and have more sex—or have sex at all because let's face it, I'm not having any."

Last night at the club, I danced with a cute guy. We danced a lot. Dirtily. And it was fun. At the end of the evening he propositioned me, which was a turnoff, so I shot him down when he asked for my number. Hannah and Jess gave me a ration of shit over it, going on about how I should "loosen up and have a good time." Jess even joked that I have "cobwebs in the nether regions."

Twisting my hands together, I pace back and forth. "Yeah, sex is nice. I miss it, but I'm not in a relationship or even dating right now, and one-night stands aren't my thing. Meanwhile, all my friends are bed hopping, which I don't judge. That's what most single people my age are doing. *I'm* the odd man out. But I don't believe anything is wrong with me."

I stop pacing and stand before him. "Do you?"

I hadn't meant to say all that, but once I started talking, every one of my thoughts spewed out.

Everett stares at me slack jawed before saying, "There is nothing wrong with you."

I blow out a breath and since I am on a roll, ask the question that springs to mind. "It's not weird that I get more excited over my next photo shoot than an offer of sex from a hot stranger?"

He chokes in response.

"It is weird, isn't it?" I ask.

"I'm—uh—a little caught off guard."

"Sorry. It's just that you are the only person I can have this conversation with," I explain. "My friends are all of the same opinion and Maren will say I am doing the right thing. She'd encourage me to stay celibate until marriage. But you… I've heard stories about you. You've lived a wild life. So *please*, tell it to me straight. Am I being too serious? Will I one day regret not being wild and crazy?"

Everett, once again his usual calm and collected self, places his hands on my shoulders. His eyes are set on mine. "If you're happy with what you're doing to hell with anyone else's opinion. As for your question about regret…" He drops his arms and takes a step back. "After all my years of being wild and crazy, I can honestly say, I don't recall a tenth of the sex I've had or the women I had it with. It was meaningless—a way to pass the time. But I remember something from every shoot I've ever been on. It seems to me you're on the right track."

The tension in my shoulder's eases. "That makes me feel better."

"I'm happy I could help." He winks and picks the packing tape back up.

"I hope I didn't make you too uncomfortable," I say and resume my work.

"You definitely took me by surprise, but like you said, we're friends. As my friend, you can talk to me about anything, but Liv," he holds a hand to his heart and laughs, "next time, give a guy a warning."

"So much for lunch at the park," I say, staring out the window at the rainstorm. "It wasn't supposed to rain today."

I spend most of my lunch breaks at the little park around the corner. It isn't much of a park. It's simply a nicely landscaped lot with a gazebo and a few park benches. Relaxing in the gazebo each afternoon has become one of my favorite pastimes. I enjoy watching people walk by with their dogs and the couples strolling hand in hand. I've overheard some very interesting conversations while sitting in that gazebo.

"You can hang out with me in the office while I process," Everett offers.

He knows I dislike having lunch at the counter. I don't wish for people to see me eating. And… as much as I love my job, I won't work on my breaks. If patrons notice me sitting there, they would rightfully expect my attention. The only other private area besides

Everett's office is the dark room slash storage closet. Eating there would be weird.

"You don't care?" I ask.

"Of course not. Is that why you go out every day? Do you think I mind having you in the office with me?"

"What if I disturb your work?"

Motioning for me to join him, he says, "You won't disturb me. Come on in."

I stand to the side while he clears away a section on the desk for me to put my food. While the gallery is immaculate, Everett's desk is pure chaos. He claims he can't find things when it's organized. I think it has more to do with him not wanting to take the time to clean and keep things in order. One thing I've learned about Everett is he never does anything he doesn't want to do.

He points to my cobb salad. "That looks good."

"I'm not much of a cook," I admit, "but I sling a mean salad."

We both laugh.

"How's the hangover?" he asks.

"The headache has passed, but I feel like garbage. Maren will be unhappy, but I won't make dinner tonight."

His eyes bulge. "You're not going?"

I shake my head. "I just want to go home and crash."

"You can't bail. I need you there."

"Why?"

"It's no secret that your sister hates me. Having you there makes things less awkward. It gives her something to focus on other than her utter disgust for me."

"It's that bad?"

"You have no idea." He holds his palms up in prayer. "Please come. If you need a nap, go home for the afternoon, but you must show up to dinner."

I'd laugh, but I feel too rotten to spend the energy. "If I'm gonna make it, I must sleep."

"Fine. Head home and rest but be sure to set your alarm because you can't skip dinner."

"Long time no see," Everett jokes as I arrive for supper.

"Too long," I reply. I slept a few hours, but don't feel any better. Nevertheless, a promise is a promise.

"And look at that!" Dex says, pointing at the antique clock on the wall. "Right on time."

Winking at Everett, I say, "I have a really cool boss. He's very supportive of my work, family balance."

"Sounds like a great guy," Everett says with a grin.

"He is." I give his arm a playful bump.

"Since you're here," Maren says to me, "you can help me bring the food to the table."

I follow her into the kitchen, ready to ask what smells so delicious, but she speaks before I get the chance.

"What the hell was that?" she asks, fists on hips, her hard blue eyes drilling into mine.

"What was what?"

"You were flirting with Everett." She gestures to the living room where we just came from. "*Blatantly.*"

"I was not."

"You were, too."

"Was not!" I whisper yell.

"I watched it with my own eyes."

"That was not flirting. It was friendly banter."

"It was flirting."

"Damn it, Maren," I cross my arms, "it was not. The last thing I would ever do is flirt with Everett in front of *you.*"

"So, you're admitting that you flirt with him."

"No!" I holler but catch myself and lower my voice. "I have never flirted with him nor he with me. Okay? We work together. We see each other almost every day. We're friends, Mare. That's it."

"Why don't I believe you?" She purses her lips.

"Because you don't want to." I slap my thigh. "You are convinced that Everett and I are having hot, nasty sex in secret. Which we're not. But if you don't quit this, I will out of spite."

She steps forward. "Don't you dare!"

"Then stop this!" I throw my fists in the air. "I wasn't flirting. I never have. But if I am going to be accused of doing things I'm not doing, then I may as well do them!"

Realizing how serious I am, Maren holds her palms up in surrender. "Okay, I'm sorry."

This round goes to me.

Or so I think.

Handing me a platter to carry out, Maren says, "Liv, your intention may not have been to flirt, but I guarantee you Everett took it that way. You must be careful not to give him an opening because he *will* take it."

Rolling my eyes, I snap, "You're the one who needs to be careful, Maren. I already told you, accuse me again and I will do it."

Right in your face.

The photos I took on the foggy day at Bear Lake turned out fantastic. I spent the entire weekend processing. When I came across this one in particular, I was astonished. Even though it was just an impromptu study shoot, I got a phenomenal snapshot. At least, I think it is. Since working with Everett, I am learning what to look for in an image.

Keen to share my photo with him, I walk into the gallery with a pep in my step.

"You are way too bright and cheery for a Monday morning," he jokes.

"I want to show you something when you have time." I wave my memory card up high.

"Show me now." He motions for me to sit at the computer. "I have something to show you too, but ladies first."

Everett stands beside me as I insert the memory stick and open my picture file. He gasps at the sight.

Fog hangs above the pine trees and dances over the top of the lake, yet you can still see the reflection of the trees in the calm water. The mood of the photo is obscure but not gloomy. Looking at the image, I can smell the damp air mixed with the essence of pine.

"Let me get closer." He bends over my shoulder, peering into the screen. The aroma of his cologne envelops me. "This is magnificent, Olivia."

"Really?"

"This is even better than City Hall."

Beyond happy that he's pleased, tingles run up my spine. "I was amazed when I saw it. It didn't require cropping or anything. The picture came out perfect."

"This belongs in your professional portfolio. Truly impressive."

I stare at him in awe. Did he actually say that? "It's because of you," I declare. "You've taught me so much. As soon as I caught sight of the landscape, I knew exactly what settings to use and the composition I envisioned."

"I gave advice and instruction, but *this*," he points to the screen, "isn't something that can be taught. This shot is far better than any I got that day."

"I doubt that." He could take a better picture than me with his eyes closed.

"I'm not blowing smoke here, Liv. This blows me away. In fact, this piece is going on the website and up in the gallery next to City Hall."

It's my turn to gasp.

"Send this to the printer for a twenty-four by thirty-six print."

I beam with pride. "I was hoping you'd like it as much as I do."

"Like it?" he asks. "I love it."

My heart skips a beat. Everett isn't easily impressed. That he's enthralled with my amateur work is a heady experience.

"I stunned myself with this one."

"You haven't stunned me. The instant I found out that print in Dex's house was yours, I knew this was the caliber of photographer you are."

I spin on the stool until we are face to face. "You did?"

He nods. "Keep this up and you could go down as one of the greats, Livvy."

Livvy? That's a first. I've never been a fan of that nickname, but I don't hate it when he says it.

"You think?"

He shakes his head. "I *know*. That is why you're here. When I witnessed what you are capable of with minimal training, I realized I had to work with you. I had to foster your gift and help it grow. Selfishly, I wanted to watch your raw talent unfold." He rests his hands on my shoulders and leans in close enough that I catch the scent of his aftershave. He smells so good. "I can't tell you how much I've enjoyed working with you, Liv. You have breathed life into me. I hadn't been excited about photography for a long time. You changed that."

While stepping back, he maintains steady eye contact. "Six months ago, I was ready to close up shop and walk away from everything. I had no inspiration. No motivation. But that changed because of you. Now, I wake up with invigoration."

I stare, mouth agape, in total disbelief of what I just heard. He has rendered me speechless. He skims my jawline with his fingers. His tender touch causes me to shudder.

"By working with you," his voice is low and smooth, "I've rediscovered my passion for photography. You've lit a fire inside me that's been missing for years. I traveled the world over seeking to relight the spark and I found it right here, in you."

My breath hitches. "In me?"

"Yeah. You." Inching closer, he swallows. "These past few weeks with you have been the best I've had in as long as I can remember. I adore… watching you… watching you work. Seeing you learn and soak in everything I say. The excitement on your face when we go shooting or when we're in the office processing. You even get excited to help clients here at the gallery. You make it new again. I see photography through fresh eyes. I look at things with a sense of newness and wonder, and it's because of you."

"I d-don't know what to say."

"You say it all, every day, without saying a word," Everett says in a deep voice. As he moves in closer yet, his eyes are glued to mine and his mouth is slightly parted.

I lick my lips. My hair rises on the nape of my neck and my body floods with heat as I anticipate his kiss. Standing less than an inch away — he's so close I feel the warmth of his breathing on my cheek. I shut my eyes.

Chapter 7

AND THEN THE DOOR OPENS.

Everett jumps backward, but our eyes remain locked for a few moments before he turns his attention to the person who has just walked in.

Damn it!

"Steve," Everett walks toward the man. "To what do I owe the pleasure of this visit?"

The two men hug. They must be friends. Or maybe family?

With a nod in my direction, Steve says, "Didn't mean to interrupt."

Everett clears his throat. "No interruption. What are you doing in Denver, my friend?"

"Family business. Figured I'd stop in and check on you and Dex."

"It's good to see you, man," Everett says. "Follow me to my office so we can catch up."

As he turns to lead Steve to his office, Everett glances my way. His expression is one of bewilderment and trepidation.

The guys stay in Everett's office for two hours. When they finally emerge, Everett tells me he will be out for the rest of the day and to lock up when I leave. The look he gives me is one of concern and discomfort. I can tell he wants to discuss what happened, or rather what almost happened, except he can't right now.

Just before nine o'clock, I get a text from Everett saying he is on his way to my apartment. Making haste, I change out of my pajamas and into and a pair of shorts and a blouse. In the bathroom, I give my hair a quick blow out, splash cold water on my face and gargle mouthwash. My pulse races as though I'm waiting for a hot date.

A couple minutes later, there's a knock on my door, ramping up my already speeding heart. Inhaling deep, I turn the knob.

"I hope you don't mind the late call," he starts, and I step aside, allowing him to enter. "I was hoping to discuss what took place earlier."

Trying my hardest to conceal the trembling in my voice, I say, "Okay."

He points to the recliner by the sofa. "Care if I sit?"

"No, please do. I should have offered," I answer and take a seat on the side of the couch nearest to him.

He looks around the room, listening. But for what? "Are your roommates home?"

I shake my head. Jess is working and Hannah is spending the night with her on and off boyfriend.

"Good." He swallows and rubs his palms up and down his thighs. "So about today… I… I got a little carried away. Lost my control. What I did was wrong. I'm sorry."

He sounds as though he's trying to convince himself as much as me.

"You don't have to apologize. It wasn't just you."

His eyes snap to mine and he arches a brow. "It wasn't?"

"We were both there."

Blowing out a breath, he drags a hand through his hair. "You are fantastic, Olivia. In every way. You're smart and sweet and ridiculously beautiful and... But I can't... with you. I just can't. I made a promise to Dex and Maren."

My heart stutters. *He* thinks *I'm beautiful? And he wants to... with me?* I scoot forward on the cushion. "But you want to?"

"Hell yes, I do." He slaps his thighs. "Shit, I shouldn't say that."

"Why not?"

He shoots me a "You know why" look and stands and paces the room. "I've ruined everything. I promised Dex I wouldn't go there with you, that I'd keep my hands to myself, but you're so... and I'm... me. Damn it! I don't know what to do."

"Do what you want to do." *Oh, please do what you want to do.*

"I can't do what I want to do." Covering his face with both hands, he continues to pace. "Not with you."

"Yes, you can."

With a pained expression, he stops pacing and turns to me. "You don't understand what you're saying, Liv. I'm a lot older than you and... There are so many reasons why it's a bad idea."

"Maybe, but I don't care." I walk to where he stands. "My sister, your best friend, I work for you, our age difference... All I know is," I can't believe I'm going to say this out loud, "I want you, and now that the feeling is mutual..." I lift my shirt over my head.

His eyes bulge, "What are you doing?"

"Undressing." I unbutton my shorts and let them fall to the floor. My brazen act takes me by surprise. This is completely out of character for me, but I must seize this opportunity. Everett was the one who said I have to answer when opportunity knocks. So here I am, answering and inviting it in. Inviting *him* in.

"You have to stop. Please." He looks away for a fraction of a second before looking back at me. His hungry stare rakes over my body and he clutches his hands, twisting them back and forth.

I unclasp my bra and slide the straps down my arms. Everett drops his hands and balls them into fists. His eyes are trained on my breasts. I loop my fingers into my panties...

"Stop!" He clenches his teeth and hisses. He's losing control. "I can't do this. You are Maren's baby sister, and I promised I wouldn't."

Despite his plea, I slide my panties to the floor and step out of them. Now, I stand before him in all my glory.

"Your move," I challenge.

Everett strides to me, taking me into his arms. "I'm so going to hell."

My bare breasts press against the softness of the shirt that clings to his hard chest. His strong hands grip my hips, keeping me in place as his piercing eyes bore into mine. "Do you enjoy playing with fire, Olivia? Because that's what we're doing."

"I want this," I say, jutting my chin out to match his ferocity.

Everett drags the back of a finger down my cheek. His usually bright blue eyes have turned a darker shade. When he lowers his head, I raise onto my tiptoes to reach his lips. His mouth captures mine, our tongues swirl together leisurely as they come together. The sensation is like a lightning bolt coursing through me. His kiss grows increasingly passionate, sending sparks of desire through my body. Our kiss deepens yet, growing wilder by the second.

Jesus, Everett's kiss completely undoes me. His untamed hunger matches my own.

His mouth, the way his fingertips roam my naked body, the heat that he radiates, his scent, his taste. All of it overwhelms me with an overload of sensation, giving me a full on high unlike anything I've experienced.

No guy has ever kissed me like this. Never made me feel this way.

But that's because I've been kissing boys. Everett Shaw is all man. A pure, raw, carnal grown man. One that knows exactly what to do. And lord, so far, he's doing it just right.

But then he tears his mouth away and I whine in protest. His breathing is fast and shallow, his lips are red and swollen.

"A better man would do the right thing and leave."

"Why? Because of Dex and Maren?" Stepping forward, I close the small space of distance between us. "I'm a grown woman, Everett. I know what I want, and no one will tell me I can't have it."

Placing my hands on his chest, I press my body to his. His erection, hard as steel in his jeans, presses into my abdomen as I place a wet kiss on his corded neck.

Smoldering with hunger, he slides his fingers up the nape of my neck and into my hair, giving it a tug. "The only things I've regretted are the things I didn't do."

"That's why we have to do this."

"But what if you regret it?" His internal battle is clear.

"I won't."

He tightens his grip on my hair as his free hand glides down the side of my body, sending shivers up my spine. The instant my lips part, he claims them with his own, devouring me with complete control.

He hikes my leg up to his hip and presses his hardness against me.

I whimper something unintelligible, but I'm not embarrassed.

Everett brings a hand to my face, holding me in place as his tongue works mine fiercely and unapologetically. "You taste even sweeter than I imagined." Somehow, he kisses me deeper yet, as though he can't get enough. I certainly can't get enough of him. He clutches my body even tighter to him. "So, so sweet," he croons huskily.

Every thrust of his tongue and the sensation of his beard against the soft skin of my face fuels the fire already raging inside me. With desire pooling between my thighs, my nipples tighten painfully, begging for Everett's touch. For the heat of his mouth. This is how a real man kisses.

"Oh, God," I moan against his lips.

As though he's reading my mind, his warm, wet mouth leaves mine as he moves lower. Everett places his lips on the swell of my breast, kissing and licking as he makes his way to my aching nipple.

His hands cup my breasts, squeezing roughly. His tongue flicks my nipple again and again before he takes it into his expert mouth and sucks. A sound akin to a growl emanates from his chest.

While his mouth continues to work my breast, his hands slide around to my back. His fingers spread as they slowly glide downward to my backside. His index fingers skim delicately between my cheeks before giving them a firm squeeze. Another groan escapes his lips.

With our bodies pressed together, I feel so small as Everett's much larger frame all but swallows mine. My hands roam his cotton covered chest and I feel every dip and ripple of his abs and impressive pecs. Underneath his clothes, he's all muscle and strength and warmth.

Everett walks backward to the couch, taking me with him. He sits and draws me onto his lap to straddle him. The only sounds are our wet kisses and moans. My hands are everywhere, in his hair, on his shoulders, under his shirt, skimming the soft flesh at his belt line. With one hand he fondles my breast, pulling and twisting the sensitive nipple, while the other caresses the curve of my backside.

Panting with ragged breaths, we continue to kiss. It's so, so good. The best kissing of my life. He breaks our kiss and presses his lips to my ear, gently flicking his tongue along the rim. "I hope you're ready for what I'm about to do to you." He grinds his erection against my wet and willing sex. "Once I'm inside you, you'll be ruined for other men."

"I'm ready," I murmur, surprising myself with the sensuality in my tone. I arch my back, giving him a full view of my breasts, and grind onto him in a desperate attempt to satisfy the ache between my legs. Never have I been this wanton.

With a smile of pure satisfaction, Everett brushes his fingers between my bosom, down my torso to my belly button. "You are so beautiful it hurts."

Silently, I will his hand to move lower. For him to touch me where I yearn for it most. But he doesn't. He sweeps my hair to one side and plants a leisurely, wet kiss on my shoulder and collarbone. My body trembles. Everything he does is magic. He hasn't even been inside me, and I already understand why women fall in love with him after a single night.

Everett lifts me with ease and lies me onto my back, my head resting on the arm of the sofa. He leans downward and nibbles on my neck, jaw, and shoulder. I run my hands over his chest, down his sides and back to his firm ass. His hands work their magic as he caresses my breasts before inching them lower, lower, and lower yet until he reaches my apex.

My breathing is shallow, and I pant as I await his touch where I need it. But he hesitates.

Shameless, I beg, "Please."

"You want my touch?"

"Yes, yes." I bite my lip.

Finally, he gives in and presses his fingers to my wetness. He glides his index finger up and down my folds, teasing me as he reaches my entrance. I buck my hips, trying to force him inside, but I fail. With a smirk, he drags his fingertip deliberately down my slit before moving upward to my clit. He circles the nub again and again without making direct contact. My frustration builds, as does my arousal.

"Please," I plead again.

"I like it when you beg," he says and then presses the pad of his thumb to my sensitive bud, working it up, down and around.

He slips a finger into my depths as he deftly works my clit. Grabbing a hold of his shoulders, I bite down and groan. My climax is already building.

"You respond beautifully to my touch, Olivia." He sinks his teeth into my neck before moving lower to my belly button, dipping his tongue in and swirling the rim. The man is a genius at foreplay. After a moment, he kisses his way back to my breasts, sucking and laving each nipple. "You have gorgeous breasts. I could spend all day licking and kissing them."

I can only imagine how many boobs he's seen. Mine are surely nowhere near as impressive as others.

"Roll over," he commands.

I start to protest, but the heat in Everett's eyes spurs me on. Eager to please him, I do as told.

My body shudders as his fingertips trail down my back, touching every inch of my skin. Without warning, he places his mouth on my ass, licking and nibbling. His fingers slide between the cheeks to stroke my wetness.

I grip the arm of the couch, lost in a whirl of sensation. My breathing is fast, and my heart pounds. The only thing I hear is the sounds Everett's mouth makes as he nips and licks my skin. His magical hands are searing hot on my flesh.

Without warning, he stands and I roll over to watch him yank off his shirt. I don't have time to enjoy the view of his torso because he is already pulling off his pants and boxers.

My mouth waters as I gaze upon the most delicious male specimen I've ever had the good fortune of laying my eyes on. He's cut and corded and ripped from head to toe, just as I had imagined he would be. His long, thick erection stands at attention and I stare unabashedly. For lack of a better word, he's perfect. The man should have his likeness carved into stone for posterity.

"If you want me, you'll have to take me," Everett says, and holds up a condom.

I most definitely want him. I sit upright and reach for Everett's hand, pulling him onto the couch next to me. Crawling onto his lap, I straddle him and remove the condom from the wrapper. His jaw clenches and fire blazes in his eyes as I roll it onto his long, hard shaft. His arm snakes around my waist and he presses the tip of his cock to my entrance.

"Take me," he growls, deep and husky.

Everett's eyes hold mine as I push down and slowly take him inside. My eyes widen as he fills me, hot and pulsing. He bites his lip and groans, all the while maintaining eye contact. My sex stretches to accommodate him. Once I've taken every inch, I sit completely still to revel in the fullness. A soft moan escapes my lips.

A deep groan erupts from Everett's chest. He tugs my hair and thrusts his hips, demanding movement. Gripping his shoulders, I lift to his tip before slamming down his entire length.

With a loud grunt, he throws his head backward. "Oh, yeah."

He places his hands on my hips as I rock back and forth, circling my hips. I work him every way I can.

Everett allows me to control the pace, watching me as though I am the most beguiling and gorgeous creature he has ever seen. The pure animalistic lust in his eyes makes me feel beautiful and sensual in a way I've never experienced. With my head cast back, I ride him with abandon, coating him with my wetness. I moan and yell his name. He's so big and hard.

He leans down and takes my breast into his mouth, feasting on the flesh. His tongue circles my nipple and he sucks once before tugging it with his teeth. The sensation sends a spasm to my core, and I squeeze his length with a vice like grip.

I graze his chest with my fingertips and find his nipples, giving them a twist. With my lips on his neck, I flick the skin with my tongue, tasting the saltiness of his sweat. He bites my shoulder as I continue to ride him. He murmurs how tight I am, how incredible it feels to be inside me. That I'm better than any fantasy he had.

Our bodies move as though we are out of control. We bite and lick and push and pull, pull hair and groan and scream. A torrent of naughty words rush from Everett's oh so dirty mouth. That sexy, sexy mouth.

As I chase my orgasm, my body becomes tense. It's. Right. There. So. Close. I want it. I *need* it.

But I don't want this to end.

"Give it to me, Olivia," Everett urges me, "Come for me."

He holds my head in place, staring into my eyes, willing me to let go. His face is flushed, and his taut expression conveys he's holding on by a thread.

His words mixed with his intense gaze push me over the edge and I detonate. Writhing wildly, I gasp at the intensity of the orgasm that is erupting deep within.

Everett's body tenses and he holds me down on his cock as it jerks inside me. "So. Fucking. Good."

My heart races faster than ever. I can't move. Can't breathe. Don't know how I'm still alive. Utterly sated, I drop my head to Everett's shoulder and collapse into him.

Breathing as hard as I am, Everett holds me, rubbing my back and brushing my hair with his fingers. We're content to sit here holding one another as he softens within me. This moment is far more intimate than the incredible, mind-blowing sex we just had.

I am indeed ruined for other men. *All* other men.

After one more round of earth-shattering sex, Everett held me until I fell asleep. In the middle of the night, he woke me with a kiss to my temple and told me he would see me at the gallery in the morning. I rolled over and fell back into my dream. A dream of me and Everett doing all the things we had done just hours before.

While I always look forward to working, today is so much better. I can't wait to see Everett and kiss his morning smile. Last night, I slept sounder than I have in my entire life. I'm sure it had something to do with having the greatest sex of my life. My body feels weightless and relaxed. Best yet, I can still feel where Everett has been.

"Good morning," I say as I enter the gallery with a bounce in my step.

Everett sits at the counter wearing the guiltiest expression I've ever seen. "Good morning."

"I brought bagels and coffee," I say, and set them on the countertop.

He smiles. "Thank you."

Written all over his face are the words he is preparing to say—words I'd rather not hear. But in his eyes lies something else. Memories and the longing he's trying and failing to contain.

"How did you sleep?" I ask with a mischievous wink, and hand him a coffee.

He swallows. "We have to talk."

Chapter 8

ARCHING A BROW, I BRING my mocha to my lips, but stop short of sipping. "Do we?"

"Last night was fantastic." His gorgeous guilty blues melt into mine. "You are incredible. And while I don't regret what happened, it can't happen again."

"I disagree."

"Liv," he pleads.

I get a cinnamon bagel, his favorite, from the bag and spread cream cheese on it before handing it to him. "We can do what we want."

"We can't."

"I can."

"Not if I'm not a willing participant."

I shoot him a playful grin. "You will be."

"I can't." He drags a hand through his perfectly coifed hair. "I want to. You *know* I want to. But it's not going to happen again."

I step close enough that my abdomen grazes his crotch. "We'll see."

Biting his lip, he groans. The sound is similar to those he made last night while buried deep inside me.

Everett spends most of his day in his office with the door closed while I stay busy in the gallery. Our few interactions are awkward and clumsy. He can't make eye contact. The man is completely undone by my presence. He won't be able to resist me for long.

To my great surprise, Grayson stops in moments before closing. He never called or texted to let me know he was coming.

"What brings you by?" I ask.

Under normal circumstances, I would be happy for him to visit, but his timing is terrible. I had planned on talking with Everett when we closed. I can't do that with Gray here.

"Two things. First, I wanted to see you in your element and second," Everett emerges from his office, keys in hand making a beeline for the exit, "I thought I'd ask if you want to grab dinner at the new Thai place down the road."

Everett comes to a screeching halt, staring daggers at Grayson.

"Hey," Grayson approaches him, palm extended, "you must be the famous Everett Shaw I've heard so much about."

Everett's eyes flit to mine, then back to my friend. Grayson's hand remains extended, but he hasn't accepted it.

Is he jealous?

Chin up, Everett responds, "I am. And you are?"

"I'm Olivia's buddy, Grayson."

Everett relaxes and his features soften. We've talked about Gray, so he knows who he is to me. Finally, he accepts Grayson's hand and shakes it. "Good to meet you, Grayson. I've heard a lot about you as well."

"This is an incredible gallery."

"Thank you. I hate to be rude, but I'm on my way out." Clearing his throat, Everett's eyes flit to mine once again. "I'm heading out early, Liv. See you tomorrow."

Everett rarely leaves first. He's doing so now to avoid me and the conversation we'd likely end up having if we closed up together.

"See you—" I don't get to finish my sentence before he's gone.

Impolite departure aside, all I can think of is the irritated look on Everett's face when he thought Grayson was some guy asking me out.

Gray spins back to me. "Well, that wasn't at all awkward."

I drop my chin to my chest and bite my lip. "Yeah."

With a forceful exhale, Gray shakes his head. "You slept with him."

I nod. "Last night."

"And now he wants nothing to do with you?"

"It's not like that."

He rolls his eyes. "Sure…"

"It isn't." I cross my arms and jut out my hip. My jaw stiffens. "In fact, he made it perfectly clear that he wants *a lot* to do with me. He's just worried about Dex and Maren."

"Are you positive it's not an excuse? He is known as a hit it and quit it type of guy."

I narrow my eyes. "That's not what happened here."

"Keep telling yourself that."

"It's true!" I sigh.

"I'm sure all the women he's left in his wake felt the same way you do right now."

Heat floods through my body as my irritation escalates. "How exactly do you assume I feel?"

"Used and tossed away." His words sting.

I point in his face. "He didn't use me, and he hasn't tossed me away!"

"Yeah, he did."

I blow out a breath and try to regain my composure. As annoyed as I am with my friend, he's only trying to protect me. His intentions are good.

"Gray, I realize you're convinced that Everett is a bad guy, but I know him better than you and I am telling you, he isn't."

He tilts his head back and glares at the ceiling. His tone is sharp. "A good guy would've kept his damn hands off you if he couldn't follow through."

"You don't understand… It's complicated."

"No, it's not!" He throws his fists in the air. "You're trying to romanticize your one-night stand into something it wasn't."

So much for calm and composure.

"That's a shitty thing to say, Gray." I go to the door and open it. "Just go."

"Liv—"

I cut him off, "I said leave!"

Not an hour after our fight, Grayson and I made up and went to the Thai restaurant for dinner. We discussed what happened between Everett and me, and I *somewhat* convinced Grayson that he did not take advantage of me. I explained that Everett came to my place to do the right thing. I was the one who seduced him.

Now, I have a new quandary. It's eleven in the morning and Everett still hasn't shown up for work. Earlier, he sent a text saying he would be in late and gave me a list of things to do.

I haven't heard from him since.

He's avoiding me and I hate it.

I drop my forehead to the counter. All the worst case scenarios run through my mind.

What if he fires me?

He probably will.

It'll be a mite difficult to work with one another if he can't be around me.

Even if he lets me go, I don't regret the night we spent together. It's impossible to regret the best night of my life.

The front door swings open and I lift my head to see Everett striding in, confident and upbeat as ever. My heart races. Normally, I would greet him, but today I wait for him to speak.

"Sorry I'm late," he says, no sense of discomfort in his voice. "I had an appointment."

If only I was as relaxed as he appears to be. "You're the boss. No need to explain."

He joins me behind the counter. "I didn't want you to think I'm avoiding you."

"Aren't you?"

"No."

I cock my head to the side, skeptical.

"I did yesterday, I admit. But I've taken time to contemplate our *situation* and decided to act like an adult." He drums his fingers on the countertop. "What happened, happened. You are still my employee and star pupil. I can't just disappear or hide in my office."

My heart sinks.

His employee.

His star pupil.

Is that all I am? I avert my gaze to the floor. "That's a very mature decision."

Everett places two fingertips beneath my chin and lifts until our eyes meet. "Liv, we can't. No matter how much we want to. It isn't right." Placing his hands on my arms, he gazes into my eyes with tenderness. "I need you to understand one thing. The other night… it wasn't me taking advantage of you. It wasn't just… It was… You have no idea how badly I wish things were different."

Me too.

And they could be if he'd let them.

Everett releases me and drags a hand through his hair. "I've grown to like you a lot, Liv. I want to ask you out and take you on a date. That's a *big* deal for me. I haven't dated in eons. But I can't go out with you. Dex and Maren will never accept it. Maren despises me. I'd lose my best friend." He steps closer. His voice is low. "Being with you was the first and only time I have ever betrayed him. My loyalty as a friend means something to me. Knowing that I've been disloyal to Dex is painful for me. I won't do it again."

I get it now. He's scared to lose Dex—the only real family he has.

"I understand." I say with a slight smile. "May I ask one thing?"

"Sure."

I pick at my cuticle. "Can we at least still be friends?"

"Of course," he answers as though I should already know.

"We'll just move on like it never happened."

Shaking his head, he swallows. "I'll never forget it happened. It just can't happen again."

I respect Everett's feelings and admire his loyalty to Dex. And despite agreeing it can't and won't happen again, I believe it will. We share an undeniable chemistry. The passion we shared that night was off the charts. When he looks at me, it's obvious he feels the same.

It's only a matter of time before we give in.

The next two days pass without another word of our tryst. Neither of us avoids the other, and we remain friendly and professional. It is almost as if nothing has changed between us. Apart from the times I notice him watching me and the instances when he catches me staring at him.

Things have changed, we're merely pretending they haven't.

Tonight is Dex and Maren's weekly dinner. Everett and I arrive at the same time. He rings the doorbell and we wait in silence until Dex opens the door. Placing his hand at the small of my back, Everett usher's me into the house. The innocent touch is enough to warm my entire body.

As per usual, once we're seated around the table, Dex asks, "How's everyone's week going?"

Monday night with Everett flashes in my mind. His dirty words. My back arched as I rode him. The tender manner with which he held me after we finished.

Everett clears his throat. "Same old, same old."

With an arched brow, I glance at him as if to say, "Really?"

Dex looks to me. "And you?"

I shrug. "Same old, same old."

"Everett told me about your Bear Lake print that he displayed in the gallery," Dex says. "I looked it up online. It's damned good."

My cheeks flush. I've never taken compliments well, especially from people with whom I'm close. "Thank you. I'm glad you like it."

"Your sister and I are considering getting a copy and putting it up here at the house." He motions toward the second floor. "Maybe in one of the guest rooms or the hallway upstairs."

"It's an incredible piece," Everett states. "It should be hung in homes everywhere."

I blush. "So, how's your week been, Dex?"

"Same old, same old," he chuckles. "My chief of surgery is still an ass and making my job a living hell."

"I'm sorry to hear that," I say.

"This is why I'm glad I work for myself," Everett says.

"I may be soon," Dex declares. "I'm putting serious thought into opening my own practice. After weighing the pros and cons, the pros are coming out on top."

"Going into business for oneself is a daunting task," Everett says, "but it's so worth it in the long run. Do it, Dex. You're a premier cardiothoracic surgeon. People come from all over the world to have you as their doctor. Mercy General doesn't deserve to capitalize on your talent."

"I agree," Maren concurs. "You should do it, Babe."

As we eat, the discussion transitions to lighthearted small talk. The men chat about their sports teams and an upcoming men's trip they have planned. Maren and I share girl talk, but as soon as I bring up the wedding, she's quick to change the subject.

"I have someone I want you to meet," she says to me. "I think you'll like him."

Everett's gaze shoots my way.

I shake my head. "No way. I hate being set up."

Besides, the man I want is sitting right across from me.

"It's not a set up," she insists. "He's coming to Dex's birthday party. You'll be there, he'll be there…"

Everett's curiosity filled eyes are trained on me.

I sigh and shift in my seat. "I don't know, Mare."

"His name is Callum," she ignores my protest, "and I am telling you, you're gonna love him. He works at his uncle's architecture firm. He's super good looking and tall. And he's a runner like you."

"I'm not really a runner." A weak excuse, I'm aware.

She shrugs. "Anyway, he saw a picture of you and asked if I'd arrange an introduction."

She picks up her phone and hands it to me. On the screen is a photo of a handsome guy. Dark hair, broad shoulders, gorgeous smile. Totally my type.

"See," Maren says with a mischievous twinkle in her eyes. "He's a hottie, right?"

Burning under Everett's stare, I hand the phone back to her.

"You have to meet him," she insists.

"I guess I will at the party."

Maren claps her hands together. "Yay!"

Everett lowers his head, focusing on the food on his plate, but I notice the tick in his jaw. After studying him for the past few weeks, I've learned his tells. He's unhappy.

"Will you be going out to Bear Lake tomorrow?" Everett asks as we shut down shop for the night.

His question catches me off guard. Today was the same as the previous three days. We worked together, interacted professionally. Sure, we stole the occasional furtive glance, but kept things strictly business.

For the first time in days, his inquiry gives me a sense of hope. Maybe he wishes to join me? My belly flutters.

"I'm considering going," I lie. I haven't thought about it. But if he wants to come along, I will make the trip.

"I think, for obvious reasons," looking to his empty hands, he twiddles his fingers, "I shouldn't join you."

I can't resist. "Obvious reasons as in…"

He shoots me a look and I laugh.

"Oh, right. You might jump me."

His eyes snap to mine. "Purely for clarification, you are the one who jumped me."

And I'd do it again right now if not for his speech about loyalty and losing his best friend. "True."

He grins, but it's gone as fast as it came. "I just think we should avoid temptation."

I tempt him… I knew it.

In my most nonchalant voice, I say, "I understand."

"Perhaps in a couple weeks once things are more… settled."

"Okay." My tone is still casual.

His shoulders slump barely enough for me to notice.

"You're not upset?"

"I'm a little disappointed, but you're right. We should limit our temptation, and if we were away *together* and *alone*, it could be tempting."

"Exactly. And I've—" He stops.

"What?"

Rocking on his heels, he scratches his beard. It's longer than usual. "I shouldn't say it."

"Well now you have to."

"It's been hard enough denying the temptation this week, don't you agree?" His eyes search mine.

He is waiting for me to admit that I, too, am grappling with ignoring my desire. I won't give him the satisfaction. He's the one who decided it—we—can't happen. If he's struggling, that's his fault. He can't lean on me for support.

"I have no idea what you are talking about," I answer in my most serious tone.

"Right. Right." He shoves his fists in his pockets and sways on his heels again. "Last night at dinner was so awkward, don't you think?"

"I thought we handled it well."

"Sitting at the table with Dex and Maren, I felt *so* guilty. It had to have been written on my face."

"It was pretty obvious."

His eyes bulge. "Really?"

Chuckling, I place a palm on his bicep. "Calm down, I'm joking."

My touch lingers as I recall clutching his biceps while in the throes of passion. His gaze falls to my hand, and he releases a shallow sigh.

"Last night, sitting across from you, in front of them, I kept remembering…" Yearning flickers in his eyes and he wets his lips. "We were on constant replay in my mind."

"That night is always replaying in my mind," I admit.

We exhale in unison.

I've reached my breaking point.

"Everett, you have insisted it can't happen. You say you want to avoid temptation. If that's the case, we can't talk about it, because if we do, I'm gonna strip in front of you again, right here and now. Is that a temptation you can deny?"

He gulps. "No."

We stand, staring at one another, each of us silently willing the other to make a move, while simultaneously praying they won't.

"I should go," I whisper, breaking eye contact.

"Yeah." Everett blows out a breath.

With haste, I grab my purse and keys from behind the counter and make my way to the exit.

"Liv," Everett calls out.

I spin around to find him walking toward me. "Yes?"

He halts at the halfway mark. "Have a good weekend."

"You too, Everett."

It's rare that both Hannah and Jess have a Saturday off, so when they do, the three of us go out. We always end up at The Thirsty Stone Ale House because Jess is in love with their main bartender, Ryan. I'm game for The Thirsty Stone because it happens to be Everett's preferred watering hole. He's known to pop in for a drink and a match of darts on Saturday nights. Dex joins him every now and then.

I hope Everett is there. I pray Dex isn't.

Not that it matters if Dex is with him. It's not like anything will happen either way. But, if Dex is there, I must keep my staring in check.

It's a moot point if Everett isn't there, which he might not be.

Maybe he is with someone tonight. I cringe at the thought.

The instant we pull into the parking lot, my eyes search the vicinity for Everett's Jeep.

Sure enough, the truck is here. My heart takes off on a sprint.

Thank God he's here instead of shacked up with a strange woman for the evening.

What if he brought a woman?

Unable to stand the idea, I shake my head.

"Isn't that McHotness's Jeep?" Hannah asks.

I answer with a nod because my mouth is too dry to speak.

As we enter the bar, my first instinct is to locate Everett's whereabouts, but I don't want to come off desperate. Still, I need to know who he's here with.

Play it cool, Liv. You're here with your girls for a fun night out.

Right. If I see him, I'll ignore him. That puts the ball in his court and disguises my desperation.

We pay our cover charge and go to the bar. To the left of the bar are the dart boards. That's where Everett usually hangs out. In my peripheral, I catch sight of the area, but don't look. We get to the bar and give our drink order to Ryan. After being served, we sit at a nearby high topper so Jess can flirt with him.

I enjoy the ambiance of this place. It's dimly lit and not so loud you can't hold a conversation without screaming. A variety of music from rock to rap, new and old plays in the background. The patrons vary in age from young to middle aged. A few men appear to be in their seventies. Best of all, there's never any trouble here.

I'm dying to seek Everett out, but I'm trying to give the impression of indifference, even though I'm the exact opposite.

"Have you seen him?" I ask the girls.

When Hannah whips her head in search of him, I clutch her arm.

"Don't be so obvious," I hiss.

Jess is a master of subtlety. With discretion, her eyes scan the room, and she leans close. "He's playing darts with a really hot chick."

My stomach clenches.

He is *here with someone.*

Unable to stand it, I must see who came with him.

Whirling around in my seat, I spot him throwing darts, facing opposite us. When I glimpse who's with him, I breathe a sigh of relief. It's just Carmen, his next closest friend after Dex. She pops into the gallery occasionally. Sometimes with her equally stunning girlfriend, Alisha. I have grown fond of her.

"That's Carmen," I tell them. "I've met her. She's a lesbian."

I watch as he finishes throwing, but spin around before he turns my way. I mustn't let him catch me staring.

"I'm not much into older guys," Hannah declares, "but that man is F I N E."

"I dig the bit of gray in his hair," Jess says. "It lends his hotness an air of sophistication."

Hannah and I giggle. She's right, though.

"That body though," Hannah moans. "I bet it's even finer in the buff."

"It is," I admit. I so badly want to see it for myself.

"Does he always wear a smoldering expression?" Hannah inquires.

Nodding, I speak slowly. "Yep. Every second of every day."

"How do you focus at work looking at that all day?" Jess asks.

"It's not without difficulty."

"I wouldn't be able to," she states.

"Especially not now that you know what you're missing," Hannah adds.

"Thank you for pointing that out, Hannah."

"Oh shit, he just looked over here," Jess shrieks, but keeps her facial features relaxed and normal. She has a great poker face, unlike Hannah.

"Do you think he recognized you?" I ask.

"He definitely recognized me."

"Is he still looking?" I ask.

"I'd have to look to find out."

"Don't look," I order. "Pretend you didn't notice."

"Isn't it weird to ignore him?" Hannah asks. "You work together. You are friends. Ignoring him implies you're either uncomfortable or you're playing games."

Again, she's correct.

"You should acknowledge his presence," she suggests. "Doing so will make you seem unaffected."

"Should I go over there?"

"No," she replies. "Give him a small wave and leave it at that."

"That leaves the ball in his court," I say.

"Exactly."

As suggested, I spin around to wave. When I do, I find Everett looking my way with a smile that leaves me breathless. I return the smile, wave, and swing back around.

A few minutes later, Ryan pops over with a round of drinks we didn't order.

"Sent by the gentleman over there," Ryan points to Everett.

Us girls hold up our drinks and mouth a silent "Thank you" to Everett.

It doesn't take long for the alcohol to hit my system. Whenever buzzed or drunk, I get a fierce itch to dance. The three of us get up from our stools and start swaying to whatever song is playing. I don't know it well. It's an eighties or nineties tune that I've probably heard five times in my life, but it has a fun beat that is easy to move to. The singer croons about angels and devils and divine things.

Lost in the music, I'm swinging my hips to the beat when a pair of hands grab my waist from behind.

Everett.

Chapter 9

LEANING BACKWARD, I PUSH MY backside against him.

I knew he wouldn't be able to resist me for long.

I raise my hands and clutch his hair. My partner's fingers wander, tracing the outline of my breasts as we continue to move. Hannah and Jess hoot and holler as we dirty dance.

So much for avoiding temptation.

When the song ends, I turn to thank Everett for the dance.

But the person standing before me is not Everett.

Oh my god.

My jaw hits the floor. I was bumping and grinding with a total stranger. A hot stranger, but not the man I assumed he was. I sway to the side. *This did not just happen.*

My eyes flit to Everett who still stands at the dart board, glaring at me slack jawed with a visible flush on his cheeks.

"You've got killer moves," my dance partner says, eyeing me up and down with appreciation.

"Thanks," I gulp. "And thanks for the dance." I turn back around to the table and my friends with my mouth hanging open.

"How about another one?" He leans into my neck.

"I'm good." I shift forward, putting space between us. "Thanks, though."

"Okay. If you change your mind," he motions to the area where the pool tables are, "I'll be right over there."

I smile, but only so I don't come across as a bitch. "I'll keep that in mind."

Once he's gone, I smack my forehead and say, "That didn't just happen."

"Yes, it so did," Jess says. "And McHotness watched the whole thing go down."

Hannah giggles. "I'm not sure whether he was more turned on or jealous."

"I thought it was him!" I shriek.

"By the look on his face, he wishes it had been," Jess states.

"Oh, yeah," Hannah agrees.

No, no, no. "What if he thinks I did it to make him jealous?"

"So what if he does?" Jess asks.

"I don't want him to think I'm playing games."

"I don't know what he thinks," Hannah says, "but you've definitely got his attention."

"Is he still looking this way?" I ask.

Both girl's answer, "Yep."

What must Everett think of me?

At least fifteen minutes pass and I am no longer having fun. I want to go home.

Ryan appears with another round of drinks we didn't order. Why on earth is Everett sending drinks after what I just did? Perhaps it didn't affect him the way my friends assumed it did. Maybe he doesn't care that I rubbed my ass all over another guy.

"You are popular tonight," Ryan says to me and points to my dance partner. "These are from Josiah."

Turning to Josiah, we three acknowledge his gesture. I hope he doesn't expect this to earn him a second dance because it isn't happening. No way, no how. The next time I feel a pair of hands on me, I'll turn around to see who they belong to.

I groan. "Everett probably assumes I shake my ass for every strange guy who approaches me." Why wouldn't he after what he just witnessed?

In her most reassuring, yet drunken voice, Hannah says, "It was one dance with one guy. It's not a big deal."

"You're a hot, single woman in a bar," Jess chimes in. "It's what we do."

"I don't want him to assume that's the kind of gir—*woman*—I am."

"Then tell him," Hannah suggests.

"Sure," I scoff. "I'll just walk on over there and tell him I thought I was dancing with him."

Jess chokes on her drink and her eyes widen as she glances at something behind me. I hear Everett clear his throat.

Suddenly dizzy, a heavy sensation spreads throughout my core. I squeeze my eyes closed. Please tell me he didn't hear that.

"You thought it was me, huh?"

My cheeks and neck are on fire. My heart races with embarrassment. Not only did Everett watch me dance with a guy, he now knows I figured it was him. Which is worse?

I turn to face him. He waits a moment for my answer, but I'm too stunned to speak.

"I can resist anything except temptation," he says. His crystal blue eyes smolder with intensity. "Let's get out of here."

Without giving me time to say goodbye to my friends, Everett takes me by the hand and ushers me through the crowded bar and out the side exit. The instant we're outside, he grips my shoulders and pushes me against the brick wall. His lips crash onto mine and he thrusts his tongue inside, tasting of whiskey and mint. He groans as our tongues roll together and my fingers slide into his hair before pulling it roughly.

When rain begins to fall, Everett pulls away, breathless. He grabs my hand and escorts me to his Jeep. He opens the door and helps me inside before climbing into the driver's side. We stare at one another, each of us breathing heavily, as he starts the engine.

Lightning strikes, followed by a loud crack of thunder as the rain picks up intensity. We're still staring.

Everett must read my mind because he reaches for me and claims my mouth once again, as forcibly and passionate as the last time. With his fingers curled around my neck, he tugs me to him. I'm still in my seat, but on my knees as we kiss. We fill the Jeep with sounds of our desperate moans and wet kissing. My hands are in his hair, on his chest, his abs. His hands slide under the hem of my shirt, grazing my abdomen, reaching higher and higher. He cups my breasts as my fingers reach his belt line.

I've never had sex in a car. I always said I never would. That I had more decency and respect for myself than to do such a thing. But Jess once said, "You haven't lived until you've had a toe-curling orgasm in the driver's seat of a car."

With Everett, I'm too wanton and desperate to care about being decent. I want, no I *need,* that toe-curling orgasm right now. Based on the unadulterated lust shining in his eyes, he needs it too.

I unzip his pants as he tweaks my nipples through the lace of my bra. He raises his hips to help me lower his jeans enough to free his erection. I take him into my palm and pump up and down before swirling the head. He lays his head back and groans. I sink my lips to his tip and give it a long lick before taking his engorged length into my mouth. He smells and tastes of man. His hands clutch my hair as I pleasure him with my tongue. As much as I crave him inside me, I'd be happy to make him come this way.

"Jeans," he grunts and tugs my hair to pull me upright. "Off now."

I make fast work of removing my jeans and panties as Everett rolls a condom onto his erection. He moves the seat back as back as far as it will go so I may climb on top.

We waste no time. We don't take it slow. The instant I'm straddling him, he presses the tip of his cock to my entrance and thrusts as he pushes me down onto him. He takes me in one swift motion, filling me to the hilt. We both cry out in pleasure. My hands grip his shoulders for purchase as I ride him fast and hard, chasing my release that's already building. When I come, it will be powerful.

With one hand in my hair and the other kneading my breasts, Everett stares deep into my eyes, his primal lust blazing as I slide up and down his length.

"So good," he moans. "So tight."

His velvety voice sends a tingle up my spine and the first wave of my orgasm propels me to ride faster. The intensity of his stare is almost too much to bear, but I don't dare turn away. I need to see when he comes.

Another shock wave is followed quickly by another. I cry out. So close. At the precipice.

"Come for me, Liv." He grips my thighs and pushes his hips upward, meeting me thrust for thrust.

My pleasure explodes within. My toes do indeed curl. I scream out his name as ecstasy tears through me.

His body tenses, face is flushed a deep red. The muscles in his neck are corded. "I'm gonna come."

With a grunt, he holds me on his cock as he pulses and jerks inside me. While he comes, his eyes stay trained on mine showing me how much he wants me—how crazy I make him. He gives me everything inside and out. It's too intimate. But I don't look away. I want him to see what he has done to me. All the things *he* makes *me* feel.

Once we're both sated, we remain joined, just looking into one another's eyes. In this moment, we are changed.

"I can't resist you," he murmurs.

The morning light shines through the window as I open my eyes. Everett lies on the bed to my right, snoring softly.

Memories of last night flow through my mind.

No sooner than we got to his place, we were stripping for round two. That round was promptly followed by a third. We slept a short while and Everett woke me for round four. The man is a machine.

I roll onto my side to watch Everett sleep. He is just as gorgeous asleep as he is awake. Perhaps more so. Lying on his back, his head is turned in my direction. One hand rests on his torso while the other lies on his hip. His sculpted chest rises and falls with each breath. His hair is mussed. A vision of utter perfection.

While I'm happy to lie here and watch him sleep all day, he wakes within minutes.

A smile of satisfaction spreads across his lips when he opens his eyes. "Good morning."

How is it possible his sleepy voice is even sexier than his regular voice?

"Best morning I've had in... best morning I've *ever* had," I confess.

"Mmm..." he closes his eyes and I can tell he's remembering our night. "The best sex is illicit sex."

Does that mean sex with me is some of the best he's had? "I agree."

"As much as I'd like more illicit sex," he turns to me with a sly smile, "I should give you a day's rest."

A day's rest...

"Does that mean I'm not getting the," I make air quotes, "this can never happen again speech?"

"Even if I said the words," he skims my jawline with the back of his hand, "we both know it would be a lie."

I nod and close my eyes, reveling in his gentle touch.

"But if you want the day off," he says, "we need to get out of this bed right now."

"I don't *want* the day off, but my ability to walk tomorrow could depend upon it."

"Okay, breakfast it is." He tosses off the sheet and stands, giving me a much-appreciated view of his glorious backside.

Walking is overrated.

I struggle not to drool as he slides on a pair of black leisure pants.

"How do you like your eggs?" he asks.

The word fertilized pops into my mind and I giggle at the absurdity.

"What's funny?" he asks.

"Nothing," I answer. "I like my eggs scrambled with cheese and hot sauce."

"My favorite," he says with a wink and walks to my side of the bed, holding his hand out to me. As he lifts me from the mattress, his greedy eyes sweep over my naked body.

Everett has me sit at the island while he puts on a pot of coffee and starts on breakfast. I enjoy watching him move about the kitchen. That he's shirtless is a bonus. Four rounds of phenomenal sex with Mr. Big has me a bit sore, but that doesn't stop me from growing feverish at the sight of him.

"Looking at me that way will only get you in trouble," he smolders.

"What way is that?"

"Like you'd rather eat me than the eggs."

"I would."

He bites his lips and moans. "I really am going to hell for this."

"Why?"

"Liv, you're forbidden fruit and let's not forget that I'm nearly old enough to be your father." He sets a cup of coffee in front of me.

"Not even close."

"I'm forty, you're twenty-four. That's sixteen years, and I was having sex at fifteen."

I do my best to conceal my shock at his admission. He started early. I didn't lose my virginity until I was eighteen.

Finally, I manage to speak. "Age is just a number."

"I'm a cradle robber." He scrambles the eggs. "I am officially a dirty old man."

Thankfully, there isn't an ounce of regret in his tone or expression.

"You're not an old man, but I have learned how dirty you can be."

"Likewise, Miss Bell," he smirks. "I have to say, I was pleasantly surprised last night."

"Oh yeah?"

"You are quite high-handed in the sack."

I shrug. "What can I say? I know what I like, and I have no problem asking for it."

"Asking?" He raises a brow. "More like demanding."

I take a sip of my coffee. "I didn't hear you complaining."

"And you never will." He leans in and kisses me with just enough tongue to be a tease. "I am more than willing to give you what you need when you need it."

"Ditto, Mr. Big." I try the nickname out loud.

"Mr. Big?"

"That's your new nickname."

He tilts his head to the side. "*New* nickname?"

"Your original one was McHotness."

"McHotness?"

"Yeah, it's how my friends and I refer to you."

He chuckles. "When did this start?"

"A while back." I don't dare tell him it was Grayson who came up with it.

Everett gets a distant look in his eyes. "Who would've guessed that we'd end up here?"

I did. "I knew I'd end up in your bed the moment I met you."

"You pretty much saw to it."

"That's me, Miss High-handed."

Everett fills two plates with eggs and fruit, sets them at the island and takes a seat next to me.

"Bon appetite," he says and digs in.

After breakfast, I hop in Everett's shower. If I'm quick, I'll have enough time to swing by my place to get a change of clothes before meeting Grayson for lunch. Surprisingly, I could eat again. My vigorous night must have taken a lot out of me.

On my way out, I lift onto my toes to plant a soft kiss on Everett's lips. "Enjoy golf with Dex."

"Just so you know, and because we haven't discussed it, I don't intend to say anything about… us." He scratches his head and looks unsure. "It's a little soon, don't you think?"

"I'm not ready for Maren to find out." She would take the wind out of my sails.

"So, we're in agreement?" he asks. "This'll stay our secret for now?"

"Yes, we are in agreement."

"I have news," Gray says once we place our orders.

"Yeah?"

"Andrea and I are officially dating."

Andrea is his boss's assistant. This is the first time he's referred to her by her name. Before they started sleeping together, she was "the bitch whose name we do not say."

"When did this happen?"

"Friday night. We were right in the middle of doing it and she stopped and said, 'I really like you, Grayson. I want you to take me on a date.' So yesterday, we went on our first date."

Always with the unnecessary extra details. He could have just said she asked him on a date. But I don't say anything because that's Grayson. "How'd it go?"

"Best date I've ever had."

"That's awesome. So, you like her?"

"I do, Liv." His sweet brown eyes sparkle. "She's not at all the person I once thought she was. Andrea's funny and self-deprecating and thoughtful."

Which begs the question… "Then why is she such an asshole at work?"

"I asked her about that, and she explained that it's because no one takes her seriously. Guys can't see past her rack and girls hate her for her looks. She puts on the tough act to be taken seriously."

"Makes sense." I pause as our waitress sets our drinks on the table. She tells us our food will be out soon and walks away. "How are things at the office with you two now?"

"We keep things professional there. No one knows we're seeing each other, and we want to keep it that way."

"That's smart."

"Speaking of keeping things professional," my friend's eyes bore into mine as though he knows what he can't possibly know, "how is it going between you and Everett?"

A wide smile spreads across my lips and I lean forward a smidgen. "We're no longer keeping things professional."

"What?" His eyes widen. "When did this go down?"

"Last night." I tell him all about what happened at The Thirsty Stone and that we spent the night together.

"But it's not just sex?" he asks.

I shake my head. I don't think it's just sex.

"So you're dating?"

I shrug, unsure. "I think so."

"You think so?"

"Yes," I change my answer to appease both of us. "We're definitely dating."

He eyes me with skepticism. "You're sure?"

No. "I think so."

He sighs. "You might want to get clarification on that."

Looking at him, it's obvious he thinks it was just another hookup. "It's new. We're exploring our connection. We'll figure it out as we go along."

"Okay," he says, "but don't let too much time pass before you figure it out. It's best to know up front."

"I'm a nervous wreck," Maren says as I help her put new sheets on her guest bed.

The sheets that were on it were already clean, but she insists they be changed out with a freshly laundered pair for her soon to be mother-in-law to sleep on.

"I see that," I say.

This is the most unkempt I've ever seen my sister. She's not necessarily dirty, but her hair is a mess, her outfit doesn't match. It's like she jumped out of bed, threw her hair into a ratty ponytail and had her eyes closed when she picked out her clothes.

"I am a fairly confident person, but Dex's mother has the ability to reduce me to a bumbling idiot."

"She can't be that bad."

Dex's mom, Sharon, is coming to visit for Dex's birthday. She arrives tomorrow and Maren called me over to aid in scrubbing her already immaculate house to make sure it's pristine. But everything I clean, she goes back over, so I'm not a hundred percent certain why I am here.

"Don't misunderstand, she's a great woman." Maren hands me one end of a blanket to lay on my side of the bed. "A *great* woman, which is the problem. She's so great that it's intimidating. Great isn't even a strong enough adjective."

"No one is that great," I assure her.

"Sharon Stevens is. She grew up an army brat and lived all over the world. She's fluent in *five* languages." Maren smooths out the blanket until it's flawless on all sides. "She was the wife of a brilliant award-winning surgeon, and raised four successful, perfect human beings, two of whom became surgeons. I'm not perfect. I am the farthest thing from perfect on the planet."

Appearing as though she will hyperventilate at any moment, she plops down onto the mattress. "I'm not brilliant. I bake for a living and only speak one language. I can't possibly be what she had in mind for her *brilliant* surgeon son."

Sitting next to her on the bed, I take her hand into mine. "You are an incredible human being, Mare. And you aren't any less than just because you aren't a well-traveled surgeon."

"Once you meet her, you'll understand what I mean. Sharon has this way of sizing you up with a simple glance. And she asks so many questions." She hides her face with her hands. "It's nerve-racking."

"She's probably trying to get to know you."

With a sigh, she sits upright. "We're not talking about, where did you grow up and where did you graduate college type of questions. We're talking, how many boyfriends have you had, when did your last relationship end, why did it end, have you ever cheated?"

I laugh. "Nobody asks those questions."

"She does. And she did."

I gasp. "Seriously?"

"Seriously."

Wow. "I understand why you're nervous."

She blows out a breath. "Please tell me this isn't how I will feel for the rest of my life whenever my mother-in-law comes for a visit."

I pat her leg and say the only comforting thing that comes to mind. "It'll get easier with time."

"Thank God she moved to Arizona. At least I'll only see her a couple times a year."

Glancing around the room, I say, "I think we've got this place spic and span."

"Thanks for helping me. You should get going. It's after eleven and you have to work in the morning."

"I don't require much sleep." Which is a good thing because I haven't averaged much since being with Everett.

"I've been meaning to ask, how are things going with Everett?"

My heart stutters and my mouth goes dry.

Does she know?

How could she?

Maybe she saw my car at his place or his at mine.

My phone pings with a text alert. The only person who texts me this late is Everett when he can't sleep. I better not check it. I can't risk my sister seeing it if it is him.

"Do you still like the job?" she inquires.

My tension releases. *Thank you Lord.* "The job… yeah, it's as great as ever."

That's a lot of "great's" in a single conversation. Are my nerves showing?

"Everett's still being a good boy?"

He's good at being bad, that's for sure. "Yep."

"You two have surprised me. I was positive you'd end up in his bed, but you've proven me wrong."

I nod.

She continues. "I guess he respects some boundaries."

I nod again. If only she knew all the boundaries he crossed last night. "I should get going."

"I'll see you at the party Saturday. Oh, and don't forget, you'll be meeting Callum. Wear something cute."

The party.

Me. Everett. Callum.

Should be an interesting evening.

Chapter 10

EVERETT AND I SPEND SATURDAY morning walking the streets of downtown Denver to partake in a little urban photography. I've tried it on my own, but every time I was approached by odd men who assumed following me around was perfectly natural. When I take friends with me, they're too distracting. They never quite understand that photography is more than point and shoot. It requires thought and focus. It's impossible to be focused with someone chatting in your ear about this thing and that thing.

When I told Everett of my interest in urban photography, he offered to go out with me since he, too, is a fan of the art form.

We come to an adorable little café on the outskirts of the city with an outdoor dining area tucked away in a quaint courtyard and pop in for a bite.

The hostess seats us at a small table barely big enough for the both of us. I slide my chair next to Everett's and link my arm with his, resting my head on his shoulder. I turn my camera on us and tell him to smile for a selfie.

"What are you doing?" he asks.

"Taking our picture."

"That's not what I mean," he says. "PDA… it's risky."

I set down the camera and twist to face him directly. "We're sleeping together, Everett. That gives me carte blanche to sit beside you at lunch. Besides, no one is here to see."

"This is a popular place." He looks around, worried. "Anyone could walk in."

"The only people we're hiding from is Dex and Maren."

"And anyone they know. Dex knows a lot of people in this city, Liv."

Slipping my arm back through his, I return my head to his shoulder. "We spend all our time cooped up in the gallery or in bed. This feels date-y. I'm taking advantage of it. Deal with it."

He chuckles. "There you go again, being high-handed."

"It's becoming my specialty."

"Tell me something I don't know."

As we laugh, the waitress arrives and asks what we want to drink.

"I'll have a sweet tea," I say, looking up at her from Everett's shoulder.

"Same," Everett states, "but add lemon to mine."

"Sounds good," she says and leans forward. "Can I just say… you are a stunning couple."

"Thank you," he and I reply in unison.

"When the two of you came in, I was blown away. You complement each other so well." Then, almost as an afterthought, she adds, "You'll make beautiful babies."

Blushing, I tuck a lock of hair behind my ear. Thank God Everett can't see my face.

Our waitress advises us she will be right back with our drinks before going inside.

"We are two very good-looking people," Everett quips.

"Indeed."

Silence.

We each pick up our menus to look them over.

Are we in an awkward silence?

Or is it just me?

Everett appears entirely relaxed.

"I wonder how Maren is holding up," I speak, needing to fill the silence. While it may not be awkward for him, it is for me. "She was really freaking out over Sharon's visit."

"Mama has that effect on people."

"Mama?" I hadn't expected him to refer to Mrs. Stevens that way.

"Sharon has been a surrogate mom to me ever since my mother passed away."

"Oh?"

"I honestly don't know where I'd be if not for that woman." As he sets his menu on the table, his gaze becomes unfocused. "She practically raised me. My dad had no use for me, and he worked all hours of the day and night. I basically lived at Dex's house. For all intents and purposes, Sharon is my mother."

"You must look forward to seeing her tonight." Isn't he? Because he spent yesterday with me. Why didn't he pop over to see her after work yesterday? I could've handled things at the gallery for a day while he visited with the woman he considers his mother.

His smile is nostalgic. "I am, but there's just one thing."

"What?"

His expression turns serious. "The woman is a living, breathing lie detector. Mama can smell bullshit from the next town. The day I lost my virginity, she knew it the moment I walked in the house. She took a single look at me, shook her head and said, 'I pray you at least had the good sense to wrap your rocket.'"

I stare at him, stunned. Perhaps Maren wasn't exaggerating about Sharon. And now she and I are in similar boats. Tonight I am meeting my boyf—Everett's—mother.

I feel faint.

Everett continues. "I've never been able to hide anything from Mama. We have to be extremely careful around her, Liv. No smiling at each other. No glances. Absolutely no flirting. Nothing. If we so much as slip up for a second, she will catch it."

I can do that. Can't I? I hope. "Got it."

"I'm serious, Liv."

Clearly. "It'll be okay, I promise."

Me. Everett. Dex. Maren. Sharon. Our secret. And Callum.

This evening will definitely be interesting.

Given that my sister is trying to set me up with Callum, I had planned on wearing a demure outfit to the party. Maybe if I come off as a quiet, buttoned up geek, he won't be interested. But now that I'm meeting Everett's mom, I've had a change of heart. Although she isn't aware of our involvement, she might eventually learn of it. I want to impress her. I want her to remember me as a polite, attractive young lady. Besides, not only am I involved with Everett, I am Maren's sister. Maren is marrying her son. I have two compelling reasons to make a great lasting impression.

I don't have many dresses to choose from. My nicest is a coral cap sleeve midi dress, which is almost perfect for tonight. I worry the side slit is a tad too high for meeting a boyfr—Everett's—mom. If she figures out that Everett and I are togeth—involved—I want to put my best foot forward. A high slit might send the wrong message, but it will have to do.

When I arrive at Dex and Maren's, I stand at the door, rubbing the back of my neck. My stomach rolls and my mouth is dry. I haven't even met Sharon yet, and she has me in a frenzy. *Please Lord, don't let her be as intimidating as everyone makes her out to be.* I do not fare well with intimidation. It brings out my timid side. When I get timid, I say the most ridiculous things. I can't be ridiculous. Not tonight.

I hear throat clearing from behind me and spin around to find a familiar face.

A face I've seen once. In a picture.

Callum.

His full lips spread into a handsome smile. "I believe you are Maren's sister, Olivia."

"Olivia Bell," I hold my hand out formally. "And you're Callum."

Taking my hand, he holds it more than he shakes it. "Callum Anderson. It's a pleasure to finally meet you. I've heard a lot about you."

"Have you?"

"It was all good, I assure you."

"That's nice to know." I pull my palm from his grip. "Shall we go inside?"

"Ladies first," he insists, and pulls the screen door open for me.

And so my interesting night begins.

I step into the entryway and Maren spies us at once and dashes over with a squeal.

"You've met!" She bounces with glee.

"We have," I say.

"Yay!" she claps and bounces again.

She must've started in on the booze.

"How are things?" I ask regarding Sharon.

"Great! Just great!" Given her overzealous response, things aren't great.

Mimicking her over the top enthusiasm, I say, "That's *great!*"

"The open bar is in the den," she says. "Help yourselves to a drink and get acquainted with each other. I'll bring Sharon by in a few minutes."

With that, she disappears into a crowd of unfamiliar people. I scan the room for Everett, but he isn't here. His jeep was outside. So he's somewhere in this house. And here I stand with my quasi date.

"I assume you know where the den is?" Callum asks.

I nod. "Follow me."

We round the corner into the den and I catch sight of my guy standing to the left of the wet bar chatting with a friend of Dex's. He notices me at once and takes in my appearance. The slight twitch in his lip conveys his approval of my dress choice.

Callum and I approach the bar, both of us requesting a glass of cabernet.

We look about the area, but find nowhere to sit.

"Why don't we stand over there?" Callum says, pointing to an empty space near a window.

"So, how do you know Maren?" I ask, trying to make small talk, with my back toward Everett so I'm not tempted to glance in his direction. I am itching to see the expression on his face.

"My uncle is friends with Dex's uncle, David. David called in a favor to have my uncle design their new house. I'm assisting on the job."

"And my sister convinced you to come here and meet me."

I don't buy her line that he saw a picture of me and asked for an introduction.

"No at all. One night the four of us, Dex, Maren, myself and my uncle met for dinner to go over our progress on the project. Dinner led to drinks. Your sister was hilarious and super charming. My uncle inquired if she had any sisters for me. She showed me your photo, and I asked her to introduce us."

"Full disclosure, Maren and I are nothing alike," I warn.

"I wasn't hoping you would be. There was just something about your smile and the way your eyes sparkled. In the picture, your happiness was… infectious." His tone is genuine. "I had to see that smile in person."

I blush. Nobody has ever complimented my smile so beautifully. "That's very sweet."

"Isn't it?" Everett's voice cuts in.

My eyes dart to Everett, who is wearing a noticeably fake smile. "I'm Everett," he extends his hand to Callum, "Dex's best friend and Liv's… boss."

Callum accepts the handshake. "Good to meet you, Everett, I'm Callum Anderson. I work with the architecture firm that Dex and Maren hired."

"Yes, I heard about that. Do you mind if I steal your date? I have business to discuss with her."

Without giving him a chance to answer, Everett leads me away by the elbow. He ushers me as discreetly as possible to the next room over, Dex's home office. Once inside, he closes the door and pushes me up against it, slamming his lips to mine.

"He's not your date," he growls.

"Neither are you," I taunt.

"I am more than a date. I'm your lover." His hand slides into the slit in my dress. "Did you have to wear this dress? It hugs *everything*."

I push my chest out. "That's why I wore it."

"For me or *Callum*?" he says the name like it's the most repulsive word ever.

"What do you think?"

He drags a fingertip down the center of my chest, between my cloth covered breasts. "You intended to tease me all night knowing I can't touch you?"

That hadn't crossed my mind, but I am pleased it turned out that way. "You're touching me right now."

Fire dances in his deep blues. "Because you, in this dress, with that cum stain junior architect drooling over you drove me to madness."

The top three buttons of his black button-down shirt are open. I undo the fourth and press my palm to his chest. "Isn't this a little risky? What if Dex or Maren walked in?"

"I'm not sure I would care." Leaning into my neck, he inhales and licks my jawline. "All I can think about is burying myself inside you to remind you who you belong to."

"I still have a reminder from this morning," I murmur.

"Seeing you smile at *Callum* had me wondering if you'd forgotten."

I reach my fingers into his hair and pull. My eyes bore into his. "Everett, you are the only man I want, or haven't I made that clear?"

His lips descend upon mine and he presses his hardness into my center. His tongue works its usual magic, rendering me weak in the knees.

A female voice behind the door asks if anyone has seen Everett. He pulls away, breathing heavily. My lipstick is smeared on his mouth. He groans silently.

"Later," he whispers and wets his lips.

"Promise?"

He points at the wall toward the den. "Shut that guy down, Liv. I can't stand to watch him paw at you."

"He never touched me."

"And he better not. Please, just shut him down."

Everett jealous is a sexy sight.

"Okay. I'll shut him down." I straighten my dress and fix my makeup in the mirror on the wall. Once finished, I swing around to find Everett watching me with eyes filled with longing and frustration. "I will walk out first. Be sure to clean my lipstick off your face and get that," I gesture to the tent in his pants, "under control before you go out there."

I pull the door open and step into the hallway. Neither Maren nor Dex are in sight. No one who knows me saw me slip out of the office.

I locate Maren in the family room chatting with her best friend, Sarah.

"Hi, Liv," Sarah pulls me in for a hug. "How's it going?"

"It's going well. Yourself?"

"My boyfriend left me today for a younger woman. He's moving out of our house and into her's as we speak."

I place my hand on her arm in comfort. "I am so sorry, Sarah."

"The sad thing is, I was expecting a proposal." A tear slides down her right cheek and she blots it away with a cocktail napkin. "I thought we were solid. I was completely blindsided."

"Oh, Sarah…"

"There you are." Callum sidles up beside me. "All done talking business?"

"All done."

"Great. I need a refill on my wine. Join me?"

"It's not a good time. Girl talk."

He flashes a million-dollar smile. "Come find me when you're finished."

Callum leaves and I turn back to Sarah and Maren.

Maren says, "You should've gone with him, Liv."

"I'll find him later."

"I'm telling you, you don't want to pass him up," she insists. "He is perfect for you."

"Jury is still out on that since I just met him."

"Spare yourself the trouble," Sarah says with a wave of her hand. "All men are worthless, untrustworthy swine."

At some point, Dex entered the room. "I take offense to that."

Dex drapes an arm over Maren's shoulder and kisses her on the temple.

"Except you," Sarah allows. "You're the one and only exception."

"My son is unquestionably an exception," a woman who looks a bit like Dex appears at his side. They have the same ivory skin and wide-set dark blue eyes. Sharon.

My palms sweat. I hope I wore enough deodorant. Just looking at her is panic inducing. I'm dating—sleeping with—her adopted son, and she hasn't a clue.

"You must be Dex's mother, Mrs. Stevens." Subtly, I wipe my palm on my dress before extending it to her.

"And you are the lovely Olivia." Shaking my hand, she holds it in both of hers. "Please either call me Sharon or Mama."

"It's very nice to meet you, Sharon."

"I hear you work for Everett." She looks me up and down with seeming approval.

"Yes, Ma'am." I hold my hands steady to hide my trembling.

By the sour look on her face, she didn't appreciate being called Ma'am. "I am also told you're quite a talented photographer."

"I'm working on it."

"You must be succeeding if Everett has taken you under his wing."

I can't keep her gaze. "I am grateful for the opportunity to learn from him."

She leans in close and whispers. "Be careful around him. Everett finds it rather difficult to keep his hands to himself around attractive young women."

I cough. "So I've been told."

"Speaking of my bonus child, I'm gonna go find him. I get the impression he's avoiding me, and I intend to find out why."

Thirty minutes later, after Sarah has left, Dex and Maren are mingling with their abundance of friends. I would hang out with Everett, but that idea has disaster written all over it. Instead, I stand in a corner, sipping wine. I've started in on my third glass.

"You didn't come find me." Callum approaches.

"I was just getting ready to," I lie.

If Everett see's us together, it won't bode well.

"It's warm in here," he says. "Care to join me for some fresh air?"

"I get cold easy," I lie, again. I definitely don't need Everett seeing me walk out with the guy.

"Maren tells me you're a photographer."

"I'm working on it. Right now I assist Everett, the gentleman you met earlier."

"Yeah." He scratches his head. "I have to ask… is there anything going on between you two? Because he seemed a little… intense. As though he didn't want you talking to me."

Unable to lie aloud yet again, I shake my head. "Everett is always intense. Don't take it personal."

Callum stares at me with a thoughtful expression.

"What?" I ask.

"I'm still waiting to see that incredible smile in person."

I flash him a quick grin.

"Pretty, but that's not the one."

"I don't know what picture you saw, so I'm not sure which smile it was."

"I guess I have to make you smile until I see it."

Admittedly, I'm charmed. If I wasn't involved with Everett, I would give Callum a chance. But I am with Everett and he asked me to shut this down. If the shoe was on the other foot, I wouldn't appreciate Everett standing with a beautiful woman who was chatting him up.

Here goes…

"Callum, you're probably a great guy, and you're good-looking and charismatic, but I'm not in a place where I'm open to meeting anyone."

"Oh." He frowns. "Maren told me you were single. If I had known you are involved…"

"I am… single. I'm just complicating-ly single."

The side of his mouth curls into a crooked smile. "Never heard that before."

Nervous, I laugh. I'm becoming timid and ridiculous.

"I apologize. Normally, you'd be precisely my type, but…"

"No need to explain. I appreciate your honesty. But Liv, I'll be keeping tabs on you. If your situation becomes less complicated, give me a call. I'd like to get to know you." Before walking away, he hands me a card with his info.

In the living room to my right, Everett wears a satisfied expression.

I hate being the first to leave a party, but I feel this one will last well into the early morning. Maren is busy mingling with her guests. Everyone here wants a moment of the birthday boy's time. I've had a few brief conversations with Dex's friend's wives, but they are all considerably older than I, married and settled with kids. Outside of our shared connection in Dex and Maren, we have little in common.

The longer I stay, the more wine I drink. The alcohol is making it impossible to stay away from Everett, or keep my eyes off him. I need to call it an evening and go home.

"I've never seen my son so happy," Sharon says from my left, pointing at Maren and Dex. "I'm thrilled they're finally engaged. It took long enough."

I nod. Maren's fear of commitment was a problem between them in the beginning. Even once she got over that fear, her aversion to marriage remained.

"I can assure you, Maren is as happy and in love as Dex is, Mrs. Stevens."

"Sharon," she corrects me.

"Sharon. Sorry."

Sharon turns to face me with firm eye contact. "What are your thoughts on commitment?"

"I'm an advocate of committed relationships."

Nodding, she steps in close. "I hear that you're a good girl. Is that true?"

Mama is every bit as intimidating as they have made her out to be. My voice shakes, "I think so."

Eyeing me up and down, she asks, "Are you promiscuous?"

Geez. Is this woman for real? "No."

"How many lovers have you had?"

Maren was right about the inappropriate questions. But what is her interest in me?

With raised eyebrows, she's impatient for my reply.

"Three," I answer apprehensively, but then remember another. "Four. It—It's four."

"Were they all men or men and women?"

I cough. "All men."

She purses her lips. "What's your credit score like?"

My credit score? What the hell?

"It's perfect." I think.

"How would your friends describe you if I asked them?"

I swallow. "They'd probably say I'm a good friend. Reliable, kind, caring, astute, a hard worker."

"Okay," she says with a smile as though she accepts my answers to her strange and intrusive questions. "You are a lovely young woman, Olivia. I'm very pleased to have met you."

Chapter 11

AFTER SHARON'S INTERROGATION, I SAY a quick goodbye to Dex and Maren and text Everett to tell him I'm going home. He responds and asks me to go to his place, that he will be close behind.

I let myself in with his hidden key, change into a pair of his boxers and a t-shirt and crawl into bed, utterly spent from the lengthy day.

Less than an hour later, Everett slides in next to me and draws me into his arms.

"As much as I loved the dress you wore tonight," he murmurs, "seeing you in my clothes is even sexier."

He kisses my neck and massages my back.

"Would you be upset if I'm too tired to pick up where we left off earlier?"

He places a soft kiss to the rear of my head. "Not at all."

Everett makes me the little spoon and pulls the sheet up around us. This is how we often fall asleep. But I have a nagging concern that won't allow me to doze off.

"Sharon interrogated me before I took off. I think she suspects something."

"Your suspicion is accurate," he admits, and I flip over to face him.

"What did she say?"

"She called me out on avoiding her. Said she caught me glaring at you with Callum and noticed how I relaxed once you shot him down."

"But she doesn't know anything for sure?"

"I came clean." He scrunches his nose. "I had to, Liv. I literally *can't* hide anything from her."

My eyes widen. I'm not upset, just very surprised. He was so adamant about keeping us a secret from Dex and Maren. Personally, I couldn't care less whether they find out at this point. "What if—"

He cuts me off. "She won't say anything. She really likes you."

"Are you sure?"

"I trust that woman with my life. If she says she won't spill, she won't."

Everett and I stay at the gallery late on a Tuesday evening to rearrange the exhibit and change out the window display. Somewhere along the way we end up making out in the office. The man has a voracious sexual appetite.

"Being with such a young woman definitely has its perks." He lifts his shirt over his head before dropping it onto the floor. "I didn't think I'd ever meet anyone who could keep up with me."

"Lucky you." I hike my skirt.

Everett pulls away. "Did you hear something?"

"No." I pull his face to mine and resume kissing.

And then we both hear the side door open and close. We snap up and he runs to close the office door as we scramble to put on our clothes.

"Didn't we lock the doors?" I ask.

"We did."

Dex calls out from the hallway. "Ev?"

Everett's eyes dart to mine. "Shit."

"What do we do?" I whisper.

He rubs his neck as he thinks. "Stay here. I'll go out and get rid of him."

"How did he get in?"

"He has a spare key."

"Everett, buddy," he knocks on the door. "It's me, Dex."

Everett mouths, "Hide under the desk."

Once I am out of sight, he opens the door.

"Hey," Everett greets Dex. "This is a surprise."

"Yeah, I was on this side of town and saw the lights. Thought I'd pop in. I brought a six pack."

"Uh… I'm right in the middle of processing. I hate to break when I'm on a roll."

"I can wait."

I catch the shuffle of feet. Someone, presumably Dex, has taken a seat on the other side of the desk.

"I need to talk," Dex says. "Maren is freaking out again. And I hardly see you these days. All you do is work."

"You know what?" Everett asks. "The processing can wait. Why don't we head over to The Thirsty Stone?"

"I can hang around while you finish. It's no big deal."

"Nonsense. My best friend is in distress. Let's go get a proper drink and you can tell me what's going on."

A few minutes after the guys leave, I receive a text from Everett with an apology telling me he will see me tomorrow.

Everett is off on his guy trip with Dex and other friends. They left this morning and I now have a full Everett-free week ahead of me. I haven't gone more than a day without him since we started seeing each other. If that's what we're even doing. We work together. We spend at least half our nights together. Still, I'm not positive this is an actual relationship. It's hard to be sure when the most important people in your life can't know about it.

We still have dinner every Thursday with Maren and Dex. Though we arrive separately, and while there, we pretend to be nothing more than two individuals who work together. Everett has perfected the art of indifference. Meanwhile, the entire time we're there, I yearn for him to take my hand and say, "This is my girl."

That may never happen.

I'm not even sure I am his girl. We haven't said we're exclusive. And though it bothers me, I don't have the guts to say a word.

In desperate need of my closest friend's advice, I've met Grayson at his place. That he's a member of the opposite sex is most helpful. He can give me a male's perspective on sex and dating. Because at this spot in time, I'm at a loss.

After cracking open a couple beers, we relax side by side on his sofa.

"Tell me what's up," he says.

Staring at the bottle in my hand, I sigh. "I figured when Everett came clean to Sharon about me, it meant we were headed toward telling Dex and Maren. But that was weeks ago, and he still insists we can't tell them."

"Have you expressed your desire to be out in the open?"

"Not exactly," I take a swig of my beer, "but he's well aware that I don't care who knows. Keeping things hush-hush was never my idea. Ever since the night in the office, I've felt like a dirty little secret."

"You need to tell him how you feel, Liv."

"But I'm scared."

"Why?"

I hate that I'm getting ready to admit my fears aloud. Until now, I've kept them to myself. Most times, I push them to the back of my mind where I can't hear them.

"Because I'm unsure how he feels about me. I mean, we've never even been on an actual date. We spend all our time at the gallery or his condo." I turn to Grayson. "I can't help but wonder if this is just sex for him."

"Do you think that's what it is for him?"

"Partly yes, partly no."

"Then ask him straight out. It's time to figure out, once and for all, what this is between you two." After a brief pause, he continues, "If you ask me, you've put it off too long."

I blow out a breath. Another admission on the tip of my tongue. Another I've never said aloud. The reason I've put off this discussion with Everett.

"I have feelings for him, Gray. *Strong* feelings. It'll kill me if he doesn't feel the same."

Grayson places a comforting hand on mine and looks at me with total understanding. "That's all the more reason to find out. You two need to be on the same page. Go to him and have the conversation."

"What if his feelings aren't the same?"

"Then you end it."

I close my eyes as my stomach twists. That's what I'm afraid of.

While he's gone, Everett keeps in regular contact. Having left me in charge of the gallery, he calls daily to receive updates. But he also sends me flirty texts throughout the day. We send each other pictures, some on the naughty side. He even called a couple evenings and talked to me as I drifted to dreamland. Surely, if he didn't possess romantic feelings for me, he wouldn't talk me to sleep.

Would he?

The evening Everett will arrive, he tells me to meet him at his condo. I know what he has in mind, but we're having our talk first. I have to find out if he wants me or just sex.

I *must* know. And I vow to myself there shall be no sex until I get my answer.

And if it's just sex, there won't be any more sex. It—we—will be done.

But the instant Everett walks through the door, my plans fly out the window. Our eyes meet and I'm drawn to where he stands. I missed him more than I realized.

Yes, we need to talk. And we will. But for now…

"I couldn't get to you fast enough." He places his palms on either side of my face and kisses me as if it's the first, or the last time he'll ever get the chance.

An undeniable need erupts within me, taking over my senses and my body. I yearn to touch and taste every part of Everett's mouthwatering body. Unable to resist, I skim my hands across his shoulders to his pecs, to his waist, and back upward. Everywhere I touch is lean, warm, taut muscle. I salivate at the memory of what lies beneath his shirt.

I slide my fingers lower, to the waistband of the jeans that hang low on his hips and press a palm to his impressive bulge. His erection jerks in my grip. Lust blazes in his eyes. Thrilled by his response to my touch, I work my hand up and down every inch of his hardened length.

"Liv," his desperate voice is barely louder than a whisper.

The thirst in his tone sends a spasm to my core.

Everett's desirous gaze sweeps over my body and he spins us around, pinning me to the door. One hand holding me by the throat, the other slides down my spine, settling on my bottom. Caressing and kneading my backside, he presses his erection against my abdomen. His mouth claims mine, swiping his tongue across my bottom lip before plundering inside. There's nothing gentle about his kiss. It's forceful and domineering. I whimper as his mouth ravages me.

Desperate to be closer to him yet—eager for skin to skin contact—I remove my shirt and bra, tossing them to the floor. Knowing what I crave, as he always does, Everett moves his hand from my ass to my breast, cupping it tenderly.

He sucks in his bottom lip and groans as he swipes his thumb across my hardened nipple.

With a shudder, I gasp at his touch. There has never been a better lover.

Everett dives in, claiming my mouth once again with a kiss that leaves me breathless. *God, I have missed the taste of him.* Needing more, I take his lower lip between my teeth and bite down lightly. His fingers grip my hair, tugging my head backward. He kisses me deeper yet, and a primal groan rumbles within his chest. The sexy as hell sound sends my arousal into overdrive.

As fantastic as the kissing is, I need his mouth elsewhere. I arch my back, thrust my chest forward and breathe his name as I pinch and twist my throbbing nipples. Taking the hint, Everett lowers his face and flicks his tongue across one pebbled nipple. He flicks it again and again, teasing me until I can take no more.

"Please," I beg.

He presses his mouth on my breast and licks and sucks just as I need him to. My head falls back against the door, my fingertips thread through his hair as I revel in the delicious sensation.

After working both breasts, he moves lower, his tongue skimming my ribs and stomach. Almost as arousing as his lips is the brush of his beard on my delicate skin. Everett slides his hands into my pants, palming my bottom. He makes quick work of removing them, leaving me in only my panties.

Everett places a trail of wet kisses up my thigh, stopping at the oh so sensitive area below the hip, giving it a few licks before burying his face into my lace covered mound. Overcome with desire, I pant his name.

"Turn around, baby," he orders.

Without question, I happily do as told, resting my forearms against the door. Unsure what he intends to do, I ready myself for anything. When the heat of his mouth meets my flesh, I moan with satisfaction.

"You have a perfect ass," he says before sinking his teeth into my backside.

Pain mixes with pleasure and my body trembles as I cry out. But he soothes the area with soft strokes of his tongue.

Everett utters words of appreciation for my firm backside and the "sexy" lace thong I'm wearing. My breathing is fast and shallow. My nipples brush the door with each breath I take.

"You have no idea how much I missed you," he murmurs.

Everett rises to his feet, his left hand gliding up my side to cup my breast. He moves in close, pressing his erection into my backside and a moan escapes my lips.

The sound of his ragged breaths thrills me. His voice is low and husky, "Do you know how many times I fantasized about you while I was away?"

"Not as many times as I fantasized about you."

He drags a finger down the cleft of my ass and back up. "I spent more time in the shower thinking of you than on the golf course."

Images of Everett pleasuring himself to thoughts of me causes my sex to spasm. My panties are soaked.

His erection twitches against me. The hand that rests on my backside moves higher over my hip to my front. Everett teases me through the front of my soaking wet thong. I shudder and clench my thighs together, desperate for any friction. It's not enough, so I push my hips forward in a failed attempt to get his touch where I need it most.

"What do you want, Baby?" he croons.

"Touch me."

"Like this?" he asks and strokes my fabric covered clit just once.

Though the touch lasts only a fraction of a second, it's enough to send a tingle up my spine. I buck my hips and beg, "Please."

"You know I can't deny you," he whispers and slips his fingers into the waist of my panties. Still, he teases me, barely brushing his fingertip across my clitoris. Once. Twice. Three times.

Unable to withstand his taunting, my body trembles. A sharp breath escapes my lips. "I need you inside me."

He thrusts a finger into my depths. "Is this what you want, Baby?"

He pushes the finger in and out and around. "Or did you have something else in mind?"

I indeed had another part of his anatomy in mind, but his finger is already doing the work. My orgasm is right there, waiting to ignite. All I need is…

Everett knows what I need, when I need it, and he always delivers. He presses his thumb to my clit as his finger slides in and out of my wetness.

My knees become weak and the room spins. Feeling wild and fevered, I ride his hand, rocking forward and backward. My breathing hitches and my body tenses as the first wave hits. With climax imminent, my sex clenches around Everett's masterful fingers.

Desperate for the taste of his kiss, I fist Everett's hair and bring his lips to mine. Thrusting my tongue into his mouth, I move my hips at a furious pace.

I'm. So. Close.

My release is… right… there…

Light flashes in my eyes and I writhe as my orgasm tears through me. My entire being pulses and aches. My heart hammers in my chest.

As the feverish passion from a moment ago ebbs, Everett's kiss becomes soft and slow. Pleasurable aftershocks continue as his hand still works me, leisurely and tenderly.

My body relaxes and I try to catch my breath as my bliss fades.

"My turn." He scoops me up and carries me into the bedroom.

"That was incredible," Everett says, kissing my temple.

"Mmm," is the only response I can manage. Covered in sweat, my heart is still racing. How on earth did I survive two full hours of continuous sex with this man?

"Thirsty?" he asks.

I nod.

When Everett goes to the kitchen, I hear a knock at the door. I pick up a woman's voice but can't make out what she's saying.

The door opens.

"Hey there," the female says in a seductive tone.

I jump from the bed and peek around the bedroom door to see a tall, blonde bombshell wearing a dress that leaves zero to the imagination.

"April," Everett says, "this is a surprise."

Bimbo Barbie flashes a flirtatious smile. "I was around the corner having drinks with my girlfriends and figured I'd swing by and see if you are up for some fun. It's been too long."

Everett drags a hand through his sweaty hair. "It's really not a good time."

"Oh," she lowers her voice, and her eyes widen, "you're not alone."

He shakes his head. "No."

"That's too bad," Blondie purrs and draws a finger down his chest and winks. "Maybe next time."

"See ya, April."

That's all?

No, "I have a girlfriend?"

No, "I'm sorry there can't be a next time?"

Just, "See ya?"

What the fuck?

See, Olivia, this is why you should have had the talk with him first.

I get back in the bed and pull the sheets up to my chin as Everett enters the room.

"She was hot," I say.

With a shrug, he climbs into the bed next to me and hands me the glass.

"Does that happen often?" I ask and take a drink.

"Not often."

But it happens.

"Would you have let her in if I wasn't here?"

"What?" He jerks back. "No."

I take another swig of the water.

"Hey," he scoots closer and pulls me against him, "Liv, I'm sorry that happened. Please don't be mad. I haven't seen April in months. I have no idea why she popped by."

She made it perfectly clear why she popped by.

I set the water on the bedside table. "I need to know something."

"Okay."

"Is this," I motion from me to him, "just sex?"

"No," he says the word as though I should know better.

"Then what is this? What are we?"

He blows out a breath and rubs the back of his neck. "I'm not a fan of labels, Liv."

My heart feels as though it shrinks, and I pull away. "We can't avoid this, Everett. We've been doing this for weeks now."

"I'm not avoiding."

"Alright, so let's figure this out. You say it's not just sex. Does that mean we're in a relationship?"

His arms tense and he looks at everything in the room but me. "I—I, uh, don't know."

"Are you scared? Because if you are, that's okay. I am too."

"Liv, I…" he hesitates, and I stare at him, waiting. "I enjoy being with you. I don't wish to be with anyone else and I haven't been since this began."

"So, we're in a relationship." It isn't a question.

A moment passes, and he lifts his gaze to mine and gives the tiniest of a nod.

"Then why not tell that woman you're with someone and there won't be a next time?"

He blows out a breath. "I was trying to get her out of here as fast as possible."

"I can't be your dirty little secret anymore, Everett. If I'm going to be in a relationship, I need to be in it out in the open. In front of my sister and Dex. Do you realize we've never gone on a public date? I want to go on dates and hold your hand and do all the things couples do." I shift my gaze to my hands. "If we can't do that, I can't do this."

"Liv—" he starts to protest but I'm on a roll and cut him off.

"I'm tired of the secrets, Everett. I won't keep lying to my sister."

"You're right," Everett says. "And you deserve those things, but I need time. Telling Dex is a big deal. It will change everything. I promised him I wouldn't touch you, and all this time I've been lying. And let's face it, Maren will never accept us, which will drive a wedge between me and Dex. Dex is the only family I have. Please tell me you understand that."

"I understand." I get out of the bed and start dressing.

"What are you doing?"

"I'm going home."

"Please don't leave." He reaches for me, but I step away.

"You said you need time." I zip my jeans. "So, take the time you need. But while you take that time, we are on hold."

"What?" His shoulders slump.

"I told you, I can't keep doing this. I refuse to be a secret. So, take your time, and when you are ready, we can pick up where we left off."

Chapter 12

"TELL ME I DIDN'T OVERREACT." I pace Grayson's living room.

I didn't sleep at all last night after leaving Everett's. I went home and tossed and turned in my bed. As soon as the sun came up, I called Grayson and told him I needed to talk. I've just finished telling him everything Everett, and I said.

"You most definitely didn't overreact."

"But he told me it isn't just sex. He agreed we're in a relationship." I come to a halt and turn to Grayson, who is sitting on the sofa. "All he's asking for is a little time."

"That's such shit, Liv." Gray smacks his thighs. "Everett knows it won't matter whether he tells him tomorrow or six months from now. Dex's reaction will be the same. He wants to keep things how they are."

"Well, that can't happen."

"I seriously hope you don't let it. You deserve better."

My stomach churns. "What if he won't tell Dex?"

"You'll have to decide. Either stick to your guns and tell him to fuck off, or continue sleeping together in secret."

I groan and pull at my hair. "I don't want to do either of those things."

"Then let's hope he does the right thing."

"He has to."

My friend pulls me into his arms and kisses my temple. "If he doesn't, I'll kick his ass."

"I miss you, Liv," Everett says, leaning close. It's Friday night and we've just closed the gallery for the day.

Pretending to be unaffected by his nearness isn't an easy feat. "Tell Dex and things can go back to the way they were."

Tomorrow will be a week since our talk. Seven days since I pressed the pause button. Every day, he's begged me to change my mind. He promises to tell Dex when the time is right. But that's when we argue. I contend there will never be a right time. He assures me there will be. I ask him to agree to a timeframe, but he says he can't.

Last night I skipped out on Maren's dinner. I lied and said I was sick and planned to spend the evening in bed. I couldn't sit across the table from Everett and pretend everything is okay.

To say it has been a tough week is an understatement. I crave nothing more than to be close to him. To talk and smile and laugh and joke like we used to. For him to hold me.

As much as I want him, I won't give in. I can't.

"That's just it, though. If I tell him, everything will change. It'll ruin everything, Liv."

With an exhale, I break eye contact. "Then maybe we shouldn't be together."

Everett closes the distance between us and lifts my chin to face him. "Don't say that."

"If we have to hide our relationship, what's the point? It can't go anywhere. It can't grow." I sigh and my insides crumble. "It's pointless."

"No, it's not. We're great together. You can't deny that."

No, I can't. And I never did. But if we can't be in a real, open relationship, it is pointless. And I deserve better than to be anyone's secret.

Squaring my shoulders, I face him straight on. I mustn't allow him to rope me in. "Come clean, and we can be great together again. Until then, hands off."

"I'm glad to see you're feeling better," Maren says as we peruse the farmer's market.

"It was probably something I ate." I stop and buy a loaf of fresh bread. There's nothing more comforting than a piece of fresh warm bread with butter. Lately, I've needed a lot of comfort.

"You missed out on a great meal Thursday. I made Shepherd's pie."

I shouldn't have come. I am so not in the mood for small talk. I'm not in the mood for much of anything. But I can't say that to Maren. It's rude and would hurt her feelings.

"Sorry I missed it."

"Are you okay?" she asks. "You seem a little down."

"I'm fine."

I'm not fine at all. Maren showed up at my place unannounced and forced me to get dressed and come here with her, Dex and Everett. Afterward, we're all going to lunch.

I was looking forward to a couple days of not seeing Everett. Working with and being near him every day this week was torture. Now here we are hanging out with the very people who are the reason we're apart. Luckily the guys are, for the most part, doing their own thing.

"I can tell something's up," she pushes.

If I don't tell her something, she will hound me until I crack under pressure. I go with the first lie that pops into my mind. "Gray and I had an argument. I hate it when we fight."

"Oh, no. What happened?"

"Growing pains I guess. He's dating someone new and I don't care for her." The lie rolls off my tongue easily.

"You know… I was convinced that Grayson is in love with you."

Many years ago, Grayson and I explored our friendship. We thought we might make a good couple, that we were meant to end up together. Two weeks and a handful of awkward kisses later, it was clear we were wrong.

Although I've told Maren, on several occasions, that Gray and I are just friends, she still clings to hope that one day we will end up together.

"I can assure you he isn't."

"Are you upset because you have feelings for him?"

"Absolutely not."

"I am certain you'll make up and be back to normal in no time. You are two peas in a pod."

"I'm sure you're right."

"Hey, Ladies," Dex says as he and Everett approach. He kisses Maren on the cheek.

That could be me and Everett if he would do the right thing and tell them about us. I clutch my back and turn away. It hurts to see their happiness when the source of my sorrow is smack dab in front of me.

"Looks like you've been successful," Dex says to Maren and points at her two large bags.

"I hope you like Rutabaga," she chuckles. "I bought a bushel."

"Not especially," he answers with a wrinkled nose. "But I love you so much I'll eat anything you feed me."

Normally, I find their affection cute and inspiring. Today, I have a hard time keeping my gag reflex in check. Everett glances at me as though he knows what I'm thinking, and it appears he feels the same.

Maren turns her attention back to me. "I still can't believe you shot down Callum. I'll never understand what you were thinking."

My eyes flit to the reason I turned him down. Everett. Unable to hold my gaze, he looks away.

"He was a nice guy, but something was… off."

"I can't imagine what that was," she says. "If I was your age and single, I'd jump all over that."

"Maybe he's more your type than mine."

Maren gives my shoulder a nudge. "Callum is every woman's type."

Dex chokes. "I'm standing right here."

Despite my crummy mood, I laugh.

"I said if I was single," Maren says. "I hit the jackpot with you, Baby."

"You're damn right." He pulls her in for a kiss.

I never got to have this with Everett. We never walked the farmer's market hand in hand. Never walked anywhere hand in hand. But we were playful and affectionate, like Maren and Dex. We laughed until we cried. We talked about everything under the sun. He knows my greatest fears and I know his. What we had was real.

Why isn't he willing to fight for us?

"If Callum and Grayson, both of whom are great guys, don't fit the bill, what exactly are you looking for in a guy?" Maren asks me.

It's a struggle not to look at Everett. I've already found what I want.

"Someone who can make me laugh when it feels impossible. Someone who makes my heart race just by walking into the room. Someone who smells and feels like home. Someone who invades my every waking thought and my dreams at night." I take a deep breath. "Someone extraordinary."

Thankfully, Everett ducked out of lunch. By the time we left the market, I was spent mentally and emotionally from acting as though everything was hunky-dory. Also, thankfully, I have the apartment to myself tonight. Jess is at work and Hannah is spending the night at her boyfriend's place.

I'm sitting on the couch queuing up a horror film on Netflix. I'm not a fan of scary movies, and I prefer not to watch them alone, but I'm avoiding romance, sadness and comedy at all costs. Horror is my only safe bet. The overflowing bowl of popcorn and bag of chocolates beside me will have to keep me company.

My phone rings. It's Maren. She's calling to check up on me and ask if I've made up with Grayson. Not wanting to tell any more lies, I reject the call. Besides, as much as I love my sister, I don't wish to talk.

I push play on the movie, and she calls again. She's persistent when she's concerned about me. I turn off the ringer.

My phone buzzes with a text message.

Maren: *Call me immediately.*

Sorry, sis. Not tonight.

Turning the phone over, I ignore any additional texts. Fifteen minutes later, there's a loud pounding on my door.

"Liv!" Everett bangs on the door. "It's me, open up."

First Maren's calls and text, now this. Something must be wrong.

"Let me in, Liv," he begs, frantic. "Please."

Oh God. Has something happened to Dex?

I hurry to the door and yank it open.

"Wha—" I start, but then I see Everett's bloody face. "Oh my God!"

There's a gash above his left eye, a cut on his lip. His cheek is red and swollen.

"I told Dex," he says with a wince.

My mouth falls open. A mishmash of feelings course through me as I'm stunned, happy and upset at once.

Stunned and happy that he told Dex.

Upset by Dex's horrifying reaction to the news.

I usher Everett to the sofa, shoving my snacks out of the way so he can sit. I switch off the television and take a seat next to him.

When my phone buzzes again I shut it off. I will deal with Dex and Maren later. Right now, I need to hear Everett's side of the story.

"He obviously didn't take the news well," Everett mutters with a somber tone. He clutches his head in his hands. "I tried telling him this is the real thing. That we're happy together. But it didn't matter. He said I betrayed him, and he'll never forgive me."

"I figured he'd be angry, but I didn't expect a fistfight."

He shakes his head. "I refused to fight him."

I gasp. "You *let* Dex do this to you?"

"I deserved it."

"No, you didn't!"

"Yeah, I did." He sighs and leans forward on his elbows. "I broke a promise and lied to him."

Heat flushes through my body. It's a good thing Dex isn't in front of me. "He had no right to demand that promise to begin with."

"He was trying to protect you, and I can't blame him."

I can. And I will. But first things first. I must find out where things stand between Everett and me. "Now what?"

"Honestly, I'm hoping I didn't ruin my friendship with Dex in vain." He leans in with a hopeful expression. "You said if I told him, we could be together again. The truth is out now."

"You still want to be together after this?"

"Of course." Everett takes my hands into his. "Liv, I found something in you I never expected to find. You have made me happier than I've ever been, but most importantly, you make me a better man. I refuse to let you go for anything or anyone. I'm only sorry it took me so long to do the right thing."

When I woke, I had half a dozen voicemails from Maren and twice as many text messages. She insists on meeting today to talk.

That's fine with me. I have a few choice things to say to her and Dex. Especially Dex.

Maren either heard me pull into the driveway or she was watching outside her window for my arrival because the front door swings open before I make it to the porch.

The instant I step inside, she hollers, "What the hell are you thinking?"

With a fierce step in her direction, I point in her face. "Don't you dare come at me like that!"

"You've been screwing Everett and lying to me all this time!"

Standing aside, Dex is poised to jump in between us if need be.

"First," I start, "we aren't just screwing and second, even if we were, that's my business! I'll do what I want with whom I want. You get no say in it."

"Jesus Christ, Olivia." Maren throws her hand up in exasperation. "How can you be so stupid?"

"Of course, that's what you think. You always assume the worst about Everett. You never gave him a chance. You don't even know him!"

Folding her arms across her chest, she juts out a hip. "I know enough."

"If you believe that, *you're* the stupid one." I turn my attention to Dex. "But what about you? You're supposed to be his best friend. What kind of person thinks so lowly of their closest friend?"

"He's the one who betrayed me!"

"He didn't betray you. You had no authority to forbid him from being with me. I'm not your property, Dex. I don't belong to you or Maren." Stepping forward, I poke him in the chest. "You are to blame here!"

"If making us out to be the bad guys makes you feel better, fine. Whatever helps you sleep at night."

"I will sleep great with Everett by my side."

Maren scoffs. "We'll see how long that lasts."

"Yeah, we will."

"When he breaks your heart," she says, "which is inevitable, don't come crying on my shoulder."

I throw my head back and laugh at her audacity and self-righteousness. "Trust me when I say, you are the very last person I'll come to about anything, ever again."

Maren balks at my words and her anger shifts to injury.

I take a deep breath to compose myself. There's something they need to hear. Something they need to understand. When I speak, I'm calm and collected.

"I have no idea what the future holds," I begin. "But what I have with Everett is real. It's not just sex. He isn't using me or taking advantage of me. He's good to me in ways no other guy has ever been. I care for him. He has brought my life into full color and focus. But neither of you know that because you haven't seen it."

"Because you've both been lying to us," Dex says.

"You made us lie!" I holler, frustrated. "You never would've accepted us together. Even if we told you on day one, your reaction would have been the same."

"Don't you dare blame us for a choice you made," Maren spits. Her anger has returned.

Ignoring her, I shift to Dex. "Everett is grieving the loss of his best friend—his brother for all intents and purposes. But you know what? He's better off. Any *friend* who would treat him the way you have is no friend at all."

Dex turns away and goes to the window on the far side of the room.

"Don't speak—" Maren starts, but I cut her off.

"Shut up, Maren," I bark, and go to where Dex stands. "And to be clear, I'm the one who pursued him. *I* seduced him. He said no. He tried to push me away, but I wouldn't let him. I went after him."

Dex looks to me, but says nothing, so I continue.

"How would you respond if someone forbade you from being with Maren? Would that have stopped you?"

Before he can answer I spin to Maren and ask, "Would it have stopped you?"

Maren casts her gaze to the floor. Observing them both, their answers are a resounding "No."

I step to my sister. "Either accept my relationship with Everett or lose me."

Maren flinches, her mouth agape. But I don't care that my words hurt her. I will stand up for myself, Everett and our relationship the cost be damned.

"What I have with Everett isn't a mistake. I've never been this happy," I declare. "I know who Everett is. I know his history, and it's not pretty. But he's so much more than the sum of his mistakes. If I can look past it all to the good in him, why can't the two of you?"

Dex and Maren stand before me, utterly speechless.

Fantastic.

I open the door to leave but spin around to say one last thing before I go. "You both should be ashamed of yourselves."

Six days have passed since my confrontation with Maren and Dex. My sister and I have texted a few times. We agree it's for the best that the four of us take a little time to think and cool down. In her last text, Maren said she refuses to lose me. That she believes she and I will emerge on the other side of this stronger.

The only way that can happen is if she changes her attitude toward Everett. But I didn't say as much. I've already made my point.

Everett and I couldn't be better. We've spent this week in our own private bubble. We spend our days at the gallery and our nights together at his condo. Tonight, we are going on our first official public date. Everett is taking me to dinner but won't tell me where. I am overjoyed. There was a time when I believed this would never happen. I pinch myself now and then to remind myself it's real.

To make it feel like an actual first date, I'm getting ready at my place and Everett will pick me up at six. Just like any first date, my adrenaline rushes. I'm breathless and impatient for Everett to arrive.

Right at the stroke of six, the knock at the door sends my pulse into overdrive. My guy is here.

He's my guy.

Everett Shaw is my *guy.*

I bounce up and down and quietly squeal with glee.

Hannah and Jess clap silently before disappearing to their rooms to give us privacy.

When I open the door, Everett offers me a simple bouquet of daisies—my favorite.

"For you, Miss Bell."

"Thank you, Mr. Shaw." I accept the flowers and motion for him to enter. "I'll put these in water."

"You look lovely," he says.

My cheeks heat up, but I'm not sure why. He's told me I look lovely, beautiful, and gorgeous a hundred times before. "So do you."

"I clean up okay."

Yes, he does indeed. In this moment, he looks better than ever, though he doesn't look any different. I've seen him in a suit before.

Just like a first date, Everett opens the car door for me. But that isn't new. I never caught on to it until now, but he always opens doors for me.

"Are you going to tell me where you're taking me?" I ask once he's seated beside me.

He shakes his head. "You'll find out when we get there."

I lean over and kiss his cheek.

"No kissing." He wags a finger at me.

"Why? We kiss all the time."

"Would you have done that on a true first date?"

"No, but—"

He interrupts. "This is meant to be a first date. We can't do anything out of the ordinary."

Oh, really? "I guess that means no sexy time for you later."

This gets his attention. His head whips in my direction. "People have sex on first dates."

"I don't."

He smirks. "We'll see."

"We sure will."

"You can't resist me."

No, I can't. "If this was a real first date, we wouldn't talk about having sex later."

He laughs. "True."

I get an idea and take my phone from my handbag. Tonight, we'll have actual first date discussions.

"Would you text on a first date?"

Everett takes issue with phones and texting when we're together. He insists we turn off notifications when we sit to dinner and phones are off limits in the bedroom. He's all about giving the other person full attention. It's a trait I like about him.

"I'm not texting. I'm researching."

"Researching what?"

"Ideas for first date conversations."

Everett chuckles. "I doubt that's necessary."

"Hey, I want tonight to be as authentic as possible." I find a website with fifty first date conversation starters. This should be a good point of reference. "Besides, I would've done this if it was an actual first date."

He smiles, fully amused. "Okay. Carry on."

We pull up to the swankiest Italian joint in Denver. I've always wanted to eat here, but it's out of my price range. When I asked Everett if he'd ever eaten here he said it's one of the best Italian eateries he's ever been to. Even better than some in Italy. He promised to bring me here one day.

One day has arrived, and not a second too soon.

Upon entering the restaurant, I feel as though I've been transported to Italy. Not that I know what Italy is like. Nonetheless, I imagine they've captured it perfectly. This is exactly what I imagine a restaurant in Italy is like. The aroma is heavenly. The dining room is dimly lit and hums with quiet conversations held by the guests. A very well-dressed host greets us, and Everett gives him our reservation information.

"Follow me," the host says and leads us to a candlelit table alongside a window.

Not long after being seated, we meet our server, Natalie. Everett orders a bottle of wine and we are left to peruse the menu. Once we've placed our order, I pull out my phone and click to the website with the date questions. As I read them over, I realize I know many of the answers. It takes a moment, but I finally find one I don't have the answer for.

"This is great," I say and rub my hands together. "Name five things you wish to do before you die."

"Five things?" Everett asks as though it's a tough order.

"Yep."

He scratches his chin. "I've done most everything I want to do."

"Then list three things."

Inhaling deep, he takes a while to think. "I'd like to learn how to meditate. Learn to play the piano. And maybe become a dad."

I raise my fingers to parted lips. The last item is certainly unexpected.

"What?" he asks when I can't voice a response. "Are those not good answers?"

"They're just surprising."

"Why?"

"One, I'm uncertain you could sit still long enough to meditate. Two, I can see you playing a piano, but not confident you'd have patience enough to endure the lessons. And three, you've never talked about having kids."

"You might be right about the first two things," he chuckles. "As for kids… it's a new consideration. Now it's your turn. What are three things you want to do?"

"I don't even know where to start. There's so much I want to do."

"Just name the first three things to pop in your mind," he encourages.

"I hope to become a successful photographer which you know. I want to travel the world. I've always wanted to visit the Colosseum in Rome. And I think I might try skydiving." I could go on all day about the stuff I hope to do in my lifetime.

"I'd be happy to help you with those."

"You're already helping with one."

Everett smiles and I look to my phone for another question.

"What's been your biggest regret in life?" I ask.

He answers at once with confidence. "I don't have regrets."

"None?" Everyone has regrets.

He shakes his head. "Not a single one."

I lean forward. "How is that possible?"

"Don't misunderstand." He slides his hand across the table and places it on top of mine, his fingertips lightly brushing my skin. "Plenty of things have occurred in my life that I wish hadn't. Many of which were my fault. But everything that has transpired brought me to where I am. If I changed any of those things, where would I be today?"

This is why I'm so enamored with this man. "I love that answer."

"How about you? Any regrets?"

"Not now." If what he said is true, and the things that have happened in my life led me to this moment with the guy of my dreams, how can I regret any of it?

"You know what?" he asks.

"What?"

"I have one regret." Clasping my hand, he gives it a gentle squeeze. "I never should've insisted on keeping our relationship a secret. This, right here, is how it should've always been between us."

And just like that, I fall deeper.

Chapter 13

MAREN CALLS SUNDAY MORNING AND invites me to lunch. She's had enough time to process our predicament and is ready to work toward healing. Before I can argue this isn't something she and I can mend on our own—that Dex needs to reach out to Everett—his phone rings. It's Dex asking Everett to meet him.

To say I'm dreading the meeting is an understatement. Maren says she wants to mend our rift, but on what terms? Is she willing to accept Everett completely, without judgment? The only way this will work for me is if she changes her attitude toward him. I'm not positive she is capable of that.

We meet at her place at twelve thirty, just the two of us. Dex is meeting Everett at the condo at the same time.

Maren greets me with a warm smile as I step into the house.

"Can I have a hug?" she asks, and I oblige. "Do you want to eat while we talk, or talk first?"

"Let's talk first." I can't eat a bite until we get this conversation over with.

"Okay. Take a seat in the living room and I'll bring us a couple glasses of sweet tea."

I purposely sit in an armchair. If I sit on the sofa, Maren may be inclined to sit next to me. Sitting beside her could be a bad idea if our discussion doesn't go well.

"I put extra sugar in it just the way you like," she says and hands me the tea. Her abnormally high pitch reveals her uneasy disposition.

"Thanks." I smile and take a sip.

Maren takes a seat to my right on the sofa. She sets her drink on the coffee table, inhales deep, and folds her hands in her lap.

She's *really* nervous.

"I'd like to start," she says.

Here we go.

I nod. "Okay."

"First, I want to say I'm sorry. Dex and I had no right to insinuate ourselves into your personal life. I—we—recognize it isn't our place to decide who you will, won't, can or can't be with. We were out of line."

I tilt my head, doubtful that she means what she says. "I appreciate you saying that but…" I hesitate because this is where things might turn ugly. History has proven that once a conversation takes that turn between us, it is impossible to course correct.

"Go ahead," she urges gently. "It's okay."

I blow out a breath. "Do you really feel that way or are you just saying it to make peace?"

"I mean it, Liv. This past week has been horrible. I miss you so much." Her voice is sincere. "I've taken this time to put myself in your shoes to understand how you feel. I set my opinions aside and focused on what you must be feeling, and it opened my eyes. You have every right to be angry at us."

I open my mouth to respond, but Maren holds up a hand to interrupt me.

"When you were here last," she says, "you asked if someone forbade me and Dex from being together, would it stop us? The answer is no. I'd never let anything come between us. But then I took your question a measure farther and asked myself how I would feel if somebody had interfered in our relationship."

She has thought this through. I'm impressed. "What was your answer?"

"I'd be furious, just as you are." Leaning over, Maren places her hand on mine. "Although Dex isn't here, I assure you, we assume full blame for everything that transpired."

Our conversation has gone much better than I anticipated. I expected Maren to apologize, but I hadn't expected it to be so heartfelt. I didn't foresee her taking full responsibility.

"That means a lot to me, Maren. This week has been painful for me, too." I didn't realize how painful until this very moment. "You're my big sister. I need you in my life."

"I am always here for you, Liv." Her lip trembles and she wipes a tear from her eye. "Please understand, I wasn't trying to control you. I was concerned about you. I only want the best for you."

"Maren, I understand that. But there are lines that shouldn't be crossed. Lines I won't allow to be crossed."

"I promise never to cross that line again."

I hope that's a promise she can keep. Maren isn't one to make promises lightly, but I've witnessed her dislike of Everett firsthand. It's difficult not to be skeptical.

"It's my turn to speak."

Maren nods, and I take a sip of my tea before starting.

"It's up to me to decide what or who is or isn't best for me. I'm going to make mistakes. Everyone does." I motion in her direction. "Take yourself, for example. You've dated your share of bad ideas. While I truly don't think being with Everett is a bad idea, I'm not stupid. I realize it could go wrong. But that could happen with anyone. I want him, Maren. I care for him. And the only way you and I can move forward is for you to accept my choice and to accept Everett."

She answers without hesitation, "I can do that."

"You have to treat him better, Maren. I won't tolerate you treating him with any less respect and concern than I give to Dex."

"You have my word."

"You can't fake it. It has to be genuine for it to work."

"I admit, I judged a book by its cover. I judged Everett based on rumors and his reputation without taking the time to dig deeper and get to know him. That was my mistake. The man is my fiancé's best friend and my sister's boyfriend, so he must have some outstanding qualities. I will make an effort to get to know him."

"Really?" I ask, hopeful.

When she nods, I stand and reach for her hand, pulling her into an embrace. This is exactly what I wanted to hear, but never in a million years thought I would.

"How'd it go with Dex?" I ask the instant Everett opens his door.

"It went well." He wraps me in his arms and kisses the tip of my nose. "He's on board. How did it go with Maren?"

"It was great." I beam at him. "She apologized and accepted all blame."

Everett's blue eyes widen. "Really?"

"I was as shocked as you are. She even says she's going to give you a real chance and get to know you better."

"She said that?" He looks kind of scared.

I nod. "Yep. What did Dex say?"

Everett leads me to his sofa and pulls me onto his lap. "He wasn't as quick to accept all the fault, not that I blame him."

"Wait, Maren told me, they accept full responsibility for what went down."

"They do, to an extent."

"To an extent?" I ask, chagrined. Was she just telling me what I needed to hear?

"Liv, Dex knows me better than anyone. He had motive for concern." Tucking a lock of hair behind my ear, Everett gazes at me with adoration. "He knew I couldn't resist you. He knew it before I did. And given my history, he went into crisis mode to protect you from getting hurt. He had no reason to believe I'd be any different with you than any other woman."

"That doesn't excuse what he did." Everett's face is still healing from the damage Dex caused.

"No, it doesn't, and Dex knows that. But it is important for you and me to understand that he and Maren did what they did with good intentions. I respect that they were trying to protect you."

With a huff, I cross my arms. "That makes one of us. Doesn't it bother you that Dex has such a low opinion of you?"

"Dex doesn't have a bad opinion of me, Babe. He just knows my past and the nefarious things I've done." He looks away with shame. "All he wanted to do was shield you from that. If I'd made it clear from the beginning that I am different with you—that our involvement is the real deal—we might've avoided this mess."

"I can't believe you're shouldering blame for their actions."

"Only a portion of it."

"Any is too much."

"Let's not lose sight of our victory here." He gives me a squeeze. "Dex and Maren have accepted our relationship. That's a big win. We have reason to celebrate."

Taking a deep breath, I lean into him. Mom always said, 'A win is a win.'

"You're right. We do."

But I still wonder whether my sister was entirely honest with me in our conversation. Perhaps taking all blame was just her telling me what she felt I needed to hear. She is known for doing stuff like that. And did she mean it when she vowed to treat Everett better and to give him a chance?

I suppose time will tell.

It's Thursday night. Dex and Maren are hosting dinner for the first time since we came out as a couple. Also for the first time, Everett and I arrive together. My heart is in my throat as we make our way to the door. I wipe my slick palms on the side of my legs.

Everett turns to me with an understanding smile. "It's going to be a great evening."

"You really think so?"

He brings my hand to his lips for a kiss. "Yes, I do."

I close my eyes and suck in a calming breath. This night is make or break for the four of us. The weight of it is heavy. "Okay. Let's do this."

Everett knocks on the door and the seconds it takes for it to open feels like minutes.

When Maren opens the door, I notice she also wipes her pants on her legs. It's a nervous habit that we share.

"Hey!" she says in her high pitched nervous voice. "Come in."

My sister pulls me in for a quick hug, as is typical, but then she does the same with Everett, catching us both off guard. Everett awkwardly reciprocates. This might be the first hug they've ever shared. She's making an effort, but going a tad overboard. Nevertheless, I'll take it.

Maren tells us Dex is in the den having a pre-dinner drink. Everett goes to join him while I follow Maren to the kitchen to help with the food. Thankfully, she has an open bottle of cabernet on the counter.

Thirty minutes and two glasses of wine later, we are all seated at the dining table. Our hosts have changed the seating arrangement. Tonight, we sit with one couple on each side of the rectangle table. My sister sits across from me, and Dex is across from Everett. Beforehand, Maren, and Dex had always sat at the ends of the table.

My nerves have gotten the best of me. I have no appetite, my mouth is dry and my muscles are twitching. Wine normally has a calming effect on me. And perhaps it's helping a little, but I'm just too nervous to tell. As I fill a third glass, Maren watches with a curious expression but doesn't comment.

Dex begins the conversation the same as any other Thursday. "How is everyone's week going?"

Everett answers first with our running joke. "Same old, same old."

Everyone laughs, and he continues. "It's been a busy week. I did an interview with Aperture Magazine on Tuesday."

"That's a prestigious photography magazine, right?" Maren asks.

"One of the most respected in the industry," Everett answers.

"That sounds exciting," she says.

Feigning nonchalance, he shrugs. He's extremely anxious over the feature. It's a big deal.

"In celebration of his career, they're featuring his entire portfolio," I explain. "It is an honor bestowed on few."

"Congratulations, Ev," Dex says. "That's awesome."

"Yes. Congrats, Everett," Maren says.

"I already said it, but congrats, Babe." I lean over and kiss his cheek. Once I realize what I've done, my face burns. In the car on the way here, we agreed to not be overtly affectionate. It's one thing for us all to have dinner together, as couples. It's another to show affection. I shouldn't rock this precarious boat.

"Liv has good news as well," Everett says.

"Yeah?" Dex asks.

"It's nothing as big as a feature in Aperture, but I've sold a dozen prints this week."

"That is fantastic, Livvy," Maren says, her tone genuine.

"Hell, yes it is. We have quite a bit to celebrate." Dex lifts his glass and we all follow suit. "Here's to Ev and Liv. May good fortune continue to shine upon both of you."

"Here, here," Maren says, and we clink glasses.

"You didn't eat much," Maren points out, as she and I clean up after dinner while the guys are out in the garage smoking cigars. "Did you not enjoy the carnitas?"

"They were great." I pour myself another glass of wine. After drinking a full bottle, I am wobbly on my feet. "I just didn't have much of an appetite."

"That's unlike you," she states. "You usually eat enough to fill a horse. Is everything okay?"

"Yeah. I…"

"What?"

I cast my gaze to the floor. "I can't eat when I'm nervous."

"You were unsure how tonight would go."

"Weren't you?" Though I've had more than enough to drink, I take a long sip of my wine.

"I was anxious, but only because I wanted everything to be perfect."

"This is excellent wine," I take another swill.

She chuckles. "I think I had better take your keys."

"No worries. Everett drove and I'm staying with him."

Maren shifts feet and makes a strange noise, like throat clearing, but not quite. She flashes a quick, false smile.

Shit. I shouldn't have added that I'm staying at his place.

An awkward silence falls over us. I go back to rinsing the dirty dishes and Maren places them in the dishwasher.

After a couple minutes, Maren speaks, "Forgive me. I didn't mean to react the way I did. The last thing I want to do is make you uncomfortable."

"I'm fine," I lie. I couldn't be more uncomfortable if I was sitting on a pin cushion.

Maren turns off the water to stop me from rinsing. "I am an idiot. Damn it! I knew I'd say or do something stupid to upset you."

"I'm not upset." It's the truth. "But I do feel uneasy."

She starts speed talking. "It just caught me off guard hearing you say you're staying there. I don't know why. You're in a relationship. Of course, you spend nights together. It is perfectly natural. But… for me… knowing you are together and witnessing it firsthand are two different things. It makes it… realer. It's a lot to digest. Do you understand?"

"I do, Mare." Swaying to the side, I pull her in for a hug. "I can't tell you how much tonight means to me. You made a wonderful dinner. You've been great. I couldn't have asked for more." I lean away to look into her eyes. "Please, forget about your reaction to what I said. It's okay."

"Yeah?"

"Yeah."

As is becoming routine, Everett and I are taking an after-work stroll around downtown. With our hands entwined, I lean into him as we walk.

"This is my new favorite thing," I say, completely contented.

"Walking around downtown?"

"Walking around in public where everyone and anyone can see that we're together."

With his lips pressed to my temple, he says, "It is nice."

As soon as our secret was out, I updated my social media profiles to reflect my new relationship status and uploaded every picture I have of us. While Everett didn't post a ton of photos of us, he changed his profile picture to one of him kissing my cheek. We aren't just official, we're social media official. Everyone we know, knows. Mostly, they've been supportive. But Everett received numerous posts and messages from shocked women, saddened that he is no longer available for late night booty calls.

"We need to get out to Bear Lake for your official shoot to finish your assignment," Everett says.

"I forgot about that. I've been a little distracted."

"Me, too." He drapes an arm around my waist. "Have you decided what scene you want to capture? Do you still prefer the sunset?"

"The fog was pretty cool," I admit, "but I already got the one great shot, so I'm going for the sunset."

"Let's keep an eye on the weekend's weather and plan a trip. We can rent a cabin and make a romantic night out of it filled with wine and candles."

A fun day of photography followed by a romantic night with my man sounds incredible. Any other time, I would jump at the offer. But other plans for the weekend popped up, and I'm hoping to include Everett.

"About the weekend," I start, "I got a call from my dad earlier. He's coming into town Friday and is staying through Sunday."

Dad still works and lives in Colorado Springs. It's only a little over an hour away, but I don't go there as often as I should. He still lives in the house I grew up in. Since my mom's passing, it's difficult for me to be there. It doesn't help that Dad kept everything exactly the same as it was when she was alive. He even keeps some of her clothes in the closet. He claims it helps him "feel connected" to her.

It has been five years, and he hasn't been on a single date. He says Mom was the love of his life and when he dies, he intends to reunite with her in Heaven. Finding another woman or falling in love would complicate those plans. While I admire and respect his choice, I worry about him being alone.

I never intend to move back to Colorado Springs. I adore Denver and intend to keep it as my home base. Whenever I suggest that he move here, he claims he's content where he is. He has said, perhaps one day when he's older and less independent he will move here to be closer to me and Maren.

Though I look forward to seeing my father, I'm anxious. He's aware I am in a relationship with one of Dex's friends and has asked for an introduction.

Nothing says, "this is a serious relationship" like asking a guy to meet your dad. We've only just gone public. Only recently declared that this is an exclusive, monogamous relationship. Is it too much, too soon? For me, it makes perfect sense. I want my dad to meet the great man I have chosen to be with.

But there's more to my anxiety than how Everett might react.

I'm a Daddy's girl. Always have been. My dad is extremely protective of me. The only argument he and my mom ever had was when she allowed me to go on my first date at sixteen. Dad insisted that I not date until after I graduated high school. He instantly despised any guy I dated. It's why I didn't have my first actual boyfriend until I was in college. For that reason, I haven't told him about our considerable age difference. I worry he will freak out.

I debated telling him first, but I don't want him to judge Everett before he meets him. If I tell him now, he will go into the meeting with a preconceived notion about Everett. That's how my father operates, and once he's made up his mind about someone, it's damn near impossible to change it. It is vital that my father meets Everett with an open mind.

"Okay, since you'll be spending time with your dad, I'll traipse over to Maroon Lake for a shoot and some fishing." He kisses my temple. "Won't be as fun as being holed up in a cabin with you, but it'll do."

I come to a halt, forcing Everett to do the same. "Actually, I was hoping you'd join me and Dad for dinner Saturday."

He jerks his head back and his breath catches. "You want me to meet your old man?"

"Yeah." I slip my hands into my pants pockets. "He asked to meet you."

Everett scratches his beard. "You told him about me?"

"Of course." There isn't a lot I don't talk about with my dad. I call him at least every other day to check in and when I do, we go over everything we've done since we last spoke.

"I don't know, Liv." Rocking on his heels, he takes a deep breath. "Historically, dads don't like me. Not that I've met many. In fact, I haven't met any since college. But none of them cared for me."

I step forward and take his hand into mine. "That was a long time ago and I think my dad will like you."

"You *think*?"

Shit. Poor word choice. "Maybe he will, maybe he won't. I still want him to meet you."

"You should enjoy your time with your dad. You haven't seen him in a while and I don't want to spoil it."

I take his other hand so I'm holding both and give them a squeeze. "You won't spoil it. Please come to dinner with us."

Everett pulls his hands from mine and rubs his neck, rocking back and forth on his feet. "We're still on precarious ground with Dex and Maren. Are you ready for another blow? Because that's what will come of you introducing me to your father. There's nothing worse than a parent's disappointment. Trust me, I am an expert at parental dissatisfaction."

I drop my gaze to the pavement. While I figured he might be hesitant, I never imagined he'd be dead set against it. "I kind of already told him I'd bring you."

His voice is soft. "Liv, I really don't think it's the right time."

The question flies out of my mouth before I think it through. "Is that because you're afraid he won't like you or because you aren't serious about our relationship?"

"Babe, I take us very seriously." Placing a palm on each side of my face, he brushes my cheeks with his thumbs. "What we have is fantastic. I just want to stay in our happy little bubble a while longer. Is that such a bad thing?"

His words ease my hurt feelings, but marginally. "How does meeting my father change that?"

"He's your dad, you're his baby girl. No one ever measures up in a father's eyes. Do you think a forty-year-old Casanova is going to fit the bill?"

"He doesn't know about your reputation, Everett, and besides you're a reformed Casanova."

He blows out a breath and draws me into his arms, peering down at me. "I am crazy about you, Liv. But I'm not ready to meet your dad. I'm sorry."

Chapter 14

"I FEEL LIKE I NEVER see you anymore," Gray says as we fold his laundry. I'm folding shirts, he can fold his own underwear. Not that he folds them so much as he balls them up and tosses them into the drawer.

Between me spending seventy-five percent of my time with Everett and Grayson being with Andrea, we don't see each other as often as we used to. It is pure happenstance that Andrea is having a spa day with friends while Everett is spending this rainy Saturday afternoon playing indoor golf with Dex.

"I know. I see you less in an entire month than I used to in a week."

"We need to be better about making us as high of a priority as we do our relationships."

"Agreed."

"Speaking of relationships, are you still in fairytale land with Everett?"

"Things are good," I sigh, "but I have a new predicament that I need advice on."

Grayson listens intently as I recount Everett's refusal to meet my dad. Once I'm finished, he takes a moment to mull it over.

"I see both points of view," he says, which I wasn't expecting. I assumed he'd be on my side. "You're excited to introduce Everett to your dad because you have strong feelings for the guy. You might even be in love with him—"

Waving my hands, I cut him off, "What? I am not in love. I have feelings for him, and I admit I'm falling fast, but I'm not there yet."

He just shrugs. His gaze becomes unfocused, and he smiles. "That's the thing about love, it crops up when we don't realize it. For some, it happens really fast and takes us completely by surprise."

I freeze, my mouth agape. "Are you talking about me or you?"

"You, for now," he smirks, his focus back on me. "We'll get to me in a minute."

"Hold the phone! Are you saying you are in love with Andrea?"

He wags a finger. "No changing the subject. We're discussing your dilemma."

"My dilemma is that I'm bummed over Everett refusing to meet my dad, not whether I'm in love."

"It's interconnected. Let me finish."

"Fine, Doctor Freud." I wave in his direction. "Finish your psychoanalysis."

"As I was saying, it's important to you that Everett and your dad meet because you're that invested in the relationship. You're at the point where you are ready to take that step, and that's okay. But as you know, you haven't been together long. The relationship is still fresh. And you're working at a handicap with Everett."

Wait. What? I stop folding. "What handicap?"

Rolling his eyes, Gray sighs as though I should have the answer. "You are his first real relationship in forever. He's lived his life single and fancy free. This is all new to him."

He makes a valid point. "True."

"Maybe he feels as strongly about you as you do for him, but maybe he doesn't." Grayson must see a disappointed look on my face because he adds, "Yet. In relationships, especially with new couples, people aren't always on the same wavelength where feelings are concerned. One usually falls first while the other lags behind."

I cross my arms and digest all he has said. "So, in a nutshell, you're saying Everett won't meet my dad because he doesn't feel as strongly as I do, and he's not as invested in us as I am?"

"No." He shakes his head. "I'm saying that *could* be the reason. Or it could be his lack of relationship experience. He has been a womanizer fo—"

I cut him off again. "Please don't use that word. I hate that word."

"What word would you rather use to define it?"

"We say Casanova."

"Fine. Everett has been living as a *Casanova* for his entire adult life. Suddenly, he finds himself in a committed monogamous relationship. He is navigating uncharted waters." Grayson pauses to let that sink in and then continues. "He's already been in a fight with his best friend over you. My advice is give the man time and don't take it personally. I don't think his reluctance to meet your dad reflects how he does or doesn't feel about you. It's probably just a lot for him to take in."

As I prepare to respond, he continues. "And let's not forget, the guy doesn't have a good relationship with his own father. He admitted that parents aren't his specialty, and not in his comfort zone."

I have a seat on the edge of the bed. "You're one hundred percent right. It's too soon. And rather than putting myself in Everett's shoes, all I've done is assume he doesn't care as much for me as I do him."

With a thoughtful expression, Grayson sits beside me. "So, you are in love with him?"

"No." I shake my head. I can't be. Not yet. That would be crazy.

Cocking his head, he arches a brow.

"I have feelings… strong feelings for him."

"And?" he presses, his eyes locked on mine.

"I sometimes wonder if he feels the same."

"Liv," he takes my hand, "the guy was willing to risk his lifelong friendship to be with you, it's safe to assume he has feelings for you."

I wrap my arms around Grayson. That was the best thing he could say. "You are the most amazing friend, Grayson Masters. So now… it's your turn. Fess up. Are you in love?"

Even though my talk with Grayson put things into perspective and dissolved my aggravation with Everett, I'm still disappointed that he's heading off for Maroon Lake. He's leaving work early because he has to check in before five o'clock. It's noon, and the drive is only a couple hours. Is he going this soon so there's no chance of being in a position to meet my dad?

"Enjoy your visit with your dad." He kisses the tip of my nose. It's one of his regular displays of affection. "I'll see you Sunday."

I nod and cast my gaze downward. My body is suddenly very heavy.

I don't want you to go.

"You said you weren't mad." He places his fingers beneath my chin and raises it so I'm looking into his worry filled eyes.

"I'm not."

He tilts his head. "You seem mad."

"I'm not mad. I'm disappointed."

"That doesn't make me feel any better," he sighs. "I thought we were in agreement."

"We are. It's just…" I turn away.

"Just what?" His gentle tone is full of concern.

"I realize we haven't been seeing each other long, and I understand and respect that it's too soon for you." My voice drops. Breaking eye contact once again, I twist my wrists. "I'm crazy for you, Everett. I was excited about the idea of you meeting my dad."

Why did I say that? We agreed that he won't meet my dad this weekend. I have no right to stand here pouting in the eleventh hour.

Stepping forward, Everett takes my hands. "I promise I will meet him. Perhaps one day soon."

I nod again. Does he mean it, or is he placating me? If I ask, it could put him on the defensive and lead to a disagreement. I've had the entire week to express how I feel. Why did I wait?

"I have a bad feeling," he says, rubbing the back of his neck. "Like you're going to stew on this all weekend and when I return, we won't be okay."

"We'll be fine. Enjoy your trip."

He leans his forehead against mine. "You know I'm crazy about you, too. Right?"

I nod. Hearing those words soothes my insecurity.

"I'm not saying no to meeting him," he says, "I'm just saying not yet."

I lean into him and he wraps his arms around my waist. "Okay."

"Do you promise to be at the condo when I get home Sunday?"

"I promise."

Dad insisted on taking me somewhere nice for dinner. Earlier this week when he told me to make our reservations for Saturday night, he explicitly said, "Make sure it's a place that doesn't have tv's on the walls." There's a quaint steakhouse outside the city that only allows people in by reservation. I can't say with absolute surety there aren't any tv's, but steak is his favorite food and their ribeye is supposed to be the best in Colorado.

"This is a neat place," he says after we've been seated, and the server has poured our wine.

Thankfully, there are no televisions hanging anywhere.

"I've never been here, but Everett says the steak is to die for."

"It's a shame he has to work. I would've liked to meet the young man."

Young man. I nearly spit out my wine. Dad undoubtedly assumes Everett is close to me in age.

Rather than tell my father Everett isn't ready to meet him, I said he had to work tonight. Which isn't a complete lie. By going on a photo shoot, he is technically working.

"Perhaps next time," I suggest. "How was brunch with Maren and Dex?"

"It was great. That Dex sure is a fantastic guy. Maren is a totally different person with him. I've never seen her so at ease and *happy.*"

Before her relationship with Dex, my sister was a bit on the neurotic side. The word calm wasn't in her vocabulary. She worked sixteen-hour days, six to seven days a week. Probably only averaged four hours of sleep a night. She was obsessive compulsive about every little detail. Dex has achieved wonders in settling her down.

"If soulmates are a thing, he is Maren's."

"You got that right. The guy is a miracle worker."

As we laugh, a tall figure appears to our left. An all too familiar scent makes my heart flutter.

My Everett.

"Is there room for one more?"

As badly as I want to jump from my chair and throw my arms around him, I keep my composure and answer with a smile, "Sure."

Dad looks to me with a curious expression as Everett takes a seat in the chair to my right.

"Dad, this is Everett my…" He's my what? Is he my boyfriend? We agreed we're in a relationship, but we've never used any terminology. Why didn't I just say, this is Everett, and leave it at that? Now, my unfinished sentence hangs in the air, waiting for completion.

I stare into space, mouth agape because I can't look at either man.

Everett extends his hand to my father. "Hello Mr. Bell, I'm Olivia's boyfriend, Everett Shaw."

"Well isn't this a fine surprise," my father says and takes his hand. "Please call me Tom."

"It is a pleasure to meet you, Tom," Everett says.

"The pleasure is all mine," Dad says. "We were just talking about you."

"Good things, I hope," Everett quips. He is his usual cool and confident self. No signs of any nerves.

"We were saying what a shame it is that you had to work tonight," I say.

Everett entwines his fingers with mine. "I can work anytime. This is where I need to be."

I smile widely. "I'm so happy you're here."

"Anything for you." He bends down to kiss the top of my hand.

In this moment, I am happier than I've ever been. Despite his not being ready, Everett put my feelings above his own and came to meet my dad. Actions truly do speak louder than words.

When my sister found out that our father met Everett last night, she insisted that I come over straightaway and tell her everything. In her kitchen, I sit at the island while she bakes. One of her neighbors hired her to bake a cake for her son's eleventh birthday. It's no wonder Maren always smells of cake batter. Confections are her life.

As usual, she has a spread of finger foods for me to nibble on while we talk. It amazes me she's so skinny given the amount of time she spends with food.

"He just showed up without telling you he was coming?" Maren asks, wide eyed.

"He tried to call, but I accidentally had my phone on do not disturb."

Maren shakes her head with a smile as she mixes the batter. "Everett has really taken me by surprise. Even Dex was blown away that he showed up to dinner."

"I was stunned," I confess. "I talked to him earlier in the morning. He was planning to go on a hike before setting up for his shoot. He told me to call him when I got home. That was the last we spoke until he surprised me at the restaurant."

Biting into one of Maren's delicious homemade jalapeno popper's, I recall the conversation we had after dinner. The first discussion Everett and I had that really proves how much I mean to him. "When we got to the condo, Everett said he was at the lake and he couldn't stop thinking about the disappointment I felt over him not being there. It nagged at him all day. He couldn't focus so he hurried to the cabin, checked out and raced home in hopes he'd arrive in time."

"What did Dad think of him?" Maren pours the batter into a baking dish. "Did he say anything? Any issues with the age difference?"

This is where I tell her my second favorite part of the night. "When Everett was in the men's room, Dad said he liked him. That he saw how much we mean to each other, and we make a nice looking couple. He asked about our age difference, but said as long as I'm happy that's all that matters."

"Wow, I figured he'd be more concerned over the age thing. Let's face it, Dad has always looked for any reason to hate the guys you date."

"True. He is usually so overprotective of me, but he wasn't with Everett."

"Maybe he's mellowing in his older years."

"I don't know, but he seemed to love Everett. I mean, they talked so much that I basically sat there listening the whole time. Dad asked about his career and travels. They spoke about me when I was little. Dad, of course, told Everett all my most embarrassing stories and promised to send him my high school pictures, which I'm sure he'll follow through with. All in all, it was a perfect night."

After sliding the cake into the oven, Maren takes a seat next to me at the counter. "It could've gone either way, but I'm glad it went smoothly."

"That makes two of us. I admit, I worried it wouldn't go well." If it hadn't, it would've crushed me.

"It surely had something to do with Everett's charisma. The man could charm Hetty Green for a million dollars."

"Hetty Green?"

"You know Hetty…" Maren nudges my shoulder. "The world's stingiest woman."

I shrug. "Never heard of her."

"Everyone knows about Hetty."

"Clearly not *everyone*."

"*Clearly*."

Giggling, we dive into the snacks before us.

"So… is now a good time to ask how the wedding planning is coming along?"

"Slowly," she drags the word out for dramatic effect. "We've secured the venue, but I still need to decide on flowers. I can't figure out what I like."

"Have you decided on colors?"

Maren shakes her head. "I'm terrible at this! I never realized how hard it is to plan a wedding. There's so many details."

"May I make a recommendation?" I ask as I chew on a mouthful of something delicious.

With her elbows on the counter, she leans forward as if she's physically exhausted. "Please."

"Don't go trendy. Stick with classics. Black, red and white is simple and romantic. Or you can do neutrals."

"I like the idea of neutrals. Everyone keeps suggesting pink or teal and pastels."

I fake a gag. "So trite!"

"That's what I thought!"

I tap my chin with my index finger and envision her wedding and the colors she should have. Neutrals are definitely the way to go. "What about bluish gray, sand and white?"

"That sounds gorgeous!" She drapes an arm across my shoulder and leans into me. "See, this is why I need you. This stuff comes so easily to you. Are you sure I can't talk you into planning the whole thing?"

"The aggravation of planning one's wedding is part of the experience. Embrace it!"

She fake laughs and rolls her eyes. "You just wait. One day it'll be your turn. Then you'll understand what I'm going through."

The difference between Maren and I is I've been envisioning my wedding since I was a young girl. I know precisely what I want.

I desire a traditional church ceremony filled with all the people I love. I will wear a great big ballgown straight out of a fairytale. My groom will be in a customary black tux. Our reception will be outside under twinkle lights, with candles and white flowers galore. I even have the wording picked out for the invitations.

All that's left for me to do is execute the plan.

But first I must find a man, fall in love and become engaged.

My stomach flutters as a vision of Everett on one knee pops into my mind.

That image is immediately followed by a picture of him standing at the alter, watching in awe as I walk down the aisle.

Unable to get oxygen, I close my eyes and rub my chest.

Where are these thoughts coming from?

Maybe one day... A long, long, *long* while from now I'll get married. At present, my focus is on my photography career. I always said I won't wed until I have a solid career. And Everett and I are new. We haven't gotten to the in love part yet. We may never get to that point. He might not even want marriage. He's gone this long without it.

What if he doesn't want it?

It wouldn't be a deal breaker.

Would it?

Do I need the actual marriage certificate? It's just words on paper. All that matters is the commitment two people make to each other. A piece of paper can't make much difference.

Can it?

Why am I even thinking about this?

It has to be because my sister is getting married and we're discussing her upcoming nuptials.

There can't be any other reason.

Can there?

Maren waves a hand in front of my face, snapping me back to reality. "Earth to Olivia."

"Sorry, I was thinking about the wedding."

"How's the toe?" Everett asks as I examine my pinky toe for swelling.

Two nights ago at his place, on my way to bed from the bathroom, I jammed my toe into the leg of the bed. It's not broken, but I can hardly walk.

This isn't the first time I've hurt my foot on his bed. There is only two feet of space between it and his dresser. His room wasn't built to accommodate a California king sized bed. The area is barely big enough for a queen.

"It still hurts, and these damn shoes don't help." I point to the nude high heels on the floor beside me.

"I told you not to wear those."

"They're the only heels I have that match this skirt."

He laughs. "Vanity over practicality?"

I roll my eyes. "Do you want me to wear flip-flops to work? Because those are the only shoes that don't cause me pain."

"You can wear whatever you choose, Babe." He pats my behind. "I don't mind."

"You're sweet." I kiss his cheek. "But it's only right that I present myself in a professional manner here at the gallery."

He picks up my shoes and walks away.

"Where are you going with those?" I ask.

"You aren't wearing these death traps with that swollen foot." He disappears into the office and comes out empty handed a second later.

"Now I have no shoes."

"You'll work barefoot today."

"I can't do that."

"You can and you will. Boss's orders." He sits on the stool next to me and pulls me onto his lap. "Besides, the fire engine red toe polish is a perfect combination of sexy and fashionable. Customers will love it as much as I do."

I shake my head. "You are something else."

Everett takes a deep breath and closes his eyes. "I've been tossing around the idea of a bigger condo. Maybe even a house. My place is cramped. We can't hang out at yours because you have roommates. It's time to find a suitable home to settle down in. What do you think?"

"That's a fantastic idea. My foot can attest to the fact you need more room." It won't survive too many more late-night trips to and from the restroom.

He ducks his chin. "Will you come with me?"

"Sure I will."

"Yeah?" He flashes a wide grin.

I rest my head on his shoulder, relishing the warmth of his embrace. I'm never more at ease than when in his arms.

"It'll be fun to help you look for a new place."

Chapter 15

EVERETT WASTES NO TIME SETTING up an appointment with a realtor. Two days later, we are out looking at listings. We arrive at the third—a custom house. New construction. Three bedrooms, two full baths, a large family room and a generous, designer kitchen. A great house, but more than Everett needs as a single man. He would have to buy a ton of furniture to fill the place.

"It's perfect for couples and small families," the realtor says.

"It is a fantastic home," Everett says. "Precisely what I had in mind."

It is?

This is isn't at all what I assumed he'd be in the market for. I imagined something akin to what he already has, but bigger. A larger living space, two decent sized bedrooms. As great as this house is, he doesn't need this much space. Although, it would be an investment and he can easily afford it.

"What do you think?" he asks, excitement dancing in his brilliant blues.

"It's a lovely home." I sweep my hand over the smooth granite kitchen countertop.

His face falls. "I detect a funky tone in your voice. Do you not like it?"

"I love it. I'm just surprised it's what you want."

"Can you give us a minute?" Everett asks the realtor, and she steps out of the room. "I love this place, Liv. I love it because when I picture myself here, I see you here with me."

I nearly choke. "What?"

"When I proposed looking for a house, I was suggesting a home for *both* of us." He takes my hands into his. "I want you to move in with me."

"You do?"

"Is that such a surprise? We're together almost every day, we spend most nights together. Living together would simplify things."

My lungs feel tight and my palms are sweating. "That is a big step, Everett."

"I'm ready to take that step, Liv."

What?

Since when?

"Close your eyes," he says, and I comply. "Now imagine you and me living in this house. Getting ready side by side in the huge master bathroom every morning. Carpooling to work. Cooking together in this gorgeous kitchen in the evenings. Decorating a Christmas tree together. I've never had my own Christmas tree. I never had a reason to get one, but if we were here *together*, I would. God, I'm excited just thinking about it."

I open my eyes.

Did he seriously just say all that? Two weeks earlier, he was reluctant to meet my father. Now he wants to buy a house together and put up a Christmas tree?

He went from first gear straight to sixth and I'm not buckled in.

Not long ago, I was fretting over whether he cared as much for me as I do him. I guess this is my answer, but it's so much more than I bargained for. He's leaping forward at warp speed.

"Can you see it?" he asks, his eyes sparkling with hope and enthusiasm.

Stepping backward, I hold a hand over my heart. "I can. Eventually."

"Eventually?"

"In a couple years or so, sure."

The excitement drains from his face. "A couple years?"

"I don't know," I back pedal. "Maybe sooner. I just had no idea this is where you are."

"I know." His excitement may be gone, but hope remains. "And I realize this is quick, but I know what I want, Babe, and I want you. All of you, every second of every day. I can't get enough of you. I don't want to spend another night apart from you."

My body sways and I become dizzy. He has all but declared his love for me, thus rendering me euphoric, yet overwhelmed.

Glancing at my surroundings, I can see myself here with Everett. I can easily imagine a life with him. But am I ready for it now?

I don't know.

Since I assumed we weren't there yet, I never considered the idea. I presumed he was nowhere near ready for this level of commitment. I had even considered that he may never be.

This is the last thing I expected.

I need a minute to process this new development. Some time to consider his proposal.

But even if I decide that I'm ready for this, there's still another issue. One that I can't remedy easily or any time soon.

"Everett, I can't afford a place like this."

"Don't worry about that." He waves as if it's no big deal.

"I won't be a kept woman." I've always been dead set against the notion.

With a forward step, he places his hands on my arms. "It wouldn't be like that, I promise. There's more to a partnership than the exchange of money."

My head swims with thoughts. This has come totally out of left field. "I'm only twenty-four. Just starting out in my career…"

"Look at all the twenty-four-year-old's who are married with kids. Their careers are new and they're just starting out. I'm sure you have friends who are married."

My heart stutters and my breath hitches. What's with all the talk of marriage? "Are y-you proposing?"

"No," he responds at once but then asks, "Why? Would you say yes?"

I walk to the other side of the counter to put space between us. Clutching my chest, I try to breathe deep. "Let's focus on one proposition at a time."

Everett speaks, his tone filled with dejection, "I love this house, Liv, but I don't want it if you don't want it with me."

"I need time to consider the idea. Can I have that?"

His posture sags and his arms hang limp at his sides. When he answers, his voice is thick. "I hear in your voice and see on your face that you're not ready. You don't want this."

Without giving me the chance to respond, Everett calls the realtor into the room and tells her this isn't the right place for him.

For *him*.

A minute ago it was *us*.

The house was our last stop with the realtor. As planned, we swing by our favorite Cajun restaurant to grab a bite to eat. Everett barely spoke three words to me on the way here. He radiates a funky, negative energy that's wholly unlike him. He's quiet and withdrawn. I've never seen this side of him.

After ordering our food, we sit in continued silence. Everett sits leaning away with arms crossed and a pinched expression, staring anywhere but at me.

"Are you mad at me?" I ask.

"No." He shakes his head, still unable to make eye contact. He picks up his phone and scrolls at something on the screen.

"It seems like you are."

"I'm not," he groans.

Lie! "Let's talk about this."

He shoots me a look. "This is the wrong place for that discussion, Liv."

Minutes pass. He continues to scroll on his phone while I squirm in my seat, picking at my cuticles. This is miserable. "I've lost my appetite."

"Me too. Let's get our order to go."

Twenty agonizing minutes later, we pull up to his condo. Everett pulls in next to my car and leaves the Jeep running.

"Carmen asked me to help her paint her living room," he says. My cue that our day together has come to an end. Funny… he never mentioned that until now.

I assumed we would come back here and discuss what happened at the house earlier. We need to work this out. "Don't you think we should talk?"

He stares, unblinking, out the windshield. "Not right now."

"Why not?"

"Because I need to think."

A burst of adrenaline shoots through my system as panic tears through me. "Think about what?"

He casts me an irritated "are you kidding me?" glance. "About the fact that I put myself out there and you rejected me."

Is that what he thinks? "I didn't reject you."

"That's sure as hell what it felt like."

"This is why we need to talk." I reach for his hand, but he jerks it away.

He grits his teeth. "Not. Right. Now."

"I am not rejecting you, Everett. I just—"

He squeezes the steering wheel. "What part of I need time and don't want to talk are you not comprehending?"

I open my mouth to respond, but the words don't come out. Instead, I get out of the Jeep and watch as he drives away. This is the first time we've parted on a sour note. The first time he didn't kiss me goodbye.

It stings.

That was the first Saturday night we spent apart.

When I called Sunday to ask if I could stop by, he claimed he wasn't home. He was spending the day helping Carmen paint. I asked if he wanted me to swing by later so we could spend the night together. Brushing me off, he said it would be a long day, that he would see me at work.

I arrived at the gallery at the usual hour and Everett wasn't here.

No call.

No text.

I've been here just shy of two hours.

This isn't like him at all.

He wasn't kidding when he said he needed space.

Except, he didn't say he needed space. He asked for time to think. And he didn't ask so much as he demanded it.

Does this mean he's still thinking, and doesn't want to be around me?

Finally, at a quarter till eleven, he graces me with his presence, looking a little worse for wear.

"Rough night?" I ask in a curious rather than condescending fashion.

"You could say that." There is zero sparkle in his eyes. Zero pep in his step.

"Did Carmen break out the bourbon?"

"Yep." His tone is clipped. He rubs his temples.

"I have ibuprofen in my purse."

"Already took some," he says. "I'm going to the office to see what I can get done in there."

"I brought bagels if you're hungry."

Without a response, he disappears.

The day passes with him in the office and me out in the gallery. We come in contact periodically, only talking business as needed. The elephant in the room is intolerable and tough to ignore. But if I bring it up, he will say this isn't the time or place. He'd be right. We can't have a difficult discussion about our relationship at work.

As soon as the clock strikes six, I lock the door and go to find Everett in the office. Regardless of his hangover, we're having this conversation. I take a seat in the chair across from him at the desk, prepared to hash this out.

"You brought up moving in together and marriage and I freaked out. You've hardly spoken or made eye contact with me all day."

No response. He just looks at me as though I am speaking a foreign language he doesn't understand.

"You don't have to be embarrassed," I say.

"Embarrassed?" He barks. "I am not embarrassed."

"Then tell me how you feel."

He drags a hand through his hair. "I already told you. I feel rejected."

Scooting forward, I reach across the desk. "And I told you I'm not rejecting you."

With his arms crossed, he sits back in his chair. "You're rejecting my request to move in together."

"That doesn't mean I'm rejecting you. It doesn't mean I don't want to be with you."

"But it makes me see for the first time that we are in very different places in our lives."

"Yeah, but we already knew that."

"I never felt our age difference until now. I am ready to move forward and take the next step and you're not." He scrubs his face with his hands. "I've never wanted this with anyone and now I do, but the girl I want it with doesn't want it with me."

"I just need a little time."

He blows out a breath. "A couple years is more than a little time, Liv."

"I'm younger than you. The prospect of settling down scares me. Can't you understand? How can you be mad?"

His tone softens, "I do understand and I'm not mad. But it is a huge reality check. I'm forty. You're twenty-four. I realize that you are just starting out in life and building a career. But in ten years, I'm gonna be fifty. I can't wait that long for the life I want."

"I never said you had to wait ten years."

"You once asked me where I saw myself in five years. Being with you has changed what I want. I see you and me in a house like the one we looked at, waking up on a Saturday morning to make pancakes for our kids. That's what I want. Can you say the same?"

I stare, slack jawed. Making pancakes for our kids?

Before I can process my feelings, he continues. "I didn't think so."

I throw my hands in the air. "Just give me a minute."

"You either feel a certain way or you don't."

"You are coming at me full speed without giving me a second to process it."

"Just admit it. You aren't ready."

"I…" Am I? If he would just allow me a moment to consider everything he's throwing at me…

"Exactly," he says. "And it's better to be honest now than invest years that I can't get back."

I cringe. With tears pooling in my eyes, my body shakes. "I can't believe you said that. Being with me is a waste of time?"

He sighs and squeezes his eyes shut. This time it's him leaning in and me pulling away. "I didn't say that."

Heat flushes through my system and I rise from my seat. My finger trembles as I point in his face. "That's exactly what you said. So let me do you a favor and stop wasting your time."

I grab my purse and keys and sprint for the back door. Everett hollers after me, but it's too late. I'm gone.

Two days have passed since I ran out on Everett. I haven't been to work because I can't face him. He's been calling and texting nonstop, and I haven't answered or responded. I need time to think things over. How do I feel about him asking me to move in? How do I feel about him saying he sees us married with kids in five years?

I need time to think about him saying that he won't waste his time with me since I don't feel the same.

Although I never said I don't feel the same. I simply asked for time.

I am staying at Grayson's because Everett has been hanging around my apartment trying to catch me. Hannah and Jess think it's cute. I don't. Now I know how Everett felt when I pressured him to talk before he was ready. Sometimes a person needs a minute to be within their thoughts and feelings to sort everything out.

Maren invited me over so we can talk. Evidently Everett confided in Dex about what happened and she wants my side of the story. I refuse to meet her at their house. My luck Everett would get wind of me being there and show up unannounced. I told her to meet me at a coffee shop close to Grayson's. I also told her if she's doing this to set me and Everett up to talk, I'll never forgive her.

Maren hasn't arrived yet, so I ask for a booth in the far back. I don't need everyone here overhearing my relationship woes.

Not five minutes after I get seated, she arrives. Before taking her seat across from me, she leans down to give me a hug.

"How are you?" she asks, her eyes filled with concern.

"Terrible. I haven't slept. I've barely eaten."

"Everett asked you to move in and you broke it off?"

"Is that what he said?" I have to keep myself from hollering. "That is not how it went down at all."

"That's just the gist that I got from Dex. I didn't speak to Everett. Dex told me that Everett asked you to move in, but you refused. That you got into a fight and you left. He hasn't heard from you since."

"Okay," I blow out a breath, "Everett said he wanted to look at bigger places because his condo is too small. He asked me to help him and I did. We went to a house and all of a sudden he was going on about us living there together and putting up a Christmas tree. Then he started talking about marriage—"

She blinks. "Marriage?"

"He blew my mind." I tug at my hair. "It came totally out of left field. Just a few weeks ago he was dead set against meeting Dad and suddenly he wants us to live together? He said he sees us married with kids in five years."

"What?" Maren's eyes bulge from her sockets and she leans forward in her seat. "Everett said all that?"

"Yes! I was as stunned as you look right now."

"Holy shit, Liv."

"I know, right? All I said was that I needed a little time to think about everything. I mean, he came at me with so much, so fast and totally unexpectedly. He became upset and told me he's too old to waste time with someone who isn't ready for the things he wants in life."

"Wow." She shakes her head. "I need time to digest it all and it doesn't even have anything to do with me."

When the waitress appears to take our order, I just order a mocha, but Maren orders two croissants. No doubt one is for me, but I have no appetite.

"He claimed I rejected him, but I didn't," I say once the waitress is out of earshot. "I only asked for a little time to think. I had no idea he was entertaining these thoughts. Had no idea he was at that point already in our relationship. I mean, we haven't been together that long. I figured, with him, it would be years, if ever, that he'd feel that way or be ready for those things."

"That's a fair point. This is Everett Shaw we're talking about. He's not exactly Mr. Commitment."

"Exactly!" I holler, garnering looks from nearby patrons. When I speak again, I take care to lower my voice. "He has to realize he took me by surprise."

"Like I said, I haven't spoken with Everett. But according to Dex, he feels terrible. He realizes his mistake and wants to work it out."

I shake my head. "I can't talk to him until I sort through my feelings."

"Do you want me to relay that message?"

"Yeah, I guess." A moment passes and I glance about the area. My thoughts are all over the place. "I don't know what to do about work. I can't work with him right now. What if I can't work with him ever again?"

"Don't worry about any of that. Take this week to think. I seriously doubt the guy is going to fire you."

The tears that are pooled in my eyes fall. Maren reaches across the table and takes my hands into hers.

"I love him." I choke on a sob. While this is the first time I've uttered the words, it's not the first time I thought them. "I didn't realize it until he said he wouldn't waste time with me. As soon as he said those words, I knew. I've never felt like this about anyone, Mare. I'm so completely in love with him and it scares the hell out of me."

Maren slides into my booth and takes me into her arms, brushing her fingers through my hair as I cry. "Oh, Livvy."

"I love him, but I can't give him what he wants. At least not right now. And If I can't, it means we can't be together. And if we can't be together…" Another sob escapes my chest.

"I don't think that will happen," she says. "It's obvious you both care deeply about each other. Differences can be overcome with compromise. Take me and Dex. We're polar opposites in a lot of important ways, but we balance each other out. We make each other better." Maren pulls away to look me in the eyes. "If you love Everett, talk to him. Tell him how you feel. Figure out what you can compromise on and what you can't. That's the only way to move forward."

I'm stunned that Maren of all people is giving advice on how to work this out with Everett. She's still not his biggest fan. I assumed she'd be happy if we broke up.

"I am unsure what compromises I'm willing to make." Sniffling, I wipe my tears with the back of my hand.

"That's okay. But tell him that. Even if it's just a text, check in with him. Let him know you haven't shut the door. That you're taking a few days to think, and you'll talk when you are ready. The guy is seriously freaking out."

"He is?"

"He is driving Dex crazy asking if we've talked to you. Dex says he's never seen him like this."

Hearing that makes me want to run straight into Everett's arms and never leave. But I can't. Not yet. I mustn't go to him until I've thought things through. But she's right. I should tell him I'm not shutting him out of my life.

Talking with Maren calmed my nerves substantially. For the first time in two days, I am thinking clearly. As soon as I get to my car, I send Everett a text apologizing for not responding to his messages, asking for another day or two before we talk. His reply is immediate. He writes that he misses me and wants to work this out. I tell him I do, too.

When I arrive at Grayson's there's a note on the entryway table saying he's out for a jog. It'll be nice to have a little alone time to decompress.

I lie on the couch staring at the ceiling for the longest time, pondering my situation. It's time to determine exactly how I feel, what I want, and where I can compromise.

The longer I think about it, I realize I am not opposed to living with Everett. I was more surprised that it's what he wants. However, I am troubled over finances. I'm still paying on student loans and will be for many years to come. I would feel guilty living in a nice house to which I can't contribute. But perhaps I can get over that. Like Everett said, there is more to a partnership than money. I can contribute in a multitude of ways. I can cover utilities and cable and help with groceries.

As for marriage and kids in five years? I can't commit to that.

Though I won't rule it out.

I suppose I can see myself married in three years. Maybe two. As for kids, I might be ready in five years. But again, I won't commit to it. It depends on how my career progresses.

I absolutely need the next two years to focus on my career.

If he will accept those terms, we can move forward.

God, I hope he will accept my terms.

Chapter 16

AT SOME POINT I MUST have fallen asleep. When I open my eyes, it's after nine. Sitting up on the couch, I look around. There's no sign of Grayson. If he was here, I would know. He's not a quiet person and I am a light sleeper. Perhaps he met up with Andrea.

My phone pings with a text and I assume it's Grayson confirming my assumption. I'm surprised to see it's Everett.

Everett: *I respect that you need time. I just want to say goodnight and that I'm thinking of you.*

Me: *I'm thinking of you too. Goodnight.*

As I press send, I decide to tell him one more thing.

Me: *I'll call you tomorrow.*

I feel good about the decision I made regarding what I want and what I am ready for. No sense dragging it out. Besides, I really miss him.

Knowing Grayson won't mind, I crawl into his bed to watch television. He can wake me up and kick me out when he gets home.

He never used to, but we've both agreed it isn't the best idea to share a bed now that we are both in serious relationships. I would be furious if Everett slept in a bed with another woman, even if nothing took place. And I don't want to give Andrea any reason to dislike me. Gray and I made a vow. As we are permanent fixtures in each other's lives, we will do everything we can to get along with one another's significant others and avoid any friction.

Andrea once asked Grayson if anything ever happened between us. He was honest and admitted we tried to date, but it turned out to be a disaster. That he and I are like brother and sister. Supposedly, she's okay with that. Although, like most people, she finds it strange that a guy and girl are close friends with no romantic or sexual entanglement.

Rather than turn the television off, I mute the sound. Quickly and easily, I fall into dreamland. A little after four in the morning, I awake to noise of the front door opening, followed by voices. And crying.

Sitting up to listen, I recognize the voices. It's Grayson's mom and dad, Lisa and Brian.

And then there's sobbing and Lisa calls out, "Grayson!"

I leap from the bed to find out what's amiss. Lisa crumples over on the living room floor clutching a framed picture of her with Grayson. The picture Grayson keeps on his entryway table. Standing beside her, Brian wipes tears from his cheeks.

"Lisa? Brian?" I say and approach the two of them.

They turn to the sound of my voice. Lisa reaches out for me. "Livvy," she cries harder.

Confused and afraid, I wrap my arms around her.

"He's gone, Livvy." She clutches me tightly. "Our Gray is gone."

Gone? Where?

"What do you mean?" My voice shakes.

Brian places a trembling hand on my shoulder. "There was an accident."

There was an accident.

There was an accident.

There was an accident.

I listen to the story, unable, or rather unwilling, to believe a word of it.

Grayson was struck by a car while on his jog.

A hit and run.

The police still haven't found the person responsible.

Grayson is gone.

Gone.

Departed.

Expired.

Dead.

Forever.

In one instant, my life has been forever altered. My heart is shattered.

I rush to the one and only person who can grant me comfort.

I never use the keys to Everett's condo without his knowledge. Not that he would care if I did. It was my decision. It was my way of respecting his space and privacy.

But I'm desperate to be near him. I need him more than ever. Now.

"Everett!" I holler through my tears, not caring if I wake his neighbors, as I unlock his door.

It's not yet six o'clock. He won't be awake.

I throw the door open. "Everett!"

Everett comes running from his room in a state of panic.

"Liv?" He sprints to me and pulls me into an embrace. "What's wrong?"

Devoid of strength, I fall limp in his arms. "Grayson is dead."

I repeat those words over and over as Everett holds me. I coat his bare chest with my tears, and he clutches me tight, rubbing my back in slow, soothing circles. After I'm all cried out, I tell him about the accident.

It wasn't a quick death. Grayson suffered multiple injuries. Broken bones, internal bleeding and a traumatic brain injury. He was conscious before they took him into surgery, but he died on the table. His parents weren't able to say goodbye. *I wasn't able to say goodbye.*

I have lost my best friend.

The pain is unendurable. Sharp stabbing pains in my stomach. A physical pain in my heart. My body is weak. How does one survive the loss of a soulmate? Although we weren't lovers, Grayson was my soulmate. We were meant to be in each other's lives for all time. How do I get through life knowing he isn't here anymore?

When I come to, I'm in Everett's bed. My clothes are drenched. The sun hangs low in the sky, casting an orange glow on everything in the room. I either passed out in Everett's arms or I spent the day in a catatonic state. Either way, I can't remember anything after recounting Grayson's accident.

"Hey Sweetie," Maren's voice breaks the silence.

I turn to find her sitting in a dining chair in the corner next to the chest of drawers.

My shoulders curl over my chest as the pain of my loss overwhelms me. Pulling my knees to my chin, I rock back and forth.

This can't be real.

He can't be gone.

He can't.

Not my Gray.

"I can't take it," I whimper. "It hurts too much."

Sliding into the bed beside me, my sister pulls me into an embrace. "I'm so sorry, Sis."

Everett and Dex enter the bedroom quietly. Dex takes a seat at the end of the bed. Everett sits on the other side of me, placing a comforting hand on my back.

"What can we do?" he asks.

"Nothing," I whisper and cling to my sister the same way I did when my mom died.

As much as I love the three people in this room, they can't help me. Not even their presence eases my pain. The only face I want to see is one I will never see again.

A face I will never see again.

A voice I will never hear again.

Never again.

The funeral was nice. Or at least that's what everyone says.

I didn't think it was nice at all.

There's nothing nice about one's untimely demise.

They say the good ones go too soon. Cliché as it is, it's true. Grayson was a good one. He was better than good. He was great. He was remarkable.

I gave a eulogy. Of course, I gave one. But I barely got through it. Everett came to the podium, and I leaned into him as I sobbed through my tribute to my best friend. It was beyond a shadow of a doubt the hardest moment of my life. I couldn't have gotten through it without my love by my side.

Since receiving the news, I have barely been away from Everett's side. I've been staying at his place. He has kept the gallery closed to be with me while I grieve. I have immense gratitude for him and all he's done.

"I don't know what I would have done without you today," I confess, lying beside him on the mattress.

With his lips pressed to my temple, he murmurs, "I'll always be here for you. No matter what."

I roll on my side to face him. "Everett?"

"Yeah?"

"I love you."

Thrown by my abrupt declaration, he gasps and blinks slowly. His sweet smile builds gradually. "I love you, too."

Hand in hand, we lie in silence, gazing into each other's eyes. When the lump in my throat eases, I continue.

"Losing Grayson so unexpectedly has taught me a lesson." One I thought I already learned, but alas… "It reminded me not to take my loved ones for granted. I'm scared, but I cannot imagine life without you. I refuse to let fear ruin the best thing in my life." Lifting myself, I crawl on top of him and straddle his hips. "You are the best thing that has ever happened to me. I want you and I love you, so if the offer to move in together is still on the table, I accept."

Visibly stunned by my speech, he swallows. "Nothing would make me happier."

In the morning I go to my apartment to tell Hannah and Jess that I'm moving out, effective immediately. If I'm going to do it, there's no sense procrastinating. Mom always said, "If you're gonna do it, do it." When I arrive shortly after ten, they are just waking up.

"Hey guys," I say as I enter the living room.

"Hey," both girls reply in unison and get up from their seats to give me a hug.

"How are you doing?" Hannah asks.

"I'm hanging in. But if I even think of Gray, I bawl." Tears are welling up as I speak.

Jess pulls me close. "We're here if you need anything."

Holding back my tears, I sniffle. "I appreciate it."

"Are you hungry?" Hannah asks. "We were getting ready to make scrambled eggs and English muffins."

I shake my head. "Everett made breakfast this morning."

"I swear, he is the perfect guy," Jess says.

I go to the chair next to the couch and take a seat, motioning for them to join me in sitting. "Speaking of Everett, I have an announcement."

Hannah flashes me a knowing look. "You're moving in with him."

"You are?" Jess asks, forlorn. "I thought you weren't ready yet."

"I've done a lot of thinking since Grayson…" I can't say the "D" word. "It feels right to move in with Everett. But I won't leave you guys hanging. I am prepared to cover my end of the rent until you find a new roommate or the lease expires."

"Actually, you might not have to worry about it," Hannah says. "McKenna is looking for a place. Her roommate eloped last week, and she has to be out of her apartment by the end of the month."

McKenna is a girl we went to school with whom we know well. Hannah is closer with her than I ever was, but she's nice. She should be a good, dependable replacement.

I breathe a sigh of relief. Moving out five months before our lease ends is a rotten thing to do. And continuing to cover rent here while living elsewhere would prove difficult.

"That's great," I say.

"But we'll miss you," Jess pouts.

"I'll miss you, too."

These girls are my tribe. I will miss our late Sunday mornings, hungover, eating English muffins and eggs. Though it has been a while since I've shared a Saturday night or Sunday morning with them. It is amazing how much one's life changes upon entering a serious relationship.

"When are you going?" Jess inquires.

"Today."

"Today?" they ask simultaneously, their shock evident.

I nod. "I need to be close to Everett right now. He's the only thing holding me together."

Thankfully, my friends are as supportive as I hoped they'd be. They each give me a hug and say everything will be okay. And I'm pleased that by moving out, I am helping McKenna.

The three of us discuss my moving plans. I will try to sell my bedroom furniture this week. Also, I am gifting them my sofa and coffee table. I have no use for it and don't want to leave them without.

Once we have hashed out the details, I go to my car to retrieve the boxes I picked up on the way here. Once I'm in the process of packing, I realize I bought too many. I have less stuff than I thought. As I am filling my last box, Maren appears in the doorway. She called earlier and asked if she could stop by to check on me. I decided to wait until she got here to share my news.

"You're packing?" she asks with big eyes.

With a nod, I reply, "I'm moving in with Everett."

"Into his tiny condo?"

"For the time being. He's calling the realtor to see if the house we liked is still available."

"Wow, Liv." Maren plops onto my bare mattress. "Buying a house together? Are you sure about this?"

"We're not buying it together. I can't afford a place like that, and I'm not ready to own a house." I sit beside her. "We'll just be living together. We're working out the financials. He says I don't have to pay for anything, but I won't be kept. I insist on paying my way as much as I can."

With a smile, she lays a palm on my shoulder. "Your independent streak is one of my favorite things about you. It's a trait we both have."

"Most definitely." Maren and I are different in many ways, but we share a need for autonomy.

"Everett has impressed me this week. He really stepped up." Looking round my barren room, she places a hand on a taped box. "I'm glad you have him to help you through your loss."

The mere mention of my loss sends a shooting pain to my gut. "I don't know what I'd do without him."

"I'm here, too. If you need to talk or cry or whatever."

Resting my head on her shoulder, I say, "I'm sure there will come a time when I need to talk, and when that time comes, you'll be the person I call." I turn so we are face to face. "But for now, I can't. My focus is on anything other than my grief."

Thank God Everett is a wonderful distraction. He knows when to keep me busy, and he knows when I need to be held. As though he is reading my mind, he gives me what I need when I need it without having to ask.

"I assumed you weren't up for company, which is why I have kept my distance. But I've been worried about you."

"You need not worry, Mare. I'll be okay." Having gone through this before, I am acutely aware of the stages of grief. I know the drill.

"There's no pressure, but you and Everett are invited to Thursday dinner if you want to come. Maybe some normalcy will help."

"That's a good idea. Let's plan on it."

"Let's do." She pulls me to her and brushes her fingers through my hair.

"You've inherited a new job."

"I have?"

"You're not just my sister anymore. I have bequeathed you the roles of best friend and confidant. Think you can handle that?"

She squeezes me tight. "I'm certain I can manage."

The news of Grayson's death was undeniably one of the worst moments of my existence. It ranks right up there with my mother's passing. A week ago, his burial was one of the hardest days of my life. But having just helped his mom pack up his place… that was hands down harder than his funeral.

Grayson no longer has a place in this world. All of his things have been packed up to be donated or given away. He is now one hundred percent completely and utterly gone from this earth.

Life makes zero sense.

There are mass murderers and child molesters alive and walking free, and my Gray is dead.

Why?

WHY???

Until God can give me an acceptable answer, he and I are on the outs.

As I sit on the floor in front of Everett on the couch, he rubs my shoulders. "Are you okay?"

"No, I'm not." I don't know when I'll be okay again.

"Is there anything I can do?"

"You're already doing it." I glance back at him with a feeble smile.

"Do you want to talk about the day?"

No, but I need to.

Oh, how I wish Grayson was still alive. If he was, I wouldn't be suffering such gut-wrenching pain and anguish.

"I wish his parents would've kept his place a little longer. It was nice being able to go there. Being around his things made me feel close to him." I point to the box by the door. "But Lisa let me keep some stuff."

"That was thoughtful of her."

"I got all his signed Bronco's memorabilia, I thought we could put it with yours in the new house."

"Absolutely," Everett says enthusiastically. He's a huge Bronco's fan. But even if he wasn't, he would let me put it on display. That's his nature.

"He has a signed Elway jersey."

"No way! That's going on the wall somewhere."

"It was one of his most prized possessions. I cried when Lisa handed it to me." But I cry over everything as of late, so it's nothing new. "I wish you two had known each other better. I think you would've been friends."

Leaning in close, he presses his cheek to mine. "I wish we had, too."

"Have you ever lost someone you loved?" I ask and then remember his mom died. "Besides your mother, of course."

"I was so young when my mom passed that I recall little about it. I don't even remember being sad, though I'm sure I was." He was only three when his mother died from a ruptured aneurism. "I've known people who died, but nobody I cared for as much as you cared for Grayson."

"I hope you never experience it. It's awful. It's worse than any physical pain I have ever felt." I've broken an ankle and a wrist and dislocated a rib. I could put all three together and it wouldn't come near the agony of losing my mom and Grayson.

"I imagine it is."

On my knees, I turn to face him. "Promise me nothing will ever happen to you."

Hesitant, he draws his eyebrows together. "I—I can't really promise that, Babe. Accidents happen."

My chin trembles as I cry. "I can't lose you."

Everett draws me into his arms, stroking my back. "I'll do my very best to make sure you don't."

"That's not good enough." I clutch his shirt with quivering fingers. "I wouldn't survive if something happened to you."

With a soft voice, he tries to soothe me, "We can't worry about what may or may not happen."

"If you felt what I'm feeling, you'd worry about it."

"I can't imagine what it would feel like if anything happened to you," he admits. "We just have to take each day on faith."

Faith!

Ha!

I sit back on my heels. "I don't have faith. Not anymore."

The next few weeks pass in a blur. I keep myself occupied with work. Everett and I stay busy on weekends. He knows idle time is not my friend right now, so he makes sure we always have something to do. I go and go all day until my head hits the pillow at night.

This morning, they gave us the keys to the house and we are moving our things in. Everett did away with everything old and we picked out brand new furniture. I say "we" only because Everett requested that I help pick it out. I didn't pay for any of it. I couldn't afford to. I was embarrassed, but Everett told me not to be. Although we aren't married, He has made it clear we are partners in every way. We are together and sharing a life. Everything is shared. It's no longer him or me. It's "we."

"Why did I think moving would be fun?" I ask and open another box. This must be the fiftieth box I've opened today. "My fingers are dried out from all the cardboard."

"I think it's fun." Everett snaps my picture for the millionth time today. If he wasn't so cute, I'd boot him in the ass.

"No, you don't."

"Actually, I do." He plops down on the bare mattress. "This is awesome. Our first house together. It's a day for the books."

"Maybe it's fun for you because you're going around taking pictures all day while I'm doing all the unpacking." I pull a slipper from the box and throw it at him.

"We have to document the experience."

"I'll tell you what we have to do." Standing with hands on my hips, I blow an unruly lock of hair from my face. "We have to find the sheets for this bed. It's after eight o'clock and I still haven't found them."

With a kiss to the tip of my nose, he says, "How about you go downstairs and help Maren in the kitchen. I'll find the sheets and make the bed."

"Deal."

But when I get to the kitchen, there's nothing to do. Maren has unpacked and put away every little thing. The pantry is stocked as only an expert could do. It's perfect. It's glorious.

"How did you manage this so quickly?" I ask, astounded.

She shrugs. "Kitchens are kind of my thing."

We both chuckle.

"What's next?" she asks.

"You've done more than enough, Mare. You don't need to do anything else."

"Nonsense! It's still early. I can work on one of the bathrooms."

"I have a better idea," I say. "Let's crack open a bottle of red."

"If I start drinking, I'll be worthless halfway through the first glass."

"That's the whole point," I laugh. "We've been at this for twelve hours. We deserve a drink."

"Should we call in the guys?"

While Everett works in our room, Dex is working in the guest bedroom. I really want sheets on my bed tonight.

"Everett is on a mission to find our bed sheets," I explain as I uncork the wine. "I couldn't find them, and I refuse to unpack another box. So he's staying put until he finds them."

Thank God for movers. I've moved a couple times in my life and always did it myself with the support of friends and family. Everett hired movers to bring everything in, so all I've had to do is instruct where to set things and unpack boxes. Unbelievably, we've finished most of the unpacking. All that's left is hanging wall art and putting out knick-knacks. Luckily, we are both anti-clutter so we don't own many tchotchkes. I, *we*, shouldn't have more than a few days work ahead of us to add the finishing touches to the house.

Our home.

My home with Everett.

I am living a dream.

Nothing has ever felt more right.

Why was I so freaked out about this?

I wish Gray was here.

Chapter 17

TWENTY MINUTES AND A FULL glass of wine later, the guys emerge.

"Hey, hey," Everett says. "What's this malarkey?"

"We decided it was time for an alcoholic beverage," I answer.

"What about us hard-working men?" he asks. "Don't we get a drink?"

When he picks up the bottle of wine from the table, I snatch it away.

"Did you find the sheets?" I ask.

"Yes, I did. I even made the bed your highness."

"Very good, my peasant. You may partake of the wine." I hand him the bottle.

"Where's the scotch?" Dex asks.

"Booze is in the bar." Maren gestures to the free-standing bar against the living room wall.

When picking out furniture for the house, a bar was one of Everett's prerequisites. I agreed as long as it was tasteful and added to the décor rather than took away from it.

After pouring himself some wine, Everett plonks into the oversized chair. He pats his leg motioning for me to sit on his lap and I happily comply.

"Where were the sheets?" I inquire, truly puzzled.

He nuzzles my neck. "In a box in the closet."

"What? I looked in every single one of those boxes." At least three times apiece.

"You missed one far in the back. It was still taped shut."

"Of course," I groan. "But it had to be the only one I missed."

Dex pours a glass of scotch and joins Maren on the sofa who is studying me and Everett.

"You guys did good," she states, glancing around the room. "This home is gorgeous."

"Thanks," Everett says. "I knew it was the one as soon as I stepped into this room."

"What do you think?" Maren asks me.

"I love this house." I lean into Everett, grateful for his vision of the two of us here.

"It's as though it was built for the both of you," she says. "It fits you to a T."

"I agree," Everett says and rubs my back up and down as I snuggle into my man.

"It already feels like home." I breathe Everett in. *He* is my home.

"You've officially won my seal of approval, Everett," my sister says. "You've made Livvy happier than I've ever seen her. And I have to admit, you look good together. Kind of like this house, you're a perfect fit."

Dex chokes on his drink. "Is that you or the wine speaking?"

"It's me," she assures him and then turns to us. "May you both share many happy memories here."

"Thank you, Maren," Everett's voice is thick with emotion. "That means a lot."

"That said," Maren adds, "if you ever hurt my baby sister, you shall incur my wrath."

Even though we all laugh, we know Maren means what she says.

The next few weeks are a dream. I never knew living in my own home and having my own space would be so freeing. When I get home at the end of the day, I can turn on the television to anything I want while Everett and I cook supper. I'm no longer subjected to lame reality tv, which isn't reality at all since it's scripted. I'm probably the only twenty-four-year-old who hates the crap. I prefer medical dramas and animal rescue shows.

Another advantage is, I don't have to coordinate what to make for dinner with two other people. As much as I adore my girls, figuring out dinner was always a nightmare. I liked Chinese, but Jess didn't. Jess preferred pizza, but Hannah wasn't a fan. Hannah liked one fast-food restaurant while I favored another.

Everett and I enjoy nearly all the same things, and he's generally content to eat whatever I suggest. As a bonus, he does most of the cooking, though he insists that I help. This morning I baked brownies using Maren's tried-and-true recipe. The first thing I have ever baked from scratch. Unable to resist, I tried one at lunch and it was just as good as if Maren had made it.

Another wonderful surprise… The two of us have meshed our lives seamlessly. We fell into a routine with ease. It helped that we'd already been spending most days and nights together before moving in with each other.

And low and behold, I love having my own house so much that I actually look forward to cleaning. Never in a million years would I have believed I'd be happy to scrub a toilet. But I take pride in keeping my beautiful home clean and cozy.

The only way life could be more perfect is if Grayson was here.

On this lazy Saturday afternoon, I'm in my backyard, getting a suntan while jamming out to my favorite tunes. I check the time on my phone. Everett should be home soon. I can't wait. He promised to grill steaks for us tonight. My stomach rumbles as I think about it.

Speak of the devil, the patio door slides open and Everett steps out. When I swing around to greet him I am alarmed by the scowl on his face. He usually comes home happy after golfing with Dex.

"Is everything okay?" I ask.

"I received some interesting information today." With legs planted wide, he stands perfectly still, his lips pressed into a firm line, and arms crossed.

Is he mad at me?

"What information?" I turn to give him my full attention.

"I learned my girlfriend, whom I'm living with, who is supposed to be my partner, is considering giving away a kidney."

Oh shit.

I scramble to my feet. Maren must've told Dex, who obviously told Everett. They probably assumed he knew.

"Everett—" I start to explain, but he cuts me off.

"Imagine my surprise when my best friend asked if my girlfriend was going through with the," he makes air quotes, "*donation.* I had no idea what he was talking about."

When I step forward, he steps back. Stepping away is his defense mechanism when he's angry. He has never been this mad at me.

"I'm not donating a kidney."

"Then what is he talking about?"

"Jess's older sister has lupus nephritis. She's in kidney failure and needs a transplant. A bunch of us agreed to get tested to see if we're a match."

"And you didn't think that information was important enough to share with me?" He pinches the bridge of his nose. "We live together, Olivia! We're sharing a life. We decide things together!"

This is the first time he has yelled at me. I don't like it. If he would just allow me to explain…

"I wasn't hiding it. It happened very fast. I was going to tell you if I got tested."

His flaring nostrils and cold, hard glare suggest that was the wrong thing to say.

"*Tell* me?" he seethes. "That's not deciding, that's *telling*!"

I hold up my hands. "That isn't what I meant."

"This is a big deal." He exhales sharply. "Giving away a kidney is a big damn deal! It makes me wonder if you're taking our relationship seriously."

"Of course, I do."

Without another word, he spins on his feet and heads for the house.

"Where are you going?" I ask.

"I need some time alone. Do us both a favor and let me have it."

An hour has passed and Everett is still locked away in his man cave in the basement. He asked for time, but I can't stand him being mad at me. We need to talk this through.

I admit, it ruffled my feathers when he came at me about this. But he is right. I should have talked to him. I wasn't purposely hiding anything from him. It didn't seem important since they had found a match and I was off the hook for getting tested. If he will listen, I'll be able to calm him down.

Inhaling deep, I count to ten before heading down the stairs.

"I'm not ready to talk, Olivia."

That's twice he has called me Olivia. He never calls me Olivia. It's usually either Liv or Babe. He's seriously pissed.

"You need to hear what I have to say."

No response.

"I never got tested because they found a match."

"That's great, but it doesn't change the fact that you were considering donating a kidney and didn't feel the need to share the information with me."

I take a seat on the couch beside him and he scoots away.

"Like I said, it all happened quickly. Maren was with me last night when I got the call from Hannah saying everyone was going in this morning to be tested. I agreed to go, but they found three compatible matches and don't need me."

"Last night, you were planning on being tested to find out if you're a match." He crosses his arms over his chest. "You had all night to tell me and you didn't."

"I never intended to keep anything from you. And I never meant to decide anything without you. I just saw a friend in need and wanted to help. Wouldn't you do the same thing if it had been Dex's mom?"

"Yes, but—"

I speak before he can finish, "I would like to think you wouldn't prevent me from helping a friend."

He looks to the ceiling and blows out a breath. "A kidney transplant is major surgery. Things can go wrong. It shouldn't be a snap decision."

"You're right. I should've told you as soon as I received the call. Please don't be mad at me." When I scoot a little closer, he doesn't move away. "I'm learning, Everett. This is my first real relationship. I've never had to include anyone in the decisions I make."

His eyes soften, and his tone is gentle. "I understand. It's just that I've never been in love before, and I love you *so much*. The idea of you donating an organ scares the hell out of me."

Finally, I can take a breath of relief. I can't stand him being upset with me. "I love you, too. I'm sorry I scared you."

"Let's make a pact, here and now, from this day forward we will make all decisions together."

"I promise." I hold my hand out for a shake.

"What's that?" He laughs a booming Everett laugh. The laugh I adore. Thank God for a moment of levity.

"We're making a pact, we have to shake on it."

"Oh no, that's not how we seal deals around here," he says and presses his lips to mine.

"Then how do we seal deals?" I ask against his mouth.

"Allow me to show you, Miss Bell," he murmurs, deep and throaty.

Just like that, I melt. All he has to do is give me *the look* and I fall to pieces, ready and willing.

Lowering his face to my neck, Everett brushes his lips over my skin before kissing me softly. "The taste of your skin is addictive."

When I purr at the sensation of his mouth on me, he quietly chuckles.

"Do you enjoy this method of closing deals?"

"Yes," I whisper.

"Me too." Pulling back just enough to gaze into my eyes with contentment, he brings his lips to mine once again.

As he kisses me, he tugs at the hem of my shirt pulling it off in one swift motion. I don't know what to remove first, Everett's shirt or his pants. I settle on the latter. It is the most important garment, after all. We can make love with his shirt on, we can't if he's in his jeans. Lust smolders in his eyes as he circles my taut, lace covered nipples while I unzip his fly.

"You in lace is my favorite thing."

Which is why I wear it almost daily.

The cool basement air gives me goosebumps. Everett pulls away, taking with him his warmth. He stands and takes off his pants, kicking them across the room, making me laugh. Gyrating his hips provocatively, he leisurely lifts his shirt over his head. He knows how to seduce me. I melt when he dances. He puts on the best strip teases. My eyes rake over the length of his magnificent body. I lick my lips in anticipation of him removing his boxers. But this is what he does. He torments me, taking his sweet time to give me what I want.

The heat of my desire alleviates any chill I felt a moment ago. I squeeze my thighs together to quell my aching need.

On the verge of begging, he hooks his thumbs into his boxers and drags them down, albeit much too slowly. Finally, his erection springs free, swollen and ready. He's always ready.

So am I.

We truly are a perfect match.

I'd wager a bet that no one on earth has as much sex as we do, and it's still not enough for either of us.

There is no such thing as enough for him and I.

Seeing Everett's naked arousal has me fit to drop to my knees to take his deliciousness into my mouth. However, the overpowering throbbing in my core demands release. I know what will push him over the edge and bring him to me, ready to fulfill my every wish.

I reach around my back and unclasp my bra, pulling it away from my skin. The moment my fingertips touch my sensitive, peaked nipples, his body is pressed against mine. He can never resist the sight of me touching my breasts, clothed or not, but especially when I'm not.

The weight of Everett's body thrusts me onto my back. He hurries to get rid of my shorts. As soon as they hit the floor, he slips a finger into the seam of my panties, sliding it from my entrance to my clit. I gasp with pleasure as he sweeps his fingertip back and forth across my most sensitive spot. His skillful touch sends sparks of electricity through my body and I clutch his shoulders.

"So wet, Babe." His voice is low and husky.

Arching my back, I pant as he rolls the tip of his finger around and around, applying just enough pressure to drive me wild. An arousing growl escapes his lips as he continues his ministrations.

I am his. All his. I always will be.

Everett brings his mouth to mine, coaxing my lips to part, allowing him entrance. He pushes my panties down my thighs as his tongue slips into my mouth, eliciting a soft moan. The taste of him is exquisite. I return every lick and stroke of his tongue with my own until he pulls away and kneels before me, positioning me the way he wants and spreads my legs wide.

Yes. Yes, yes, yes.

If I died with this man's face between my legs, I would leave this earth a happy woman. Our eyes meet for a moment, each of us conveying our longing for the other, before he buries his face into the apex of my thighs. Everett draws a long, agonizingly leisurely stroke up the length of my slit to my clitoris.

My toes curl and I moan as my core clenches and spasms. "Oh, yesss."

Gripping my hips, he devours me, working me into a frenzy. And then he slows and presses his tongue to my nub and licks just once. With the first flutter of impending pleasure, my pelvis bucks. He repeats the act. Another wave crashes over me, this time stronger. He blows cool air onto my sex. A signal that he's not going to allow me to come this way. He's selfish sometimes. He wants my orgasm to come from him being within me. I don't mind. As much as I love oral sex, nothing is better than coming with him inside me.

Everett moves us to the floor and hovers over me, his blue eyes trained on mine, piercing my soul. He claims my mouth with passion, my taste on his lips. "You are everything to me, Liv."

My heart stutters. He's told me he loves me many times, but he's never said this. Before I can respond in kind, his mouth is back at work, worshipping me. His hand skims my hip, making its way to my thigh and hikes my leg up to his waist. When he pulls back, his eyes search mine.

"Tell me you love me," he pleads with a hint of desperation in his voice.

"You know I do." I brush my fingers through his hair.

"Tell me. Say the words, Baby."

"I love you." So much. Too much. I kiss his wet lips, wrapping my arms around his neck, pulling him closer to me. "I'll always love you."

As I gaze into his gorgeous blue's, he positions himself at my entrance. He hovers longer than I would expect. It isn't like him to hold back.

"I need you," he whispers. He's not talking about sex. He truly *needs* me.

"I need you, too."

"Always?"

"Forever."

This seems to mean more to him than my confession of love. Finally, he pushes into me inch by inch, slowly filling me until he's settled all the way inside. We each suck in uneven breaths. Everett stares down at me with a deep adoration and sincerity.

After Grayson's passing, we quit using condoms. A mutual decision. I'm on the pill and we're both clean. As great as our sex was before, it's magnified by a thousand since ditching the latex.

"We fit together perfectly," he croons.

He withdraws little by little and sinks back in just as deliberately, setting a steady tempo, making delicious love to me.

"Do you feel it? The power of our connection?" he asks, repeating the slow, arduous motion intensifying my need for him.

"I do," I murmur. I've felt it from the very first time we connected.

He continues his steady, controlled thrusts and I slide my fingers up and down his back, kneading the firm flesh.

"There's nothing better than making love with you," he says. "I wish we could spend every second together just like this."

"Me too," I breathe.

I'm consumed by the sensation of Everett moving in and out, back and forth, the rotation of his hips edging me to the precipice of release. He peers down at me with pure reverence. His patience and self-control to maintain his exquisite, unhurried pace make me love him even more. He makes perfect, sweet love.

His face glistens with sweat. Although we are moving at such a leisurely speed, I imagine it's taking him a considerable amount of willpower and restraint to do so. I cup his cheeks as he gazes down upon me, his body trembling as he pushes in and pulls out. His erection twitches inside me, the first sign that he's on the brink. My sex tightens around him and he gasps, blowing out a ragged breath.

"I'm close," he groans and thrusts in, grinding into me mercilessly. The intensity of his stroke has me chasing my orgasm. It's right there… If only I just raised my hips and met his strokes… But this is his pace. He's in control. And he's taught me release is abundantly sweeter when I wait for it.

He moves in me, once, twice, three times… Every nerve ending in my body buzzes as I teeter on the brink.

"Come with me, Babe," he says and jerks forward, losing control. His delicacy is ebbing as he reaches the point of no return. Resting his forehead on mine, he slams into me. Buried deep inside, he rotates his hips, pushing into me hard. He knows just how to push me over the threshold to my bliss.

I cry out his name as I shatter beneath him.

Everett quickens his last few thrusts as he finds his own release. "I'm coming," he grunts and drives into me one final time, his erection pulsating as he fills me. His body stills and he collapses on top of me.

In this moment, I am utterly complete. I couldn't want anything more than to be sharing this life with this man.

Chapter 18

"THIS PRINT HAS GOTTEN A LOT of traction," Everett says in regard to my Bear Lake photo.

As we speak, we are packaging up four prints and two canvases of the print that have sold.

"I can't believe it," I say. "But it's only because it's in your gallery and on your website."

With a groan, he rolls his eyes. "When are you going to stop being so damn modest about your talent?"

"I'm not being modest," I insist. "I love the picture and I am super proud. But, if it was on my own website, I doubt it would sell like this. It probably wouldn't sell at all. Your name and visibility made this possible."

"My name may be helping with visibility, but my clientele wouldn't buy the print if it wasn't good." He finishes taping the box he's working on.

"True." He does have a very selective, affluent clientele.

"You should submit it for the IPA," he suggests, with complete nonchalance, as though it's no big deal.

I scoff at his absurd suggestion. The IPA is one of the most prestigious photography competitions. One doesn't enter it willy nilly.

"Liv, we've talked about this," he says. "An important step in building a photography career is entering competitions."

"Yes, but my work isn't IPA good yet." My plan is to start with small contests. Maybe even local.

As though I've annoyed him, he glowers at me with exasperation and stops working. "Yes, it is, Liv. If you don't submit this photo, I will."

He'll do it, too. Everett never says things he doesn't mean. The idea makes my muscles twitch and I wring my hands. "And when I lose, I'll feel rotten."

"You could win, Liv. And even if you don't get first place, I'm confident you'll place." He comes to where I stand and places his palms on my shoulders. "I wouldn't recommend entering the contest if I didn't think you have a real chance."

It is an excellent shot, I'll give him that. It's as good as any I've seen in magazines. We got a call from a respected gallery in New York a couple weeks ago that offered to put it on display. I just received an email from them this week with a picture showing it hung in their show room. The gallery owner claims it has garnered a great deal of interest and positive feedback.

"Can I think about it?"

"No." He crosses his arms. "Either submit it, or I will."

With my hands on my hips, I jut out my chin. This isn't his choice to make. "You don't have the right to decide that."

Stepping close, he gazes at me adoringly. He gives me this look whenever he wants something. It almost always ensures he gets his way. "Have I ever steered you wrong when it comes to your work?"

I bite my lip. "No. But…"

"You have one week to send in your submission, or I'll do it for you."

I fold my arms across my chest. "Now who's being high-handed?

"You can thank me later." He plants the sweetest kiss on the tip of my nose.

Maren arrives right on time to pick me up. We're going to the florist to make a final selection for her bridal bouquet. The last time we went, she narrowed it down to three arrangements. She's taking me so I can make the choice for her.

It's pouring rain so rather than come to the door, she honks the horn and waits in the driveway. When I get in the car, her face is red and splotchy, and her eyes are blood shot. She's been crying.

"What's the matter?" I ask.

"Nothing." She tries to play it off with a smile, but she can't hide her puffy eyes.

"What happened?" I press.

With a sigh, she relents. "Dex and I had an argument last night and it carried over to this morning. He slept in the guest room and isn't speaking to me."

"Mare, that's horrible. What was the fight about?"

"Same old crap." Her lip trembles. "My insecurities got the best of me. I accused him of being like every other man alive."

"You didn't." Dex isn't like every other man alive. He's not like *any* other man alive.

"I did." Her voice cracks. "He said he refuses to spend the rest of his life trying to convince me he is faithful."

"What does that mean?"

"I pushed him too far this time, Liv." She shakes her head as fresh tears spill. "He's not going to marry me."

Dropping her face into her palms, she sobs. I pull her to me, rubbing her back in a soothing motion. As the rain pelts the roof and the windows, I hold her while she cries.

"Everything will be okay, Mare. Dex loves you."

"What's wrong with me, Liv?" She clutches my blouse. "Why am I this way?"

"There's nothing wrong with you. We all have baggage."

"You don't." She sniffles. I imagine there is a fair amount of snot on my shirt right now.

"Sure I do."

"You're the perfect girlfriend. You'll probably make a perfect wife." She pulls away and wipes her eyes. It's a good thing she isn't wearing mascara or her face would be streaked with black. "You would never put Everett through the crap I've put Dex through. I mean, you've converted a manwhore into the ideal monogamous boyfriend."

"I am not perfect, Mare. My relationship isn't perfect. If you recall, it wasn't too long ago that I almost lost Everett because I freaked out. You and I might have more in common than we realize."

"Why do I needle him?" She wipes her nose with a tissue. "I question him about every little thing. I'm continuously looking for that one fatal flaw. Always expecting him to let me down even though he's never given me any reason to feel that way."

"Do you think maybe it's time you tried therapy?" I ask and lightning strikes.

We've had this conversation a few times. The last time was a disaster. Maren isn't proponent of therapy. I happen to believe everyone could benefit from a little self-reflection and guidance. It helped me immensely when my mom died.

Ignoring my question, she pulls away and stares out the windshield. "We were doing so well for so long. I don't know what set me back."

"Perhaps talking to someone would help you figure that out and avoid future triggers."

"I'm talking to you."

"I'm not a professional."

"Do you and Everett argue?"

I nod. "We have disagreements."

"Are you ever unreasonably jealous or insecure?"

She's hoping I will say yes. It would validate her feelings. Help her feel less screwed up. But I cannot lie.

"No."

"See. I'm such a mess!" She clutches her head in her hands. "I'm with the best guy on the planet. A guy who has probably never once even considered cheating on anyone and I can't trust him. You are with a guy who's most likely slept with thousands of women and you feel one hundred percent secure."

Thousands of women. The thought makes me nauseas. She's probably right about the number. Still, out of all those women, he chose me.

"Our relationship is new. We're still in the honeymoon phase. Our time is coming, I'm sure."

"I never assumed we'd make it this far," Maren confesses. "I never thought he'd choose me. I'm not good enough for him."

I gasp at her admission. "You don't actually feel that way, do you?"

She nods and wipes her nose with the back of her hand. "I always have."

"You get that thought right out of your head, Maren Bell," I demand. "You are good enough. You are *more* than good enough. Dex knows this, which is why he chose you. It's time you realize it too before you lose him."

"What if I already have?" Her eyes are so sad and fear laden.

"He stayed home last night," I point out. "You haven't lost him. Now take your ass back home and do whatever it takes to make up with him."

"What about the flowers?"

"I will take care of it." I was going to anyway, and we both know it. She was just coming along out of duty.

"Really?"

"You've been stressing about the damn flowers for weeks. I'll go pick them out. They'll be perfect, I promise."

She pulls me in for a hug. "I love you, Livvy."

"Love you, too. Now get the hell out of here."

I open the door to step out of the car but have a final thought. One that might help her.

"Nobody ever imagined Everett would settle down," I say. "No one believed he could, but he did. If Everett of all people has found his way, so can you."

Picking out Maren's flowers doesn't take long, so on the drive home I make a quick pit stop at my old apartment to visit the girls. I want to check in on Jess and see how she's doing. Her sister is set for her kidney transplant in the coming week which has her frazzled.

My visit ends up turning into a marathon girl talk session. Hannah and her boyfriend broke up again. Things are heating up between Jess and Ryan. And they want all the details about my new domestic bliss with Everett. It's as though they view me as an old married woman, although I'm nowhere close to getting wed.

Almost five hours later, I arrive home. I am starving and can't wait for Everett's world-famous lasagna. I've never had lasagna anywhere that is half as good as his. He picked up the recipe while traveling in Italy. Recipes from the mainland are always better than any Americanized version.

I enter the mudroom through the garage, kick off my shoes and go to the kitchen. Everett is nowhere to be seen. No lasagna in sight.

"Everett?" I call out. When there's no reply I try again, "Babe?"

With his jeep in the garage, and all the lights on, he must be around here somewhere. Opening the basement door, I holler his name.

Still no response. Maybe he's asleep or in the shower.

As I approach the stairs, I notice the back-porch light is on. When I get to the sliding doors, I see him on the deck, leaned back in a chair, staring up at the sky.

"Hey, you," I say and step outside.

"Hey." He turns to me. There's a glass of scotch on the table beside him, along with the bottle.

Is he drunk?

"I thought you were making lasagna."

"So did I." He takes a swig of the booze.

"What's wrong?" I pull a chair in front of him and place my hands on his thighs.

He sighs, leans forward and encircles my wrists with his fingers.

"It's been an interesting day," is all he says.

Even through the shadows on his face, I can make out his ashen color. His palms are clammy, his shoulders are tight, and he can't hold eye contact. I am frightened to ask what has happened.

"Do you wish to talk about it?"

"Not really."

"Do I need to worry? Are you okay?"

"I'm okay."

That doesn't answer my first question, but I'm afraid to press.

"I'm sorry I didn't cook," he slurs. "We can order Chinese if you want."

"No big deal." My appetite is rapidly diminishing as I study him. Something is wrong. Something serious. I'm nervous to find out what it is, and he's obviously hesitant to tell me. "Should I leave you be?"

Jutting forward, he cups my face with his palms. "No. Will you sit with me for a while?"

"Yeah, I can do that."

He rests his forehead on mine.

We sit in silence for the longest time before he suggests we go inside and scrounge something for dinner. The two of us whip up a couple grilled cheeses and canned soup. Once we've eaten, we agree to call it a night.

We get into bed and Everett pulls me close, whispers how much he loves me and makes soft, slow love to me to prove his point. Afterwards, we fall asleep in each other's arms.

"Liv," Everett says, rousing me from my slumber.

"Mm-hmm," I mutter sleepily and roll over, ready to accept him. It's common for him to wake me for sex in the middle of the night.

"I can't sleep. I need to tell you what happened."

This gets my full attention and I am suddenly wide awake. "Okay."

When I move to turn on the lamp, Everett stops me and pulls me close.

"You know how much I love you, right?"

Oh God.

Oh.

God.

He cheated on me.

My heart races and tears well behind my eyes. I'm glad he didn't allow me to turn on the light. It's better that I hear this in the dark.

"Just tell me," I croak.

He sucks in a deep breath and even in the darkness, I see him rake his hand through his hair. His words come out in a rush. "An eighteen-year-old girl showed up here tonight claiming to be my daughter."

Relief washes over me.

He didn't cheat.

I can deal with this.

I think.

"Your daughter?"

"I figured it was a joke at first, but I was once involved with the woman she claims is her mom. And… she looks a hell of a lot like me."

"You have a daughter…" It isn't a question. My Everett has a daughter not much younger than me.

"I might."

I turn to him, flummoxed. "You just said she looks like you. You believe she is yours."

"It's a possibility, but we shouldn't freak out yet. I'm getting a DNA test."

"What if it's true?" I ask, although I already know the answer to the question, and I don't like it.

What does this mean for us? Would things change? It's not like she's a toddler. She is an adult, technically. Though when I was eighteen, I didn't feel like an adult.

"I haven't thought that far out yet," he answers. "Haley—that's her name—said her mom died two years ago. She's been living with her aunt who recently told her the truth about her parentage, and she wanted to meet me."

I am dizzy and my body tingles with discomfort. Is this really happening? My Everett is a dad? I rock back and forth and try to calm my breathing.

"Are you okay?" he asks and scoots closer, wrapping a strong steadying arm around my waist.

"We shouldn't freak out yet," I repeat his words. "Not until you get the DNA test."

"I have to tell you something, but you absolutely cannot say a word Dex."

"My lips are sealed," Maren assures me.

Everett doesn't want Dex to learn of his predicament until we have confirmation of Haley's parentage. He said if she's not his kid, there's no reason for Dex to find out about this.

Everett cares about his friend's opinion of him. They've been closer than ever these past few weeks since Dex and Maren found out about our relationship. Dex sees Everett in a whole new light. Views him as a mature, responsible adult. He insists he never thought lowly of Everett, he just saw him for what he was. A hard-working guy who cared deeply for his loved ones but happened to be a carefree wanderer, bedding women around the globe.

I respect Everett's wishes, truly I do. But I must talk about this with someone. Now that Grayson is gone, Maren is my go-to person. As much as I adore Hannah and Jess, they can't be my confidants. They wouldn't understand the complexity of the situation. For them it would be black and white. They'd say, if she's his daughter, pack your crap and leave.

I am concerned this will injure Maren's newfound respect for Everett and her approval of our relationship. Nevertheless, I need her. I called her this morning and asked her to meet me at the park after work, but not to tell Dex we are meeting. When Everett inquired on my plans for the day, I lied and said I'm getting together with Hannah. As much as I hate lying, it was the safe bet. If I'd told him I was meeting Maren, he'd fret about me telling her. He'd have reason to worry because that's what I am about to do.

I swallow and take a breath in preparation of the bomb I'm fixing to drop. "An eighteen-year-old girl turned up at the house yesterday, claiming to be Everett's long-lost daughter."

Maren chokes, her cerulean eyes bulge. "What?"

"I'm freaking out. We both are."

"I guess so." A moment passes in silence as she digests the information. "Did you meet her?"

I shake my head. "I was at my old apartment when she showed up."

Thank God I wasn't there. How would I have reacted if I'd opened the door to Haley and received the news straight from her lips? It wouldn't have been good, I'm sure.

"Everett's getting a DNA test," I explain, "but I can tell he believes her. He says she looks just like him."

Maren nods but remains silent. It's not a "I'm so shocked I can't speak silence." It's a "I don't want to say the wrong thing and tick you off" silence.

"What are you thinking?" I ask.

"I am thinking I'm not surprised. This is Everett we're talking about. He could have a dozen kids roaming the earth."

I instantly envision a gaggle of blonde haired toddlers living in different cities and countries, each with different moms. The vision makes me cringe. "I hadn't considered that possibility."

My sister shoots me her dead serious look. "My advice is, you better prepare yourself for life to change."

"Do you think she's his?"

She nods.

"At least she's an adult," I say. "She has been raised. It isn't like she will live in my house."

"Perhaps not," Maren says, and I hear the "but" before she says it, "but she'll be a fixture in your life from here on out. And children alter the dynamic of relationships. Everett will be taking on a new role. He'll be spending time with her, getting to know her and learning to be a father. He'll likely expect you to be a part of it all. Are you up for that?"

Sure as I sit here, I know I don't want any part of this. I have zero interest in meeting the girl. I don't want to know her. I didn't create her. I didn't bring her into this world. I don't owe her anything. I enjoy having Everett to myself and prefer not to share him with anyone, including a daughter.

Yes, I am selfish. I don't care. If that makes me a bad person, so be it. Haley's sudden arrival has threatened to throw my perfect life into complete disarray.

"No," I answer honestly. "I'm not."

"Then you need to talk to Everett, and the sooner the better. He needs to know where you stand."

A sinking feeling grows in the pit of my gut. I rub my face and groan. "This sucks so bad."

"It surely does."

"How do I tell him how I feel? That I don't… that I'm not…" I can't even speak the words out loud to myself. I lean forward clutching my head in my hands.

"You just say it." Maren pats my back. "Tell him you're freaked out. That you worry about how this will affect your relationship."

As I sit up, I blow out a breath. "There's still a chance she isn't his."

Tilting her head to the side, Maren eyes me with concern. "Better to prepare for the worst than cling to hope and be let down."

That's so the opposite of what my mom would say. But, in this case, it is solid advice.

Maren spends the next hour giving me ideas of how to discuss my feelings and concerns with Everett, and does her utmost to convince me it's a conversation he and I must have at once. By the end of our talk, I am even more nauseas than I was when he told me about the girl.

Before we part ways, I make Maren promise me at least a dozen times not to utter a word of this to Dex. Once I'm confident she won't spill the beans, I get in my car and drive home.

Chapter 19

TO SAY THINGS ARE AWKWARD at home would be an understatement. Everett and I try to keep everything as normal as possible, except under the surface, nothing is normal.

It's been three days since I learned about Haley. Against my better judgment, I never had my talk with Everett. I've been too scared and upset.

He is leaving soon to pick her up for the DNA test. I have been sick to my stomach all morning and didn't sleep a wink last night. With my appetite in the toilet, I've lost five pounds. As it gets closer to time for him to leave, my symptoms worsen. My chest is heavy, I'm dizzy and I can't stop shaking. I feel useless and devoid of all energy.

Please let it be a slow day at the gallery.

Standing in front of the bathroom mirror, I study my reflection. There isn't enough makeup in the world to cover my lack of sleep and anxiety.

"You're gray," Everett says from behind me. His expression is one of concern as he rubs my neck. "Are you okay?"

"As okay as I can be given the circumstances."

"Talk to me, Liv." He spins me slowly to face him.

Everett has been trying to get me to divulge my true feelings to him for days now, but I am not comfortable voicing them. But like Maren said, I must. The only way we will survive this is with open communication.

"I hate this," I confess, and drop my gaze to the floor. "I do. I feel like, when you get the results and they confirm she's yours, everything will change." And not for the better.

"Some things will, but not everything." Cupping my chin, he gently lifts my face to his. "We will still be us. We'll still be living our lives. I'll just have an added family member."

"A daughter is more than just a family member, Everett."

"I know." His voice is soft. "But Haley's grown. I won't be raising her. She won't be living in our house."

"I get the feeling you're excited about this."

"After getting to know her these past couple days, I admit I am." His eyes sparkle when he smiles. "She's a clever girl. She's got spunk. A lot like me in some aspects. I think it'd be fun to be her dad. I truly think you will like her."

My exhale is so sharp, it comes out as a groan. "I'm going to say something that you may find offensive or hurtful."

"Okay."

"I'm twenty-four years old. I'm not ready to be a mother or a mother figure especially to a girl who's barely younger than I am."

He nods, but I can tell he's seriously considering my words. "That's understandable." He squeezes my shoulders. "I really don't believe there's anything to worry about. She has—she *had* a mom. All I ask—if it turns out Haley is mine—is that you stand by my side. I want you to go along with me on the journey. And it would mean the world to me for both of you to get to know one another and become friends."

He has resigned himself to being her father.

As have I.

Ready or not, this is happening.

"Of course, I'll be by your side."

As for becoming her friend… we'll have to see how that plays out. Friendships can't be forced and I am not fake. Even if she and I don't become friends, which we could, but if we don't, I will always be kind and respectful toward her. But in this heavy moment, it's best that I not say all that.

"Thank you, Babe." He pulls me into an embrace. "I love you."

"I love you, too."

He leans away just enough to make eye contact. "What do you say we invite her over for dinner tonight? We can put burgers and brats on the grill. It's the perfect opportunity for you to meet her."

My heart rate spikes. I am not prepared for this. "I don't know…"

"You have to meet her."

"I know. But I assumed it would happen after the test results came in."

Everett steps back. His calm and patience has vanished and been replaced with disappointment. "You're hoping she's not mine."

With my gazed fixed on the tile floor, I twist my hands together. "I'm sorry. I'm not trying to upset you or be unsupportive."

He drags a hand through his hair. "Who would've thought my having a daughter would affect you more than me?"

That's a good question. I am damn surprised he's taking it so well. I would've imagined news such as this would send him into a panic attack.

"I'd like to have her over for supper tonight," he reiterates. "She's here in Denver all alone. She spends all day and night in her crappy hotel room, probably eating fast food for every meal. I want to do something nice for her."

I can't say no. That would be wrong. And besides, there's no sense putting off the inevitable. "Okay, let's invite her."

His lips spread into a sweet, thankful smile. "It'll be great, you'll see."

I spend the entire morning at the gallery priming myself, getting in the appropriate frame of mind for tonight's dinner. Everett's right. I have to meet Haley. What difference does it make whether it's tonight or two days from now? Waiting would only delay the unavoidable. My dad raised me to never procrastinate. If something needs done, do it straight away. And always tackle the difficult tasks early so you don't waste time dwelling on them.

Just as I begin to feel confident and prepared, the front door swings open and in strides Everett and a ridiculously beautiful blonde teenager.

Haley.

I gasp and my chest tightens.

I'm not at all prepared for this.

Why didn't he give me a heads up?

"Instead of dinner," Everett starts, "Haley and I figured we'd bring you lunch."

His eyes beg for understanding and he kisses my cheek.

I gape at him, then Haley, then him again. When I speak, I try my hardest to conceal my irritation. "This is a surprise."

The gorgeous girl hands me a sack of food. "Everett says you love Thai food."

I gulp. "I-I do, thank you."

"I made him bring me here," she says, "I couldn't wait to see the gallery. When I saw the website, I couldn't believe it. It's so cool that my dad is a famous photographer."

Her dad?

The results aren't in yet!

Doing my utmost to appear calm and collected, I keep my thoughts to myself with a smile.

"This place is awesome!" Haley squeals and skips around the room, examining the prints on display. "It must be amazing getting rich with something as easy as taking pictures."

Did she really say that?

As though Everett just runs around clicking his camera with zero thought or effort? As though what he does isn't actual work? As though he isn't truly brilliant?

What a little bitch.

If she says one more stupid thing, God help me, I will need to be restrained.

What's worse is Everett doesn't seem to be the least bit bothered by her offensive comment. He simply follows her around with a silly grin, staring at her like she's the most remarkable creation on the planet.

"I bet I could do this," Haley declares smugly with her chin jutted in the air. "We can turn this into a family business, and I won't need to worry about money anymore."

If it was possible for my jaw to hit the floor, it would. Her statement is preposterous. Absurd. Ludicrous. Does she assume she can show up on the scene, out of the clear blue, and make all this hers?

Everett continues to follow her like a lost puppy. "If you're interested in photography, I'd be happy to take you under my wing."

Is he blinded by his adoration for her? She's now made two reprehensible and ridiculous remarks, and it's like he didn't hear them. I can't believe I'm witnessing this.

Looking at me, Haley says, "Only if I don't have to do any cashier work. I'll take pictures, but I've been a cashier, and I hated it. No offense, Olivia."

Excuse me?!

Excuse! Me?

She called me a cashier!

My annoyance must be on full display because Everett looks at me with a pleading expression.

"She isn't a cashier, Haley," he says. "We both work in the gallery. It's fun."

"It doesn't look very fun."

"Maybe being a photographer isn't for you," I suggest.

She ignores me.

"Who's hungry?" Everett asks, changing the subject.

"Not me," I answer. "I have work to do in the office. Please excuse me."

"Today didn't turn out as I had hoped," Everett says as we slide into bed later that night.

It is astounding the toll stress and anxiety can take on one's body. I'm exhausted, although I haven't done anything physically strenuous.

"You know what they say about expectations." I stare at a wooden beam in the ceiling.

"Yes, I do. Still…" He's also staring at the ceiling. "I can't believe how badly it went."

I replay the afternoon in my mind. Things continued to worsen as the day progressed. Haley was out to offend and irritate me.

"I recall you saying she was clever and spunky. You said nothing of her snark or downright bitchiness."

"Liv…" he chides me.

Chides me! As though I'm in the wrong.

I whip my head in his direction. "It's the truth!"

In his eyes lies a warning. "Please don't talk about my daughter that way."

I scoff. "We don't know if she is yours yet."

"I do."

I fold my arms over my torso as my stomach tightens. "Really? How?"

"I feel it," he insists with his hand resting over his heart. "She's mine."

"And that gives her the right to say the things she did to me?"

"She was probably nervous or intimidated."

I find it astonishing that he has the audacity to defend her after what went down today.

"Intimidated? By me?" I ask, incredulous. "No one, especially myself, could intimidate that little urchin."

"Olivia, please don't do that."

Olivia… My name calling struck a nerve.

Unable to contain my anger, I sit up and spin to face him. "It's okay for her to call me ugly, but I can't comment on her nasty attitude?"

He groans and drapes an arm over his face. "She didn't call you ugly."

"Um, yeah, she did."

Twenty minutes after I excused myself to the office to calm down, Everett coaxed me to join them in the gallery to talk and get better acquainted. The very first words she spoke to me upon my return were, "Don't take this the wrong way, but you're not at all what I imagined when my dad said he had a girlfriend."

Out of curiosity, I asked her what she had imagined. She said, "I pictured someone hot. My mom was hot and, like, *super* voluptuous. I get my looks from her to give you an idea. So, you can see why you are the opposite of what I expected."

I was done with her after that.

Everett sighs and pinches the bridge of his nose. "I admit, she was a little *snarky* as you said, but I really think it's because she was nervous to meet you."

"Is this how it's going to be?" I ask.

"What do you mean?"

"She can speak to me and treat me however she wants, and you'll defend her? And I'm expected to take it with a smile?"

He waves me off. "That's ridiculous. You're overreacting."

"I am not! I've heard horror stories about kids treating their stepparents horribly."

"You've made it abundantly clear that you have no intention of being a stepparent to her, so don't worry about it."

"I won't allow her to mistreat me, Everett. Not even for you."

His face is tight, and he clenches his jaw. "Can we please not get ahead of ourselves here?"

"That's rich," I laugh.

"What is?"

"You telling me not to get ahead of myself when you're already calling her your daughter and you don't even have the DNA results."

He rolls over, facing away from me. "Good night, Olivia."

I stare at his back, dumbfounded. How can he can possibly be mad at me when I am the wronged party here? "I can't sleep."

"Well I can, so either turn out the light or go find something to do."

"Everett."

"I said goodnight."

I'd like to say we calmed down and became less antagonistic towards each other in the following days, but we haven't. I am constantly on edge. Most of our conversations lead to arguments. At this point, when we speak, it's only out of necessity. Everett has done me one solid, and hasn't brought Haley around again, though he's been with her each evening.

Today they get the results of their DNA test. I'm a wreck. Though our lives have already changed, today, the change becomes official. Neither of us slept. He was awake brimming with excitement. I was filled with dread.

The test result is available online, so Everett called Haley over to read it together. My fingers are still crossed that it is negative, but a part of me feels guilty for it. Whenever Everett talks or even thinks about Haley, his face lights up. He's overflowing with pride and joy over her being his daughter. I want him to be happy, but I'm frightened. We already have so much tension between us. Once that result comes in—if it confirms that he's her father—how will we overcome it? How will we navigate these new waters?

As an act of kindness, I am making brunch. I called Maren for a couple of her recipes that are simple enough for me to prepare. Everett mentioned that Haley loves waffles, so I've made some. I also picked up pastries and bagels. There's enough food for eight people.

"This looks great," Everett says when he walks into the kitchen. His shoulders relax and he pulls me into a one arm hug. "You went all out. Thanks, Liv."

"I wanted to contribute something nice to the day for both of you."

"I appreciate it." He flashes a genuine smile, the first I've seen in days, and kisses my cheek. "And Haley will too."

"I hope so," my voice shakes.

"How are you doing?" His tone is soft as he peers down at me with concern.

"I'm fine."

He tilts his head to the side. "You can be honest."

Can I?

"I'm okay." What else can I say? The truth would just hurt him.

Standing before me, he rests his palms on my shoulders. "I know things are off kilter, but we'll get through it. We'll be okay."

God, I pray he's right. I nod and the doorbell rings.

"She's here." His eyes twinkle and he hurries to the door.

Too anxious to wait, Everett and Haley agree to check the test result before eating. Everett sits in the chair at the desk and Haley stands behind him as he navigates to the lab website and logs into his account. Standing on the far side of the room, my entire body trembles.

If there was ever a time when I needed Grayson, it's now. I try to imagine the advice he would offer. I'm sure he would tell me to count to ten and breathe. That one way or another, everything will work out. One way or another meaning, either Everett and I will get through this together or we won't. But either way, life will go on. And it is up to me to make the most of it. It's up to me to do what I think is best and what will make me happiest in the long run.

As I glance at Everett and Haley, my heart thunders in my chest and my stomach rolls. I shouldn't be in here. This is their moment. I am nothing more than a fly on the wall observing a very important occasion in the lives of two people. I am not one of those people.

"Here we go," Everett says with a nervous smile.

"Let's see it," Haley urges, confident and excited.

Everett clicks the link.

Looking away, I screw my eyes shut and hold my breath.

"Yes!" Haley exults.

"You're mine!" Everett shouts, and I hear him jump from his seat.

When I pry my eyes open, the two are embracing.

It's done.

It's official.

Everett is a dad.

"Get over here." He waves me over to them.

I swallow and force my cemented feet to move. Then I remember, I should smile and will my lips to do so.

Everett pulls me into their embrace.

"We're a family," he says.

No, we're not.

You two are family.

I'm just… here.

I'm an interloper.

Facts are facts.

With results in hand, so to speak, the three of us travel downstairs to partake in brunch. I'm not hungry, but how will it look if I don't eat the meal I prepared? Not wishing to draw attention to myself, I make a plate and join them at the table.

"You mentioned the possibility of staying in Denver for a while if the results were positive," Everett says to Haley. "Do you still plan on doing so?"

She nods. "Yeah. I have nothing to go back to, anyway. My aunt kicked me out right before I came here."

"What?" he snaps, incensed.

"She never wanted me to begin with, but she had no choice. She promised my mom she'd take care of me before she died. But the moment I turned eighteen, she told me flat out she doesn't want me around anymore."

"That's terrible, Haley." He places his hand on hers.

She drops her chin to her chest. "You're all I have."

Everett kneels next to where she sits. "I'm here for you and I want you to stay here with me. With us."

With a quivering lip, she appears to be crying except her eyes are bone dry. "Really?"

"Absolutely."

Ogling her surroundings with greedy eyes, she looks like she just stepped into the lifestyle of the rich and famous. "I can live *here*?"

My heart thuds. *What? No. No, no, no.*

"Sure," Everett replies in his newly discovered dad voice.

No! Where is my say in this?

"Oh, thank God." Haley closes her eyes and draws in a breath. "I was freaking out. I didn't know what I was gonna do. I have no money. The only time I've eaten since being here was when I was with you."

Everett gasps, horrified. "What? Why didn't you say anything?"

I should chime in and show my support, but I'm reeling. I feel terrible for the girl being kicked out and broke with nowhere to go. It must be frightening to be in that predicament. And yeah, offering her shelter is the right thing to do, if only temporarily. But still… I am suddenly sharing my home with Everett's eighteen-year-old daughter, who I didn't even know existed until a few days ago. Adding insult to injury, she's a rude girl who has zero respect for me.

My life made a one-eighty in a matter of days.

Is this really happening?

If I had a dollar for every time I've asked that recently.

"I wasn't comfortable asking for help until I was sure you're my dad."

"You should have said something, Honey." Everett's term of endearment strikes me as odd, though it shouldn't. She is his daughter, after all. "I would've helped you. I'll do everything I can to help you."

"I'm so relieved to not be alone anymore."

Everett pulls her into an embrace and her face relaxes, almost into a smile. And then she shoots me a look that says, "Game on."

What the…

"I'll drive you to the hotel to pick up your things," he offers.

"Actually, it's already in my car," she says. "I only had the room through today."

The rest of the day passes in a blur. I can't recall anything after brunch. I spent the entire afternoon and evening on autopilot. The one thing I remember, right after we ate, I snuck to the bathroom and texted Maren an update, telling her we will call them tomorrow to set up a get together to share "exciting news" with her and Dex.

After Everett and I get Haley set up in the guestroom—I suppose it's her room now—I draw a hot bath to soothe my stiff muscles. Though it's only nine o'clock, I am ready to pass out.

As I finish getting dressed for bed, Everett steps inside, closing the door behind him.

"Haley's squared away," he says.

"That's good." I yawn, stretching my arms overhead.

"Do you mind running the gallery alone tomorrow? Haley needs a few things, so I'm taking her shopping."

I shrug, though I am mega curious what "things" she needs. Or is she milking her rich daddy for all he's worth? "Okay."

"Do I detect a tone?" he asks. "You've run the gallery without me before."

"It's not that." I pull the blanket back and sit on my side of the bed.

Everett sits beside me with worry in his eyes. "What is it?"

I speak low so only he can hear me. I hate having to lower my voice in my own home. "What happened to us making decisions together?"

"What do you mean?" He appears genuinely confused.

"You invited her to move in without even discussing it with me first."

"What else could I do? She has nowhere to go. Should I have said, too bad, so sad?"

"No." I pick at the blanket. "But she's a stranger, and she is living in our home."

"She's my daughter."

"Yeah, but we don't know her. And I suspect there's more to the story of her being thrown out than she's telling us."

"Look," Everett takes both of my hands into his, "the arrangement is only temporary. I'm sure she doesn't want to live with people she hardly knows. I'll help her find a job and get a place of her own. It won't be more than a few weeks, tops."

Chapter 20

"YOU HAVE A KID, WOW," Dex says.

Everett and I sit poolside with Dex and Maren on their deck. Us girls are enjoying sangria while the guys drink their typical scotch.

"I know, right?" Everett says. "Who would've thunk it? Me, a dad."

Maren clears her throat, but recovers with a smile. "Congratulations."

"Thanks." Everett beams.

"Where is she?" Dex inquires.

"She's at home," Everett answers. "I figured the introductions were better saved until after I told you about her. I didn't want to overwhelm anyone."

What about me?

I am beyond overwhelmed.

"So, Liv," Maren starts, "how are you feeling about everything?"

"I'm… fine," I lie. Honesty would instigate a conversation that isn't appropriate for the current setting or company. "It's a shock, but I'm glad for Everett."

"I thought I'd never have kids," Everett says, brimming with joy, "but I'm so excited about Haley. I had no idea how happy having a kid would make me. I finally have a family. I can be the father I never had. Hell, I'm ready to make babies and start living the dad life."

I choke. "What?"

"Just joking, Babe," Everett squeezes my hand. "Kind of. It would be cool to be a stay at home dad."

He's got to be kidding. "Yeah, I won't be having kids anytime soon."

"Well, when you're ready, say the word." He winks playfully. "I'm raring and ready to go."

Rendered speechless, I stare in silence. Who is this man next to me?

Everett turns to Dex and Maren. "I can't wait for you to meet Haley. She is fricking awesome. And stunning. I make beautiful kids, but that's no surprise."

Dex and my sister laugh while I sit stone-still, reeling from what just transpired.

"When is she returning to LA?" Dex asks.

Averting my gaze to the floor, I stay quiet.

"She's not," Everett replies. "She's staying with us."

"With you?" Maren asks, voice high pitched.

"We agreed it's best for her to stay here," Everett answers. "She's only eighteen, with no job, so staying with us is the only viable option for now. And it'll give us time to get to know each other and foster a relationship."

"How are you doing with all this, Liv?" Maren asks me directly.

I repeat a portion of what Everett said, "We agree it's the only viable option."

"I see." She picks up on the fact I mentioned nothing of how I feel.

"It's going to be great," Everett says with a wide grin. He wraps an arm around me and pulls me close. "Me and my two girls."

"A few weeks tops."
Famous last words.

It has been five weeks. Haley still lives with us and *still* doesn't have a job. Well, she *had* a job. A week after she moved in, Everett set her up to work as a receptionist in an upscale salon owned by a friend of his. She lasted a week and a half. She claimed the smell of the hair products made her nauseas. Everett had another receptionist job lined up for her in a friend's law office, but she said she hates receptionist work and asked her father to hire her at the gallery. I put my foot down. Technically, I have no say over what he does with the gallery. It's his. He can employ whoever he wants to do whatever he chooses. But I pleaded with him that it is too much for the three of us to work together and live in the same house. Thank God, he agreed it had potential to be a disaster.

I learned Haley's never held down a job. She bagged groceries part-time in a couple different stores back in LA and worked a few short-lived stints as a waitress. She refuses to do either of those things again as they are "beneath" her. Everett and I sat her down and explained that with such little work experience, any job she gets will be entry level. If she doesn't find anything better in the next two weeks, she promises to "consider" the receptionist job.

It's a Friday night and the moment I walk into the house, it is plain to see Haley didn't complete any of her chores. The carpet isn't vacuumed and her mess from last night still blankets living room. I glance at my kitchen where there are dirty dishes stacked everywhere. A dirty kitchen is my pet peeve, which is why I cleaned it before going to work. My labor was a waste of time since it's even messier now than when I woke! There are enough dirty dishes here that it looks like five people ate.

Perhaps five people ate here. Haley has made friends with some girls who live on our street, and they congregate here often. Hence the mess. She and three of her new friends had a marathon movie session that lasted until four in the morning. I sent Everett downstairs three times to tell them to take their hollering down a notch.

Speaking of movies, I can't recall the last time I could sit in my living room and watch anything. Last time I tried, Haley whined and complained about how boring my movie was, so I tossed her the remote and went to the bedroom to read instead.

It wasn't very long ago that I was Haley's age. I don't remember being a quarter as disrespectful as she is. I'm starting to understand why her aunt kicked her out.

"Hey," she says as she comes down the stairs. "Sorry about the house. I woke up late and then spent the day at Kelsey's."

"Spent the day at Kelsey's?" I ask, skeptical. "The kitchen is demolished."

"We ate lunch here since we have better food than she has at her house."

We. I sigh inwardly. "Please at least pick up the living room."

"I was just getting ready to."

Yeah, right.

My blood pressure rises as I make my way to the kitchen to clean it for a second time today. Haley does nothing of importance all day, but can't be bothered to pick up her own mess? Instead, I have a good hour's worth of cleaning ahead of me after working the entire day.

Forget cooking dinner. That would just be more for me to clean. Tonight, we will order takeout.

Moments later, Everett steps in from the garage.

"What's for supper?" Haley asks him.

Not, "Hi, how was your day?" Not, "Sorry I didn't clean up."

"I don't know yet," he replies and looks around, taking in the horrid sight. Then his eyes find me, slaving away at the mess in the kitchen.

If he dares to ask me what's for dinner…

He walks toward me with eyes full of contrition. He takes a plate from my hand. "I will clean this. I'm sorry."

After a sharp exhale, I whisper yell, "*You're* sorry? *She* should be sorry. *She* should be the one cleaning this mess."

"I'll have a talk with her."

"We've had talks with her." I force myself to keep my voice low enough that Haley can't hear me. "She was supposed to clean today and instead spent all afternoon with Kelsey and the other bimbots."

Bimbot is the name I've given Haley's friends. It's fitting since they're a bunch of promiscuous bimbo's with robot-like personalities.

"Babe… I promise to handle it. And I'll get this place spic and span in no time."

"Order take out for dinner," I sigh. "I'm gonna throw in a load of laundry."

Laundry is another point of contention. I run the washing machine daily since Haley moved in. She changes her clothes no less than two times a day, claiming she has to because of the humidity. And she can't be bothered to wash her own. First, she claimed she didn't know how, so I showed her. Then, she whined and complained that the washing machine is too complicated. Now, she just throws her "dirty" clothes on the washer for me to deal with.

An hour later, I am in the bedroom recliner, feet propped up, engrossed in a mystery novel. I've read more books these past few weeks than in the entire year prior. Reading has always been an escape for me when I'm stressed out.

My blood pressure is down and I am almost relaxed when the door swings open. Praise God, it's Everett. Haley has a bad habit of entering without knocking.

"The living room and kitchen are clean as promised and I ordered Thai for you."

He's trying. "Thank you."

Everett kneels in front of me. "I realize this has been a tough time for you. Having Haley here has been… harder than I expected."

No shit. I assumed her being here would be difficult, but she has managed to surprise even me.

There's a knock on the door and rather than waiting for us to say something, Haley charges into the room.

"Guys, I'm going to Maddie's to spend the night."

"Haley," Everett chides, "we've asked you not to enter without permission."

"I knocked first."

"And instead of waiting for an answer, you barged in," he says.

"Sorry, geez." She rolls her eyes. "I guess you should be glad I'll be gone the rest of the night." With that, she stalks off, slamming our door behind her.

My blood pressure surges once again.

"Babe," Everett says, his hands resting on my thighs, "I'm sorry."

"You apologize on her behalf every single day."

Sighing, he throws his head back. "I don't know what else to do."

Perhaps I should give him a clue.

"She has been here over a month. Still has no job. She eats us out of house and home. She's disrespectful. She complains about everything. She freeloads and destroys our home daily. I can't take anymore."

"I know. What can I say? I'm trying to get her a job but—"

I cut him off. "She doesn't want to work. She wants to live on your dime."

He sits on his heels and rubs the back of his neck. "I'm starting to see that."

"We have to figure something out, Everett. This cannot continue."

"I agree, but what can we do? I don't want to push her away. She's my kid and I only just found out about her."

"What we allow is what will continue." It's a quote I saw on social media the other day, which rings very true in our present circumstance.

"What should I do, Liv?"

"Try a little tough love. Set ground rules. Tell her it's time to accept the receptionist position. That the stipulation for being here is working, and chores are not optional. If she won't do those things, she is on her own."

"I can't say she'll be on her own. I wouldn't mean it."

"Put your foot down with her, Everett. Assert your authority. This is your house and in order to live here, she must abide by your rules. That's how it is in any household with adult children. I had to follow my dad's rules when I lived there. I still do when I go to visit."

He rubs his forehead. "I doubt she'll take kindly to an ultimatum."

"I don't take kindly to any of the things she's done. Does that matter at all?"

"Of course it does. But can't you understand my predicament? Haley barely knows me. I have to tread carefully or risk losing her."

"I understand that, but Everett, do you realize we haven't had sex in over two weeks? She's either barging in on us or we're too tired or I'm too stressed."

I'm not trying to compare lack of sex to loss of a child, but it's imperative he recognizes that Haley has negatively impacted every single part of our life and our relationship.

"Trust me, I realize it, and I hate it as much as you do."

"We have no privacy. No time to ourselves." I stand and pace the room. "You spend most of your time outside of work with her. I spend most of mine in this bedroom by myself. Inviting Haley to stay here *temporarily* was the right thing to do. But based on the way things are going, it's plain to see she has no intention of getting out on her own." I stop pacing, coming to a halt in front of Everett, who is now standing. "And in the honor of full disclosure, I resent you for putting me in this situation."

"I hate that you to feel that way, Babe," he clutches my wrists, "but I understand why you do. I feel awful for it."

"I don't have the answer for fixing things, and I don't expect you to either." With my eyes closed, I tug on my hair. "I'm just saying, we need to figure out something because things can't continue as they have been."

"Agreed. We'll figure it out. I will start by talking to her tomorrow and telling her chores aren't optional." Draping his arms around my waste, he pulls me to him and kisses me on the nose. "And I'll install a lock on our bedroom door."

Maren and I enjoy some of her famous sweet tea outside on her back deck. A gentle breeze blows and the sun hangs low in the sky. Closing my eyes, I inhale. This is the most relaxed I've been in days.

My sister has taken well to being my full time confidant. I think she prefers it this way. One thing is certain, it has brought us closer. Not that we weren't close before. But by opening up to her, she understands how much I trust her, which means a lot to her.

"How is it possible that you have gone through more with Everett in the short while you've been together than I've been through with Dex after years together?"

"I wish I knew," I sigh.

"To be fair, I can see Everett's point of view."

"You can?"

"She's his daughter. He missed out on her entire childhood and is trying to make up for lost time. And he fears upsetting her or letting her down which is only natural."

"What are you suggesting? That I should accept the status quo?" I'm not upset. I want to know what Maren thinks I should do because I haven't a clue.

"I'm saying you may not have a choice. Or, the only choice you might have is to remove yourself from the situation."

I shake my head vehemently. Haley has taken enough from me as it is. "I am not breaking up with Everett over her."

"I didn't say break up, I meant move out," she clarifies. "Just temporarily. You can be together and live apart while he navigates this new chapter in his life."

"I don't want to do that either," I pout. This is horribly unfair. No one is taking me and my feelings into consideration. Why am I being put out and forced to make changes to accommodate her?

"I know, but when kids are involved, it gets complicated and sticky and the kid will *always* be the priority."

I hang my head. "I've figured that out."

The kid should be the priority. I'd never expect Everett to choose me over Haley or to put me above her in his choices. That would be unrealistic. But he should stick up for me when she's in the wrong. He's letting his fear stop him from doing what's right.

"It wouldn't be forever," Maren says. "Maybe in six months or a year she'll get her crap together and be in her own place. Perhaps she will be back in LA by then. In the meantime, you can stay with me and Dex."

"You guys are about to get married. I can't do that to you."

"Married, shmarried." She flicks her wrist. "It's just a piece of paper, and neither of us would care in the least."

"I worry Dex might feel the same way about me as I feel about Haley if I moved in."

"I can assure you, he won't. Dex loves you like a sister."

As much as I hate to admit it, Maren might be on to something. Perhaps the best thing I can do is remove myself from the situation. It will allow Everett time to focus on his daughter and fostering their relationship rather than playing referee between the two of us. I will still see him every day at the office. And I'll be far less aggravated. We'll definitely get along better.

But how do I break the news to Everett without hurting him? I have to convince him it's just a temporary living arrangement. That I will move back in as soon as Haley has moved out.

Regardless of my explanation and the promises I make, he will still be hurt. He was so excited about us moving into the home and sharing our lives. But when I decided to live with him, he didn't have a daughter in his care. If he had, I never would have agreed to live together.

Perhaps my moving out is the push he needs to get her straightened out.

When I walk into the house, it's strangely quiet. Everett sits on the sofa, staring into space. I ask, "Where's Haley?"

Please say she is staying with a friend and we have the place to ourselves for the night. The two of us can make popcorn and cozy up together on the couch for a movie like old times.

Like old times…

But then I notice Everett's anxious, worried expression. Did his talk with Haley go badly? Perhaps she packed her stuff and left.

"What is it?" I go to where he sits.

The television is on, but muted. He clicks it off. "I sent Haley to Kelsey's so we can talk."

My stomach tightens. "Talk about what?"

He pats the cushion next to him and I take a seat.

"As you know, I had a talk with Haley today. I told her what we need from her while she's here. That she has to be better about cleaning up after herself and that she needs to settle on a job."

I rub my hands back and forth on my thighs. "Based on the look on your face, I'm assuming she didn't take it well?"

With a sigh, he rubs his forehead with his index finger and thumb. "She's pregnant."

My heart sinks into my stomach. "What?"

"She hid it from us because she's afraid. It's the reason her aunt kicked her out. She didn't want any part of it."

I remain silent as I digest this information.

Everett continues. "She hasn't been keeping up with chores because of her morning sickness. She's sick day and night. As for getting a job, she isn't sure she'd be able to hold one down with the way she has been feeling."

While it is clear he believes her explanation, I'm skeptical. And exasperated. She hasn't appeared to be the least bit sick since she's been here. She has plenty of energy for going out with her friends and staying up all night.

I slap my thighs. "Pregnant women work, Everett. They cook and clean and they have jobs."

"She's scared, Liv. She's scared about being pregnant and alone. Scared of being a mom if she keeps the baby. She came here so she won't be alone in this. I am all she has."

I think I might vomit. This situation goes from bad to worse every single day. What's next?

"She's just a kid," he reminds me. "How would you feel in her position?"

I wouldn't be in her position, but I don't say as much. "So, what now?"

"She begged me to let her stay throughout her pregnancy. She promised she'll do better and will try to earn her keep."

"So she's staying… here… for…"

"For as long as she needs."

I roll my head back and groan. "This is a never-ending nightmare."

"Olivia!" Everett snaps.

Jumping up, I point in his face. "You don't get to be pissed at me! I'm the one who's pissed! You made yet another decision without discussing it with me."

"I didn't see any other answer, and I'm confident this is the right thing to do. It's the sort of thing you would do." He stands and takes my hands into his, looking at me with pleading eyes. "Being with you has taught me what it means to be selfless and generous and good. I'll get us a bigger house where we can all have our own space, if that will make things easier. I'll hire a housekeeper and a cook. I will do whatever it takes to make this work."

"Everett!" I holler and yank my hands away, clutching my hair in my fingers. "I was barely ready to live with you, let alone your grown daughter and now soon to be grandchild. It's too much! I'm not ready for all this."

"You were ready to give a kidney to your friend's sister! This is what you do for the ones you care about, right?"

Silently, I count to ten and speak in a calm voice. "I understand why you're doing this. It makes sense for you. But it doesn't make sense for me. Did you even consider that? Or is Haley your only concern?"

Everett drags a hand through his hair. "Don't make me choose, Liv."

"Why? Because you'll choose her?"

After a moment, he answers quietly, "Yeah, I will."

Tears flow down my cheeks. As deeply as I love the man before me, and as much as I want to be with him, this hurdle is insurmountable. I walk to him, raise to my toes and kiss him gently. "I love you, Everett. So much. But this can't work."

Chapter 21

MOVING IN WITH MAREN AND Dex is a monumental failure on my behalf. I'm twenty-four years old, jobless and living with my sister and her fiancé. To placate myself, I insist it's only temporary. I will find a job, any job, as soon as possible and get my own place. But I must find roommates unless I land a position making enough to afford an apartment. I'd prefer a place of my own. Even if it is just a tiny studio apartment. I crave my own private space.

Thankfully, the transition to Dex and Maren's has been easy. I didn't have much at Everett's. All the furniture we had he bought. All I had were my clothes, my camera equipment, and a few family heirlooms. It took Maren and I all of three hours to move me out of the house.

Dex has assured me at least a dozen times that I'm welcome to stay as long as I need. He also claims he's not choosing sides. He simply said he's sorry for the way things turned out and that he will help in any way he can. And like a big brother would, he hugged me and let me cry on his shoulder. He truly has become the brother I never had.

Everett hasn't called once. When I told him it was over, he assured me he wouldn't chase me. That if I left, that was it. It was done. We were done.

He meant it.

I'm surprised.

I thought he'd at least *try* to save us.

I should be glad he hasn't. Returning isn't an option. I'm not ready to be a stepmother or a grandma. And selfishly, I wanted Everett to myself. I don't want a part-time boyfriend who's a full-time father. That isn't what I signed up for. His life took a different path than we planned and as such, he must go his way and I'll go mine.

What's done is done.

But it hurts like hell. My first broken heart is a pain unlike any I've experienced.

"Do you have everything you need?" Maren asks once I'm settled into the guest room.

Not even close. "I think so."

She sits beside me on the bed. "Do you want to talk?"

I need to talk, but the person I want to talk to is Grayson. Oh, how I wish he was here. He would have the perfect thing to say, even if it didn't seem perfect at the time.

Grayson knew me better than I know myself. Without fail, he would know what to do, he would hold me and listen. He would assure me I've made the right decision. And he would undoubtedly find a way to make me laugh.

But Maren is my person now.

For some unfathomable reason, I have the need to explain myself. As though I'm trying to justify a horrible mistake. "I wasn't ready for it all. What else could I do?"

"You did the right thing, Liv. You and Everett are in two entirely different places in life."

"Isn't love supposed to conquer all?" I pull a pillow onto my lap and squeeze it to my body. If only I could fill the emptiness… "That's what my mom always said. That with love, you can get through anything."

"I'm of a different opinion on that," Maren admits. "I believe that sometimes love isn't enough. There's so much more to a relationship than being in love. Sometimes, life gets in the way. And timing can be off."

That was precisely what I needed to hear. Life definitely got in our way, and the timing was way, way off. Our love wasn't enough to keep us from crashing and burning. A sob rips from my chest.

"I really loved him—I love him—Mare. And he loves me."

She pulls me into her arms and strokes my back. "Oh, Livvy, I know."

"I've never wanted anything more than I want him. I will never love anyone else this way." So many times, I've heard my friends say that and every time, I resisted a powerful urge to roll my eyes. I never understood. Because I'd never loved anyone, I couldn't comprehend the depth of their despair. I get it now. I'll never again mock anybody with a broken heart.

"Maybe you won't have to."

Pulling back, I peer into her eyes. "What do you mean?"

"I believe you two were the real deal. That you love each other as much as anyone has ever loved another. But the timing is wrong." She sweeps my tear-soaked hair from my face. "Perhaps once he's gotten things squared away with Haley, you'll find your way back to each other."

Oh, how I wish she was right. I'd do anything for that to happen. But it won't.

"He won't take me back," I shake my head. "I hurt him so bad. He accused me of abandoning him when he needed me most."

"Couples get mad at one another. Dex and I get mad at each other all the time. It doesn't stop us from loving each other."

It isn't the same. "But you never walked out on Dex."

"Actually, I have."

I gasp. "What?"

"I've broken up with Dex a couple times."

"I never knew."

"You know me, Liv. I'm a mess. I constantly let my insecurities get the best of me."

"Why didn't you tell me?"

"Because I was too embarrassed. And Dex never let me go for long."

My voice is small, "Everett said he was letting me go. That if I left, we are done for good."

Maren clasps my hand. "He only said that out of anger, Sweetie. He didn't mean it."

"He meant it," I sniffle. "He meant every word."

"Oh, Livvy. Come here," she says and pulls me close once again. "It's going to be okay, I promise."

I haven't seen Everett, nor have I heard a peep from or about him. When I asked Dex about him, he explained that because he loves us both, he isn't playing middleman. He's not telling Everett anything about me, and he isn't talking to me about Everett.

Thursday evening dinners are on hold at present. Everett doesn't come to the house. Dex either meets him out or sees him at Everett's home or the gallery.

I miss working in the gallery almost as much as I miss Everett. I reached out to my old boss a week ago and to my amazement, she was eager to rehire me. My replacement wasn't getting the job done. While I'm not excited about the work, at least it's a paycheck. And she's paying me substantially more this time around. It would seem she has a newfound appreciation for the excellent work I did as her assistant and recognizes my worth.

With my earnings, I should be able to afford my own place. Apartment hunting is next on my to-do list. I don't want to encroach on Maren and Dex any longer than necessary.

It's Friday night and Dex and Maren are out with friends. Is Everett one of those friends? Or is he spending his evening with Haley? Or… is he with someone new?

That's a frequent thought these days. Will he be quick to move on? Will he return to his old ways? Has he already?

When I shared my concerns with Maren, she told me to brace myself. If he hasn't yet, it shouldn't be long. My guess is she knows something but can't tell me because of Dex. Then again, it's possible she's just being a dutiful sister and giving me sound advice. My mind works overtime twenty-four hours a day, considering all the worst scenarios.

But who am I to freak out about what Everett's doing or with whom? I'm the one who ended it. If I hadn't, I'd still be there, and he would be with me tonight.

But I couldn't stay. I was miserable. We all were.

I made the right choice.

I must stop thinking of him incessantly.

My phone pings. Jess and Hannah have been calling and texting all day trying to convince me to go out with them. Their hearts are in the right place, but the last thing I feel like doing is hitting the club. Besides, if I get drunk, I'll just turn into a blubbering mess. Which is what happened last weekend. I spent the entire Friday night crying over Everett and what was and probably never will be again.

Glancing at the screen, I do a double take when I see a text from Callum.

I'd all but forgotten about him. I haven't spoken to him since Dex's birthday party. How did he get my number? Or do I even need to ask?

Callum: *Maren told me about your breakup. I'm sorry. I'm also sorry if it's too soon for me to reach out, but I don't want to miss my chance to say I am throwing my name in the hat. When you're ready, I'd like to take you out.*

It is too soon.

Way, way too soon.

How do I respond to such a message? Do I type "Thank you" or "I'll think about it?"

Before I decide, he sends another text.

Callum: *We should get together as friends. One can never have too many friends. What do you say? I guarantee to make you smile. Maybe even laugh.*

He is as charming as I remember, even via text. Not an easy feat. Perhaps it would be fun to hang out with him. I liked him when I met him. And it would be nice to be around someone with whom I'm not tempted to talk about Everett.

Me: *I could do with a good laugh. A real one that comes from the belly. If you think you can manage that, we can hang out.*

Callum: *I'm confident I can manage that.*

Me: *Okay, but so we're clear, it's not a date.*

After clicking, I worry I may have come across too harsh. I hurry to type another text.

Me: *I'm not ready to date yet.*

Callum: *I understand completely. But a fair warning. Most women find me irresistible. So while I can promise not to come on to you, I can't promise you won't make a move on me.*

Callum: *Just joking.*

Callum: *Kind of.*

Me: *You must be quite the Lady's man.*

Callum: *Nope. I'm a one girl kinda guy. My mom would kill me otherwise.*

Me: *I see. You're a mama's boy. No amount of charm can overcome that hamartia.*

Callum: *Hamartia… Let me google that… Fatal flaw. Ouch! That stings. For the record, I am not a mama's boy. I was just raised to respect women or else get my a** beat. I'd wager she'd still give me a whooping if I did anything wrong.*

I laugh out loud.

Me: *You made me laugh. Not a belly laugh, but you're off to a good start.*

Callum: *Outstanding! So when are we hanging out? Tomorrow?*

Me: *Sure, why not?*

Callum: *Pick you up at six? We can grab a bite to eat.*

Me: *Let's meet. Picking me up is date-y.*

Callum: *That would be a serious hamartia. We can't have that.*

Me: *Haha, laughing again.*

He texts me an address.

Me: *See you there at six.*

As soon as our text exchange ends, I am overcome with guilt. How would I take it if Everett was meeting up with a hot chick who was into him? I'd hate it. It would annihilate me.

But who's to say he hasn't? For all I know, he has already had sex with someone. Grayson once told me it's what guys do when they break up with somebody. Especially if they were in love. They can't handle the pain, so they hook up with the first acceptable and willing female they meet. Knowing Everett's reputation, he's sure to have hooked up with someone by now. Probably Bimbo Barbie that showed up at his door that night so long ago.

Why should I feel guilty about having a platonic dinner with Callum?

I refuse to feel guilty.

Except I do.

Really guilty.

I'm going regardless.

"Atta girl, Liv!" Hannah gives me a fist bump. I've just finished telling her and Jess about my date with Callum. Yes, it turned out to be a date. It went well. *Too well.* "The best thing you can do is get back on the horse."

"Technically, it's a different horse," I say.

"Even better," Jess says. "Show us the picture again."

I pick up my phone and scroll to a selfie Callum took of he and I trying to cook.

He definitely gets credit for most interesting first date. For our date, we went to a cooking class dinner. We prepared our own meal together, following the instructions of a chef. There were three other couples in the class. Except we aren't a couple. Callum got a bunch of pictures and videos. We made quite a mess of our dinner. Neither of us are very good cooks.

"He's gorgeous." Jess pretends to drool.

"He really is," Hannah agrees.

"They say the best way to get over a breakup is by having hot, nasty sex with someone else," Jess says. "Your boy, Callum, looks like he could definitely deliver in that department."

I snort. "You're awful, Jess."

"No, I'm not. I'm honest. And it happens to work."

Hannah Chuckles. "You know this how?"

"I've tried it," Jess answers. "A few times."

I love that she's not the slightest bit ashamed.

Still… "I'm not having sex with anyone for a long while."

"Please say you at least kissed him at the end of the night," Jess says.

I shake my head.

"Girl, that's your loss." She points to Callum's face in the photo. "Those lips beg to be kissed."

I laugh. "I can't kiss Callum when I am still in love with Everett."

"Yes, you can," she assures me. "And you should. I'm telling you, the faster you move on with another guy, the sooner you'll get over Everett."

Others have said the same thing. I don't know if I believe it. I imagine it's akin to putting a bandage on a gaping wound that actually needs stitches to heal properly. All it does is control the bleeding and prolong the healing.

Besides, I'm not looking for a rebound and if I was, I wouldn't choose Callum. Callum has relationship potential and by rebounding with him, I'd kill any chance at ever having something lasting with him.

If that's what I wanted.

Right now, I'm nowhere close to being ready to even consider another relationship.

"I think it's best that I keep Callum in the friend zone until I am over Everett."

"Better not keep him there long," Hannah warns. "That boy probably has lassies chasing after him all over town."

"Lassies?" I snicker.

She nods. "I'm single, I might be one of them."

"You better move over," Jess gives Hannah a shove, "because I'm first in line!"

"I can't believe you didn't tell me you went out with Callum!" Maren playfully swats me on the arm as I join her on her bedroom floor to wrap wedding favors.

"It was a last-minute thing. Not a big deal."

It never occurred to me that Callum might tell Maren about our night out. But why wouldn't he? She's my sister and they are working together on her and Dex's new house.

"He sure posted a lot of photos to his social media for it not being a big deal," she smirks. "You looked like you were having so much fun, Liv. I haven't seen you smile like that in so long."

"It was fun," I admit.

"Are you going out again soon?"

"We aren't dating, Maren. We're friends."

She shrugs. "I'm just happy to see you out enjoying yourself. I worry about you being cooped up in your room all the time."

"I am not in there *all the time*," I protest.

She shoots me side eye. "You only come out for work and sometimes to eat dinner with me and Dex."

She's mostly right. "I needed time to myself while I nursed my broken heart."

"Judging by the pictures I saw, Callum gives the impression of an effective and *fine* nurse." She winks and bumps my shoulder.

I throw my head back and laugh. "Oh my God, you sound just like Hannah and Jess. I'm gonna tell you what I told them. Callum is a great guy and we are hanging out, but that's all it is. I'm not ready to date."

"Whatever it is between you two, I approve, and I hope you'll make," she makes air quotes, "hanging out a regular occurrence."

I stop wrapping. "Can you promise me something?"

"Let me guess, don't tell Dex."

"I don't want it getting back to Everett."

"It won't. Neither of us talks to one about the other. You know that."

"Still, I'd feel more comfortable if this stayed between you and me."

"Why?" She also stops wrapping. "Because you think it'll ruin a chance of a reconciliation?"

"I—I..." Yes. The answer is yes, but I can't say it out loud. It's hard enough admitting it silently to myself.

"Is that where your mind is? You want to reconcile?"

Unable to make eye contact, I pick at a wrapped package in front of me. "I just don't want to kill the possibility down the road."

"I had no idea that's what you were thinking."

"Of course, I am, Maren." I look to her. "I love him. I will never stop loving him. And I will never love anyone else the way I love him."

"Liv, honey," she grips my hand, "we've all said that about people we've since gotten over. Give it time. You'll move on and get over

Everett and you will find someone perfect for you who will make you forget all about him."

She's never been more wrong about anything in her life.

"Even if I'm never with Everett again," I say, "I could never forget him."

He's my first love. One never forgets their first love.

My boss's strictest rule is that I can't have my phone in the studio. It is to be turned off and left in my purse while working. Never mind that hers sits out ringing and pinging and buzzing every three minutes all day long.

While on my lunch break, I take my food out to my car. If I don't leave the premises during my break, she doesn't respect my time and troubles me with work.

Once in the car, I turn on my phone to check for messages. there are a few texts and two voicemails. The texts are from Callum. He sent me a funny selfie and a quote about not being able to find his Monday motivation. I chuckle and move on to my voicemails. The first is Maren asking if I mind swinging by the grocery on the way home to pick up a couple things she forgot yesterday. I send her a quick reply before listening to my next voicemail.

My heart skips a beat when I hear Everett's voice.

He finally called!

"Hey Liv, it's Everett." As if I wouldn't recognize his voice. "Sorry to call, but I have an inquiry on your City Hall print. A lady saw it here when it was on display and asked if she can buy a canvas print. It'd be a large sale. If you want, I'll call the printer and have it done. Call or text to let me know what you wish to do. I told her I'd get back to her by tomorrow. Thanks."

My heart plummets to my stomach. He was just calling about business. His tone was completely professional, not a hint of interest or emotion.

When we broke up and I quit working as his assistant, we both agreed that I would no longer offer my prints in his gallery. A clean break was best, and if I'd kept my prints there, we'd have to be in contact with one another. That could be complicated and potentially "messy" according to Everett.

That he's willing to sell the print for me should make me happy. He doesn't have to do it. He could have told the client it's no longer available.

But I'm not happy. For a moment I thought he was calling to talk. Or perhaps tell me he misses me and wants us to work out our differences.

He didn't say anything. Didn't even say he hopes I'm doing well.

Oh, but the sound of his voice…

I listen to the voicemail again.

And again.

God, I miss the deep rumble of his voice.

I miss everything about him.

My heart races as I stare at the phone screen, debating whether to call or send a text. I want to hear his voice. Perhaps this is a push from God for he and I to talk. If I call, maybe it'll lead to an actual conversation about us.

But I'm a bundle of nerves.

Am I ready for that discussion? Nothing has changed. Haley continues to live with him. Our lives are still on different paths. Besides, do I wish to be with someone who makes all the decisions in what is supposed to be a shared life?

It can't work between us right now. The timing is wrong. Or perhaps we aren't suitable as a couple.

But none of that changes how much I miss him.

How much I love him.

How much I want him.

How much I *need* him.

I take a deep breath and count to ten before tapping "call" on the screen. My foot bounces on the floorboard and I shift in my seat. My fingers are like ice cubes, though I'm not the least bit cold. Last month, I never would have dreamed of being this anxious over calling him.

I've called his cell phone out of habit. It would have been better to ring the gallery. Too late now.

"Hello," he answers formally, although he must realize it's me. Only weeks ago he would have answered with some derivative of "Hi, Babe."

"Hey," I try to control the trembling in my voice. "I just got your message."

"Yeah," he clears his throat and cuts to the chase, "a client wants a forty-eight by sixty of your City Hall photo. What do you want to do?"

My mouth is bone dry. "If you don't mind having it done for her, sure."

"She's buying a print of mine, so I'd like to do it for her."

"Okay. Do you still have the file for printing?"

"It's on the computer. I won't do anything without your permission, but if you want me to delete your files after today, I will."

"It's up to you. I trust you."

"Mmm…" I detect cynicism in his tone. "I'll get her set up and will mail you the payment check, minus my commission, of course."

He doesn't sound like himself. He's distant and cool.

What else did I expect after breaking up with him and moving out during the most important time in his life? I recognize my fault in this and I own it.

"Of course," I repeat his words and swallow.

"Okay, I'll—"

I cut him off. He is preparing to end the call, but I can't say goodbye. "Everett?"

"Yeah?" His tone is clipped.

"I—uh… how are you?"

"Seriously?"

"I know we broke up but—"

It's his turn to interrupt me. "I'm not doing this, Olivia. I will not sit on the phone making idle chit chat with my ex-girlfriend."

"Okay…"

"I'll take care of the print and delete your files. I gotta go."

With the deafening sound of a click, he's gone.

That hurt.

Gaping at my phone, tears spring to my eyes. My chest aches. How will I find the strength to go back into the studio and work for the next five hours?

Chapter 22

ANY PROGRESS I'D MADE, OR thought I'd made, since my breakup with Everett was undone by our phone call. I've reverted to spending all my time in my room feeling sorry for myself and trying not to cry.

People, Maren included, say time heals all wounds, including broken hearts. How can that be true when my pain is more intense now than it was the day we broke up?

Before speaking with Everett, I had plans to hang out with Callum today. We were going to hike the Mesa Trail. I texted him last night saying I need to change my plans. He seemed okay with it and said he'd see me another time, hopefully soon. But for the past hour, he's been texting and ringing my phone off the hook. All I want to do is lie in this bed wallowing in the misery I've created for myself. It's what I deserve.

Maren has tried to coax me out of my room. She asked me to go with her to the farmer's market since Dex has plans for the day, but I refused. She even pulled the, "If you don't get your butt out of bed, I'm gonna throw ice cold water on you," line and it still didn't work. I just shrugged and told her to do whatever she needs to do.

It's almost two o'clock and all I've done is eat a bowl of cereal and brush my teeth. I wouldn't have eaten, but Maren pleaded with me to eat something. She prattled on and on for an hour about how worried she is for me. Finally, I caved.

As I drift into a much-appreciated nap, the doorbell rings. Moments later, I hear footsteps coming up the stairs and sit upright in the bed. *What now?* No doubt my sister wants me to come down and entertain her guest.

"Liv?" Maren knocks on my door.

I suppress a groan. "Yeah?"

She opens my door and pokes her head inside. "You have a visitor."

A visitor? I haven't invited anyone over. "Who?"

"Callum."

"What?" I holler.

She steps into my room and closes the door. "You will not be rude to guests in my house, so get out of bed, fix yourself up and get downstairs. You have ten minutes."

"What is he doing here?" I grit my teeth.

She puts her hands on her hips. "I invited him."

"Then he's your guest, not mine."

She rolls her eyes. "Don't be juvenile. He's here to see you."

I whisper yell. "Because you told him to come!"

"Because I will not let you wallow in sorrow any longer. So get your ass out of that bed and go downstairs pronto!"

As Callum and I start our hike, I ask the question that has nagged me since we left the house. "What did Maren say when she called and asked you to stop by?"

"I'll tell you, but you gotta promise not to get mad at her."

I can't make that promise. "It was that bad?"

"No. Your sister loves you. She's worried about you."

It was that bad. "Now you *have* to tell me what she said."

We quit walking and he turns to establish eye contact. "She said you're having a really hard time with the breakup, but it seems you have fun with me. Her exact words were, please come and make Livvy have some fun."

"That's all she said?" As if that isn't cringeworthy enough.

"Pretty much, yeah." His smirk tells me there was more.

I cross my arms. "Pretty much?"

A group of hikers approach and we step to the side of the trail so they can go ahead of us. At first, they're laughing and carrying on until they notice our serious expressions. They probably think we're an arguing couple. I force a smile and say "Hi" as they pass. Once they're out of earshot, Callum answers.

"She said the only time she's seen you smile since your breakup was in the pictures I took when we went out."

Jesus, Maren! "She's being overdramatic."

"I'm sure she is. That's her way. But it gave me an excuse to see you."

I grin despite myself. "I guess this is better than sitting in my room."

"That's what you were going to do today?"

Shit. Now he knows I canceled our plans for no good reason. "I'm sorry, Callum."

"Don't be sorry, Liv. I get it." Looking to the ground, he kicks a rock. "I've had a broken heart. I know what it feels like."

It seems everyone joins the broken-hearted club sooner or later.

"Can I ask a question?"

"Sure."

"How long did it take to get over it? To stop hurting?"

"It seemed like forever." He glances up to the sun. "It was a solid year before I started feeling normal again."

"That long?" My stomach rolls. I can't go on like this for a year.

"My circumstances were a little different. Alicia and I were happy and in love when she died of leukemia."

Suddenly, I view Callum in a whole new light. I have a newfound respect and appreciation for him. He's a kindred. He knows the pain and grief that death of a loved one leaves in its wake.

Having his heart broken that way must be far worse than my mere breakup. "Oh, Callum, I am so sorry."

"Thanks," his smile is sincere, "but I'm okay. It's been three years. I still think of her and I miss her, but I've made peace with it. Maren told me a good friend of yours recently died in a tragic accident."

I nod. How much have these two talked about? "Grayson was my best friend."

"I'm sorry for your loss, Liv." He gently encircles my wrist with his fingers. "For both losses you are presently experiencing. Just know, the pain eases over time. You'll eventually reach a point where it'll hurt less when you think of them. Eventually, you'll just have fond memories of the time you spent together."

His words are the most poignant and honest that anyone has offered amidst my suffering.

"Thank you, Callum," I peer into his kind, sapphire eyes. "I'm glad you showed up today."

"Me, too."

As the days pass, I find Maren was right. I do smile when I'm with Callum. Spending time with him isn't just fun, it's effortless. We enjoy many of the same things. The time I spend with him is similar to hanging out with Grayson, but with an added physical attraction.

A strong attraction I was unable to deny after three glasses of red wine last night.

Turning to my side, I find Callum sleeping peacefully beside me. I roll to my back and scrub my face with my hands. With my stomach in knots, I scream at myself internally. *What is wrong with me?*

Sliding out of bed as quietly as possible, I grab my clothes from the floor and tiptoe to the bathroom. In the mirror is the reflection of a woman I don't recognize. A hideous, shameful trollop.

I've just led Callum on in the most horrific way. Sleeping with him indicates that I want something I don't. Yes, I like him. Yes, I feel a powerful attraction to him. But I'm not ready for a relationship, and I'm not the kind of female who sleeps with a guy I'm not in a relationship with or at least want a relationship with. I still hope to one day reconcile with Everett, despite how unlikely the possibility.

I take a deep breath and after staring at the shower stall for several long moments, turn on the water. Maybe I can wash away my wickedness.

But when I step out of the shower, I feel no cleaner. No calmer. No less ashamed.

I brush my teeth using my finger and gargle with mouthwash. Surprised to find that Callum has a hair dryer, I blow out my hair. Once I am reasonably presentable, yet thoroughly embarrassed, I head out to the kitchen where I hear Callum moving about.

My heart hammers in my chest. I'm not prepared to face him, but we need to talk. It's crucial that I set things straight. I can't let him think last night was something it wasn't or that we are something we're not.

"Hey there," he says with his gorgeous as ever smile.

You can to this, Liv.

You have to do this.

"Hey." I clasp my hands behind my back, wringing my fingers together.

Thank God he doesn't move in to kiss me. That would be awkward.

"I have little in the way of food," he says, his expression a mixture of embarrassment and contrition. "I hope frozen waffles are okay."

"Actually, I'm not hungry." I point to the coffeemaker and the array of creamers and sugar he has sitting out, along with an empty mug. "But I'll have a cup of coffee."

Once I have my coffee in hand, I ask Callum to join me at the dining room table. As I open my mouth to begin my speech, he speaks.

"I see the regret in your eyes," he starts. "I wish I could say it doesn't bother me, but it does. However, I do understand. It was too soon to sleep together."

Thank God he understands. "I shouldn't have let this happen. But I was caught up in the moment and there was wine and you're *so* great." I motion back and forth between us. "Obviously, there's an attraction here. But I'm not ready."

"I know," he clasps my hand with his, "and it's okay, Liv. We can take a step back. I can't pretend like this didn't happen. I can't pretend it wasn't a fantastic night for me, anyway. But I don't want it to mess up our friendship."

"I can't pretend this didn't happen either, and last night was great," I confess. "*You* are great. And I don't want it to come between our friendship, either."

"So, we agree to take a step back?"

As the tension leaves my body, I exhale. "It would be wonderful if we could."

"Liv, I like you. I *really* like you." With his eyes trained on mine, he scoots closer. "You're the first girl since Alicia that I've liked this much. And it's not about sex. I genuinely like you as a person and I enjoy spending time with you. But I understand and respect that you need to ease into your next relationship. I am a patient guy and I'm in this for the long haul."

Damn, why is he so perfect? "You are too good for me."

"Actually, I think I am just right for you. And you're just right for me." Raising my hand to his lips, he plants a delicate kiss on my skin. "And when the time is right, we'll be just right together."

He certainly says all the right things.

Maybe he is right for me.

If I had met Callum first, would I still have fallen for Everett? Or would I be blissfully happy with the wonderful guy sitting here with me?

On my way to work this morning, I received a text from Carmen inviting me over this evening. Since we haven't spoken since the breakup, her request comes as a complete shock. Though I doubt the invitation is so we can hang out and share girl time. While she and I were friendly when Everett and I were together, she is his friend, not mine. Her loyalties are with and to him, as they should be.

"You know me as a straight shooter," Carmen says almost as soon as I step into her house. "So, I'm gonna tell it to you straight."

I gulp. "Okay."

"I like you, Liv," she says. "I especially like you for Everett. Everett was the best version of himself when he was with you. It was a version I have never known in all the years I've been his friend."

Given the way the Carmen began the conversation, I was expecting a harsher speech. I hadn't realized I was so uneasy until all my pent-up anxiety washes away and my muscles relax.

"I believe you care for Everett as much as he cares for you."

It isn't lost on me that she speaks of our feelings in the present tense, and I appreciate it. "I do."

"Then put an end to this ridiculousness! Call the man and makeup already."

If only it was that easy. "The last time we spoke, he made it perfectly clear he doesn't wish to talk to me."

With a groan, she sweeps her long raven tresses to one side. "He's hurting, Liv. The guy is a mess. I have never seen him so low."

"He didn't seem to be hurting when we talked." He was impatient and irritated.

Shifting her weight from one foot to the other, Carmen rubs her temples. "Of course he didn't. He doesn't want you to see how much he's suffering. But let me assure you, he is. He's *broken*."

"I didn't do this to hurt him, Carmen." Gesticulating wildly, I pace the length of her living room. "I didn't know what else to do. We were in a mess. Our life and our home was in shambles and I was powerless to do anything to change it or make it better."

"I know. And now he knows. He realizes he messed up. That he gave Haley too much power." She sighs and crosses her arms. "Don't even get me started on that girl. The moment you were out of the picture, she turned up the dial on her manipulation. I had to all but smack him in the face to make him see it."

While I'm sorry to hear that, I'm not surprised. I realized she was out to take advantage of him on day one.

"But that's not why I called you here," she says. "I called you here to warn you."

"Warn me?"

"You have about thirty seconds to fix this with Everett or he will revert to his old womanizing ways, except this time it'll be a thousand times worse."

Carmen's words are sobering. He hasn't been sleeping around. Yet. But the pain is eating at him, the same way it's eating at me. That ache pushed me to sleep with Callum. It could easily push Everett into another woman's bed. If I don't want that to happen, now is the time to act.

But the thing about me is, I can't lie. I can't keep secrets. I've slept with another man. One way or another it will come out and once it does, Everett will hate me.

"I'm not sure it's possible to fix things now."

"Sure, it is." Carmen moves closer, her eyes drilling into mine. "Everett loves you so much, Liv. It's all he talks about. You wouldn't even have to live together. You can put the brakes on those plans until the situation with Haley gets worked out. He just wants you back any way he can have you."

He does? Did he actually say that? If that's how he feels, why hasn't he told me? Why won't he talk to me?

If Carmen is saying it, it must be true. But I messed up. I believed Everett was done with me. That he didn't want me anymore. I have made a gargantuan mistake.

I tuck my chin to my chest with shame.

"Please don't tell me you're seeing someone," she pleads. "You know what, it doesn't even matter. Drop the guy. You love Everett. You belong with him."

"I'm not seeing anyone," I confess. "But I've met somebody and I… I slept with him. I can't lie to Everett and once he knows, he'll never forgive me."

Carmen's eyes widen more from shock than judgment, though I detect at least a smidgen of the latter. "Wow, Liv. I wasn't expecting that out of you."

"I'm not proud of it." Unable to stand any longer, I drop onto the sofa and hold my head in my hands. "I hate myself for it."

"Forget it," she waves her hand. "We all make mistakes. Everett has made more than his fair share. There's no need to tell him. It happened while you were apart, so it doesn't count. It's not his business. And what he doesn't know can't hurt him."

She sounds as though she's trying to convince herself as much as me. She knows as well as I do that Everett will never accept me sleeping with someone else.

"I've never been able to lie," I explain. "Never. I'm terrible at it. It will spill out at some inopportune time. Probably while in the middle of dinner in a crowded restaurant. It'll bubble to the top until I can't take lying to him any longer."

"But it's not a lie," she reasons. "A lie would be to say no if he asks if you've slept with anyone."

"And if he were to ask?" There is a chance that he could.

"I seriously doubt he will, but if he does, I guess you'll have to… fib."

As if changing the word from lie to fib makes it less punitive. I shake my head. "I don't even know how to go about talking to him. He was so cold and distant last time."

Carmen sits beside me and places a hand on mine. "And he'll probably be that way again, but it's just an act, Liv. He's putting up a front to spare his pride. But that man loves you more than anything on this planet. If you love him even half as much, go to him and work this out."

As I pull into the gallery parking lot, my entire body trembles. My heart races and pounds hard. I can't believe I'm about to do this.

By the time I left Carmen's yesterday, she had me convinced that what I shared with Everett is salvageable. But if we are to save it, it must be now before any further damage is done.

My boss wasn't happy, but I took off work a half hour early so I can get to the gallery before Everett closes for the day. We need privacy for this conversation, so going to his house isn't an option.

I arrive five minutes before closing. There isn't a second to waste. With an upward glance, I whisper a prayer before opening my car door and stepping out.

As I walk toward the entrance, I hear Grayson's voice. "You can do this. It will be fine. He loves you."

Feigning confidence, I sturdy my posture with my shoulders back and chin high. I shake my hands and flex my fingers before pulling the door open.

Chapter 23

THE BELL RINGS AS I enter. I spy Everett sitting at the front counter wearing a sullen expression. He looks up with tired eyes, but they widen with surprise once he realizes it's me.

"Hey," I say, testing the waters.

"Hey."

I hate that this is so awkward. "I'm here to talk."

"Okay…" He clears his throat. His eyes are glued to me with a probing stare as I move toward him. His walls are up.

There's no sense beating around the bush, so I get straight to the point. "I miss you."

"I…" He rubs the back of his neck. "Liv—"

Holding up a hand, I cut him off before he can rebuke me. "I was hasty in my decision to walk away. I made the wrong choice in the heat of the moment."

As I walk closer, he stands from his stool. For the smallest moment, I catch a spark of hope in his eyes before his guard is back up.

"I was overwhelmed," I continue, "and didn't know what to do. I can't tell you how sorry I am because there aren't words to express it. But I am so deeply sorry. If I could go back in time, I never would've left. But I can't go back in time, so all I can do is beg for forgiveness."

Everett's shoulders relax, and the slight smile on his lips tells me I've said the right words. "I'm just as guilty. I should've talked to you first. I should have included you in the decisions I was making. We should've decided together, but I honestly thought it's what you would do."

His cellphone rings but he ignores it.

"It was the right thing to do, and had we discussed it, I probably would have agreed to it, but…"

"But what?" His iridescent irises penetrate mine.

I stare at him, apprehensive, afraid I'll say the wrong thing to upset him and ruin the opportunity to work this out.

"It's okay," he coaxes me with a gentle voice and closes the distance between us. "You can say it."

"It still wouldn't have been an ideal situation. Not for me."

He nods. "I know, but I could've made it easier for you by putting my foot down and not allowing Haley to trample all over us—over you. I should've set boundaries and laid out rules for living in our home."

"Or I could have stayed with Maren and Dex for a little while to give you time with Haley."

He shakes his head. "You shouldn't have to leave your home… You shouldn't have been run out of your home."

"I admit I felt like a second-class citizen there."

He winces at my words and sighs. "I feared pushing her away, so I let everything fall on you and that wasn't fair." He turns away and drags a hand through his hair. "By trying not to push her away, I pushed you away instead and then had the nerve to blame you for it."

Placing a palm on his arm, I turn him to face me. "We both made mistakes."

"If I could go back in time, I'd do things differently, too."

"But we can't go back."

"What should we do then? I miss you, Liv. Being apart from you is killing me."

That is all I wanted to hear.

"Me, too."

His phone rings again and he squeezes his eyes shut with irritation. "I'd stay here all night and talk with you, but…"

"You have to go."

"I promised Haley I'd take her somewhere. Forgive me?"

I nod. As disappointed as I am that he has to leave, I'm overjoyed that we've had this talk and are in the process of working through our issues. All is right in the world again.

"Don't be sorry. You weren't expecting me."

"I'm so glad you came."

"I should've come sooner."

He steps closer, and I am enveloped by the warmth radiating from his body. "I want to kiss you."

"Then kiss me." I angle my face upward, the way I have so many times in the past when awaiting his kiss.

With palms on either side of my face, Everett gazes lovingly into my eyes. Oh, how I have missed having him look at me this way. As though he's trying to soak in every second of this moment, he moves in slowly, placing soft kisses on each side of my mouth before pressing his lips to mine. When he sweeps his tongue across my bottom lip, I whimper at the sensation I have yearned for. Everett pulls me to him until our bodies are flush and his hands move into my hair, tugging as he moans into my mouth. His lips are demanding as his tongue dances with mine. When his phone rings yet again, Everett groans and squeezes me tighter, kisses me harder. When he finally pulls away, it's with reluctance. He doesn't want to leave me anymore than I want him to go.

"I'll call you later," Everett says as he walks me to my car. He opens my door and kisses me tenderly before I get inside.

He stands, hands in his pockets, and watches me drive away. Nothing could remove the ridiculous smile on my face. However different our lives are, despite how complicated things may be, I am certain we can make this work.

Everett called last night to wish me sweet dreams and asked me to meet him at the gallery after I get off work. The day has moved at a snail's pace. I am eager to see him and finish the discussion we started. I have no doubt we will come to a resolution and decide how to move forward, together.

The moment the clock strikes six, I say a quick goodbye to my boss, grab my purse and keys and hurry to my car. I force myself not to speed like a maniac on my way to the gallery. I'm too excited to see Everett.

My Everett.

I pull into the parking lot, and not caring how I park, take up two spaces. I jump out of the car and dash to the door, unable to get inside fast enough. The instant I step inside, our eyes meet and he greets me with a smile wider than my own.

"Finally," he says and draws me into a tight embrace. "This day dragged on forever."

"I thought six o'clock would never come."

He playfully kisses my nose, followed by a slow but passionate kiss on my lips. "I'll lock up. Why don't you head into the office?"

The instant he steps into the room, he wraps his arms around me. "I haven't been able to stop thinking about seeing you since last night,"

"Same here."

"Let's never breakup again." He gazes adoringly into my eyes.

"Are we back together?"

"You're damn right we are. We never should've been apart."

I snuggle close, my cheek pressed to his chest where I can hear his steady heartbeat. "This feels so good."

"I want to hold you all night."

"You'll get no complaints from me."

He pulls back to establish eye contact. "We should talk before we get carried away."

Standing to the side, I watch as Everett arranges the armchairs in front of the desk so they are facing each other. Once finished, he gestures for me to sit.

"I promise you," he begins, but stops and shakes his head. "no, I swear on my life to never make another decision that affects you without first talking with you."

"Thank you." With a smile, I reach for his hand. "I promise to never again walk away if things get tough. I will communicate my needs and feelings in a clear yet respectful manner."

"We definitely need better, more open communication. And I'll stop assuming that I can read your mind."

"I think our biggest obstacle is lack of experience. Neither of us has been in a serious relationship. We've never lived with someone or had a partner. We have to learn to think in terms of *we* instead of *I*. I know I've been guilty of that."

He nods. "I've been guilty of it many times and for that, I apologize."

"Another part of our problem is we jumped right into the deep end. We forged full steam ahead in our relationship. This time, we should move slowly to build a solid foundation."

"That's not a bad idea." His smile is small and almost sad. "As badly as I want you home with me, Haley will be there for at least six months. She hasn't yet decided whether to keep the baby. If she does, she won't move out right away. I'm guessing you aren't interested in living with me, Haley *and* a newborn."

I shake my head. "Not really, no."

"All that matters to me is that we work this out." He squeezes my hand and scoots his chair closer. "We don't have to live in the same house to be together. But I would love for you to come back to the gallery. You have to admit, we work well together."

"Yes, we do, but I can't bail on my boss so soon. I should give her a couple months to find a replacement."

"That's a bummer, but I understand and respect your choice. You can return when you're ready."

"As much as it sucked, we both learned a lot in our time apart."

Tugging at my wrist, he pulls me onto his lap. "Yeah, we did."

While playing with the curls in his hair I notice it's longer than usual. "So it's official. We're back together."

"It was official when I kissed you yesterday." He rests his forehead on mine. "I love you, Liv. More than anything."

"Ditto." I lean in for a kiss, but he pulls away.

"Say it," he pleads. "I need to hear it."

"I love you, Everett. I always will."

With a slow smile, his gaze darkens as he cups the back of my head with both hands. He smells so good, just as I remember. His delicious scent and hypnotic eyes have me intoxicated.

Everett leans in, placing his lips on mine, and within a moment he's subtly devouring me. His warm, wet tongue flicks and rolls with mine. Lord, I have missed this man. Sliding my fingers into his hair, I give it a tug. Suddenly, I am panting with an undeniable ache between my legs. I position myself so I'm straddling him and grind down onto his bulge. He's ready. As always.

Our kissing grows wild and carnal. Unable to wait another second, I tug at the hem of his shirt and lift it over his head. As soon as it hits the floor, I pull mine off. Something raw flashes in Everett's eyes before he leans in and takes my mouth softly and slowly.

If mouths could make love, that's what this is.

"I missed this," I murmur.

Throwing my head back, I graze his naked chest with my fingertips. His eyes close as he revels in the sensation of my touch. Mimicking my movements, he strokes my bare abdomen up and down.

"I've missed touching you," he says. His eyes open and he cups my cheek. In his eyes is a mixture of hunger and tenderness. He guides my face to his and kisses me again, slipping his tongue inside so slowly, as though he's savoring me.

Everett unfastens my bra and eases the straps over my shoulders before dropping the garment to the floor. With his eyes glued to my breasts, he sweeps his thumbs over the hardened peaks of my nipples. A shiver runs down my spine and I moan with satisfaction. He knows just how to touch me. I continue to brush my fingers over his chest and abs as he caresses my breasts.

Everett was born with perfect genetics. He's gorgeous with a muscular athletic build. I take pleasure in exploring the grooves of his muscles as my palm slides low, low, low until it hovers at the button of his jeans. We make eye contact and his all but beg me to unzip his pants and take him into my hand.

I am happy to give him what he wants, but will take my time doing it. With my eyes still locked on his, I unbutton his jeans and leisurely pull the zipper down. To taunt him further, I dip just the tip of my index finger into the waistband of his black boxer briefs. The thought of touching him after all this time has me feverish. Still… I take my time. For us, foreplay was always as exciting and important as the main event. I get high from the yearning in his eyes.

Finally, I slip my fingers into his boxers and find his hot and hard length. I tug once and he groans before claiming my mouth once again. I stroke him up and down, eliciting deep moans of his approval. His breathing quickens and his body shudders. He's getting close already, so I remove my hand. As much as I want to satisfy him, that pleasure won't be from my hand.

I stand and take off my pants along with my panties, and Everett shoves his pants and boxers to the floor. We're both naked, and he stands in front of me stroking his erection, staring at me as though he's a predator and I his prey.

Everett steps forward, closing the distance between us and kisses me again, this time hard and fast. He's losing control. The room spins as I become high from his touch and the joy of being his once more. His strong arms circle my waist and he lowers us to the floor. The tile is cold and unforgiving, but I don't care. All that matters is that I am in Everett's arms, being loved and worshipped.

The brush of his fingertips against my bare skin is heavenly. He bends his head forward and licks and sucks the skin of my neck. My back arches and my body twists in pleasure.

"You taste so good, Baby," he croons and lowers his mouth to one throbbing nipple.

I spread my legs so he's cradled between them, his hardness pressed into my center, and clutch his hair. He drives me wild with the way he nips and sucks with his mouth and pinches and caresses with his fingertips.

"That feels good," I whimper when he rolls his tongue around my nipple. I tug at him to bring his face to mine. I'm ready. Needing him to be inside me, I curl my fingers around his shaft and bring the tip to my entrance. With my legs around his waist, I squeeze, trying to pull him inside me.

"I've never wanted anyone the way I want you," I say. "I'll never want anyone but you. You're the only man for me."

Never in my life have I regretted anything as much as I regret sleeping with Callum. But having done so makes me realize how profound my love is for Everett. Now, more than ever, I believe that I belong with this man.

Something flashes in Everett's eyes and he squeezes them shut.

"I love you so much." He presses into me. "So much, Liv."

"I love you, too," I reply, rocking with him as he moves within me.

His eyes remain closed, which is odd, but maybe he is overcome with emotion. I certainly am.

"You're everything to me," he murmurs as he pulls out and pushes in slowly. "No one compares to you. No one feels as good as you."

He opens his eyes and gazes down at me. He looks worried, but why? Everything is perfect. Or at least it should be. We are together.

He stops moving but stays inside me.

Something isn't right.

"Are you okay?" I ask.

His voice is thick with emotion as he says, "I love you."

"I love you, too."

Softening within me, he pulls out.

"What's wrong?" I ask.

Dragging a hand through his hair, he drops his head. Is being with me making him emotional? Or is he feeling regret?

"I can't lie to you, Liv."

My heart stutters. He doesn't want this. He's unsure about us. But just moments ago, when he declared his love for me, he seemed as sure as ever.

"You can talk to me."

With a shake of his head, he stands and pulls on his jeans. Following suit, I stand and get dressed.

"I need to tell you something," he says, "but there's a good chance it will ruin everything."

I'm struck with the realization of what he is preparing to say. As much as I hate it, it oddly makes me feel a little better.

"What is it?" I ask gently. "It'll be okay, I promise."

He looks upon me reluctantly with eyes full of shame. "I slept with someone."

I blow out a breath. Though it sucks to hear the words, I'm relieved that we can be honest with each other. I reach for his hand. "It's okay. I did too. I didn't know how to say it, and I hated keeping it from you. But this is good because we've canceled each other out."

Everett yanks his hand away and his expression is one of devastation and repulsion. "You slept with someone?"

I stand stone still, confused. Didn't he just admit to the same thing?

He repeats his question, this time louder, "You slept with someone while I was hurting?"

Wait. How can he be upset with me when he is guilty of the same?

"You slept with someone too," I remind him.

"You broke up with me!" He has never yelled at me so loudly. "*You* walked out on *me*!"

"Everett…" I start but, what do I say? I knew the truth would hurt. His truth isn't the highlight of my week either, but I'm willing to deal with it. I accept it. "It was a mistake. It meant nothing."

"Just… Wow." He looks me up and down with cold, dead eyes, his lip curled back in disgust. "I can't even look at you. Get out."

"Everett—" I reach for him and he jerks away.

"I said, get out."

Chapter 24

NINETEEN DAYS HAVE PASSED SINCE our last and seemingly final breakup. I've tried everything I can think of to get Everett to talk, and he refuses. He wants nothing further to do with me. He's even blocked me from calling or texting his cellphone. I wrote him a letter explaining my side, pleading for him to speak to me. He marked the envelope 'return to sender'. We are really and truly over this time.

I am astounded by his hypocrisy. How can he justify being so angry and unforgiving when he did the same thing? I can't reconcile it. He's completely irrational. According to Maren, I don't have to understand it, but I must accept it. My dad says it sounds like "sage advice."

Whether or not Everett wants to, he'll see me this afternoon. Today is Dex and Maren's rehearsal dinner. Dex spoke with Everett, and his request was that I not engage with him. He has nothing to say to me, and if I play my part, there will be no drama. I promised Maren I would comply.

Tonight will be pure and utter hell.

Nevertheless, I will do my utmost to plant a smile on my face and be a chipper and dutiful Maid of Honor.

Dex and Maren have chosen an outdoor wedding at a friend's estate just outside Denver. It's a ten-bedroom fifteen-bathroom mansion nestled on a thirty-acre wooded lot. Their ceremony will take place in front of a seven-acre pond.

Given the small size of the wedding party—Maren, Dex, Me, Everett, and the parents of the bride and groom—we are all staying here for the next two days. The idea is party tonight, have the ceremony tomorrow afternoon, celebrate again tomorrow night and leave the following morning. The plan sounds fabulous except for the part where I will spend two days under the same roof with Everett.

I can do this.

I can *do this.*

I will keep my emotions in check.

I will not cause unnecessary drama.

Maren's wedding will be perfect.

I've endured worse things than being in my ex-boyfriend's presence. I survived the deaths of my mom and my best friend. If I can do that, I can do this. And I'll do it with a smile on my face.

But then Everett arrives. He exchanges greetings and hugs with everyone except me. He doesn't even look in my direction. Did someone drive a dagger through my heart? I can't breathe.

Maren glances my way with concern. With a nod and a smile, I signal that I'm okay, although I'm not. While the guys chat, she comes over to me.

"I hate that this is hurting you," she says with pronounced pity.

With a shrug, I flash another smile. "What doesn't kill you makes you stronger."

"On the way here, we adjusted the wedding procession."

I arch a brow.

"You won't be walking down the aisle with Everett. My mom will go first. Then Everett followed by Dex and Sharon. You will go next, followed by me and Dad."

Guilty and ashamed, I lower my gaze to the floor. "You don't have to change your wedding for me, Mare."

"It's no big deal, Liv." She brushes my arm with the back of her hand. "Besides, the less contact between the two of you, the better."

"It's your wedding. You do what you think is best." Squaring my shoulders, I face her with confidence. "But I'm a big girl. I can walk down an aisle with Everett without falling apart and bawling my eyes out."

"No, you can't," she declares. "Weddings are emotional as it is Liv. Throw in a broken heart and bodily contact with the man you love but can't have, and you've got a recipe for disaster. Besides, it isn't just you we're worried about."

Before I can ask what she means, in walks another guest.

Sharon. Mama Stevens.

During my time with Everett, I got to know her well. She's a fantastic woman. She's fierce but hilarious. We spent a lot of time on the phone "shooting the shit" as she would say. Everett acted like he hated it, but he loved it. My close relationship with her thrilled him. He once remarked that even though he thought he'd never end up in a serious relationship, he knew if he did, the woman would need to earn Mama's seal of approval.

When we told everyone about Haley, Sharon was the first to call and speak with me, asking how I felt and how I was holding up. When I moved out, she called to say she was pulling for us to work it out. She believed that Everett and I were made for each other.

So did I.

We were wrong.

Sharon greets Dex first with hugs and kisses, telling him how much she adores him and how proud she is of him. Next she embraces Maren and tells her how she loves her like a daughter and can't wait for it to be official. Then she goes to Everett, pulling him close before examining him from head to toe. She hugs him again and whispers something in his ear.

Finally, she turns to me with a halfhearted smile.

"Baby Girl," that was the nickname she adopted for me. "It's so good to see you."

"You too, Sharon."

"I still wish you'd call me Mama." She draws me into a hug and squeezes tight. When she pulls away, she examines me the same way she did Everett. "How are you doing, Dear?"

"I'm good. You?"

"You know what I mean."

"I'm fine."

She eyes me up and down with concern. "You've lost weight and your eyes are dark. Try lying to someone else."

Despite my aching heart, I laugh. Leaning in close, I whisper, "How about I say, I'll be okay."

Unlike me, Sharon speaks loudly, making sure Everett hears, "Yeah, you will be. Just as soon as you and Everett work things out."

"Mama?" Maren interrupts. "The butler is ready to show you where your room is and take up your suitcase."

Mama gives me another squeeze. "We'll talk later."

I'd been dreading this weekend for weeks. I dreaded staying under the same roof with Everett and not being able to speak. I dreaded his probable looks of disgust and being blatantly disregarded.

But I've had a change of heart.

Since I'm here, I might as well make the most of it. There is a chance, however miniscule, that being near to me will prompt Everett to reconsider our breakup. Perhaps being in my proximity amid the romantic ambiance of a wedding will drive him back to me.

A girl can hope.

Without hope, what is there?

After all the guests arrive and they have shown us to our rooms, everyone convenes on the rear patio to begin the rehearsal. While I should be relieved not to be walking down the aisle, arm in arm with

Everett, I'm not. I hadn't realized it, but I was looking forward to walking alongside him. I was eager to be near him. To feel him and soak up his warmth. It was likely to be my last chance, and now the opportunity has been ripped away.

Dex, Sharon and Everett wait on the expansive back porch while Maren and I, along with her mom Lauren and our dad, are inside at an exit on the other side of the manse.

This is our first walk.

When the processional music begins, I'm stricken by a surge of overwhelming emotion. Maren has chosen a song that has great personal meaning to me. She doesn't know, but it was mine and Everett's song.

A couple weeks after I moved into his condo, after we'd exchanged our first "I love you's," Everett set up a candlelight dinner for us with Carmen's help. It was a Friday night, and as we closed the gallery, I asked if we could go out for dinner, but he said he was tired and just wanted a low-key night at home. I was worried he was getting sick because he's always up for going out after work on Friday. But when we arrived home, she had transformed the condo into a romantic oasis covered in white linen with red roses and twinkle lights galore. My Everett poured us a glass of wine, put on some music and asked me to dance...

"Does the song sound familiar?" he asked as he held me close.

"It does."

"It's from the last movie we went to."

The last movie we'd been to was days before I freaked out over him asking me to live together.

"Yes, I remember now. You hated the movie."

"But I loved this song. When I heard it... that's when I realized I'm in love with you."

With a gasp, I stared into his love-filled eyes.

"Every word in this song speaks what I feel for you. Being yours is a privilege I will never take for granted. I've been waiting for you my entire life. Your love is what I live for."

It has been our song ever since. I haven't listened to it since we broke up. It brings up too many beautiful yet painful memories and emotions. But Maren loves the melody. She was so excited to use it in her wedding procession. I didn't have the heart to tell her my story or the heartache I feel when I hear it.

The procession begins. Everett walks followed by Dex, who walks alongside his mother. Next, following a brief pause, Lauren starts her march and once she gets to the halfway point, I begin mine. With a fake smile, I force my gaze away from Everett. As painstakingly difficult as it is not to look at him, I walk most of the way with my eyes closed. Time crawls by as the music continues. Why, oh why did Maren choose this song? Tears spring to my eyes and though I try with all my might to hold them at bay, it's no use.

This will never be me.

The only man in the world I would ever consider marrying will not have me.

My hopes of a lifelong love are forever dashed.

I cry harder.

And then Maren steps out with our father. She beams at Dex with undeniable love while he looks at her with unabashed adoration.

My tears fall faster.

The rest is a blur.

Maren was right. It's a good thing I didn't walk with Everett. I would've begged him, there on the spot, to forgive me and maybe even ask him to marry me.

I might still.

"I bet that was some fresh hell," Sharon says from behind me.

With a shriek, I jump and clutch my hand to my chest. I just came into my bathroom to splash water on my face and fix my streaked makeup. I had no idea anyone was here.

"Sharon, you scared me."

"I'm sorry, kiddo. I wanted to check on you. You were a blubbering wreck out there."

More tears threaten and I fan my cheeks with my hands. "I thought I could rein it in."

She pulls me into an embrace. "Holding in your pain is the worst thing you can do. Just feel what you're feeling."

"I don't want to ruin Maren's wedding."

"Everyone cries at weddings, Baby Girl. No one will think anything of it."

I pull away with a sniffle. "You did."

"Only because I know what's going on."

The pain is as strong now as the day Everett told me to leave. My lungs constrict and I gasp for air. Clutching the countertop, I let it all go. "It hurts, Sharon. So bad."

"Oh, Sweetie."

In between incontrollable sobs, I mutter, "I… love him… so much. What… am I… s-supposed… to do?"

"I'll tell you exactly what to do. Keep at him. Show him how much you love him and that you aren't letting go without a fight."

"H-How?" Crying so hard, I can barely speak. "He won't t-talk to me."

"He doesn't have to say anything. You can do the talking. He'll hear you and eventually, it'll get through to him."

"How are you so sure?"

Sharon guides me to the bed and takes a seat next to me, holding both my hands.

"I know my son. Make no mistake, I may not have given birth to that beautiful boy, but he is my son. He loves you more than anything on this planet. He's hurting every bit as much as you are."

"He seems to be just fine."

"It's an act." She shakes her head. "He's putting on a show for you. He wants you to think he's unaffected, but inside he's broken. I saw his lip trembling up there at the alter. I see the sorrow in his eyes."

I didn't notice his lip trembling because I never once looked his way. If I had, I'd have lost all composure.

To calm myself down, I breathe in deep. "Do you know what happened between us… most recently?"

With a sigh, she nods. "You both slept with other people while you were apart, and he's too prideful to get over it. I gave him hell over it, believe me."

"How can he be so unforgiving?"

"He's a man." She blows out a breath of exasperation. "It's basic caveman bullshit, Liv. Another man touched his prized possession, and it has him seeing red. He's lost sight of what's important. He's lost perspective and the ability to rationalize. But it'll return. That's why you must keep the lines of communication open, so when he's finally thinking clearly, he'll know the door is open to come crawling back."

I shake my head and wipe my nose with the back of my hand. "You really believe there's hope for us?"

"There's more than hope," she squeezes my hand and gives me a reassuring smile. "You two love each other too much to stay apart."

"I pray you're right."

"Baby Girl, if my word was a check, you could take it to the bank and cash it for a million dollars."

The wedding was beautiful and went off without a hitch. I cried, but not as hard as I did at the rehearsal. I stood beside my sister with poise, joyful for her happy ending.

But I never once looked at Everett. If I had, things would've gone differently.

The reception is in full swing. There has been much drinking and merriment. The bride and groom have shared their first dance. In their original wedding plans, they were to include a dance with the entire wedding party and the parent's. They scrapped that idea because of me and Everett.

He probably told them he wouldn't dance with me.

The four of us are seated at the head table in front of Dex and Maren's one hundred and fifty guests. The room is gorgeous with the only light coming from the twinkle lights strewn above and the candles burning at the tables. Open windows and doors allow a faint breeze and romantic music plays in the background.

The time that I've been dreading has arrived. It's time for speeches.

Everett clinks his glass and stands to get everyone's attention.

I allow myself a quick peek. My first of the day.

Lord, but he's handsome in his tux. And that smile…

But I see what Sharon was talking about. The once ever-present twinkle in his eye is missing.

He begins, "There comes a time in everyone's life when they meet their one true love. Their soulmate. The person who's going to love them for the rest of their life. That moment came for Dex thirty-three years ago when he met me."

The room erupts into laughter and cheers. Even I manage a chuckle. For a moment, I thought he was going to deliver a mushy, heartfelt speech.

"Perhaps I should introduce myself to those of you who don't know me. My name is Everett. I'm Dex's best friend and brother for all intents and purposes. To be asked by Dex to stand here today as his best man is an honor. It's an honor for him as well. He has finally admitted that out of the two of us, I truly am the best man."

The guests laugh once again. All except for me. I'm transfixed on the sound of his voice while trying desperately not to look his way.

"I'd like to take a moment and acknowledge how beautiful *most* of you look tonight. It's nice that some of you made an effort. But speaking of beautiful," he turns to Maren and waves in her direction, "the bride, Maren, is stunning. It's clear to see why Dex is so enchanted by her. Her exceptional beauty makes Dex a little more handsome than he actually is." Everett chuckles and turns to Dex. "Sorry Buddy, but it's true."

Dex nods. "You'll get no argument from me."

"For those of you who don't know, growing up, Dex and I were polar opposites. He was smart and driven. I was the funny goofball. He was a bit of a nerd. Always reading books and dissecting critters. I was athletic and was and still am incredibly good looking."

With a nod, Dex joins the room in laughter and says, "Another truth."

Everett could go on speaking forever for all I care. With my eyes closed, I revel in the deep timbre of his voice.

"Our distinct personalities led to a few fight fights. My being so athletic meant I was much bigger than him, so I had to go easy on the little fella. Still, he never missed an opportunity to pester the crap out of me. I have many cherished memories with my brother. One of my favorites is of playing in the yard after the rain and trudging mud onto Mama Stevens's freshly cleaned floors and getting chased with a wooden spoon. I think I still have welts from the beating we took. Nevertheless, we learned nothing because it was a repeated offense."

Mama laughs with misty eyes. "I'd do anything to have those days back."

"Throughout high school, Dex and I were thick as thieves. Whatever trouble I'd gotten into, he was right there with me. He tried to talk me out of my shenanigans but always failed and in the end, joined in on the mischief."

Everett pauses, and in my peripheral I see him rub his chin. He's saying all this off the cuff, from the heart. No notes. I'm impressed.

"Then came time for college," he continues. "I went to one side of the country and he went to the other. I was on the west coast being wild having the time of my life while he was in the east being a diligent student. We could have drifted apart, but we didn't. If anything, our bond as best friends and brothers became stronger. He called almost every day to make sure I was at least putting in minimum effort, and when my grades slipped, he was the first one to get in my ear about it. Mama, of course, was right behind him."

The room is filled with awe's and people clapping for their close bond. Everett turns to Dex to address him face to face.

"A couple weeks ago, we were at the golf course and were discussing the wedding. You said, 'I'm really glad you and I have stayed such close friends through all these years.' We don't have many heart to hearts, so I was caught off guard by the comment, but I agreed. I too am pleased that we are still so close. But then you said something to me that I'll never forget." Everett chokes up and rests his hand on Dex's shoulder. "You said, 'I want you to know you will always have my friendship. I will always be here as your brother. I am now and forever will be your biggest fan.' Well, brother, I can say the same for you. I am always here and my love for you will never waver. Through thick and thin, good and bad, you are my brother. I look up to you and I admire you."

The two men clasp hands and share a meaningful look before Everett goes on. This time, he addresses Maren.

"Maren, I couldn't be happier that you've come into our dysfunctional, but devoted family. The two of you together make it complete. I wish you nothing but love, happiness and success for the rest of your years together."

The room claps.

"Please, everyone raise your glasses to toast the happy couple, Dex and Maren. Love is a force more powerful than any other because it is invisible. It isn't tangible, but you feel it. It can't be seen, but it can transform you in an instant. It brings more joy and fulfillment than any material possession or financial success ever could. Consider yourselves two of the luckiest people on the planet for having found it and do your best to hold on to it. Congratulations. I love you both."

The two men exchange a hug and what I assume are heartfelt words before Everett moves in to hug Maren. He also says a few things to her privately. Once she and Dex sit back down, Everett extends the mic to me. Our eyes meet briefly before he casts his gaze downward.

My heart pounds as I hold the mic. The notes I've written for my speech shake in my hand. I hadn't expected to be this nervous. Suddenly I'm overwhelmed with emotion. I glance at my notes and take a deep breath before raising the microphone to my mouth.

"Before I begin, I'd like to thank everyone who is here tonight celebrating Dex and Maren. Many of you have come from afar. A few from other countries. It means so much to Dex and Maren that you are all here with them for their special day."

The crowd claps.

"For those of you who don't know me, I'm Maren's Maid of Honor and little sister, Olivia. Those who know me call me Liv. This is where most MOH's—that's short for Maid of Honor—would crack a lame joke about how she just wrote her speech an hour before the wedding. I'll be honest, I've spent months thinking about what I would say tonight. Basically, since the second Maren told me she was engaged, I've been planning this speech. Also, to be honest, I still have no idea what I want to say. But that's Maren's fault because she gave me a list a mile long of all the things not to say which left me with very little I can say. Those of you who know Maren aren't surprised. She can be a tad controlling."

Laughter erupts in the room.

"I'll also have you know, I'm only the MOH—again, short for Maid of Honor for those of you who can't keep up—by default. Not because I'm her only sister, but because she knew she'd never be able to plan this wedding without me. The flower bouquets and beautiful floral centerpieces you see… I picked them out. The wedding colors, I chose them. The only thing Maren contributed to this most perfect wedding is the cake. Basically, this is my wedding with the exception of the groom." I turn to Dex with a smile. "No offense, Dex."

"None taken," he laughs.

"I remember when Maren told me about this incredible guy she was seeing. He was funny and smart and ridiculously hot—I have no idea what happened to that guy. I never met him. But Dex, you're pretty okay, too. I mean, you're okay for a guy who collects pencils."

Maren and Dex laugh with the crowd.

No longer nervous, I continue to jab at him.

"That's weird, right? Pencils… Seriously though, Dex is the perfect guy. Perfect for someone who can live with drawers filled with pencils. Displays of pencils on the walls and on shelves. There are pencils literally everywhere in their house. The other day, I opened the linen closet for a towel and what did I find? Pencils! The good news for you Dex is, our family is pretty laid back. We have exceptionally low standards and expectations, so since you're a brilliant, award winning surgeon, we can forgive your weird fetish."

The room roars with laughter and this time, I hear Everett join them.

"This is the part where I am supposed to tell embarrassing stories about Maren. But she has a lot more dirt on me than I have on her, so after careful consideration, I'll skip that part. What I will say is she was always gracious and the very best, most patient big sister. Many of you know Maren is older than I. We grew up in separate houses and didn't see each other as much as I would've liked. Still, I looked up to and admired my big sister so much." I turn to my sister and stare at her with love and appreciation. "I know I annoyed the heck out of you. Whatever you did, I wanted to do. Wherever you went, I wanted to go. You always let me tag along and never once complained or made me feel as though I was a third wheel. You have always been and will always be a terrific sister, friend, and person. I love you more than any words could ever express."

"Thank you, Livvy," she says with tears brimming in her eyes. "I love you, too."

"As for you, Dex… It was a rough start between you and me," I deadpan, "but you've really grown on me over the past week or two."

Again, the room bursts into laughter and Dex nods, loving the joke. He and I hit it off instantly and have been close since the day my sister introduced us.

"As I finish, I know I'm supposed to offer some marriage advice… but who are we kidding here? Not only am I single, I live with the bride and groom. Any advice from me is useless. What I will say is this… Just keep doing what you're doing. Keep loving each other the way you do. You both are an inspiration to all us single people. I, for one, hope to one day have a love as strong as yours. Everyone, please raise your glasses."

I wipe tears from my eyes as the guests hold their champagne flutes in the air. "Here's to love, laughter and happily ever after."

Chapter 25

As promised, I never spoke to Everett. We spent the entire reception ignoring each other. The closest we came to one another was during the wedding photos and even then, we interacted as minimally as possible and never once came into contact.

I was tempted. So many times, I was tempted. Especially once I'd had a couple glasses of bubbly. I'd sneak looks at him talking to guests or dancing and muster enough courage to approach him. But I'd hear Maren's voice in my head reminding me to maintain my distance. If it had been any other occasion, I would've at least said hello to the man. But it was Maren and Dex's special day and I did what they asked of me.

Dex's friends, our generous hosts, have said to take our time getting up and around this morning. They are serving brunch and everyone is welcome to stay the afternoon and enjoy the indoor pool if we so choose. As good as a nice breakfast and a swim sounds, it's best that I head home. Last night, I overheard Sharon saying she'd like to spend the day here and Everett agreed to keep her company.

Besides, I look forward to having Dex and Maren's place to myself for the next week. They woke early this morning and took off for their honeymoon in Cabo. Tonight, it's just me, their giant television and Thai takeout.

I've woken up early so I can sneak out unnoticed. Bag in hand, I step out of my room and into the hall, coming face to face with Everett. Literally, face to face. We nearly run into each other.

"Pardon me," he says as though I am a perfect stranger and steps around me, being careful not to touch me.

"Seriously?" I bark.

He comes to a halt and I stare at his back, waiting on his response. He just stands there.

"Pardon me?" I repeat his words as a question. "You're acting like a child."

He spins on his heels to face me. "How can you be so blasé about this?"

"I am not being blasé!" I holler and we both look around, hoping our hosts haven't heard.

Everett motions for me to step back into my room. Once we're inside, he closes the door.

Finally, we're talking.

"If anyone is being blasé," I point at him, "it's you!"

"I'm anything but blasé!"

"You won't even speak to me!"

He throws up his hands. "Because I can't! And trust me, that's not a blasé reaction."

"You're right." I stand, hands on hips. "It's a childish reaction."

"I'm not childish, Olivia. I am angry and I'm hurt."

"So am I!"

"Then the best thing we can do is go our separate ways and leave each other alone."

"How do you propose we do that?" I challenge. "I'm Maren's sister and you're her husband's best friend. We are in each other's lives whether or not you like it."

He narrows his angry, unforgiving eyes. "I don't like it!"

I flinch at his hurtful words. "Answer me one question and I swear I'll never bother you again."

He groans. "What?"

"How can you write me off for doing the same thing you did? Do you think it doesn't kill me that you slept with someone? Do you think I'm not hurt and angry? Because I am." Holding a palm on my chest, tears pour from my eyes. "I've never suffered like this in my life! And that's saying something given my losses. I can accept losing my mother at a young age. I can accept that my best friend is gone forever. But I can't accept you living right across town and refusing to talk to me!"

With his head hung, Everett clasps his hands around the back of his neck. When he speaks, his voice is low and gentle. "I realize I'm being a hypocrite, Olivia. But knowing you were with another man… I can't get past it."

"You were with another woman—maybe more than one, for all I know—and I'm willing to look past it." I step closer to him. "I will do that because you mean too much to me not to."

When he looks at me, his angry expression has been replaced with one of sorrow and exhaustion. His tears haven't spilled, but his eyes are glazed. "I just can't, Liv. I can't. When I look at you, it's all I think about… It's all I see… it makes me sick."

"So it's just over? Even though we love each other?" Choking on a sob, I clutch my abdomen. "Please explain to me how that is easier for you than working this out."

"It isn't easier." His voice breaks. "At all. But when I say I can't get past it, I mean it."

My lip trembles. "Because you don't love me enough."

"That's not it." He reaches out but stops short of touching me. "What I did was expected. It's what I've always done. I fell back on old habits. But you… you don't sleep around. You're a good girl. I can't reconcile how, if you love me the way you claim to, you could be with someone else."

More hypocrisy and it makes my blood boil. "I was hurting, that's how."

"You're the one who ended it." His expression reverts to anger. "You left and broke my heart."

My shoulders slump as numbness falls over me. I inhale slowly and exhale. "We can't fix this? Can we?"

Looking to the floor, Everett shakes his head. I swear I see his lip tremble if only infinitesimally.

"Am I supposed to avoid you forever and never speak to you again?"

"Perhaps one day—"

With the wave of my hand, I cut him off and finish his sentence, "We can be friends."

"It's better than nothing."

That will never be possible. I could never be *just* his friend after what we've shared. And sure as I stand here, I know beyond a shadow of a doubt I will never stop loving him.

My body quakes as I cry. At this point, I don't care if he sees me cry. I want him to see my anguish. "How can I be your friend when I love you the way I do?"

Everett steps forward as though he might embrace me, but stops shy of where I stand. He drags a hand through his hair. "You won't always love me."

You may not always love me, but I will always love you. "Yeah, I will."

Everett closes his eyes and takes one last step forward, reaching for my hands.

This is it. This is our final goodbye.

He whispers, "I never imagined it would end like this."

I can hardly speak through my tears. "I never imagined it would end at all."

His thumbs sweep softly across my knuckles. "They say sometimes love isn't enough."

"You might agree, but I don't."

"I'll always have love for you, Liv."

I glance down to my hands that are in his and realize this may be the last time we ever touch. The pain of that realization is unbearable. How can anything hurt this badly? A broken heart is by far more painful than any physical pain one could endure.

A million thoughts course through my brain as I search for words to say that might change his mind.

But there's nothing I can say. He has made up his mind. There is no going back.

We have come to our end.

There is no more us.

There is him. There is me.

Separate.

Never to be together again.

To dull the ache of my breakup, I've thrown myself into photography. I work all week in the studio and spend all weekend shooting. I spend any remaining free time building a website to display my portfolio. If I want to be taken seriously as a photographer and build my career, an online presence is a necessity. Since my collection is small, it won't be long before the website is up and running. I've also reached out to a few galleries asking to be displayed and have a few deals in the works. It helps that Everett featured me in his gallery and I have a history of sales.

I recently moved into my own apartment. It's a tiny loft, sparsely decorated, but it is mine. Dex and Maren gave me some of their furniture to help me out. They claimed they were planning on buying new, but I don't believe them. I am thankful for their generosity.

I'd like to say the pain of my breakup has gone away, but it'd be a lie. Though I'm still smarting from it, it gets easier with each passing week as I grow into acceptance.

I haven't seen or spoken to Everett since the morning after the wedding. Last night, Maren told me he asked about me recently and said he hoped I was doing well.

She also informed me he is dating. Not sleeping around. Not womanizing. He's actually dating. He met an anesthesiologist through Dex and they hit it off. They started seeing each other three weeks ago.

The news is a crushing blow. Imagining Everett on a date hurts worse than the thought of him having casual, meaningless sex. Sex is sex. But dating leads to feelings. If he develops feelings for someone else, he won't love me anymore. The mere notion of him loving anyone other than me… I can't take it.

I hadn't been expecting that report. It has thrown me for a loop. My initial response was to pick up the phone to call him. To find a way to reinsert myself into his life. I even considered telling him I'm ready and willing to be friends.

It's only been two months. He couldn't have fallen out of love with me yet.

Could he?

Is that why he's moving on? Because he no longer loves me? Perhaps he realized his love for me was never very strong and that's why he is ready to move on.

If he felt anywhere near as strongly about me as I do about him… if he missed me as much as I miss him… he wouldn't be able to move on.

I have my answer.

It's officially time that I let him go. I must stop clinging to hope.

Callum and I stayed in touch. I came clean and told him I went back to Everett. He also knows what a colossal disaster our reunion turned out to be.

We don't spend an inordinate amount of time together. We've met for lunch a few times. He joined me on a hiking photo shoot a couple weeks ago. We text daily. He's still interested, but respects my need for time to heal.

If my heart didn't belong to another man, Callum is absolutely the kind of guy I would date. He possesses all the qualities I look for. If only I'd met Callum first, he might be the one I love instead of Everett. Maybe I would be crazy happy rather than a broken-hearted shell.

Perhaps I could still be crazy happy.

It isn't a totally asinine idea.

As my mom would say, "Nothing ventured, nothing gained."

What do I have to lose?

"Do you think it's too soon for me to date?" I ask Maren as we peruse the Denver Central Market.

This is the first weekend I've taken off from shooting. Maren has been begging me to spend time with her. She worries that I spend too much time working and not enough enjoying life. She doesn't understand that working is what has kept me sane. Nevertheless, I can't alienate my loved ones.

"Not at all," she replies. "I think it'd be a healthy thing to do. Do you have someone in mind?"

"I do…" I pause for dramatic effect. "Callum."

"Yes!" She claps and throws her hands in the air. "That's a *spectacular* idea!"

"I like him, and he's been a good friend these past couple months."

She gives my shoulder a good-natured shove. "They say the best relationships are born of friendship."

"Maybe, but I worry about turning him into a rebound. The first relationship after a big breakup never lasts."

She waves off my statement. "That's nonsense."

Maren comes to a stop to look over some fresh strawberries.

"Many people have found it to be true."

Almost everyone I know says it. Hannah and Jess are convinced I shouldn't date Callum yet. They recommend I hook up with someone else first. But I don't want to "hook up." Hooking up will never be my style. Not even to help mend my shattered heart. To each their own, but I'd rather be alone. However, being alone is proving to be difficult.

"They only say that because they hooked up with the wrong people." She pauses to pay for her berries. "If you're with the right person, it won't matter when you start dating."

Isn't she the one who once said bad timing can kill a relationship? But that's not a debate I wish to get into at present.

"That's just it, what if he's not the right person and then I ruin a great friendship?"

And what if I'm seeing him for the wrong reasons? Sure, I like him, but is that why I want to date him or is it a result of my loneliness? When I'm with him, I'm less lonesome. And there's also me not wanting another girl to come along and snag the one guy I'd consider being with. Those aren't good motives for getting involved with someone.

"You won't know if he's the right person until you give him a chance."

Tugging on my ponytail, I sigh. "I hate dating."

Maren's chuckles. "Me, too. Thank God I don't have to anymore."

An awkward silence falls over us. By her expression, I can tell she regrets her words. When we spy an artisan sandwich shop to our right, we come to a stop. I offer to buy lunch and after receiving our order, we grab a nearby table.

"It's okay to be happy about your marriage," I say. "You *should* be happy. It's not your fault I'm a disaster in the relationship department."

"I just don't want you to feel as though I'm rubbing my happiness in your face. I know how much you're still hurting over Everett."

Covering her hand with mine, I say, "If you're happy, be happy. Scream it from the rooftop if you want. That's what I want for you."

"Thanks, Liv," she says with a smile. After a brief pause, she speaks again. "I'm going to say something that is a total cliché, but I'm saying it because it happens to be true."

I brace myself for what's coming. With Maren, there's no telling what it might be. "Okay."

"Time really does heal all wounds," she begins. "And though you don't believe it now, you will get over Everett. You'll stop loving him and move on. And one day you'll be happy, and this will be a distant memory."

That's what everyone with breakup experience says. And while I'm sure it's true, I'd like to put my feelings into perspective for her. "Imagine Dex left you. Cut off all communication and made it clear there is zero chance of a reconciliation. How would you feel?"

"I'd feel precisely the way you do. It would break my heart into a million pieces and I would feel like I couldn't survive it."

"Exactly, so when someone tells me how one day I'll be over Everett and happy, it means nothing to me because right now, I'm miserable." I cast my gaze down to my hands resting in my lap. "I can't picture my future without Everett, and I don't want to. And having somebody tell me about my happy future that won't include him makes my misery worse."

Maren nods. "I'm sorry, I didn't mean to hurt you."

"I know and it's okay. You're just trying to give me hope because you love me and are worried."

"I do love you and I do worry." She reaches across the table, but I don't reciprocate. "You can't imagine how upsetting it is to see you hurting so badly."

I push my food away. My appetite is gone. "Can I be honest with you?"

"You already know the answer to that."

I shouldn't tell her this, but I need to say it out loud to someone and Maren is my person now. "I feel like maybe there might still be a small chance for me and Everett."

"Liv—"

I throw a hand up and cut her off. "I know what you're going to say, so please don't."

She motions for me to continue.

"I still feel connected to him. I can't explain it. He's in my soul, my bones, my every waking thought and my dreams at night. He is my universe. I love him. I'll never love anyone the way I love him. So if there's even the slightest chance that we could get back together—"

This time she cuts me off. "There isn't a chance, Liv."

I sigh. "You don't know that."

"Actually, I do. I've seen him with Amy." She pauses and takes a breath. "He really likes her, and from what I understand, they spend a lot of time together… This isn't a rebound for him, Liv."

My entire body goes numb. This is a bitter pill to swallow. They've been dating less than a month. "They can't be that serious."

Can they?

"I can't say how serious they are, but at the risk of hurting you more, I'll tell you they went away this weekend."

Perhaps they are that serious. He moved lightning fast with me once we went public.

Oh God, has he already found my replacement? The one he will love after me?

I might vomit.

"Are you okay?" Maren comes to my side of the table.

"He's really moving on," I whisper while holding back a flood of tears. "He's not just sleeping around for fun. He's dating. He's moved on with someone else."

So now not only do I have the agony of our breakup to contend with, I have the realization that he's begun a relationship with someone new.

"I'm not supposed to tell you this but… Being with you changed him, Liv. He talked with Dex about it. He's ready to meet someone and settle down. He even discussed having a family."

And just like that, the dam breaks and my tears flow.

"You aren't ready for marriage or kids and might not be for a long time." She pauses. "He's come to realize it will never work between you two."

I nod. She's right. He's right. Our lives are too different.

I whisper because I can't find my voice. I'm too weak. "There's no chance for us."

"I'm sorry, Sweetie."

Chapter 26

CHRISTMAS AND NEW YEAR'S WERE miserable, but I persevered. It took me a solid two weeks to stop smarting from my conversation with Maren. While I needed the wake up call, it almost killed me.

Breaking up is one thing. Accepting that it's over is another. One can't move on until they've reached acceptance.

I've finally accepted it.

Hannah and Jess spent hours last Sunday convincing me there's no harm in dating even if I'm not ready for a serious relationship. Lot's of people date for fun. I'm young and this time in my life is for having a good time. They insist that if I let my twenties pass me by, I will look back on it with regret. Hannah shared a story regarding her aunt. Her aunt got married too young, had kids too soon. Was divorced by thirty, finished raising her kids as a single mom. She is in her forties now and doing embarrassing things with guys half her age. Hannah's cousins are mortified by their mother's inappropriate behavior. Do I want to be her in twenty years? If not, I need to have fun now and get it out of my system.

Callum is a good guy and I enjoy his company. I met up with him a few days ago and we talked. We've decided to start seeing one another. We'll take things slow and see where it goes, keeping it casual unless it organically turns into something more. Callum being the decent and respectful person he is understands it might be a long while before I'm ready for anything serious.

Tonight is our second first date. We're having dinner at a comedy club. A while back, I confessed I've never been to a comedy club, and he insisted on taking me.

"Ooh, front row seats," I say.

"I want you to get the full experience." He winks. "You're guaranteed to get picked on in the front row."

My eyes widen. "What?"

"The comedians always roast the people in the front row."

"Maybe we should move to the back. The *far* back."

"Where's the fun in that?"

"They don't ask people to come on stage and do stuff, do they?"

When I was a little girl, my mom and dad took me to a magic show. We sat in the front row and I was called upon to help with a trick. Never in my life had I been so self-conscious. I could hardly breathe, and when I spoke, it was more of a squeak. The magician had a field day with me. To this day, I hate being the center of attention.

"Sometimes," he laughs.

My cheeks are on fire.

"The good news is, there are a dozen chairs in the row, so you only have a one in twelve chance of being called on."

Funny guy. "You're not making this better."

With a smirk, he rubs his hands together. "This is going to be so much fun."

Draping an arm around me, Callum hugs me to him. It's at this precise moment that I notice Everett sitting at the other end of the row with a woman I assume is Amy. His girlfriend.

My replacement.

She's pretty. Ridiculously pretty. Well kept. Very classy. And from what I can tell, she has a sizeable rack. He must love that.

When our eyes meet, he is every bit as taken aback as I am.

Do I wave? Do I say hello?

Everett looks at Callum, who hasn't noticed Everett, then back to me before raising his hand in a quick wave. When I return the gesture Callum looks to see who I'm waving to.

"Shit," he mutters. "I wasn't expecting that."

I smile at Callum and shrug. "It is what it is. With him being my brother-in-law's best friend, I was bound to run into him at some point."

Thanks to my typical bad luck, it happened when we are both on dates.

"We can leave if you wish," Callum's tone is gentle and sincere.

"No." I shake my head. "I've been looking forward to this show. Besides, how would it look if I left?"

"Who cares how it looks?" he asks, with eyes full of concern. "I don't want you to be uncomfortable or upset."

"I'll be okay." I pat his leg. "If this comedian is any good, I won't even remember he's here."

Actually, that's not likely. The stage is rounded, and the front row seats surround it. Everett is in my direct line of sight.

Callum takes my hand and we face the stage as the lights dim. "Let's hope he's good."

The comedian was good. Good enough to keep my mind off the fact that my ex-boyfriend is sitting ten chairs down from me. Well… most of the time he was able to. There were occasions when my traitorous eyes wandered to where Everett sat. And whenever they did, he was also looking at me. My heart leapt from my chest with every shared glance.

Nevertheless, I laughed more tonight than I have in a very long time.

I did get picked on. A few times. The worst of it was when the comedian pointed us out as the most handsome couple in the room. He called us the quintessential beautiful American couple and assured us our children will be even more beautiful given the combination of our impressive genes. He only hoped our children didn't inherit my nail-biting habit because the way I'd been gnawing on mine, he wanted to check and see if I had any fingertips left.

The room erupted into laughter with the exception of me and Everett.

Had I been biting my nails?

I must've been more nervous than I thought. I'm not a nail biter. I only do it when I am on edge.

"What did you think?" Callum asks as we leave.

"It was great. I'd definitely do that again." Minus Everett and *Amy.*

"Then we will." He entwines his fingers with mine and walks me to his car.

Callum opens my door and closes it once I'm inside. When I reach for my seatbelt, my eyes land on a pair of spellbinding blue irises. Eyes I've looked into several times tonight. Except this time, they're only four feet away in the driver's seat of the car next to me. I can't read his expression. I've never seen it before, but it's filled with emotion. Is it sadness? Anger? Longing? Regret? He doesn't smile. I don't smile. We just stare into each other's eyes and like any time he's near, I feel drawn to him, needing to be closer. If he isn't close enough to touch, he's too far away.

Callum's voice brings me back to reality. "What do you say we grab a nightcap before I take you home?"

I turn to my date. The man who should have my attention. "That sounds great."

"That had to be awkward!" Hannah says.

She, Jess and I are at my place eating ice cream and catching up on the latest gossip. I've just finished telling them about seeing Everett while out with Callum.

"It was," I admit. "But the most unsettling part was when I got into the car and we saw each other. The way he looked at me… it was so emotional."

"He regrets letting you go," Hannah says.

"Maren insists he's happy with Amy," I grumble. "They even went on a trip together."

"He might like her," Hannah says, "but he *loved* you. You were probably the guy's first true love. You never get over that."

"If that's true, I'm screwed," I say.

"I meant to say, you never *forget* it," she back-pedals, "but you can get over it. If not, we'd all be walking around with broken hearts for the rest of our lives."

"What she should've said," Jess chimes in with a mouthful of chocolate ice cream, "is that he's probably not over you yet. And seeing you out with another—super hot—guy drove him crazy."

"Seeing him with *Amy* definitely had me feeling a certain way."

It undoubtedly bothered Everett to see me with someone else. But that's normal. It doesn't mean he wants me back. He's made it clear that's not the case.

"What you must ask yourself is," Hannah starts, "do you want to go down that road again?"

As I poke at my melting ice cream with my spoon, I don't even need to consider my answer.

"If Everett knocked on my door tonight and confessed his undying love for me, I'd probably take him back." Why did I say "probably?" I would absolutely take him back.

"But would that be smart?" she challenges, her head tilted to the side.

I shrug. "We'd definitely need to come to an understanding on some things. I'd have to give a little and so would he, but all relationships require compromise. What we had is worth fighting for." With a sigh, I squeeze my eyes closed. "It doesn't even matter because he won't be knocking on my door."

If there was ever any chance of that happening, it would have already.

That ship has sailed. Right into the waters of a gorgeous anesthesiologist who's probably ready to marry and procreate.

Glaring at the bowl in my hand, I grind my teeth. The thought of Amy pregnant with my Everett's babies makes me want to shot put my dessert across the room.

"For what it's worth," Jess says, "I think you'll be happier with a guy like Callum. You are close in age, you're both building your careers. You are on the same wavelength. As much as you loved Everett, you were never on the same wavelength."

I almost correct Jess's use of the word "loved." My feelings aren't past tense. But since she hit the nail on the head with her other points, I let it pass. "You make a valid point, Jess."

"What did Callum say about Everett being there?" Hannah asks.

Leaving my uneaten ice cream on the coffee table, I fall back onto the sofa. "He offered to leave and take me someplace else. He didn't want me to be uncomfortable."

Jess asks, "What did he think about you staring at Everett all night?"

"I didn't *stare*," I correct her with a smirk. "But if he noticed me looking, he never said anything."

Hannah asks, "Did he seem uneasy with the situation?"

"No, and I doubt he was. Callum's a confident guy."

Jess raises a brow. "Confident as in cocky?"

"Not at all," I answer. "Callum is the nicest, most humble guy I know, but he recognizes his worth. He's a catch."

Callum has loads of girls chasing him. His friends try to set him up all the time. And though I've been in limbo, brokenhearted over Everett, he has waited for me. He insists I am the only girl he's interested in. He thinks we have real potential as a couple and will be great together. When he dropped me off after our date, he gave me a soft kiss and told me it was worth the wait and that he would've waited even longer. The guy certainly is a charmer and best of all, it comes from a place of sincerity. He isn't just trying to get into my pants.

"He is definitely a catch." Hannah grins. "When do we get to lay eyes on this stud?"

"Yeah," Jess exclaims, "we need to meet him!"

I laugh at her eagerness. "I promise to bring him around soon."

"Oh, no," Hannah wags her finger at me. "I know you too well. If we don't make plans, it'll never happen."

"It's true," Jess concurs. "So tell your boy we're going on a triple date. Me and Hannah are both off Saturday after next."

Unsure of the term, I ask, "Triple date?"

"Three couples," Jess explains.

My eyes dart to Hannah who, after her nasty breakup, is also hurting. "But…"

"Oh, that's right," Jess says, "you haven't heard about Hannah's new, hot musician lover."

"What?" This most definitely is news to me.

"Girl," Hannah fake pants, "I've got a story for you."

As I fasten my earring, my phone pings with a text. Callum just left his place and will be here soon to collect me. He's running behind for our triple date because they admitted his grandfather Joe into the hospital this afternoon. The man had a heart attack and is in serious, but stable condition. I offered to cancel our date, but his grandfather wouldn't hear of it and demanded that Callum "take his girl out and have a good time."

Callum is especially close to his grandpa Joe. They go fishing every Sunday, weather permitting. In the winter, they watch football together in place of fishing.

He doesn't live far from my apartment, so it shouldn't take him more than fifteen minutes to get here. I've spoken with the girls, letting them know we are running late, and they offered to wait to order dinner until we arrive.

Not five minutes after his text, I am taken by surprise by a knock at my door.

"Did you run every red light?" I ask and open the door.

When I see who's standing at the threshold I jump back with a yelp.

Chapter 27

"EVERETT…" I HOLD MY PALM to my chest.

How does he know where I live?

Dex…

"May I come in?" he asks, sheepishly.

"I—uh—sure, I guess." I move aside, allowing him to enter.

Why am I letting Everett in when Callum will be here any minute?

More importantly, why is he here?

Something must be wrong.

"You look nice. I always loved that skirt on you." His tone is wistful. "Are you going out?"

"Callum is on his way."

With a nod, he drops his gaze to the floor.

The suspense is killing me. "What brings you by?"

Everett swallows and looks back up at me with regretful eyes. His voice is thick with emotion, "I'm still in love with you, Liv. I tried not to be, but it didn't work. Please give me another chance. I swear I'll get it right this time."

Unable to move any other part of my body besides my eyelids, I stand, blinking. The room spins. My mouth drops open and my arms hang heavy at my sides. "What?"

"Seeing you at the comedy club… with Callum… it woke me up. I realized if I didn't act, I'd lose you forever."

Blinking again, I raise a hand to my heart. I search my brain at rapid speed for a reply, but he has rendered me speechless.

"Haley returned to LA," he continues. "She made up with her aunt and she missed her friends."

"Oh…" I clasp my hands and fiddle with my thumbs. It's a stupid response, but I am still digesting that he said he wants me back.

"It's for the best." He shifts his weight from one foot to the other. "I'm glad she came… mostly. I mean, it was nice to have had time with her to get to know her. But she was only here to sponge off me. You were right about her motives. She was much more interested in my money than in me."

"I'm sorry, Everett." While it pleases me he has seen the light, his disappointment is upsetting. I didn't want him to get hurt.

"It's okay." His smile is small and sad. "My point in telling you is to say there's nothing in our way now. We can be together again, the way we were before everything got messed up."

Can we?

"The last time you broke up with me because—"

Pressing a finger to my lips, he cuts me off, "I was an ass, Liv. A stupid idiot who made the biggest mistake of my life. It was just plain old senseless pride. Can you please forgive me?"

Is this real? Am I awake or am I passed out somewhere dreaming this? Perhaps I slipped in the shower and banged my head.

"What about your girlfriend?" I clear my throat. "Maren said you're pretty serious."

He shakes his head and steps forward. "I ended it with Amy. She's nice, but she isn't you." His voice exudes sincerity and regret. "You are all I want, Liv. I miss you. You're the only woman I have ever loved."

I can't believe Everett is in my living room standing two feet from me. As I glance at the door that Callum will knock on any minute now, guilt washes over me. The very thing I've wanted, that I have dreamt of for so long is finally happening. But Callum will be here soon and he needs me. I can't turn my back on him. Only a heartless person would breakup with someone when their loved one is gravely ill. While I may not be perfect, I am not cruel. "I—I'm seeing somebody."

"I know," Everett says, his eager eyes permeating mine. He moves closer yet, nearly closing the distance between us. "But I'm your soulmate, Liv. And you are mine. I love you."

My chest caves in as tears spring to my eyes. *What do I do?*

A knock on my door snaps me to reality.

"He's here." My heart pounds. My eyes dart from Everett to the door and back to Everett.

Resting his palms on either side of my face, Everett speaks in a hushed tone, "I've said what I came to say. Take time to think about it. I'll wait to hear from you."

There's another knock at the door. I close my eyes, torn between the man in front of me and the one on the other side of that door. This is one of those times when what I wish to do, conflicts with what I know is right.

Suddenly I hear my mom's voice, "Do the right thing, Sweetie."

"I have to go."

"I will hide so he doesn't see me," Everett offers. "I'll let myself out after you're gone."

"Okay," my voice shakes. I mustn't let my tears fall or Callum will know something is wrong.

"I love you, Liv." Everett kisses my forehead. His intoxicating scent envelops me. If only I could lean into his strong arms and stay there. "I am so sorry for hurting you. I hope you will find it in your heart to forgive me."

I watch, breathless, as Everett disappears into my bedroom. Once he's out of sight, I open the door to Callum.

"Hey." He flashes his gorgeous smile, but it doesn't hide his anxiety.

"Hey," I say, trying to ignore the fact that Everett is in my room, probably hanging onto our every word. Maybe I can talk Callum out of our date. He has a lot going on and suddenly, so do I. "Are you sure we should do this tonight?"

"Yeah," he nods. "It'll be a welcome distraction after a stressful day."

"As long as you're sure. I'd understand if you need to reschedule."

With the shake of his head, he reaches for my hand. "I want to go. Besides, I've been looking forward to seeing your beautiful smile all day."

On our way out of the apartment, I glimpse my bedroom doorway. My Everett is in my bedroom and I'm leaving with someone else. What world am I living in?

I spend the twenty-minute ride to the restaurant in a catatonic state, reeling from what just transpired. I can't wrap my mind around Everett showing up unannounced, declaring his love and begging for another chance. It doesn't feel real. While Callum talks about his granddad, I do my best to follow along and respond accordingly.

Upon arrival at the restaurant, I introduce Callum to my friends and their dates, but it's as though I'm on autopilot. I have no idea what pleasantries we exchange because I can't focus on anything other than the barrage of thoughts in my head.

Forty minutes into dinner, Callum receives a phone call that his grandfather went into cardiac arrest and is on life support. Cutting the evening short, we rush to the hospital and spend three hours at the ICU while doctors work to stabilize Grandpa Joe.

Exhausted and overwhelmed with stress, Callum doesn't want to be alone, so I allow him to stay the night. Nothing happens. We don't even kiss. Still, I feel like I'm cheating on Everett by allowing him to sleep in my bed. I mustn't let anything ruin this last chance with Everett. What would he say if he knew I let Callum stay?

Callum leaves early in the morning to run home and shower before returning to the hospital. When I ask if he wants me to go with him, he says he plans on staying at the hospital all day along with his mom, but maybe we can grab lunch later. On his way out, I affirm that I am here if he needs me.

No matter what, I will keep that promise.

He may not be the man I will end up with, but I do care about him. He's become a good friend. The least I can do is stand by him during this difficult time. I understand his sorrow and his fear better than anyone. How would I feel if my boyfriend ditched me at a moment like this? And I guess that what he is... my boyfriend.

That said, I can't ignore the bright, neon pink elephant in the room. Against all odds and just when I'd given up any hope, Everett has accepted responsibility for what he did and asked for another chance. I need to speak with him.

My stomach flutters as I ring Everett's doorbell. He answers promptly. Even though he smiles, it doesn't conceal his nerves.

"Hi." He leans in for a clumsy hug. He wasn't anxious last night. Last night he was confident as ever. "Please, come in."

As I enter my old living room and look around, I'm overwhelmed with nostalgia. I remember our first day here and how we disagreed on where to place the sofa. I won. Everything is exactly the way it was when I moved out. Despite our troubles and the short time I lived here, we made many wonderful memories.

"Can I get you a drink?" he asks. "I made sweet tea."

"That'd be great."

While he goes into the kitchen, I take a seat on the sofa, legs crossed, hands resting on my knee. Do I appear as unnatural as I feel? I can't recall the last time I was this nervous, though I have no reason to be. I am here because Everett wants me to be.

"Thanks," I say as he hands me a glass.

Everett takes a seat in the chair to my left, leaned forward with elbows on knees and hands clasped. He's every bit as unnatural as me. "I'm surprised you called this morning. After seeing you last night, I wasn't sure when or *if* I'd hear from you."

"I still can't get over you showing up on my doorstep."

"I have no right to ask for it, but Liv, if you give me just one more chance I promise I'll get it right." His voice trembles. "Things won't be perfect. No relationship is, but I believe we're meant to be together."

He certainly wastes no time getting to the point. But he never was one to beat around the bush when he wanted something.

"I believe that too."

His eyes widen and he blows out a breath that he'd apparently been holding. "You do?"

"Of course I do, but—"

He cuts me off and in one swift movement he bounds from his chair and kneels before me, pressing his lips to mine. The kiss is urgent yet tender. With his lips on mine he murmurs, "Please don't say but."

As the kiss deepens, I melt into him. He tastes familiar and oh so good.

But Callum's face flashes in my mind. I can't kiss Everett when I am technically seeing someone else. Placing my hands on Everett's shoulders, I gently push him away.

"I'm with Callum."

Crestfallen, he breaks eye contact and bends his neck forward. "Is that why you're here, to tell me you're staying with him?"

How can he think such a thing? I brush my fingers through his hair. "No."

My answer restores the hope in his eyes, but he stays silent.

"You are the only man for me," I assure him, "but Callum is going through a hard time and he needs me. To breakup with him right now would be cruel. I can't do that to him. I'm hoping you will understand and allow me the time I need."

He rocks back onto his heels. "So you're saying that once he gets through whatever it is, we can be together?"

I nod. "But I can't tell you when. It might be days or even weeks."

He places his hands on my thighs and gives them a light squeeze. "I understand, and I am prepared to wait as long as it takes. I'm not going anywhere."

Still, I have to ask, "You won't get mad if it doesn't happen right away? Because I won't survive another breakup with you."

He lays a hand over his heart. "As God is my witness, I am never breaking up with you again, Olivia Bell. You're stuck with me until the day I die."

"Is that a promise you're sure you can keep?" Please, please, please.

Everett places his palms on either side of my face. "You're the only woman I've ever loved. The only woman I *will ever* love. This is a done deal, Babe. Signed, sealed and delivered, I'm yours. Hell, if I sensed you'd be up to it, I'd fly us to Vegas and get married tonight."

My heart skips a beat and I stare, mouth agape. He's not bluffing.

"Don't worry. I know you aren't ready." The corner of his mouth turns up. "But when you are it's game on."

I shrug. "I don't know… I might be ready."

He chokes. "What?"

Sure as I sit here, if not for Callum and my need to do right by him, I would hop on that plane to Vegas and wed this man. He's all I want. All I will *ever* want. But even I am stunned by the idea I'm entertaining.

"Losing you changed me," I say. "It opened my mind to a lot of things. Sometimes you have to throw caution to the wind and go with the flow. Besides, Olivia Shaw has a nice ring to it."

"Don't tease me, Liv."

I reach for his hand. "I wouldn't tease you about that."

He arches a brow, still skeptical. "You'd fly to Vegas and marry me?"

I don't hesitate, "I would. But you know what I really want?"

"What's that?"

"I want a real wedding with all the trimmings and a thousand guests to witness our vows."

He lifts back to his knees to face me. "You can have whatever you want."

"I just want you." I lean my forehead on his. "You and me. Forever."

"Then that's what you'll have."

"I love you."

"I love you more." Everett wraps his arms around me and holds me tight. He presses his face into my neck and inhales deep. "Babe?"

"Yeah?"

"Does this mean we're engaged?"

Epilogue

IT'S A SNOWY CHRISTMAS EVE and I'm surrounded by the people I love most. Everett, our baby boy Everett Junior, Maren, Dex and their two kids, my father, Mama Stevens, and even Haley and her precious little girl Ariella who calls me "Gigi" are all here. While Mom and Grayson aren't here in person, they are always present in spirit. On this most joyful night, I am thankful for a happy and healthy family that continues to grow.

Thinking back on the conversation Everett and I had so many years ago, when we were first getting to know one another, Everett got his wish and so did I. He's a semi-retired stay at home dad. The only work he does is to help me at the gallery a day or two a week. I have Everett to thank for much of what I've achieved. He is my ace in the hole. Being married and having a baby never slowed me down. I have it all—a thriving career, happy marriage and kids. Traveling isn't an option for now, but there's plenty of time. Though being honest, it's not as important to me as it once was. I'm content with what I have and what I'm doing.

Me, Everett, Dex, Maren, and our kids spend a lot of time together. It's fantastic to raise children along with my big sister. And against the odds, Haley and Ariella are integral, beloved members of my family.

If someone asked me five years ago, what my life would look like today, I would've given an entirely incorrect answer. Five years ago, I never would have imagined I'd be married with a one-year-old and a baby on the way. Five years ago, that was my ten-year plan.

But that's the thing about plans. They change without a moment's notice. It's important to be flexible and open to change. Otherwise, we may miss out on incredible life experiences. I've come to learn sometimes, the life we plan for ourselves, isn't what is meant for us, and that's okay. In fact, it can be a blessing in disguise.

So if I could give anyone any piece of advice, it would be this... Go with the flow. And never, ever deny the heart what it wants.

BOOKS BY TEIRAN SMITH

Double H Romance Series
Rooter
Becoming Jace

Standalone Romance Novels
What the Heart Wants

ABOUT THE AUTHOR

Teiran is obsessed with the written word. When she's not writing, she's reading. She can get so lost in a story, be it one of her own or someone else's, that she won't even break away to eat, drink, or sleep. By the time she gets up from a story, she's usually dizzy from low blood sugar, suffering blurred vision.

Whenever she's not writing or reading, you will find her working in her art shop. In addition to being a writer, Teiran is also an abstract artist. Her free time is spent with her husband, Scott, and their four legged child, Lada.

Please visit:
Author website: www.teiransmith.com
Email: teiransmith@gmail.com
Facebook: www.facebook.com/TeiranSmith

www.ingramcontent.com/pod-product-compliance
Lightning Source LLC
Chambersburg PA
CBHW020921110726
47900CB00001B/249